Only
the Dead

Only the Dead

A Levantine Tragedy

T.J. GORTON

QUARTET BOOKS

First published in 2019 by Quartet Books Limited
A member of the Namara Group
27 Goodge Street, London W I T 2L D

A catalogue record for this book is available from the British Library

ISBN 9780704374607

Text design and typesetting by Tetragon, London
Printed and bound in Great Britain by TJ International Ltd, Padstow, Cornwall

When the sun is shrouded
and the stars are put to flight;
when the mountains wander,
the seas will seethe and boil...
Then, each will come to know
what he has wrought.

ADAPTED FROM THE QURAN,
SURAH 81 ('THE COVERING')

Only the dead have seen the end of war.

GEORGE SANTAYANA

Foreword

Vartan, like his story, is mostly fictional. But not entirely. One man, if he were still with us, would recognise in Vartan's story key episodes of his own life, especially at its extremities. I hope and believe he would not have been offended by the liberties I have taken, and it is to him, the man I knew as 'Amo', that this book is dedicated.

1

Beirut: May 1983

Gᴏᴅ, ɪᴛ'ꜱ ꜱᴛᴜꜰꜰʏ *in here, with all the windows closed. When old Bustros built this house, it was surrounded by gardens. He did it right, all this marble and stucco, just look at that ceiling. It would be even stuffier in a modern place, but it is really warm for May. As warm as that... that year.*

Vartan looked at his hands. Hands he saw all the time but never looked at. Now, for no particular reason, they caught his attention. He took a moment to consider them, turning them this way and that. Spots, veins, knobby knuckles, clumps of grey hair: 'Tfou.' *When I think what Maria used to say: 'You have the body of an ox and the hands of a lady, or of an artist – white and small.' Artist, I preferred to think. Now, the hands of an old man, all right – of course, it had to come. I just never noticed.* He leaned back in his chair, the overstuffed once-white armchair that had sat like a throne in the vast hall of the old Beirut house for a generation.

The library was dark, too dark for reading, odd rays of afternoon Mediterranean sunlight filtering through the shutters and probing the shadows. *New glass in the windows, thank God, with the infernal traffic outside, but why fix the shutters when they will just take more bullets or shrapnel? Poor little Maya, the daughter of Bechir Gemayel. They blew up his little girl as she was driven past this house. Must have been a big bomb, to judge by the crater. I was lucky to lose only windows, though I don't think I will ever get the library organised again, now that Nubar is gone.*

Dust motes danced in the sunbeams. Leaning back, he watched their senseless, ceaseless movement and for some reason thought again of old Bustros, the patriarch of a great Greek Orthodox tribe. *He would be amazed to see his house today, nearly two hundred years after he built it; surrounded by roads and overlooked by an office block, its gardens bulldozed for another road that never happened, was never intended to happen. Turned into a no man's land where the militias dump bodies, sometimes burning them. Another reason to keep the windows shut, the oily smoke reeking of petrol and barbecue. As though anyone cared to identify yesterday's victims. It's tomorrow's they're worried about.*

Dark thoughts and the sadness he often felt after sinking into the past, reliving events of sixty or seventy years ago – more vivid to his mind now than those of last week – led him back to one place only: Persia, his nights with Dashti. He could see the gaunt face, oversized forehead, high cheekbones over sunken cheeks, eyes set in deep sockets but burning bright as cigarettes in the night. Their nights of drinking wine and reciting poetry, master and pupil making themselves dizzy with the sinuous rhythms and haunting rhymes of the quatrains, mostly those of Rumi and Khayyam. *Dashti recited this one when I called him 'teacher'…*

yek chand ba-kaudaki

There was a time I studied at the Master's feet
Then for a time, was drunk on my own mastery;
Listen till the story's end, and see what became of me:
I came like water – and turned to dust.

Now he was marooned in the big house as Beirut tore itself to pieces again, a civil war that had already raged for longer than the Second World War. *We thought they were fighting over territory and wealth, that they would never destroy the hotel district or the banks, the banks for God's sake; else what was the point of fighting? But we missed the point. The newsreels – seven years ago already, or is it eight? – grinning bearded guerrillas pouring fine wine down the drain at the Hotel Saint-Georges before torching it. The banks looted and burned. They took her jewellery, the pearl necklace and ruby and sapphire parure I bought for her in Tehran. Not that she wore it more than twice.*

He sighed and looked up at the sunbeam, now coppery and horizontal as the sun must have sunk almost to the sea out past the old merchants' quarter of Gemmayzé that sloped down the hill to the port. Could be a searchlight for all he knew, with the windows closed and shuttered. *It's so stuffy in here I can hardly breathe. I'll go to the kitchen and open the window – hopefully Maqsud will not chatter.*

Maqsud: a tall Egyptian from Assouan, a black man of indeterminate age, somewhere between forty and sixty. Terrible posture made him look older than he probably was. You always knew when he was coming by the creaking of his long black shoes: 'SQUEAK' went the left one, a milder 'squeak' went the right, 'SQUEAK squeak SQUEAK squeak'. *'At least he can't sneak up on one,' my niece would say with her impish grin. How I miss her! It feels like this house has had no feminine presence in decades. Actually that's not far off – well, a decade anyway. Makes me feel all dried up, ready to blow away.*

In the kitchen Maqsud was listening to the radio, the BBC Arabic Service. *At least the BBC presents a nice, predictable distortion. Now the Americans are trying to prop up the so-called government of this so-called republic; the newsreader, probably a Palestinian to judge by his accent, sounds ever so slightly amused. What a tragedy, the American embassy bombing last month. What a year! First the Israeli invasion in June, then Gemayel, then Sabra and Shatila. One horror after another.*

'I'll have a coffee, Maqsud, bring it to the library. Any news?'

'No, *khawaga*, nothing much, the Americans are giving arms to the Lebanese army but the 'Progressives' are too strong for them in the Shouf; there is going to be a lot of trouble there. They say Kissinger has agreed with Israel to divide Lebanon up into cantons, with Syria taking the Bekaa, Israel the south up to the Litani River. Beirut will be an international city.'

'Is that what they said on the news, Maqsud?'

'No, *khawaga*, that's what they say in the souk. The radio just talks about conferences and meetings – *kalam fadhi*, empty talk.'

Vartan left the kitchen with the radio babbling: the French foreign minister at the airport, affirming his country's unshakeable attachment to the 'sovereignty, independence and territorial integrity of Lebanon'. He shook his head as he walked back to his chair to wait for his coffee. *Sovereignty and independence indeed. How many coffees is that today? I really ought to cut down. But Maqsud makes the best Turkish coffee in the world.*

The dust motes seemed to be slowing their dance as the sun buried itself in the sea, turning its rays the colour of blood; soon he would have to turn on the lights, if the electricity was not cut. It usually was around this time of day, just when you needed it. Maqsud would have to crank up the old generator – or bring the hissing Coleman lantern with its circle of intense white light. He would tell him to bring the lantern and save the diesel, which is getting harder and harder to have delivered, not to mention the ridiculous price the bandits make one pay. He liked reading by lantern light. He had rummaged through the pile of books that erupted from their bookcases a year or two ago, when little Maya Gemayel was killed, until he found his beloved volumes of Rumi, Khayyam, Hafez, Saadi and Firdausi. The Quran he loved to read for its poetry, especially the *surahs* revealed in Mekka. A couple of her favourite French novels (Stendhal's *Le Rouge et le Noir*, *Belle du Seigneur* by Albert Cohen). Some English humour: *Three Men in a Boat* and old bound copies of *Punch*. The rest he left where they had fallen, a pitiful, colourful jumble of bindings, little numbers on their spines harking back to Nubar's now obsolete catalogue – itself a casualty. *An evening of Rumi, the dizzying mysticism of the ghazals or the lilting panoply of the* Masnavi.

If there was one good thing about all those years in Iran, it was that I learned Farsi and discovered its poetry, mostly thanks to Ali. I was so fortunate in having a friend in Ali Dashti. We were so young then! 'Dogs go home to die,' *he said, and in a way I made the same choice. I remember comparing our ailments and aches in this very room; as usual he illustrated his thoughts with a quatrain:*

bar pusht-e man

You've loaded on my shoulders a heavy load of years:
Nothing but evil comes of anything I do;
I caught my soul packing its bags – told it: 'Don't go!'
'What can I *do*?' it said; 'The house is falling down.'

Vartan sighed. *Why did he have to go home just at the wrong time, my poor friend? Why, for that matter, did I come here just in time for their bloody civil war? And we thought we were clever. Just look at all the stupid moves I've made, right from the beginning, maybe. Should I regret that? How did it start?*

2

Aleppo, Ottoman Empire: May 1915

I ENTERED Bab al-Neirab through the decrepit remains of the old city gate. Like any Aleppo boy I knew where it was; a rough Muslim neighbourhood, one best avoided by Christians, especially at night, which it soon would be, and alone, as I was. I found myself in an open space, with weeds and rubbish piles, a skinny dog nosing for scraps. At first I could see no one, and thought I had come on a fool's errand, quite literally. Then I spotted a middle-aged Arab with a dark green headcloth wound into a turban, squatting on a step and watching me. I thought this must be the 'Alevi in a green turban'. He stood up, hawked and spat, then looked around and beckoned to me, calling loudly: 'Come on, young *khawaja*, come taste the finest ripe dates in Syria, *tamr* sweet as honey, just what you need to fill that basket of yours.' And before I could answer, off he went down an alleyway, surprisingly agile. Gathering my wits, I hurried to follow him before he disappeared from sight. Soon we were deep into the maze of dank and smelly alleys. I tried to keep count of turns: ninety paces then left, fifty paces then right, hoping I would be able to find my way out again. Finally, the man stopped and knocked on a worm-eaten door into an *abu*, a vaulted storeroom under an apparently abandoned building. Most of its windows were crudely boarded up, any glass long since gone. Above the door, the stone supports of an enclosed balcony had crumbled away to give the façade a dangerous appearance, as though the balcony were only kept from collapse by the rotting remains of wooden latticework.

A key groaned, the door opened and I followed my guide inside; whoever let us in seemed to have disappeared. I tried my best to look grown-up and calm. When my eyes got used to the dim light, I saw that we were in the disused storeroom of an ancient *khan* or caravanserai, still littered with dusty bales of spoiled cotton. The man turned towards me and stared, our faces not more than a foot apart. His beard and eyebrows were stained red with henna. I tried not to recoil from his hostile gaze as well as the rank smells of body and breath. After an uncomfortable moment, I reached inside my waistcoat and drew out a roll of coins. The man held out his upturned palm, but I held the roll close to my chest and offered him the empty basket with my other hand.

He gestured to me to wait – right hand upwards, with fingers and thumb joined – and called up the battered wooden staircase: 'Ya Abdessalam, bring the dates!' With his green turban, thick shape and reddish beard, the man who appeared at the top of the stairs could have been the other man's twin. Maybe he was. He came down empty-handed, fixed me with his own unfriendly stare, then took the basket without a word, the stairs creaking loudly as he climbed.

I looked around the desolate and dirty room: a perfect setting for murder. They could cut my throat, take the gold, and no one would ever know a thing about it. I tried to think of my important errand, but could not get rid of the icy knot in my stomach. The wait was probably only a few minutes, but seemed like an hour. Alevis: my father used to say they would come down from the hills to sell their daughters into domestic service, and that they revered not just the Prophet's son-in-law Ali, as you would guess from the name, but the Devil. I didn't know how much of that to believe; my father Hovsep had been a man of strong opinions and prejudice but very little education.

Finally, Abdessalam appeared and came down the creaky staircase with my basket, now obviously much heavier. A chequered rag partly covered the contents; I lifted it by one corner but did not disturb the dates. I knew by the weight of the basket that it was not really full of dates. Even if I looked underneath and found stones, was I going to argue with two wild-eyed cutthroats deep in the most dangerous quarter of Aleppo? I handed the roll of sovereigns to Abdessalam's nameless twin, who squatted on a bale and counted them one by one, holding them up to a ray of sun and squinting at them to see if they had been clipped. My eyes were drawn to his feet: the knobbiest ones I had ever seen, horny toes looking more like the claws of some huge fowl than those of a human. He looked up, nodded a grudging approval, wrapped the coins back up in their paper and pocketed them, then barked up at me: 'Yallah, now off with you before night catches you here!'

I hoisted the basket and tried to look self-assured, but my goodbye was too loud. Scowling, Abdessalam pulled the door open and propelled me out into the street, slamming it shut behind me. The key turned in the lock as I looked up and down the darkening alley. To my relief no one was there. My hastily memorised itinerary of paces and turns served its purpose, but there was one tense moment when my path crossed a pair of shifty-looking, ragged men who stopped talking to stare at me. I kept my eyes firmly ahead, striding as though the dates were late arriving at the table of someone important.

By the time I passed back through the Bab al-Neirab gate, the sun had set, the city was beginning to settle down for the night. The merchants in the souk were tidying their stalls, getting ready to lock up what they could and carry home the rest. The call to evening prayer rang out from half a dozen minarets. I usually liked listening to it, but tonight it sounded sinister to my ears.

Just as I passed through the alley of the soap sellers' stalls, still piled high with fragrant, edible-looking green cakes of Aleppo soap made from olive oil and laurel, I was startled by the sight of a tall, turbaned Arab, walking straight towards me and staring malevolently. I froze. 'Gutter!' he growled, and I was relieved to realise that he only wanted me to make way, to step off the dry side of the alley into the open sewer that ran down the middle.

I turned away from the soap and perfume souk into the millinery and general clothing alley, dominated by colours rather than smells, and stopped to wipe the fog off my glasses. Then I trudged north through the *souk al-nahhasin*, the copper-beaters' area, trying to shield my basket from banging against anything. The makers of brass coffee pots and decorated trays had stopped their hammering and chiselling for the day, and were busy stowing away their tools and wares.

The souk was still crowded, it being a Thursday: tomorrow would be the Muslim Sabbath. I felt eyes staring at me from all sides: surely someone was going to guess that I was not delivering dates. Shouts of buying, selling and bargaining filled the close atmosphere of the enormous covered market. 'The Empire's at war,' I thought, 'people are dying not so far from here, and look at all these Aleppines busy buying a bar of soap as though their life depended on it.' Suddenly my thoughts were roughly interrupted, as something shoved me forward, nearly causing me to drop the basket. I clutched the wicker handle with both hands and lurched out of the way, relieved to see that it was only a muzzle-shove by a donkey, bristling with a clattering bouquet of tin pots and kettles. A barefoot boy was hurrying it along, whacking its backside with a stick and shouting *balak!*, watch your head! It was hot, more like July than late May. 'This year is in a hurry to get somewhere,' I thought, 'God knows where.' The long walk with my heavy burden made me sweat profusely, irritating rivulets running down my forehead under my black felt cap and continually fogging up my glasses. I told myself that's all it was: heat, not fear, though I was afraid, my stomach in a knot, an acrid taste in my mouth. 'How did I get here? Why did I jump into this crazy mission, without thinking, as usual? An Armenian caught carrying bombs though the bazaar, at this stage in the war... Best not to think what would happen if I got caught, not just to me, but to Mayrig and the children.'

As I walked, I tried to distract my thoughts from the queasy fear that pinched my stomach; everybody seemed to be looking at me suspiciously – ready to shout the alarm for crime or blasphemy, starting the hullabaloo which the bazaar loves to indulge in from time to time. 'Just not today, *please*.' Suddenly, Omar was there, right in front of me. My best friend, but I was not glad to see him. 'Why, today of all days, can I not just walk undisturbed through the souk?' I thought.

'*Ya salam*, Varo, what in the world are you doing here at this hour?'

'Fetching dates, are you blind? Mayrig is making *tamriya* tomorrow, and if you touch so much as one I'll pull out both hairs of that ridiculous moustache with my fingernails!' Omar laughed, darted forward to pluck a date from the basket and looked strangely at me for a second, before turning on his way to pray at the Umayyad Mosque as he did every day at this hour, spitting out the date-stone as he went. My excuse was a stupid one: Mayrig did not cook sweets at home and Omar must have known it.

I left the souk for the comfortable Christian quarter of Jdeide. I still felt uneasy, but not on account of the bombs in my basket, as I had deep in the bazaar. Here I was on safe terrain. 'I'm such a bad liar,' I thought. 'I could see it in his eyes. Why did I have to lie, anyway? Can't I even trust *Omar*?'

I was soon passing the ancient Armenian church of Forty Martyrs, with its ugly modern belfry stuck on; I never saw it without thinking of the forty thieves in the Aladdin story. I was close to home now, and did not mind that it was pitch-dark by the time I entered the tangled lanes of Atawi Saghir, our small and mostly Armenian neighbourhood. I climbed the outside staircase to the front door, above the vaulted *abu* where my late father – a gunsmith – had had his workshop. Mayrig opened the door before I could knock and looked around carefully before closing it, to make sure I had not been followed.

'Did you have any trouble, Varo?' she enquired, after kissing me on both cheeks. She left her wrinkled hand on my shoulder a little longer than usual.

'No, Mayrig, all went smoothly. But where are the *shabab*, the young men?'

'In the cellar. Bring the basket.' We went down the stone staircase to the ground floor, then across the workshop to a door revealing spiral stairs down into the basement, the cool, dry room where the housewives of Aleppo keep their precious provisions. Our cellar had a further, secret room, a small windowless space behind a heavy oak wardrobe; this had been pushed aside to expose the improvised dormitory and provide fresh air.

The current occupants had knocked on the door earlier that day, saying they came on the recommendation of distant relations of Mayrig's mother back in Cilicia. Mayrig did not hesitate when they asked for sanctuary. 'Of course you can stay. In you go now, quickly; I will bring you a ewer to wash your hands and faces and then you will tell me what is happening.'

The two men, or rather the young man and the boy of about twelve, made a strange sight in their torn and dirty city clothes. They picked at the stuffed courgettes Mayrig put before them. The older one spoke in Armenian, with what to me was a strange accent. 'My name is Garabed Boyajian – my brother, Bedros. We are from Harput, perhaps you've heard of it?' 'I have,' said Mayrig, 'there's an Armenian school there, isn't there? Somewhere up north. You have *walked* all this way?' 'We have, but the issue is not us. The whole nation of Armenians in Cilicia is being destroyed. Most of our people are going quietly to their fate, like so many sheep. Some are refusing, and have organised as *fidais*, resistance fighters.

'More than food, and before talk, we need help. Urgently. A trustworthy local person who is not afraid of undertaking a risky mission in the service of our nation, of Hayestan.'

I had never heard anyone talk about 'Hayestan' in that way. I knew it meant Armenia, but I was not sure where it was, or even if it was a place at all. Garabed continued: 'I have joined the *fidais*, and have been sent on a mission: to collect a parcel of hand grenades from a Muslim quarter outside the walls. We could go ourselves but not knowing the city or more than a few words of Arabic, we would be unlikely to succeed. A dangerous mission for anyone, but vital to our cause. Do you know anyone, Marie, a reliable person who would do us this service? We can pay, we have several pounds left besides the gold we brought to pay for the bombs.'

Without thinking, I blurted out: 'I will!'

'Wait a minute!' interjected Mayrig, silencing me with her sternest frown. 'What will you do with these hand grenades, Garabed? Surely you don't imagine you can take on the Ottoman Empire with a few grenades?'

'We are not fools, Marie. We will not use them to kill the lowlife scum of *chetes* and *zaptiehs*, there are too many of them and too few of us. As much as we hate those curs, we must strike at the heads, the *valis* and *mütesarrifs*, the politicians and army officers. Their orders are used to justify the massacres. That is what we can do now. Some day we will strike at the really guilty parties, Enver and Talaat and Jemal.' His voice quavered with hate as those names passed his lips. I had heard of them, of course: the 'Young Turks' who had taken control of the Empire and dragged it into the war on the side of Germany and Austria.

I looked at Mayrig, and she looked back at me for a moment, her face stony as always. Finally she nodded her agreement.

'All right then, Vartan,' said Garo, and told me how to find the contact, an Alevi in a green turban. 'You will give him this roll of coins once he has filled your basket with the bombs. Twelve of them, that's the agreement.' Garabed stopped, looked at me, then at Mayrig. 'He is young to be doing this, Marie. Perhaps we should find someone else.'

'My son is capable, do not worry. If you have prepared correctly he will succeed.'

'Please tell me more about what is happening,' I asked Garabed, after he had finished inspecting the small, round, not particularly vicious-looking grenades. Garabed and his young brother sat on one side of a bench at the old cellar table of knife-scarred wood. He spoke in Turkish, our only common language since my brother Halim had always refused to learn Armenian, other than a few words of 'kitchen talk' and the odd phrase mumbled during mass.

Garabed sat with his face in his hands for a moment. With the first part of his mission accomplished, the weeks of fear and tension seemed to catch up with him. His voice failed him several times. 'For our home town, Harput, the fateful day came towards the end of May. We were awakened by the town crier, accompanied by a boy beating a drum, announcing that all Armenians had twenty-four hours' notice to abandon all they possessed and leave.'

'Just like that?' I asked.

'Just like that. The local mayor, a friendly Turk who had often

visited our house, promised that our lives and property and honour...'
Garabed paused, looking across at Mayrig as though he would choke
up, then looked back down at the table and went on. '...Our lives
and property and *honour* would be protected. Well, I will not tell
you exactly how they went about protecting us. Only, by the time
we got down to Malatya there was nothing left to steal. Most of the
younger women had been taken away by the *chetes* and other thugs...'

He went on and on, and as I listened my mind lost its ability to
focus. The horrors were beyond belief, and yet he had seen them.
Finally he, too, seemed unable to cope. He closed his eyes and sat
silently, struggling to continue, stifling a sob.

'I will finish telling you, you *must* know what is happening to our
people. They found one pretext or another for taking away any men
and boys old enough to fight, and Father and I decided that rather
than die in the *taburlar*, Bedros and I would run away that same night.'

'The *taburlar*?' I interrupted. '"Brigades"? What could that mean?'

'My God, you *are* lucky here in Aleppo! Forced labour gangs, put
to do work no free man would ever do: working them literally to
death on the railway, or just breaking stones. But the real purpose is
breaking – killing – men. All those who drop from hunger or fatigue
are killed on the spot; shot and buried in the ditches they have dug.'

Halim had been fidgeting, obviously bored. Finally he got up,
excusing himself. I knew he was going out to find his friends, a gang
of mostly Christian boys who spent their time hanging around the
cafes in Jdeide.

'Father gave us what money he could. We did not tell Mother
as she would have been too agitated. We waited until late at night,
when we could hear the *zaptiehs* snoring, and then crept away from
the convoy. We made our way through the forests and mountain
valleys, crossing rivers by night – thank God it's not winter – to a
place called Chelik-han. We had heard from someone on the convoy
that there was a group of men and boys hiding in the hills above the
lake, and we did not have to find them, they spied us crossing the

river at a shallow place and called out to us in Armenian. If we had answered in Turkish they would have shot us for sure. We stayed a few days with them and told them we wanted to get to Aleppo where we had relatives. They asked whether we wanted to join their resistance movement: you can imagine our reply.

'One of them came with us as far down the mountain as Killis, where we made contact with another group of fugitives.'

'Killis!' exclaimed Mayrig. 'My home town. What did you see there?'

'Nothing good, *hanum*. The Armenians had all been deported, and their houses were mostly open to the four winds, looted of all they had contained. Some had been taken over by Muslim refugees, poor Greek-speakers from the Balkans. Anyway, that's where we met the other, larger band of *fidais*. These were mostly Armenians who had deserted from the Ottoman Army or escaped from the *taburlar*, joined by a few who had escaped from deportation columns, like us. They told us about the Alevi bomb makers and asked us if we would help, assuming we made it to Aleppo. Of course, we agreed.'

'Why would the Alevis want to help *us* against the Turks?' I asked, remembering the henna-bearded twins.

'A good question. We were doubtful at first, too. The *fidais* told us that, being Muslim, the Alevis were conscripted into the regular army, where they could steal gunpowder and other weapon-making material for their own ends. Or for profit in this case. Armenians have money but are forbidden from possessing weapons of any kind. That is our story: I will spare you the close calls, the dogs barking in the dead of night and raising the alarm, the gunshots. We hardly slept for two weeks; as you can see, poor Bedros here is still in a state. Please let him stay with you while I take this basket to the safe house.'

'No, Garo! Don't leave me! I'll go with you!' Bedros jumped up from the steps leading up to the *abu*. Those were the first words he had spoken since arriving. His brother went over to him and took him gently by the shoulders.

'Listen Bedros, two of us outsiders will attract more attention than one. I'll take the basket to our friends, they are waiting near the train station. Now I must go, they will be waiting for me.'

I stopped him: 'I'll come too. You don't speak Arabic, anybody can see you're a stranger. First, you will change those rags for some of my father's clothes, you're just about his size. Then we will go, but not until the morning. The streets around the station are dangerous at night, and they won't be expecting you to come at this hour. And when we go, I will stay with you.'

Mayrig stared at me, but did not object. I think she was surprised to hear me talk like that. Actually, I was surprised too. Everything seemed to be changing on this unreal day. 'All right,' agreed Garabed. 'You can come with me as far as the meeting place, but then you must turn back. I promised to come alone and they will not meet me if you are there.'

The next morning, Garabed changed into a shirt, jacket and trousers that had belonged to Hovsep and put on a round black cap of Halim's as my father's fez was two sizes too big. I had hardly slept; when I did doze off towards morning, I dreamed I was in the shadow of a looming volcano sending up smoke and sparks, and threatening to spout flames and deadly rivers of lava.

When we were within sight of the house in front of the Italian consulate, Garabed turned to me. 'You go home now, it will be better if they do not think I have brought anyone.'

'All right Garo. You remember the way to our house? We will wait for you there.' I walked back a hundred yards or so, then turned to see if our friend had found his contact. But he was gone, and I thought I caught a glimpse of the door to the small house just as it shut. Garabed did not return from his errand and sent no word.

By the end of June, Aleppo was an oven by day, merely airless and sweltering by night. One Sunday, my Uncle Sarkis – my late father's younger brother – came to Atawi for a visit. Sarkis was my favourite uncle: a burly man of medium height, with round glasses on his big Armenian nose. He was about forty and, unusually for a mature Levantine gentleman, clean-shaven. I had always hated facial hair, vain and unsanitary. I couldn't help imagining that I would look like Sarkis one day, if I should live to be as old as he was. The prospect of looking like him did not displease me. His face already had a few lines, but they were laugh-lines, evidence of his jolly temperament, so unlike his morose late brother Hovsep. But not on that afternoon in May.

'How are you, my dear Mayrig?' he began in Armenian, then switched to the Aleppo Arabic that was more comfortable for both of them, spiced with the occasional Turkish or Armenian word. 'How are the children? It has been months since we saw each other!'

'We are well, here in our cosy house, but how can anyone be happy with what is going on out in that *deli dunya,* that crazy world? But where is your wife?'

'Ah, she has another of her migraines. They seem to afflict her whenever I suggest a visit to you. It has been too long, much too long; so this time I told her to take a sleeping powder. I had to come, especially now that things are happening so fast. I need to talk to someone with a good head on their shoulders and, besides, we need to stick together, now of all times.'

Sarkis paused, uncharacteristically searching for his words. 'Marie, we all said it would never come to this. Armenians are loyal Ottomans. There are members of our nation in high positions in the government at Constantinople, remember? Why would they want to destroy us? Well, listen. They are not only doing it, they are dressing it up in legal form. The Sublime Porte has issued a decree calling for the Armenians to be deported, their property confiscated. Everything they have that could be sold, the houses and furniture and livestock and land and bank accounts and shares and jewellery, all are to be seized and liquidated...'

When he finished, there was a long, heavy silence. Mayrig stared ahead, as though trying to fathom what the future held. Sarkis shook his head.

'And here we sit drinking coffee as though everything was normal.' He finished sipping his coffee, then sat looking at the patterns in the dregs of his cup. As he returned the cup to the table, I could see his hand shaking. Sadness made the laugh-lines on his face look almost clownish.

The next day after Sarkis's visit, I went to the Sebil, the main railway station, to see for myself. Bedros tagged along as usual, still mostly speechless. The place was a madhouse, teeming with all kinds of armed men: soldiers, *zaptiehs,* policemen and, worst of all, the irregular militia known as *chetes.* I had never seen such chaos in my city, with people shoving and milling around, women and babies crying: bunches of refugees, ragged family groups, clusters of desperate women who had lost their men and children, a few frightened children huddling together. A train had stopped at the platform, and there was quite a ruckus going on with refugees trying to get off and soldiers pushing them back on. I asked a policeman where the train was going. 'Ras al-Ain, but our "passengers" will go on by foot from there, headed for Deir az-Zor, my boy. We'll be underway as soon as we finish loading the coal.' The engine was already beginning to hiss.

Suddenly a pair of black eyes caught mine from the half-open window of a nearby carriage. They belonged to a young mother, who looked hardly older than the oldest of the four or five children clinging to her floral dress; a shawl covered her head and shoulders, not quite hiding her long chestnut hair. Her face would have been pretty were she not obviously exhausted and hungry. '*Efendim,* good sir!' she shouted in country Turkish, never taking her gaze from mine. Why, I cannot say: she had no way of knowing I was one of hers. 'Help us please!'

'What is it, *hanum?*' I answered, also in Turkish, coming close to the window.

'That policeman took our money and promised to bring a *teskere*. Now the train is getting ready to leave and he has done nothing! Please!' The policeman, who must have overheard, had already started to move away, but I caught his arm.

'Captain, a moment please! This poor mother says you promised her a permit to remain here, and paid a fee. Would you be so kind as to explain?'

'She gave me five *para*, *efendim*, not half enough for a *teskere* for such a family! Let them go to Deir az-Zor, they can remain there all they want!'

'And how much would a *teskere* cost, Captain? Would ten *para* on top of what she paid suffice?'

The policeman looked at me suspiciously. 'Ten *para*? Certainly, but what are they to you, *efendim*?'

'Just a poor mother and her children, who could be my sister or yours, Captain Efendi.' With that I counted ten *para* from my pocket into the palm of my hand, which I closed when I saw his eyes brighten. 'I will wait right here for you to return, and it will be yours as soon as they are off the train. *Tamam mı?*'

The train was in the last stages of preparation for departure when he returned; the young mother at the window was becoming more and more agitated. I held up my fist with the money and pointed to her. Scowling, he opened the carriage door, pulled her and her children off and roughly shoved them aside, slamming it shut before any other miserable creatures could follow. I dropped the coins into his hand in exchange for a paper I didn't even look at: at least they were off the train, which began hissing and groaning and very gradually moving away. The young woman gripped my arm with one hand and her youngest child with the other, while the two middle ones still clung to her skirts; they all stared at me. I was afraid I had just acquired a family. What was I to do with them? First to get out of the

Sebil, swarming with armed ruffians just looking for trouble. Finally, I remembered that the Forty Martyrs church was acting as a sort of clearing house for refugees, so I took them there, the young woman embarrassing me with her tears of gratitude, and headed home.

'And how much of your money did the scoundrel take, Varo?'

'Ten *para,* Mayrig. I am sorry but they looked so miserable…'

'Of course you had to. But we cannot do that every day, else we will not have food ourselves. If you want to help, I suggest you go to the church and offer your services.'

And so the long, hot summer nightmare of Aleppo began with a vengeance. Along with the deacon of the church and other volunteers, we worked long days and sometimes nights, bringing new arrivals disembarking at the Sebil or straggling into the city at the end of a long and deadly march. One day in what must have been early July, Mayrig came home with a whole family, or what was left of one: a grandmother, her daughter and two small children, all thin and ragged and shocked by what they had witnessed and lost and suffered during the long weeks of their march. They were from faraway Diyarbekir, a hard country in the far east of Anatolia. The mother looked at the clean, cosy Armenian household, the furnishings decent but by no means luxurious.

'So you live like this, safe, while the rest of our people…' she sighed bitterly, her eyes blazing. She did not go so far as to insult us, but we could read and understand her emotions.

Over the next baking dusty weeks, the schools, convents, churches and homes filled up. The haggard survivors of what had been families slept on the street, begging for their bread. There were outbreaks of cholera, typhus and typhoid. In the midst of all this, an unusual man came into our lives: a Protestant pastor named Hovhannes Eskijian, an unassuming middle-aged man with a goatee and pince-nez.

Originally from Aintab, he had known Mayrig's family in nearby Killis. We were not Protestants, but it was no time for labels. He and his wife Gulenia were spending long days helping the refugees find shelter and food; when they could they would let Mayrig bring them around for a homely meal of kebab in yogurt, or 'liar's *dolma*' – vine leaves stuffed with rice rather than meat, moistened with olive oil and lemon. Conversation was slow as they would arrive tired and shaken by the scenes they had witnessed.

During one such dinner, I asked the pastor if there was anything I could do to help. 'Well, Vartan,' he said, 'I could use a dragoman. As you can tell, my Arabic is better than it was, but not yet fluent. Maybe you could help me improve it as well as helping with all the other work we do.' And so I did, but it was a lot more than just interpreting and translating: distributing food and money collected by the Protestant congregation (and not just to Protestants, by the way), getting one of the few Armenian doctors in town to attend to homeless refugees and so on. I was constantly on the move, often together with the pastor, always followed by my shadow, Bedros. Partly thanks to my efforts, he was by now able to get by in pidgin Arabic and had mostly lost his shyness through helping us communicate with the refugees from the north and far east of Armenia. We could still hear him calling out for his brother in his sleep.

One afternoon Eskijian said, 'Vartan, today we are going to visit the American consul. His name is Jesse Jackson, a native of some place called Ohio, but he has lived in the Empire for many years.' I was hesitant. I had seen a few Americans in Jerusalem, but they hadn't impressed me. Large, red-faced people, only interested in touring biblical sites, not in anything to do with the living inhabitants of the region. They seemed to have more money than sense, and were often taken in by locals peddling fake biblical souvenirs or tall tales, taking them to Noah's tomb or the beach where the whale spat up Jonah. Out of deference to Eskijian, I went along, deferring the errands Mayrig had sent me on.

Jackson's office was a large, bright room with bookshelves filled with leather-bound books and a massive desk covered with maps and papers. Of the man, I had a very different impression from the other Americans I had seen. Large, tall but not heavy, with the kindest face you could imagine: intelligent grey eyes set deep in a tired face. He greeted Eskijian in good Turkish, and me in broken Arabic. I answered in English: 'Pleased to meet you, sir.'

'Aha! Now that was well said, young man. Where did you learn to speak such good English?'

'In Jerusalem, sir. I spent five years at an Armenian school there, and the only subject I really paid attention to was English.'

'Well, I must say it's nice to meet someone local who can speak my language, in a city like this where they – especially the Christians – seem so keen on speaking nothing but French.' We had a long chat about all kinds of things, and I had a feeling I was being interviewed, else why would a consul spend so much time with a boy who was just seventeen?

A week or so later I was invited back, this time on my own. Jackson closed the door to his office and sat me in the leather-clad chair across from him; my glasses fogged up as usual. 'Young Vartan, I wonder if you could spare time from your activities helping the good Pastor Eskijian, to lend me a hand as well? Just between us, I don't fully trust the consular dragoman. It seems that the Sublime Porte – the government in Constantinople – knows what I am doing and who I am seeing before I even write my reports to Ambassador Morgenthau. And I don't want to write anything unless I have seen it with my own eyes. Trust is a scarce commodity around these parts, and according to Hovhannes I can trust you. What do you say?'

'Of course, ah, Excellency...'

'Now let me stop you right there. None of that "Excellency" flim-flam. You will call me Mr Jackson and I'll call you Vartan or, better, Nakashian; it wouldn't do for the staff to see us being *too* informal, but we Americans don't have truck with fancy titles when a name will do. You were saying?'

'Well, Mr Jackson, I hear that the Americans, and especially your ambassador in Constantinople, are the only ones who tell the truth about what is going on with the Armenians, and who dare to stand up to the Turks. Anything I can do to help you, I will, gladly.' Jackson's weathered face lit up in a smile.

'Excellent. Let me call in Ferhat Bey, the official dragoman. Getting along with him will be your first challenge; but he is, well, a permanent fixture. Since the war began, the Ottomans have insisted on appointing consular dragomen. He speaks English like a Victorian textbook, but he's not a bad sort, wherever his loyalties may lie.' He banged his large hand on a bell in the shape of a bronze turtle, and told the *chaoush* to bring in Ferhat Bey. Directly a middle-aged Turk in a fez and European suit came in, a small man with a carefully tended moustache.

'Ferhat Bey, this is Vartan Nakashian. I have asked him to assist me, and you, with certain minor tasks of interpretation, simple things that are not important enough to warrant your expert attention. I am sure he can learn much about the trade of a dragoman, if you will be so kind as to share your extensive experience with him. In order not to disturb you I shall call on him directly when I need his services.' I promptly held out my hand; the Turk pursed his lips and paused for an eloquent second or two before taking it, looking down at the floor as though required to do something distasteful. I saw that he wore the nail on his right little finger about an inch long, to show that he was not involved in manual labour, as though it were not obvious from his prissy appearance. He said nothing, but disengaged his hand as soon as it was decent, nodded sombrely towards the consul, and exited through the still-open door without waiting to be dismissed.

Jackson cleared his throat. 'Ahem, ah, Vartan, you will want to guard your flank with that one. Though you begin to see what

I mean.' I nodded. 'Now if you are free, perhaps you could accompany me up to the northern suburbs, beyond the train station. It seems a caravan of refugees in terrible condition has begun to straggle in, and I want to see for myself, like I said. Will you come?'

Together we walked as quickly as we could up to the outskirts of the city; the consul's long legs made him hard to keep up with. I smiled to myself, thinking how Ottoman men of real or would-be standing cultivated a stately walk, and never carried anything in the street: like the dragoman's long fingernail. Americans are different, if this one is anything to go by; but how can they compete with the lizard-men of the Levant?

By the time we were past the Sebil, we began to see them. Dozens of them: only women and girls, with more straggling in from the north. I have never seen such misery: the lucky ones were in tattered and filthy clothing, but others were almost completely naked, trying to hide their shame with a few rags. Jackson asked me to find out where they were from. I approached one woman, a dark-skinned mother who looked quite numb, with two exhausted little children, a boy and a girl, clinging to the remnants of her clothes. I asked her in Turkish, '*Hanum*, where have you come from?' She did not answer, so I asked again in Armenian; she was beyond speech and I realised she was about to drop from exhaustion. I looked around and saw an older woman on her own, still decently clothed but her face horribly sunburned. I asked in Armenian first this time and she looked up at me wide-eyed. 'From Harput, my son. We were a thousand in the convoy. They took the men and older boys. So many fell.'

'Harput,' I thought. 'Poor Garo: if he could see the women of his town, what has become of them. His mother or sisters could be among them, for all I know. Or among the fallen ones.' She went on, as though needing to tell, pausing to look around.

'The *zaptiehs* turned us over to a band of Kurdish *chetes* who took away the young women, even some of the children. They killed those who refused. Beat and stripped the rest of us, making us walk all this way half-naked, under the burning summer sun. Just look at us!' I could hardly bear to look at them, wretched creatures with sunburned skin peeling off in great blotches. Many had wounds of various kinds, and several, like the young mother I tried to talk to, looked like they would not survive long.

I translated all this for Jackson and was struck by his face. Ashen from shock at what he was seeing, lips pressed tight, he took furious notes in his notebook. When he finished writing he looked up at me. 'I will of course report all this to Morgenthau at once. It will not be the first such report, but this is abominable. The American and European governments cannot be ignorant of what has been happening. The press, especially in England, France and America, makes much of it, and public opinion is aroused. But,' he went on with a mournful look, 'the governments, each for its own reasons, have done nothing. Still, we must do what we can. Let us go and find Eskijian and see if the women from the church can organise clothing, medical help and some sort of shelter for these wretches.'

As we walked to the church, Jackson said, 'Here is something I just heard today. It may be a rumour, of course, and it is pretty hard to believe. Still, I have fairly reliable information that six villages up on a mountain called Musa Dagh have rebelled against all this, and are, or were, holding off a Turkish army besieging them. I will try to find out if it is true. If so, this could be important. We westerners love an underdog, but *only* if he shows pluck. It's all so cynical.'

Summer is always hot in Aleppo, cramped and stewing within its thick walls – but that summer was the hottest anyone could remember, even old people. It never seemed to end. Added to all this was an unheard-of thing, a plague of locusts. Clouds of them came from the desert and stripped trees bare in hours. It was worst in Palestine and southern Syria, but Aleppines with farms in the fertile areas south of Damascus told of crops and pistachio trees devastated in a day. The price of wheat was up by half at the end of the summer. As the endless days of heat dragged on and on, the situation in the crowded city got even worse, with the steady arrival of pitiful groups of death-march survivors and other refugees adding their own woes to the general misery.

Until then, I thought I had known more than my fair share of suffering. Three siblings and our father, all dead within a few years of each other. I never knew Badi, who died before he was properly born, or Rafiq, who died of dysentery when he was two. Little Haiganoush was a dark-eyed beauty, even for an Armenian, and her death from tuberculosis at five was a heavy blow to us all. And then my father's sudden death from a heart attack when I was twelve. All this made me feel I had borne more than most people. Seeing Mayrig's suffering was the worst part. The horrible scourge of consumption seemed to haunt our family.

Now there was Anahit. My sweet, delicate sister, with her brown hair and such light skin that she hardly looked like one of us, except for her large, black, very Armenian eyes. Full of love and concern for others, a much better person than me, I know. Despite that, she and I are sort of soulmates, understanding each other without talking, doing our best to help Mayrig cope and take care of little Krikor, our lively younger brother. He's too young to remember our father, maybe that's why he looks up to me with adoration. Anahit loves reading and, when we had a quiet moment, would read me poems in Arabic or French, which she had learned at the Franciscan Sisters' School before they asked her to leave. Her nagging cough worries me and terrifies our mother, though she never mentions it.

Grieving had transformed Marie into Mayrig, 'Little Mother'. A name they usually call grandmothers, and actually she looked and acted old beyond her years. She was only thirty-seven when Rafiq died, but after his funeral she put away all her dresses except black ones. That was how we children had always known her, all in black except for the white apron she wore during the day, with its pocket heavy with the keys to the house and her pantries and storerooms. A black headscarf whenever she left the house. Her long curly hair, dense coal-black when she was young, was now deeply streaked with white. She always pulled it back into a single severe tress or tied it up in an even more severe bun. Her eyes went up at their wrinkled corners, looking almost East-Asian, while her forehead was traversed by wrinkles deeper than mere lines of age. Her high cheekbones gave way to wagon-ruts that ran down past the corners of her mouth, giving her face a chiselled look like that of a stone statue to Motherhood, or maybe Grief. Grieving Motherhood. Old Stony Face, I used to call her to myself.

Late one afternoon, I was coming up the stairs to the front door, after spending the day distributing bread to the homeless families camped in the city's public spaces. I was tired, not just physically, but worn out by all the misery I had witnessed. The front door opened suddenly and Halim came out, dressed in what looked like new clothes, with a bandana tied raffishly around his neck. 'Where have you been, Vartan?' he asked. 'You look like a beggar as usual. Don't you have any pride?'

'*You* ask me that?' I shouted. 'You who waste your time and our money loafing in cafes, playing tric-trac and smoking with those worthless, loutish friends of yours when our people are suffering and dying?'

Halim laughed. 'So you're going to save them with a few loaves of bread? You're just putting off the inevitable, and not by much. The Armenians in the north are in league with the Russians, the government *had* to do something. Anyway, they are no more my people than they are yours. *I* certainly don't speak their language, and if you do, so what? What do you know of these illiterate farmers? Go ahead, go talk to the ragged refugees then, and see where it gets you: prison, maybe, if you're lucky; or the plague. We have to be good citizens of the Empire; if we don't interfere, if we don't make trouble, they will leave us alone. They need the work we do and the taxes we pay.'

'What taxes do *you* pay, miserable layabout? What work do you do, for that matter? All you do is spend money when poor Mayrig is killing herself to feed us and help the refugees on a pittance, mostly charity from Uncle Sarkis. Don't help, if you don't care; but at least get a job so you are not a parasite – you're almost twenty, for God's sake!' Halim shoved past me and headed down the stairs. Reaching the bottom, he turned back to look up at me and snarled:

'I'm going to work at the Town Hall, for your information. My name is on a list for a job in the city administration, the *belediye*, as a scribe or, with a bit of luck, *bashkatib*, a senior secretary. So there, Mister Superior Vartan!'

Speechless, I turned away and went into the house. *My own brother, agreeing with the Ottoman justification for the deportations. His heart closed to the misery all around us. And going to work for the* Turks! *Or so he says. Probably just another of his lies. Better a lie than the truth in this case. But how* could *he be like that?*

My thoughts went back to our father, that last horrible day five years ago. I saw him lying there swaddled in a sheet, inert except for those questioning eyes, he who was always so active and decisive, even harsh and dictatorial. Now helpless, while everyone stood around and stared. Looking so much older than his age, his skin waxy, almost yellow, his eyes sunk deep in his skull. He told me to come close. I leaned my face down close to his, ashamed to feel disgust at the sour smell. 'You are responsible for the family now, Vartan. You must take care of your mother, your sister and brothers. Swear!'

And of course I swore. For the hundredth time now, I asked myself: 'Why did he *do* that, burdening a boy of twelve with such a weight? Why not Halim, the oldest brother? I know, of course; I even knew it at the time. Halim is not capable. He was then, and still is now, a flighty, selfish boy, lacking in maturity. We cannot count on him to help with the daily chores. Even physically, we are so unalike. If I did not know Mayrig, I would almost wonder if we have the same father. Unless there *is* something to that bizarre idea, and that's why Father put me in charge. Halim, so much taller than me, slimmer, with straight black hair instead of my curls, tight as astrakhan. Better-looking, I know: his straight nose so unlike my beak. But I could always beat him in a fight, once I got to be about nine. Finally, all I had to do was look at him. Maybe that's why he dislikes me so much.'

A day or so after that encounter with Halim, I was walking past the Great Mosque when a barefoot boy waved at me the day's edition of *al-Muqtabas*, the main Damascus daily. I started to shoo him away, when a headline caught my eye: 'Failed terror attempt in Adana.' I gave him a *barghout*, took the paper and read. It told of an attempt on the life of Jevad Bey, former *vali* of Adana. The name was familiar: I remembered Sarkis spitting when he mentioned the man supposedly behind the massacre of Armenians and other Christians in his city a few years before. Two young men, it said, had thrown hand grenades at his car; one failed to explode, while the other bounced off the car window and exploded on the pavement, killing a young girl and wounding several passers-by. The two perpetrators of this fatally botched assassination attempt were caught and hanged in the town square; one was named as 'Garabed Boyajian, from Harput'. I felt as though I had been kicked in the stomach. My eyes started to swim but I fought back the tears. On returning home, I told Mayrig, and together we decided not to say anything to Bedros.

August finally turned to September, the year of our Lord, as they say, 1915. It was evening, and Mayrig and I were at home, trying to stay cool behind closed shutters, drinking coffee and minding Krikor, when someone knocked at the door. I opened it to find a ragged and emaciated young man who looked as though he was literally about to drop. Before I could say anything, Mayrig came up and took him by the arm, guiding him towards the divan. He stopped, wavering on his feet as though about to faint, and called out to her by name, his voice barely audible.

'What is your name, my son?'

'You do not know me, *tante* Marie? I am Minas, your nephew, Artin's eldest, from Yoghun-Oluk.'

'Good God, Minas, of course it is you, but what has happened? Where are you coming from? I have not seen you since Hovsep's funeral, you've grown so tall – but just look at you!'

She sat him down and sent Anahit to fetch him a glass of cool *ayran*. He drank a little, and then put the glass aside. 'I will tell you the whole story later, but first I have something to do. If you haven't heard, our six villages up on the mountain refused to be deported. The Turks tried to crush us but we beat them back every time. After three weeks we started running short of food, then running out. We could see the Turkish troops beginning to drag up several cannons. The leaders decided to try something desperate. Two of us boys, me and my cousin Arpag, are – *were* – the strongest swimmers, when we have enough to eat. They asked us whether we would volunteer for a dangerous task. Of course we did. We were to swim out to sea, around the bend under Musa Dagh, nearly ten miles, to where the plain is less marshy and one could walk along the road at night, at least, or even in daylight if there were no enemies in sight. From there we were to make our way to the city, with a letter for the American consul. The United States is, how do you say, neuter, but the people are sympathetic to the Armenians. We hope they will send a message to the British or French, begging them to send a warship to rescue us.'

I heard this open-mouthed. 'So you swam all that way? And then walked all the way here? And where is Arpag?' Minas put his face in his hands and sobbed. Mayrig put her arm around his bony shoulder.

'I lost sight of him. The wind got stronger; the waves were with us, which helped us at first, but after a while the sea got too choppy and we were separated. I felt my own strength flagging and put off worrying about Arpag until I could get to shore. Soon I was in the breakers rolling in towards the beach, then my feet found the stony bottom. I crawled through the surf, and once on the sand I collapsed. Suddenly I remembered Arpag. There was no sign of him! I strained my eyes for what seemed like hours. Finally, I had to accept that he had given up. We each had a copy of the letter for the consul wrapped in oilskin and sewn into our belt, so I had to continue the mission alone. I felt lonely and sad for Arpag and his family. But I have seen a lot of death in the past month.'

He let Mayrig take him in her arms. She tried to soothe him, but he broke free and sat up straight, his eyes wild. 'Do you know where to find the consul? Can we go now?' He moved as though to get up, but sank back on to the divan; Mayrig took his ruined shoes off and pulled a rug over him. He did not, could not, object. He slept through the rest of the evening and all through the night. At first light he was up, looking better but painfully thin. Mayrig made him a breakfast of olives, bread and cheese, with a glass of sugary tea. He was just Halim's size, so we soon had him looking like a *halabi*, a Christian boy from Aleppo. Together we set off for the American consulate. As we entered the antechamber, Ferhat Bey saw us heading for the door of Jackson's office, and, visibly alarmed, tried to bar the way. 'The consul is busy, he is in a meeting, you cannot…' I knocked once and opened the door, to find Jackson alone but surprised. Minas and I went in and I closed the door in Farhat's livid face.

'Vartan, what's the matter?' said Jackson, his usual ready smile turning sombre when he had had a good look at Minas.

'Mr Jackson, this is my cousin Minas, from Yoghun-Oluk. One of the villages you mentioned on Musa Dagh, the farmers who refused to be deported.' Minas blurted out his story so fast I could hardly follow his Armenian, but I tried to get the gist across. The consul's lined face was drawn with emotion.

'Such courage, in the face of such terrible odds! We had indeed heard rumours last month, but assumed, sadly, that the huge Turkish army would have reduced such a small band of mountaineers by now. I am glad to be mistaken. When did you leave, young Minas?'

'The day before yesterday, Excellency.'

'So they are still holding out after all!'

Minas then pulled the letter from his pocket, crumpled and damp but still legible. His hand trembled slightly as he handed it over. Jackson unfolded it and began to read:

To any English, American, French, Italian or Russian admiral, captain or authority whom this petition may find; we appeal in the name of God and human brotherhood.

We, the people of six Armenian villages, about 5,000 souls in all, have withdrawn to that part of Musa Dagh called Damlayik, which is three hours' journey north-west from Souedia along the coast.

Sir, you must have heard about the policy of annihilation which the Turks are applying to our nation. Under cover of dispersing the Armenians as if to avoid rebellion, our people are expelled from their houses and deprived of their gardens, their vineyards and all their possessions...

Jackson's eyes went down the page, through paragraph after paragraph detailing horrors and abominations.

The Government some forty days ago informed us that our six villages must go into exile. Rather than submit to this we withdrew to this mountain. We have now little food left and the troops are besieging us. We have had five fierce battles. God has given us the victory, but the next time we shall have to withstand a much larger force.

Sir, we appeal to you in the name of Christ!

Transport us, we pray you, to Cyprus or any other free land. Our people are not indolent; we will earn our own bread if we are employed.

Please, sir, do not wait until it is too late!
Respectfully, your servant, for all the Christians here,
> September 2.
> *Dikran Andreasian.*

Jackson looked down in silence for a few seconds. 'My friends, I understand. But what can be done? The United States is neutral. I must not be seen to be taking an active part in any rescue mission, assuming that such a mission is feasible under the guns of the Ottoman Army. The French and British and Russians have all closed their consulates in Aleppo. All communications are monitored by Jemal Pasha's spies.

'I know Jemal well. He is full of contradictions. But even if he were disposed to soften the lot of the deportees, as some say he is, he could not tolerate insurrection such as that on Musa Dagh. Appealing to him or any other Ottoman official would lead nowhere. I don't see *any* way of getting the message out in time, even if the Powers were disposed to intervene, which is far from certain. Were it in my ability to help, I would do so without hesitation, even if it meant violating my country's neutrality. But I just don't see *how*.'

I translated the consul's words for Minas. Our faces must have expressed our disappointment. Minas spoke in Turkish, slowly so there was no need for translation. 'We also understand what you say. We had hoped that America would care, and would help. We will go now, and thank you for your time and concern. However, *please* give our request some thought. Please see if you can think of a way to get a message out. Your government must have contacts with Britain and France, if it cannot act directly.'

'Minas, eat some more *fatteh*. Don't you like it?' Mayrig pressed.

'*Tante*, it is delicious, but I can't stop thinking about the others, up there, my people – our people. Do you know what they eat up there?

I must go back; I have been here for five days, they must have assumed the worst, even worse than it is.' She put her hand on his shoulder.

'Go back? What for? To end up like poor Arpag? What good would that do anyone?'

'Maybe none at all, but I *cannot* stay. I—' A knock at the door. It was Abu Kemal, Jackson's *chaoush*. 'Please could the young men call on Consul Jackson, as soon as possible.'

'Now?' I blurted out.

'If possible you are to return with me, *khawaja* Vartan.'

At the consulate, Jackson told us what he had been doing, or rather trying to do. He had sent the same Abu Kemal, a Muslim from Tripoli, in Lebanon, to Beirut. He was instructed to call on the governor of Mount Lebanon, Ohannes Pasha Kouyoumjian, with a secret verbal message from Jackson.

'Ohannes, being Armenian, has just resigned. His position was, as you can imagine, untenable; he is a good man and I hoped that he could take our message about Musa Dagh to the British or the French. Unfortunately, he had left for—Aleppo, of all places. Abu Kemal rushed back here on the first train but they are slow, as you know. We tracked the governor down to the Baron Hotel; I went to see Onnig Mazloumian, the hotel keeper, and found that Kouyoumjian and his wife had left the day before, for Constantinople.'

Minas looked at me, with shock and disappointment on his face: such an opportunity had been missed by so little! Jackson's sad frown suggested he felt the same.

'Finally, it will be up to those on Musa Dagh to attract the attention of the civilised world to their plight,' he told us. 'There must be some way of displaying a message which would be seen by passing warships, isn't there? What about painting a plea for help on white sheets, in very large letters, and hanging them from trees, or spreading them on the hillside under the ramparts you described? And another, with a huge red cross the warships could see even from a great distance? I don't think there is much I can do from here, but if at all possible, I will get a message out to the French and British to have their warships blockading the coast watch for such a signal. Ships are not likely to ignore a distress signal, even if it comes from the land.'

'Perhaps,' said Minas, after a moment's thought, 'it could be done, though we haven't seen any ships so far. Not one, and God knows we have been looking.' He turned towards Jackson: 'Everything would depend on your warning them to watch out for our signal. But that means I must get this message back up the mountain. I will go back as I came, I am much stronger now. I will leave at once.'

'No you won't,' I stopped him. 'Not alone. Just as you and Arpag came as a pair, and one of you managed to get through, so we will go together and hopefully get through together. At least one of us will, *inshallah*, God willing.' I surprised myself with that 'God willing'.

'Goodbye, Mr Jackson,' I translated for Minas; 'please do whatever you can.' The consul nodded and seemed strangely moved; I looked up from the street and saw him watching us go from his window. My worry was what to tell Mayrig. I couldn't go without seeing her – I hoped to leave with her blessing, though I knew it would be hard on her, still grieving for the other children she had buried. Her stony face looked like one of those old marble masks they find in the ruins, but she did not hesitate long.

'Of course, you must go with Minas. I will make you packages of food. And Varo, you must take *al-hanash* – Viper.' I had not thought about Viper in a long time. This was one of Father's last productions, one I knew he considered the most artistic thing he ever made. Not just a knife – a dagger. A blade of Damascus steel, honed sharp as a razor and mostly straight but with a slight, deadly curl upwards just before the point. The handle was a work of art; ebony with silver filigree chased into the wood, half-circles looking for all the world like the scales of a snake, beginning at the hilt and right up to a knob like a snake's head, with its mouth ever so slightly open.

The thrill of the day Father asked me to handle it, even to throw it at a wooden target, to test its balance. Which was perfect.

In the serpent's mouth, barely visible behind the silver fangs, you could just make out something dark green which, almost hidden, was an emerald the size of a pigeon's egg. If you didn't know, you would never have guessed. That was what Father said it was all about: hidden, secret beauty. He had made it for one of Aleppo's most important citizens, Hajj Abdul Wahhab al-Mudarris. Then when he died, Mayrig could not bear to part with it. Father was a stern man, and hated spending money. While he was alive, she used to have to feed all of us on an allowance that was really too small, and Father appeared not to have left any savings. It was a big sacrifice for her to send back the price of Viper, which the Hajj had paid in advance. A servant brought back the money the same day, with a message saying it was a present to honour the memory of her husband, and offering to help if she ever needed anything in the future. 'That's what it means to be an aristocrat!' I remember thinking.

Mayrig showed me how to fit the scabbard of stiff leather to the small of my back, held in place with a linen belt under my shirt. That way it was completely invisible, but did not hinder my movement. I practised reaching back and drawing it with one gesture, first putting my hand under my shirttail, which I wore outside my trousers. Mayrig surprised me with a long hug, and sent us on our way with small packages of food – and nothing else, since we would soon be going for a long swim. '*Tsedesoutioun*, Mayrig.' I said 'goodbye' in Armenian, as it had to be, though we usually spoke Arabic in our family. My voice broke a little and I left quickly before embarrassing myself even more. She was reciting a prayer to Saint Sarkis, supposed to protect travellers. I glanced up one last time at the foot of the stairs, and saw she was crying, something she didn't even do when Father died.

3

Beirut: October 1984

Asrar-e azalra

You'll never know the secrets of eternity, nor will I
You'll not decipher that obscure script, nor will I;
They're talking about you and me, behind that veil –
But when the veil drops, there's no more you, no more I.

VARTAN HELD the volume of Khayyam's *Rubaiyat* open
on his lap, but most of the quatrains came to him from
memory, across four or five decades. *Isn't that the paradox?
By the time you find out what's in store for you, there's no more 'you'.* He
looked up at the ceiling, the stucco voluptes with their gilded high-
lights faintly visible beyond the upper reaches of the lantern's circle
of light. *I love Rumi. But he is so full of divine ecstasy, of the music of the
spheres, that I cannot completely give myself up to him. I am irretrievably
earthbound. I can identify with Khayyam, I feel his poetry as though I had
written it. Rumi I love to read or listen to or recite, as I know and love
certain pieces of music I know I could never have composed.*

*There are some verses knocking around in my memory, I can't remem-
ber whether they are by Khayyam or Rumi or Razi. Does it matter who
the author was – or even if I remember it correctly? When a bird sings
where does its song go? Does it die with the bird? Khayyam is a soulmate.
Sometimes I feel as though I could compose a quatrain like his, even one
that he might not disavow. Maybe I should try to write my own* ruba'i.

Vartan thought for a while, playing with verses and rhymes, and finally recited out loud:

> The nightingale sings for us on a summer's day
> The summer soon passes, as soon must the singer;
> Where's the song we treasure, once the bird has flown?
> Where the song when the bird – and we – are dead and gone?

'Tfou.' *Flat. Not as easy as it looks.* He got up stiffly, joints thickened by age, bulk and hours of sitting, and went to the old oak drinks cupboard, a survivor of their brief stay in London. Several empty bottles, one quite full of vieille prune, one half-empty of Talisker, another quite empty but formerly home to Ardbeg, his smoky favourite. He poured himself a generous slosh of Talisker and returned to his chair. He repeated this a couple of times, and was beginning to feel pleasantly drunk, when – as so often – his thoughts drifted back to Aleppo soon after the war. The one they thought of as 'The War' at the time. He was carried away with reconstruction, of houses, of lives, of a nation that had come within a whisker of annihilation. Then they called it the Great War, when it was finally over; then the First World War after the Second raised its ugly head. *Now 'La Guerre', here at least, is this Lebanese war, which we first called the 'Events', then the 'Troubles', until finally it was yet another war. Not a global one, but it might as well be for those who are trapped in this place. Like me. As though all the events of my life conspired to have me end up here, holed up in this battered palace with the world ending all around. Conspired? I chose to come back, cannot blame a soul. What did Kafka say, wishing he was where he was by 'accident rather than design'?*

in kohne ribat-ra

> This threadbare inn they call the world,
> This piebald couch of dawn and night,

Is mere leftovers from a hero's hundred feasts –
A place where a hundred others took their rest.

He looked at the shadows beyond the circle of light, fluted marble columns rising towards the ceiling like the trunks of palm trees, dissolving in the darkness just short of their Doric capitals, too Palladian for the ornate Venetian style of the house. *Just as well not to see them more clearly.* He took another sip of the whisky, felt its warmth spread from his gullet to his middle and let himself drift. The old house in Beirut faded away, along with half a century. It was a dry winter day in Aleppo, with a cold west wind blowing dust and small bits of rubbish down the narrow streets, making him raise the collar of his jacket.

A boy came to the building site where he was overseeing the construction of homes in the new Armenian quarter north of the centre, north of the Sebil station of sad memory. 'Your wife wants you, the baby is coming.' The baby! Over a month early; he was not sure what to think of it, what it meant other than that he should be with her as soon as he could. He told the foreman to take over and started on his way without even stopping to wash his hands, white as they were with lime from the bag he had ripped open when a workman was struggling with it: 'my hands are small but stronger than his,' he had thought. Indulging his vanity when she was probably in pain or danger. He remembered Mayrig's last childbirth. Her cries had distressed him: 'If it hurts that much why do they do it?' the boy he was had thought.

Finally, he arrived at Ramadaniyye. They had considered fixing up the old Atawi house but she could not bear the thought of living there. Today there was a terrible silence in their new house – not usually a particularly noisy place, but there was always some activity, sweeping or dusting in the living room or something being chopped in the kitchen. The look on her face, and that of the servant Armenag, said it all. The baby had come before its time, his time, for it was a boy. Not yet ready for this world. He had tried to console her, to say that they were still young, that there would be others, stillborn words that hung in the air without penetrating her grief, what he would soon realise was her unshakeable, perhaps self-fulfilling conviction that they would never have a child together.

He shook his head, trying, failing to chase the morose thoughts away. *Then Tehran: I thought the change would be good for her. Iran was the land of opportunity, a new Shah who wanted to modernise his country, but a country that was not even medieval in its society, its roads and communications. That first trip with her in the Model T, across desert tracks from Aleppo to the Euphrates. Our so-called guide, Hattab he was called, almost naked with weird tattoos on his chest. He was a Nusairi, I think, worshippers of the devil or something just as strange. Every time I asked him how much longer it would be before Deir az-Zor, he looked into the distance, standing on the running board, and said 'An hour!' When it started getting late he got more and more agitated and then when we slowed down to cross a gully, he just ran off into the desert and that was the last we saw of him. He just couldn't get his bearings while travelling by car.*

We found Deir az-Zor without him in the end, though I have never felt so surrounded by ghosts. Almost ten years it had been since the massacres. A boy in the khan *said there were places in the desert where bones stuck up out of the sand, the killing fields where they finished off the Armenians who made it all the way there. He offered to take us there. She was afraid I would accept, I think! But why wallow in all that? We were trying to go forward, to get on with our lives, a new beginning. Certainly, that was my idea. But can one ever start afresh? The baggage always follows, like a trunk that missed the boat.*

Vartan leaned back in the old white chair and stared up at the ceiling, not at anything in particular, just up, his thoughts dissolving into the deepening darkness like the soaring columns.

4

Near Aleppo: September 1915

M Y MIND was buzzing as we walked out of Aleppo on the road towards the sea. I was worried about our chances. Not afraid, exactly, but I knew that if we both drowned, our message would never get through. The last, slim chance would be lost. There had to be another way of getting there, and I suddenly realised I knew of one. 'Minas, I'll share my thoughts with you. I know you are a strong swimmer, but you are not up to your normal strength, you know that. There is a good chance that this time, neither of us will make it: we will have to swim against the wind, which almost always blows onshore, pushing the waves towards the land. The long swim will be dangerous and exhausting, and I doubt either of us will make it no matter how hard we try. Let's take a different road, not to the bay facing Musa Dagh, just south of the Turkish camp, where you swam. Instead we will walk down to the village of al-Basit, further to the south but just as close to here. I know there is, or used to be, a sailboat. We will sail to Musa Dagh, avoiding both the swim and the Turks. I am not afraid to swim, but we have a duty to succeed, and by drowning we won't help anyone.'

Minas stared at me. '*Sail*, Varo? Just the two of us? In what kind of boat? *Whose* boat? I've never even been in a sailboat. Maybe you should try that if you really want, and let me swim back, at least I know I can swim across. Our mission is too important to take chances.' I stopped walking and took my cousin by the shoulders.

'Minas, trust me. I would only suggest such an idea if I were sure it was better than swimming. It's my Uncle Sarkis's boat, I have sailed in it many times with him. If for some reason it is not there or is no longer seaworthy, we still have plenty of time to go back to the original plan.'

'I don't know, Varo. I don't like it.'

'I don't *like* it either. But can you honestly tell me you feel up to swimming back against the waves?'

Minas looked down and thought for a moment, his forehead creased in a frown. He finally shook his head and looked up at me. 'I am ready to swim back, to do my best in the hope at least one of us gets through. But you are right, it has to be riskier than last time. If you are so sure, I suppose we don't lose anything by trying. We can always get out of the boat and swim for it if it doesn't work right, can't we?'

In fact I was secretly worried. A couple of swimmers would likely avoid the attention of anyone who was not looking for them, but never a sailboat. Nor did Minas look completely convinced, but I could tell he was also dreading the return swim through the waters that had swallowed his cousin.

The boat was in its place, tied up and bobbing against the ramshackle dock along with two other pleasure boats and a half-dozen fishing caiques. The little boat's sails had been tightly furled along the boom, which was lashed in place, like the tiller, to keep it snug in the face of winter gales. The boat had apparently not been used for at least a season. There were a few inches of water in the bilge: I tasted it – rainwater, nothing to worry about. We walked back and forth along the dock, whistling and looking all around, not just at Sarkis's boat, scanning the few fishermen's cabins for signs of life. Seeing none, I nodded to Minas and we clambered in and began untying the mooring ropes. While Minas was doing that, I freed the tiller and loosed the mainsail from the reefing lines, then began hoisting it. There was the usual offshore breeze blowing, so we would have to tack off against the wind. I knew it would take a while to get outside the bay, which was broad with a small island about half a mile offshore. Once past it, we could bear away on a more comfortable point of sail. Until then, we would be an easy target for rifle fire from the shore, if someone were to notice what looked like thieves stealing Sarkis's boat.

We pushed off the dock, clumsily and without gaining enough momentum to get free; our sail flapping, the wind blew us back heavily against a fishing boat. I pulled the sail in far enough this time, shoved off with my foot and, with Minas on the tiller and me pulling on the sail, we tacked hesitantly away from the harbour at an oblique angle off to the north, under the mainsail alone. I handed the mainsheet to Minas and went forward to deploy the headsail, which had been folded and lashed to one of the two seats. The rigging and tackle proved to be still sound, and before long both sails were up and filled. We had come about once and were sailing briskly along, heading out to sea on a starboard tack that would take us clear of the headland. I had to smile, thinking how much fun it would have been to be on the water on such a warm late-summer day if we had no mission. It seemed years since I had thought of doing anything simply for fun.

I decided we would sail until the sun set, in about an hour and a half, and then set a course for land, looking to come ashore when it was too dark for us to be noticed. Minas looked worried when I told him.

'Sail at night? How will we know where we are going? How can we find the right place to land?'

'Minas, don't worry about that. While it's light, you need to look carefully at the coast under Musa Dagh and figure out where the best place to come ashore would be, close to the path you came down. I will figure out our course by the stars once the sun is down and try to steer as close as I can to the spot you have chosen. So for the next hour or so there is not much to do. There are some things

I didn't understand from your story. Tell me, how did the villages of Musa Dagh come to rebel, when every other Armenian village and town seems to have just accepted their fate?'

'I would say it all started with Pastor Andreasian…' I listened spellbound as my cousin told about the modest Protestant pastor who found himself leading a peasant rebellion against the mighty Ottoman Empire. The town meeting where the decision had been taken; the departure of those who chose obedience rather than the unknown. Then the frantic preparations of the hilltop site where four thousand farmers moved in one night, bringing their flocks of sheep and goats and everything it would take to improvise accommodation and defence. How they repulsed the first assault that saw the enraged Turkish attackers charge up the mountain, baying for blood. And then the siege, where as the weeks wore on, hunger and dissension compounded the danger they faced. Then the second attack, an all-out assault that had been defeated with heavy losses.

'What a story, Minas,' I said at length after his feverish account gave way to a heavy silence. 'Your parents are there, I am sure, and most of your other relatives?'

'Only a few other than Ma and Pa, most of them chose to follow the sheep to slaughter. There's Shoushan, a girl from Aintab; a cousin of mine, you must have met her years ago. One elderly aunt who died of grief when her son was killed in the second attack. But it's like we are all family up there, you'll see. I hope you will, I mean, if they are still holding out, and if we actually make it up there.'

Slowly, as we talked, the sunset set fire to the distant towers of cloud far out to sea, then faded. Soon we could just make out the two distant mountains against the starry sky, not in themselves but as black holes in the field of stars. We began to shiver as the temperature dropped, but the thrill of being out among the wind and stars and sea on such a night, mingled with excitement at what lay ahead, made us ignore the cold.

Minas had told me to aim just to the left of the main bulk of the mountain, and the plan worked, up to a point. I set a comfortable course riding the sea breeze, which had fallen off after dark, towards the coast. The problem was we could not see the shore on this moonless night, and I was not actually all that sure that I could make an accurate landfall. I could just make out the white flash of phosphorescence in the gentle waves breaking on the rocks about a hundred yards ahead. 'Any thoughts, Minas?' I asked, on the off-chance he could make out some landmark to guide our course closer towards the path than to the Turks. Before he could answer, the little boat was in the shallows, its keel scraping on the pebbles, then lurching on to its beam as it ground to a stop. I was dumped on the beach, Minas in the shallow water. We tossed our food-parcels on the dry sand and pulled the boat a bit further up, its sails flapping.

'What about the boat?' asked Minas. 'It will give us away as soon as dawn breaks. They are sure to send soldiers to investigate. We will never find the trail in the dark so we have to spend the night down here somewhere. Why didn't you think of this?' I looked at the boat, which indeed would be very visible in the daylight.

'It will sail away by itself, Minas. Let's get it back afloat.' We dragged it back into the water and swung it around. In water up to my waist, I held the gunwale to windward, set the sail for a broad starboard reach, tied the mainsheet to an oarlock and lashed the tiller amidships. The little boat pulled away from my hands and sailed slowly away on the soft sea breeze, towards the south. The sail soon disappeared in the darkness, and with it our only means of escape. I wondered where Uncle Sarkis's boat would end up, as it would surely blow on to the coast during the night. I knew he would approve.

After devouring Mayrig's cheese and bread, we crawled into the underbrush, curled up as comfortably as we could and tried to sleep. The night was warmer on the land than on the sea, so we were not cold, but I could sense that Minas was as sleepless as I was, looking up at the same stars and imagining what the coming day would bring. First to find the trail, then to climb without attracting attention, then to avoid being shot by the defenders, who would not be expecting friendly visitors. I must have fallen asleep at some point, for I awoke with a start. It was already light enough to distinguish shapes. Minas was sound asleep; reluctantly, I shook him awake. We ate the last of our picnic, then crept up on to the closest large rock to take a look around. 'Well, Minas, where do you think we are?' I asked.

My cousin studied the still shadowy landscape, gradually becoming more distinct. 'Look at the plume of smoke over there: that's where the Turkish camp is, just where the coast turns out towards us. We must be pretty near the path but we will need to explore to find it. I think it's further along to the left from where we are, so let's start that way.'

Minas soon located the trail. 'It took me and Arpag about an hour to reach the coast from the top, I think that climbing up will take us twice as long, or nearly. Let's get started before it gets any later.' Stepping up from rock to rock, we would use a branch of scrub pine to pull ourselves up to the next foothold. Goat droppings here and there were often the only clue as to which way the trail led. It was strenuous but we made good progress for about an hour. 'Let's stop for a minute, Minas,' I said. 'What a beautiful place!' His face darkened.

'Wait until you see how they are, up there, how they have been living for six weeks. Wait until you taste grass stew! We must help them, we are their only hope – and just look at us. Two idiots with nothing but a crazy American idea about spreading sheets for ships to see, ships that aren't even there. They'll just make good targets for Turkish cannons!'

We carried on. Suddenly a shout echoed across the hillside in Turkish: 'Who goes there?' My blood froze. Before we could react, a shot rang out, the bullet ricocheting off a rock not ten paces away.

Another crack of rifle fire, a dull smack from an umbrella pine off to the right. The scrub pine and cedar had given way to tall pines as we climbed, shading the path and providing partial protection from the sentinel who must have been two or three hundred paces below us. We heard his frantic, nasal Turkish shouts for assistance. Scrambling as fast as we could up the stony path, we scurried from one tree to the next. Another shot rang out; I felt a violent blow to my right hip, lost my balance and fell heavily forward. I lay with my cheek on the ground, my left eye looking straight at a purple thistle. I clenched my teeth to bear the intense pain in my backside without moaning.

Minas, who was ahead of me, must have heard me grunt; he was suddenly bending over me. 'Are you all right?'

'Be quiet,' I said in a loud whisper. 'I seem to have taken a hit in the buttock.'

'Let me see,' he whispered. 'I have seen a lot of wounds during the past weeks.' I heard a tearing sound and felt a new stab of pain. 'You will live, Varo, or at least this bullet in the arse won't kill you unless you bleed to death. Do you think you can walk?'

'Do I have a choice? I'll walk, but not as fast as before. I can feel that. You *must* go on ahead with the message. I will catch up at my own speed. Now *go!*'

'No way, *kardeshim*. I lost Arpag but I will drag you up the mountain if I have to.'

Another shot rang out, whistling through the trees above us, then a whole volley as the sentinel was joined by others, all shouting at the same time, their voices closer now. Minas put his arm around my shoulders, one hand under my armpit, and joined together we hobbled through the pine copse on three legs, turning left at an orchard: figs and pears and plums, trees heavy with ripe, unharvested fruit which, in another time, another world, we would have gorged ourselves on. Now all I could think about was the pain and need to keep going.

The firing continued, but was wild; they seemed to have lost sight of us since we left the orchard. The path was more distinct up here, and the climb would have been less arduous if only I could pull my weight. A stony outcrop offered some protection but occasional shots from what sounded like a single rifle were getting louder. At least one shooter, I thought, was trying to follow us up the trail. I tried to focus all my thoughts and strength on the need to keep going despite the pain – and the rivulet of warm blood I could feel running down the back of my leg, leaving a trail I could see when I looked back, a line of red blotches that would lead the Turk straight to us.

Then the path took a turn to the right. More gunshots, but now further away. Minas tried to reassure me: 'Another five minutes and we will see the ramparts on the south side of the Damlayik, the plateau where my people, our people, are camped. In ten minutes the old doctor will fix you up, just keep going, keep walking, *kardeshim*.' I began to feel light-headed and vaguely sleepy. The pain seemed less but I had an ominous feeling it was due to loss of blood.

Soon a new voice rang out, from above us this time, and we could make out the torso of a man holding a rifle. 'Who goes there?' but this time in Armenian. Minas answered: 'Minas *yem*! Minas and Vartan from Aleppo! Vartan has been shot, get Doctor Altouni, fast!' Shouts rose from behind the stone and rubble rampart.

'It is Minas! Minas is back!' Strong hands were bearing me up, over the stones and pickets, but roughly and the pain was unbearable. Then we were on the flat; I felt the world going dark and beginning to turn in circles. I had very little impression of the scene we were passing through. A bearded old priest, standing with bright but slightly crazed eyes, his fists clenched by his side; ragged men and women, skinny children thronging the empty space between the huts. A woman wailing uncontrollably. 'Maybe Arpag's mother,' I thought, 'Minas must have told her.' I felt unbearably sleepy. The pain subsided as I sank into darkness.

50

When I awoke, I was on a makeshift cot, in a tent. My hip was painful but the pain was dull, not the unbearable searing pain of before. I still felt weak and slightly dizzy. I had no idea whether or not it was still the day of our arrival. Probably not. A middle-aged lady, who must have been forty, stood near the head of my cot, watching me wake up. 'Well, young Nakashian, you will live. A Mauser bullet in the backside is not enough to kill an Armenian, even a city boy like you. Fortunately we still have tincture of iodine, that's all a flesh wound like yours needed. But you will have a permanent souvenir of the event – two of them, in fact.'

She spoke in Armenian, the soft dialect of Cilicia like my mother's. I felt myself blush; my posterior must have been examined by this lady and who knows how many others. She laughed: 'We have few secrets up here, packed into this meadow like so many sheep. I wish I had a good broth for you. Until what passes for the evening meal is cooked, all I can give you is this. We call it "tea" but it's anything but, just boiled roots and leaves. At least it is warm. Here, drink.'

The pain when I sat up was much sharper, but I tried not to show it. I drank the bitter, watery liquid. 'Well, young man, you have put yourself in a real pickle; your backside is the least of it.' Her eyes were large, dark Armenian ones. I was sure they were made even bigger than normal by the dark circles under them, by her thinness.

'And you, Auntie?' I asked.

'I am Mrs Altouni, wife of the doctor. Call me Antaram.'

'How long have I been here?'

'You slept for two days, my son. You had lost a lot of blood but the doctor said you were strong and well fed and this wound will not be what kills you.'

'I must make myself useful. Please tell me where to go to find out what I can do.' She reached down and smoothed my hair.

'You are not going anywhere today. You must rest and make some more red blood cells, if you can on what we feed you. Tomorrow we shall see.'

Suddenly I realised something was missing, that familiar presence against my back. I felt with my hand: no Viper. I looked at her and she guessed my thoughts. 'Your beautiful dagger is safe, young man. We wrapped it in its belt and put it under your clothes, under your cot. You will have need of it soon enough, I am afraid. For today, you will rest.'

I looked around what was clearly the infirmary tent, with two rows of four or five improvised cots, most of which were occupied by men much more severely wounded than me, some with heads wrapped in bloodstained bandages and some with half a leg or only one arm. One of them was constantly moaning, an unbearable sound. Just then Minas came in. 'Ha! Up and chatting already, Varo! I'll bring in Pastor Andreasian, he wants to hear from you about our meeting with the consul, as well as what you have seen in Aleppo.'

'Minas is trying to be cheerful,' I thought. 'He looks as though he hasn't eaten since we arrived.' Minas went out again, which gave me the chance to extricate myself from the bedclothes. I wanted to look ready to get up and pitch in, feeling stupid that perhaps the only properly fed person in the camp should be hindered by a superficial wound.

I stood up, quite a painful business, and straightened the long cotton shirt that had replaced my own bloodstained one. 'I wonder who undressed me?' I thought. I took up my trousers and found they had been washed, no longer stiff with salt water, the bloodstains fainter; two neat holes in the seat showed where the bullet went in and out. I managed to pull them on without disturbing the bandage, and was just trying to get my shoes on when they walked into the tent. My eyes were drawn to the pastor, whose appearance surprised me. Slightly built, mid-forties, I thought; clean-shaven except for a neatly trimmed moustache. A person with no commanding presence or military swagger. Light greyish-hazel eyes gave him a slightly foreign air. Hunger had set his eyes deep in their sockets and drawn sharp lines around the corners of his mouth.

'Welcome, young Nakashian. You sit back and leave your shoes for now, all we need is for you to start bleeding again. Well, well, I didn't imagine we would acquire any new recruits at this stage. By the way, I know your mother's family from Killis. I'm pleased to see that Marie's son is such a fine young man. But you have done wrong to come here, to join a doomed enterprise. As a resident of Aleppo you had no need to do that. Your widowed mother needs you more than we do.'

I looked up at the solemn eyes, kinder than the stern message, though for an instant my mother's face flashed through my mind, crying on the doorstep of our home. I pulled myself up straight and said, 'Do not believe that just because they are not deporting Armenians from Aleppo, not yet at least, we don't care about what is happening to our people. I would not want to be anywhere else. All I ask is to be given a task so that I can pull my weight in your – our – struggle. My mother is a strong woman and I have an older brother who is with her.' I had to banish a fleeting mental image of the effete and selfish Halim. 'Maybe he will act more mature now that I am gone,' I thought.

The pastor approached and put his hand on my shoulder. 'We will talk about all that when you have regained your strength and can move about freely. From what Altouni says, your wound is not serious; but you must be kept quiet until it has healed enough that it's no longer liable to bleed you to death. But tell me about things in Aleppo – the survivors who reach the city, what happens to them after arrival? Have you heard of any coming from Zeitoun or the deportees from our six villages, for that matter, the ones who chose not to come up here with us? And especially, your impression of the American consul and his intentions. His desire and ability to do something for us.'

I had not spoken so much Armenian since leaving Jerusalem more than a year ago. What came out at first was a mixture of Cilician dialect I learned from my mother, and the formal language of the

Brothers. With Minas I had spoken Turkish, but up here I did not want to use the language of our torturers. Gradually I relaxed and despite the occasional stammer began to speak with a fluency that surprised me. What it sounded like to their ears I cannot say.

'In Aleppo our life was comfortable enough. When the first refugees started to arrive, we could not believe our eyes. Survivors from Zeitoun, Marash and Aintab, hardly one in ten of those who had set out. The ones from your villages must have come through the city, but I was not aware of them and cannot say where they were sent. The ones from Killis were among the luckier ones, having bribed the guards to let them get off the train in Aleppo. The most miserable ones came from further north, from Harput and Trabizon and Sivas, Erzerum and Van. Their road had been so long and hard, those who made it to the city seemed like walking corpses. Many of them died before they could either be helped or sent on.' I stopped and looked at Minas. 'You were there, Minas. Why don't you tell about our meetings with Jackson?'

'I did,' he said. 'But you know the consul better than I do, you speak his language. Please tell the pastor what you really think he meant for us to do and, especially, what if anything he intends to do himself.' I explained his idea of the sheets and messages of distress. The pastor made me repeat his promise that he would try and get a message out to the French and British blockading fleet, that they should watch for such a signal and do whatever they could to help. I made it sound like a little more like a promise than what it was, a wish.

'Even if he wanted to, and even if he did try,' asked the pastor, 'do you think he can get such a message through despite Ottoman control of the telegraph, roads and ports? The consulates of the Entente Powers are all closed, not just in Aleppo but in Beirut and everywhere.'

'Ah,' I said, 'that depends on whether he takes risks on our behalf, plus luck. I trust him and believe that we must put the signals where they can be seen, as soon as we can.'

'Actually, we've been discussing just such an idea ourselves: my wife Araxi has started sewing black letters on a huge banner made of two sheets sewn together: "Christians in Distress, Rescue." A red cross is an even better idea, and I will get her to work on it right away. However, for all our watching, there has not been a single ship or even a plume of smoke, not in the nearly six weeks we have been up here. We must not lose hope, but do what we can and pray for help with what we cannot.'

I grew heartily sick of the infirmary, but had promised not to leave my cot until Doctor Altouni said I could. I had plenty of time to think about everything that had happened during the past few months in my city. If it had not been for leaving Mayrig and the children to face unknown troubles, I felt almost glad to be where I was, dangerous or not. At least the people on the Damlayik were fighting back. At least here there would be some sort of resolution, even if it must be deadly. It would not be a humiliation.

As I lay on my cot with all these thoughts buzzing in my head, the tent flap was thrown back and a girl appeared. A slim girl about my age, with a mass of frizzy coal-black hair pulled back and woven into a single plait. Her oval face was made striking by large, dark, intense almond-shaped eyes which met my own without a trace of shyness. Her cheeks must normally have been rather full, but were sunken, her cheekbones prominent.

'You are Vartan from Aleppo?' she said in the soft Cilician dialect.

'I am, and you?' I answered. I could feel a deep blush creeping up my cheeks.

'I am Shoushan, did Minas not tell you about me?'

'Er, no, I mean, yes, ah, you're the girl from Aintab?'

'I'm from Aintab, all right, but that's not all I am. I'm a niece of Minas's mother, and you're a nephew of his father, so we're almost cousins, you and I. Our family name is der Markar: have you never even heard of us, Vartan Nakashian?'

I looked for words but none came. I only blushed deeper. 'Yes, of course,' I finally managed to stammer. 'Only everything that happened before last spring seems so far away. How did you come to be at Yoghun-Oluk?'

'I'm a wanderer, like you, it seems. Aintab is so boring! Or at least I used to think so. I was visiting Minas's family, my aunt Azniv, when the troubles started; they kept me with them as there was no way I could safely travel back home. My own family was deported with all the others from our town, and I have had no news of them since June, when I heard that they went by train to Aleppo. That is the last I heard; I thought – I hoped – you might know something.'

'No, I'm sorry.' I pushed my glasses up and looked at her, then at the floor, wishing I could give her good news. Any news. Find anything to say. I had not known many girls. In Jerusalem the school was rigorously segregated; back in Aleppo I had been busy helping Mayrig until the deportations began, then events just swept me along. I thought of females as either children or middle-aged or beyond, like Mayrig and the widows she kept company with. But here was something different. I was at a loss for words, which I at first resented but then I had to smile to myself for being so stupid.

She sat cross-legged on the floor near my cot and we talked. And talked, as though we had to hurry up and cover every possible subject. Before long I had lost my embarrassment. She had chores that took her away for an hour or two here and there, but when she could, she came back. She was exactly my age, born two years before the turn of the century, like me, but in May rather than February.

'Tell me about life in Aleppo, Varo,' she said. At first I didn't know where to start.

'It's a big town, very old, with the oldest part squeezed in behind the city walls. An old citadel dominates everything. It's a military area, but my friend Omar and I used to sneak in when the sentinels were patrolling elsewhere.'

'Omar?' she interrupted. 'A Muslim?'

'With us, Shoushan, there was no "Christian" or "Muslim", we were just friends. His father is an important man and they are much wealthier than us, but that didn't matter either. We used to laugh that we were as alike as brothers, but as it was we didn't have to be rivals about anything. Of course, we lived in different neighbourhoods. All the neighbourhoods are divided up by religion and money. Ours, Atawi Saghir, is mostly Armenian, modest people but not poor. We don't often go into the richer Christian quarters, and no wealthy merchant or landowner would dream of visiting Atawi. And no Christian would venture into the poor Muslim areas.'

I stopped talking and looked at her to see whether my long speech was boring her, but her face said otherwise, looking up at me with those huge dark eyes. I felt like I could – like I wanted to – drown myself in them.

'In a way, then, our lives have not been so different. I grew up in the Armenian part of a Turkish town; we were about half the population, artisans and farmers, and got along fine with our Turkish neighbours. So we thought, anyway. They grazed sheep and owned land or houses which they rented out, so there were business relations. But it was definitely "them" and "us". We would take them *lokoum* for their Bayram, they would bring us *maamoul* cakes for Easter. We attended their circumcisions, they came to our christenings. And funerals of course. When they went back home there was a lot of gossiping, and I am sure they did the same. But tell me one thing, Vartan. Why did you come up here? Did Minas really need you to find his way back? You would have been safe in Aleppo. Here we are probably going to die, one way or the other. And don't you dare say you wanted to see if I was visiting from Aintab!'

I couldn't help laughing, and blushing. 'No, it was not on your account, *Miss* Shoushan. Minas was exhausted and I was worried about him making that long swim. Staying in Aleppo while people were being massacred all around was painful. Pastor Andreasian said the same thing, that I should have stayed with my mother. From one point of view he was right, and I feel guilty. If you had met Mayrig, though, you would know she is strong as any man. Anyway, I never really thought about it, maybe not as much as I should have. Sometimes you just have to do something. All those people who went to their deaths without really resisting the butcher's knife. That's why Musa Dagh is so important. I would not want to be anywhere else than here with you.' I added quickly, 'I mean with *all* of you.'

Shoushan was quiet. 'I am glad you are here with us. With all of us. *And* with me.' With that she left. Two days later, Dr Altouni made one last examination of my wound, put iodine and a fresh dressing on it and said I could get up, provided I moved around carefully and avoided sudden contortions. I dressed in my own clothes, strapped Viper in its place under my shirt and hobbled out to find Minas, and to get an idea of this strange makeshift town on a mountain top.

Strange is a weak word. A tent city with neat rows of accommodation and no solid buildings except for the church, a surprisingly sturdy wooden construction. There was an ancient priest in full ceremonial robes standing in front of it, the one I had glimpsed on arrival. I think he must have been senile; he was chanting something to himself, his eyes gone vague, his cheeks sunken and his lips pulled back from protruding teeth, like the skull he would soon be, 'one way or the other' as Shoushan had said. All around the perimeter were the ramparts, makeshift obstacles of rubble and logs, with protruding platforms like a caricature of an old fort. I passed a woman carrying a large, heavy bundle of washing; her face was drawn with hunger and fatigue, but she smiled when I took her burden and carried it, limping, to the washing tub. She said Minas was down at the lower pasture, helping to slaughter one of the last remaining animals, a donkey.

When I got there I found my cousin and a burly fellow with the look of an executioner holding the mane of the bedraggled and very thin animal. It had large, glassy, sad eyes that made it look as though it knew it was about to die and was grateful. 'Not much more than gristle and bone,' Minas told me, as he held the beast's head while the other man pierced its jugular with a long, pointed knife. 'And so many mouths to feed. But it won't be long now.'

'What do you mean?' I asked. 'What has happened?' The donkey slowly sank to its knees, lowering its muzzle almost to the widening puddle of its own dark blood.

'I mean,' Minas said, 'either the Turks who have been massing troops and artillery for a week now do a better job of attacking us than they have before and finish us off. Or the sheets with the distress message and red cross actually work and a ship miraculously comes to save us. If neither of those things happen, then we will starve to death: the weak and very old or young within a week, and the rest not many days later.'

'Can you show me around?' I asked. The burly man told Minas to go, he would take care of the butchering. We climbed back up past the ramparts and followed them around to the southern side; I saw a man on lookout duty on each corner of the zigzagging wall of rough stones and timbers. Just below us, draped on a huge old fig tree, the sheet with the red cross was fixed to a branch at each corner. The second sheet covered another tree, a sapling ten paces further along: 'Christians in Distress – Rescue', appealing to an empty blue sky. The haze was burning off as the sun climbed; but the sea was bare, empty all the way to a horizon so distant it appeared to curve. Only a few seagulls shrieked in the sky above, while the odd swallow flitted past, close to the ground. The air was sweet with pine and sage.

I was amazed at the organisation, the amount of building, the cleanliness of the camp. Besides the rows of tents, there were wooden huts for storing munitions, others for food and supplies. Nothing was locked. I could only imagine the amount of work and thought that had gone into creating this village out of nothing in such a short time. Four thousand people on this mountain! And they all moved up in one night. As we continued our tour, by the mountainside, the flat area through which the Turks had tried to attack, I saw other lookouts manning the trenches; everyone, regardless of age, sex or condition, seemed to be doing something. The only really unusual thing was the silence: except for the barking of a few dogs and the occasional children's shouts, the men and women went about their work with quiet concentration. Hunger had repressed the usual garrulous chatter of Armenian women, the banter of the men. The atmosphere was determined and sober; grim, perhaps, but not weepy or morose.

Minas took me to see his parents, my Uncle Artin and Aunt Azniv. I remembered them, but vaguely. Him I found much older, stooped and thin, with pince-nez; she had been fat, and was still portly, still just as talkative but as kind as her round, sweet face. 'Vartan Nakashian, welcome!' said Artin, while Azniv looked at me with brimming eyes. 'You have chosen a strange time to visit us, Vartan. We…' Suddenly, a most unlikely sound interrupted her, a rousing and clumsily played Ottoman Army bugle call.

'That's the general alarm!' cried Minas. 'It must be the attack we've been waiting for.' He took me by the sleeve and pulled me as fast as I could hobble to one of the makeshift wooden buildings, obviously the munitions store.

He turned and stopped me just before the door: 'Can you shoot?'

'Of course I can shoot!' I exclaimed. We waited while the men ahead of us received rifles and cartridge belts, then it was our turn. The quartermaster handed Minas his gun and bullets, then froze as he looked at me in surprise. He had obviously not heard of my arrival.

'Who in the world might *you* be?'

'Vartan Hovsep Nakashian, from Aleppo,' I answered, 'nephew of Artin Bedrossian,' and held out my hands to receive the antique Mauser and its cartridge belt.

'*Baron* Nakashian, from Aleppo! Now I have seen everything! Welcome to Paradise, crazy *halabi*.'

Minas led me to a staging post near the church. A grizzled old man with an army helmet and an air of command looked at us and barked, 'southern rampart, middle post'. We hurried as fast as we could to our position, which gave us a clear view down to the coast. I thought I could see, far below, the bit of beach between two rocks where we had landed our little boat. To the left we could see brown gaggles of troops moving along the shore, two more or less orderly bunches of regular infantry dragging a large artillery piece, which I supposed to be a cannon or machine gun on wheels, followed by a disorderly mass of irregulars. These were followed in turn by a rabble of civilians armed with hunting rifles and pitchforks.

'This will be the second time they attack like this, an organised assault led by regular troops,' said Minas. 'We were afraid they would send in the whole Fourth Army against us. The machine gun is new, we have not had to face one of those before, but I still think we can cope with this, except that our men are much weaker than last time and our supply of cartridges is dangerously low. We must make every bullet count. From where we stand, that swathe of the hillside is our responsibility,' he said, pointing down the mountain towards the beach, a strip of pine copse with a clearing and an orchard with what looked like mulberry or fruit trees, perhaps the one we had crossed on the way up.

'What is our plan, or do we just wait for them to attack?' I asked.

'The idea is to wait until the first ones reach the orchard, where we can get a clear shot at them; that's when we choose our target. Then we follow him in our gunsights until he almost reaches the thick ground cover, and fire. Then we move on to the next in line, and so forth. The men on the salient to our right and left will catch them in a cross-fire, so it is not up to us to stop them all. You work from right to left and I will do the opposite. I will fire two or three rounds, then you start and continue while I reload.' He showed me the breech of his gun. 'The tube holds eight rounds and it takes nearly half a minute to load, but you can add new cartridges to the breech without using up the rounds in the magazine. That's what I do when there is time, as we need to fire accurately rather than fast.'

I practised loading the magazine as well as inserting a single round into the breech and took a closer look at my rifle. These were old Mausers, made in Germany for the Ottoman Army in 1893, according to the inscription. The sights appeared to be excellent, calibrated with Ottoman numerals. Minas saw me examining it.

'The Turks have much more recent guns, also German, and all the ammunition they could wish for. And now that mobile machine gun we saw being rolled along the shore. We will have to be clever as well as careful!'

We could no longer see the machine gun, but we could see the brown uniforms of the advance troops working their way up the mountainside, firing their guns wildly as though trying to give themselves courage.

Suddenly Shoushan was there, pulling on my sleeve. 'Vartan, you never told me you were up and about!'

'I just left the infirmary an hour ago, and haven't had time to do anything except get my gun and take my place down here. Now off with you, we have some visitors to attend to!'

'I'll go, but only to bring ammunition where it is needed – that's my responsibility. We are all helping with the fight; don't be so arrogant just because you have a gun!' At which she turned and went back up the hill with a hint of a flounce, leaving me distracted for a moment. A word from Minas brought my concentration back. 'Watch the orchard, Varo!'

Just as Minas had predicted, in a few minutes the first Turks reached the relative clearing around the fruit trees, and a few seconds later the defenders fired their first rounds. A brown-uniformed soldier threw down his rifle, clutched his chest and sprawled backwards down the slope. 'I have just seen a man killed,' I thought, yet I felt no emotion. A few seconds later I found the chest of an attacker in my own gun-sight, which I had adjusted for a distance of four hundred metres. The Mauser barked, kicking harder than I expected against my shoulder. The Turk glanced up as the bullet whined over his head, and I saw Minas glance in my direction. Then I remembered what Uncle Sarkis had taught me, that firing down an incline would reduce the height the bullet will lose. Aiming by the two hundred metre notch, I fired again. This time the soldier stopped climbing, dropped his weapon and stood up straight for an instant, wavering before collapsing in a heap.

I never stopped to think that I had just killed a man. I found another brown figure in my sight, brought him down, and looked for another, feeding a cartridge into the breech after each shot. Minas was firing steadily too, as were the defenders on the salient closest to us, on our right. Soon there was a pause as an officer halted the advance; I think he realised that the orchard had become a killing ground. The clearing was strewn with bodies lying in grotesque positions, mostly dead but there were a few wounded, trying to drag themselves to the relative safety of the underbrush. Others twitched or thrashed in the throes of death.

We waited to see what the enemy would do next. About half an hour later, the first shots fired to any effect by the attackers rang out; they had spread out and climbed through the brush to various places from which they could fire up towards the ramparts without being seen for longer than it took to fire. Then, much louder, the machine gun began to chatter, its rhythmic tat-tat-tat punctuated by the irregular reports of rifles being fired on both sides. It first failed to find its range, shredding the branches of the trees just below the ramparts, then sending bullets whining overhead. But then it began to sweep our bastion, interfering with our firing and killing a man off to our right.

'Find the bugger!' came a shout from the salient nearest us. I fought my natural instinct to duck the next time the machine gun fired, and about two-thirds of the way down the hill I could just make out the tell-tale rhythmic flash from its muzzle. They had set up the gun between two umbrella pines, protected from most angles of fire. I could clearly see one of the gunners, the one holding a belt of cartridges and feeding it into the gun. It took all my self-control to aim, with those deadly flashes seeming to point at me, the bullets ricocheting off the stones of our ramparts. One hit the wall just near us, sending stone fragments flying, one of which grazed Minas's cheek, making him cry out. I caught his eye and was reassured it was not serious, then concentrated on the gunner.

I calculated the distance at about three hundred metres, set the sight for half that and gently pulled the trigger. The heavy rifle banged my shoulder, but the Turk only looked up as the bullet fell short and went on feeding ammunition into the chattering gun. I had wasted another cartridge. Now I aimed by the two hundred-metre notch, and this time the Turk pitched over backwards; the big gun fell silent. His place was soon taken by another soldier, who did not have time to feed more than five bullets into the gun before my rifle barked and he too crumpled.

There was a marksman, just a little older than me I thought, posted along the ramparts to the left of our position. I had noticed him as we took up our places: he wore a beret and a trim moustache, which I imagined made him look French. He started joking about the donkeys in uniform we were using for target practice, when the next second there was a loud 'splat' and a grunt. He dropped his rifle and fell over backwards with most of his face missing, instantly turned into a gruesome, bloody mess. I started to move towards him to see if I could help but Minas grabbed my arm: 'Nothing you can do, Varo, it's too late. Stay at your post.'

There was a lull as the infantry continued climbing the mountain, this time spread out and scrambling from one bush or tree to the next, no longer providing us with convenient targets. An occasional rifle shot from one side or the other broke the tense silence. I couldn't see the machine gun, which they must have repositioned under better cover. 'This is going to be a long day; God knows how it will end,' I thought. Just then we had a surprising visit. A swarthy middle-aged man in an Ottoman sergeant-major's uniform of all things. He climbed down on to our platform, inspecting the defences generally but I thought he seemed interested to meet me. Minas had mentioned him, an Antakya Armenian named Mounir who had fought in the Ottoman Army in the Balkans in 1908, returning home with a medal – 'For Valour' – and a bugle.

Minas introduced us: 'My cousin from Aleppo; he's the one who found the machine gun; this is Mounir.' The barrel-chested soldier smiled at me with a gap-toothed grin and gave me a friendly clap on the shoulder.

'This is only a practice battle, not a final assault,' he said. 'The Turks are probing, bringing their camp closer to the foot of the mountain, moving up a few pieces of mountain artillery Jemal Pasha has spared for them. Thank God the Fourth Army is having trouble crossing Suez, a much more important objective than a few ragged Christians holed up on this mountain.'

Suddenly a shout rang up from the furthest point of the southern salient: 'A ship! A *ship*! Looook!' And sure enough, a long grey shape had appeared about halfway to the horizon. Its four funnels sent up black smoke that hung in a pall behind it as it steamed, it seemed to me, straight towards us. The warship must have been visible for some time, but our attention had been concentrated on the battle – or probing action, which felt to me very much like a battle.

'Wave the red cross!' shouted Mounir. Two boys immediately ran to the tree, pulled down the sheet bearing the large cross, and started waving it as best they could, as it kept flogging in the strengthening wind. Directly, two or three rifle-shots rang out from down the hill. One of the boys, who cannot have been more than seven or eight, was struck in the chest, flailing his arms as he fell backwards. The banner flapped uselessly in the wind as the other boy tried to wave it by himself, ignoring the intensifying enemy fire.

The firing subsided, as the Turks must have seen the ship as soon as we did. Many of the villagers had run to the southern rampart to see this miracle for themselves and I had the impression everyone was holding their breath. We could now see its French colours, and soon its name: *Guichen*. In its wake steamed an even larger warship, a long grey fortress bristling with long guns. Flanking it, another smaller ship. Soon we could make out the flag on the huge cruiser, also French, and its name: the *Jeanne d'Arc*. The smaller ship – which even to me, who had never seen a naval warship before, looked like a relic of an earlier time, hardly a warship at all – was flying British colours, its name gradually becoming legible: HMS *Anne*. A fourth French cruiser followed behind: the *Desaix*. The *Jeanne d'Arc* was making signals of some kind with flags.

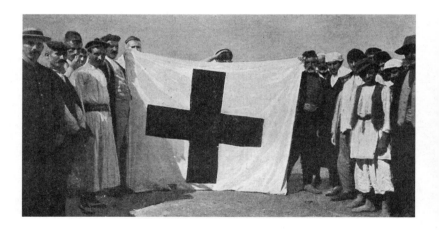

A huge 'boom' rang out and a puff of smoke briefly decorated the mouth of one of *Guichen*'s cannons. Then another, and another, and then one of *Jeanne d'Arc*'s long grey guns also fired. The thunder of a naval bombardment rolled up the mountain, and to us it sounded like music; like deliverance. Another detonation and a shell arced over the water all the way to the town of Souedia where the Turkish army had its base. It looked as though order was breaking down, the soldiers fleeing in a panic. From our vantage-point we could see the artillery pieces, abandoned where they stood. All firing died out from the land as the troops fled, many throwing down their rifles in their haste. Then silence, as we watched a boat being lowered from *Guichen* and another from the *Jeanne d'Arc*.

The surf held up their landing for what seemed to us like an eternity, but can't have been more than half an hour. Suddenly I realised that Shoushan was next to me. We both stared silently down at the miracle unfolding, the miracle that came from the sea when we least expected it. I felt her hand gripping my arm. Finally, there was a lull in the breakers and the boats found a patch of sand to beach on. A few minutes later, we could see two parties of nattily dressed French marines climbing up towards us, while others guarded the beach where the boats lay stranded. Pastor Andreasian came up, having put on his clergyman's dark suit, now a size too big; *Bashchaoush* Mounir had buttoned his uniform jacket with the incongruous Ottoman medal. My uncle Artin, one of the few French speakers in the camp, was sent for, and also came in what used to be his best suit, now rumpled and baggy. They were joined by the ancient priest with his colourful vestments and vacant expression, still mumbling to himself. Such was the committee that stood at the top of the path, waiting.

The ragged and hungry villagers in their hundreds were all clustered around the edge of the Damlayik to see the arrival of their saviours just as many of them had given up hope. Some wept openly, others asked their neighbour whether even such ships as these could possibly make room for four thousand refugees. There was an audible gasp as the sailors appeared; we all gestured to them to climb over the rampart where it was lowest, and soon the first contingent was on the plateau, facing the welcoming committee, completely surrounded by the motley, noisy crowd of Armenian farmers and their families.

'*Le Lieutenant de Vaisseau* Arnaud, at your service. I bring you salutations from *Le Capitaine de Frégate* Brisson, who has the honour of inviting a delegation to visit his flagship and discuss the modalities of your evacuation from this place.' Uncle Artin translated for the others and was chosen to lead the delegation. It also included Dr Altouni, who was anxious to request medical help for the numerous sick and wounded. Pastor Andreasian preferred to stay with the people, some of whom were in a state of excitement and turmoil near to hysteria, while others sat staring into space, weak with hunger and numb with disbelief.

By the time the delegation had picked its way down the path to the beach, embarked, motored to the great cruiser, climbed the ladders up the sheer grey sides, met with the captain and returned, it was late afternoon. Cicadas provided the only sound; eerie after what had come before. Artin stood on a tree stump in the clearing near the church and addressed the throng of villagers. 'People of the six villages of Musa Dagh, our prayers have truly been answered, our sacrifices and struggle rewarded. The evacuation – of every one of us – will begin early tomorrow morning. This will be our last night on the Damlayik; the ships will launch all their boats for the operation, weather permitting. The sick and wounded will go first, in a boat reserved for them; then anyone suspected of suffering from a contagious disease; and then the general embarkation will begin. The French marines will come back once more before nightfall, bringing bread and tins of corned beef, hopefully for each of you to have a small share.

'Tomorrow will be the start of a new life, free of persecution and privation after fifty-three days and nights on this mountain. The ships will take us to Port Said in Egypt, where the English will house us temporarily in a camp under their protection. Are there any questions before we go to the church, where Pastor Andreasian and the priests will lead us in a prayer of thanksgiving?'

Were there questions! A thousand of them, all shouted at the same time, most of which dealt with the future and which Artin could not answer. Those who had personal possessions they prized wanted to know what they could carry with them. Artin looked amazed to see how people's attachment to possessions suddenly became an issue after nearly two months during which no one had had time to think about such things, indeed about anything other than survival.

For a while all that was forgotten again, as Pastor Andreasian, flanked by the three Apostolic priests, held the strangest worship service I had ever seen. It was neither Protestant nor Orthodox. The priests led the standing congregation in the Lord's Prayer, and then the people came forward and asked one or the other of the four clergymen, with perhaps a small preference for Andreasian, '*hayr, ohrnetzek*, Father, bless me', and the blessing was duly given. The pastor at first pulled his hand away when people tried to kiss it in the Orthodox way. I think he realised though that he could not disappoint these people, who had been through so much, and soon his hand was being kissed just like those of the priests.

'Our Father, who art in heaven…' I found myself mouthing the words of the prayer, and could hear Shoushan murmuring them by my side. 'For Thine is the kingdom, and the power and the glory forever, Amen.' I did not feel this to be formal religion, which normally left me cold; it was a vital need, to say 'thank you' to someone. Anyone. 'Perhaps that is what it's all about,' I thought. 'We create someone for us to thank – or blame. And maybe it doesn't matter if there is no one listening.'

After the service, Shoushan and I walked hand in hand, silently, back to the ramparts to look at the miraculous fleet of warships gleaming in the sunset as the sea, now quiet as the wind had dropped, gleamed like burnished copper. 'Did you see how busy everyone was, packing and sorting their belongings?' she asked me. 'A few months ago, they were living their country lives as their parents and grandparents had, never suspecting what was coming. Now, who knows what the future holds for them, and for us, for that matter. An English camp in Egypt? How long can we stay there, and where will we go? There's no coming back here, that's for sure. Will I ever know what happened to my parents?'

Her face was drawn with worry, the uncertainty on so many fronts. Now the only sure thing was that we were going far away. I had no answer to her questions; I put my arm around her shoulders and pulled her close to me. If anyone saw us, they took no notice; rural Armenians are as narrow-minded as Turks, but these were hardly normal times. We leaned against the parapet near where I had stood that very morning, killing people, strangers; seeing a comrade die, then a little boy cut down just as liberation was near. We could see a small flotilla of the ships' boats returning, presumably with the promised provisions. Shoushan looked at me with a soft expression that made me melt. 'Whatever happens, however long we stay in Port Said and wherever we go from there, will you stay with me?'

I did not hesitate. It was like some ancient force took control of my voice: 'Always, Shoushan. Come what may.' She moved her face close to mine, our eyes drank in each other's gaze. I don't know if one of us took the initiative but, if so, I don't think it was me. Our lips came together in a kiss, my first and I imagine it was hers too. Then another one, longer, and I felt powerful feelings I had never felt before welling up within me. Shoushan gently pulled away and, taking me by the hand, led me back to the encampment; I had never felt so befuddled, in a way that was both wonderful and frightening. We made our way to the tent where Minas's family were bundling up their clothes and a few meagre possessions for the next stage of their exile. They were quite subdued; I asked Aunt Azniv, 'Why do you seem sad, Auntie?'

She stopped her packing and looked at me with a sigh. 'Not sad, Varo, but you are young. We have already left the home we built, the earth that holds our fathers and mothers, everything we had. Now we will go into real exile, living on the charity of strangers, while the world goes on fighting this insane war. Of course we are relieved this long ordeal is over, that we somehow came through it all right even if others didn't. But no, it's not a time for joy if that's what you mean.'

I could think of nothing to say to that. When they had finished packing their bundles, Artin said, 'I think we should get some sleep, tomorrow will be a big day. Varo, you can stay with us, no need to go back to the infirmary now, is there?' And so Shoushan and I slept in opposite corners of the tent, but I know my thoughts were all tangled up with hers, with that first kiss, the uncertainty about a future that was not all bad, for us at least, since we had found each other.

In the morning, at first light, I looked across the sleeping family members towards Shoushan; she had raised her head and was looking towards me. Without a word, we rose, put on our shoes, tiptoed out of the tent and hurried down to the rampart hand in hand. The sun was rising from behind the mountain, its golden light spilling downhill towards the sea. We watched as a swarm of boats set out from the warships. The camp soon became a hive of activity. Pastor Andreasian joined us on the rampart. I had not seen him smile before. Gradually, the evacuation began. The weakest were not able to walk, but tightly wrapped on stretchers which the marines carried down as gently as they could. Others were helped on the descent by the arms of their relatives, babies swaddled in the swaying backpacks of their mothers.

By mid-afternoon, the camp was nearly cleared of civilians; a few armed young men patrolled, including Minas and me, just in case some Turks should try to take advantage of the now mostly deserted defences and have a last go at us from the land side. Towards the end of the operation, Captain Brisson came ashore for a tour. He did not look like my idea of the commander of a great warship. He was rather slight, with no beard (why did I expect one?), just a modest moustache, and had a rather subdued uniform without medals or dangly epaulettes; but he did have a *bearing*, a quiet but powerful presence that inspired respect and obedience. He and a group of white-uniformed officers walked solemnly around with the pastor, Uncle Artin translating; Minas, Shoushan and I tagged along as close as we could. They expressed their amazed admiration at the achievement of these ordinary farmers facing the armed and hostile might of a vast empire. The captain turned away and wiped his eye at the sight of the cemetery, with its fresh graves and wooden crosses. A few women were still weeping quietly, or just sitting with bowed heads on the ground near an earthen mound.

The captain had his marines mine the gun store, so that the rifles and munitions, such as they were, would not fall into enemy hands, and spike the two small cannons which had been captured during the second Turkish attack. As the long day turned to dusk, the last villagers, even the sad old ladies from the cemetery, began to make their way down the mountain to the waiting boats. Once the Damlayik was nearly deserted, a sudden explosion, followed by a smaller one that must have been the nearly depleted gunpowder store, marked the end of the weapons that had saved them from certain death. Well, not every weapon, as I could see many men carrying a poorly camouflaged pistol or rifle as they slid and stumbled down the rocky path. There was no rejoicing, either among evacuees or sailors.

Minas, his family, Shoushan and I trudged down the path together, among the last to leave. As we went through the orchard, we saw the corpses of the Turkish soldiers someone had dragged out of the way, contorted like discarded dolls. Maybe I had cut short the life of some of them – I kept my eyes from lingering. At the bottom of the trail, a marine was directing villagers to one or the other of the launches pulled up on the beach. Those from the French warships had steam engines; the smaller ones from the British ship were rowed. The marine looked at me and pointed towards the British tender, while Minas and his family were directed towards a large launch with 'Jeanne d'Arc' on its bow. I don't know what came over me, but I took Shoushan by the arm and guided her with me towards *Anne*'s tender; I caught the eye of Uncle Artin, who nodded his agreement. His face looked kindly, even more so than usual. Only Minas frowned and I thought he was tempted to object, but he turned away with a brusque movement and headed for the launch.

The sailors rowed us quickly across the calm expanse of sea to the *Anne*. We had to climb up rope ladders, which was fun for us young people but the older ones found it a trial. All of our boatload made it safely. At the top was a typically English-looking officer with a pipe stuck in his teeth and a gruff expression on his face. He shook his head at the tattered clothes and emaciated condition of the refugees he watched clambering aboard his ship. He ordered his men to collect, unload and store all the odd weapons the men had refused to leave behind. The loaded flintlocks were really dangerous, as the only way to unload them was to fire them and the only people who knew how to do that were the mountaineers themselves.

'You gentlemen will be so good as to ensure that all firearms are safely unloaded before handing them over for storage,' he announced, an order that was met with blank incomprehension. I could tell he was getting angry at this impasse and offered to interpret. He looked surprised to hear English: 'Please do, young man!' Once I had relayed the orders to the farmers, they obeyed reluctantly. One ancient musket went off prematurely, the bullet whizzing past the officer's cheek. 'Christ almighty, three hundred and fifty savages to house and feed and deliver all the way to Egypt and they nearly blow my bloody head off!'

He became even more irritated when he saw an elderly woman climb with difficulty over the gunwale, bent under the weight of the antique sewing machine on her back. 'We have no room to stow such baggage, Madame, you will drop it overboard this minute!' He turned to me: 'Will you tell her the captain says to drop that contraption in the sea?' So that was the captain himself! I turned to the uncomprehending old lady, but before I could translate, her wrinkled face lit up in a broad gap-toothed smile at the attention.

The captain scowled and said, 'Oh, never mind, it's not *that* that'll sink us.'

'And your name is?' he asked, turning to me.

'Vartan,' I replied, 'Vartan Nakashian.'

'Please see the officer over there, Vartan, and help him get these people to understand where they are to go.' The officer was a pink-faced young Englishman trying his best to allocate the refugees to one or the other of the ship's lower decks by waving his arms and shouting English monosyllables. With my help we soon got everyone below. Shoushan was given a bedroll in one of the women's sections; my billet was with the men on the deck below. According to the captain's instructions, only married men were allowed to enter the women's deck to see their wives and children, and women and children were not supposed to appear on deck. I did not see her again for the first two days at sea.

I soon became accustomed to the slow, rolling motion of the ship, so unlike the short bouncy feel of the waves under Artin's little sailboat. Most of the men and boys spent their time either being sick, waiting to be sick or just lying around looking miserable. I loved looking over the railing at the sea, alluring and ever-changing, while trying to put some order in my thoughts after the life-changing events of the past week. After the indescribable relief of being rescued, the future seemed unknowable, vague and utterly beyond my control. I fiercely wanted to talk about all this with Shoushan. Finally, I sent a message with one of the married men who occasionally went below to see how his family was faring, asking him to find her and suggest we meet in the passengers' mess an hour after lunch.

We arrived at almost the same time. The waiter was giving the tables a cursory wipe, but ignored us as we sat at a corner table. There was so much to talk about! She told me about life on the family deck, general seasickness among the adults and the impatience of the children, gradually recovering their boisterous energy as they gained strength and weight from the diet of filling, if unpalatable, shipboard food.

'What will we do in Port Said?' she wondered. 'Where will we live? Will we just be put on the streets of Egypt? At least there is no war there! Do you know what the Egyptians are like?'

'I met several Egyptians in Aleppo, mostly domestics of rich men who came to order or collect elaborate pistols for their employers,' I told her, taking her hand in mine. 'They are darker than us, and speak an amusing Arabic, but treated me kindly. Each one seemed to feel he was as important as his master, which we laughed about. As for the *Ingleez*, I cannot imagine they will just dump us on the streets, if the ones in Egypt are anything like those on this ship. But what they will do with us, I cannot say.'

She was quiet for a moment, and we drank in each other's gaze; I at least was mesmerised by those liquid black eyes. Every part of my body wanted me to take her in my arms, though of course that was out of the question. So we just talked about this and that, as we had on Musa Dagh. Then she hesitated a moment, and asked, 'Vartan, are we forever?' That was too much for me. I looked around and saw the waiter was on the other side of the large room with his back turned. I drew her to me and kissed her, briefly but with all my soul. 'Of course we are, *janim*.'

5

On board HMS Anne: *September 1915*

A S IT turned out, I was the only English-speaker among the refugees, and there wasn't a single member of the ship's crew who spoke Turkish or Armenian, except the Egyptian cook. He spoke pidgin Turkish but was frantically busy in the galley trying to prepare food for ten times the number of mouths he had provisions for. So, one or the other of the sailors would find me, usually standing at the railing looking out at the sea, and ask me to translate. Once or twice this was for the captain himself, Captain Weldon as I learned.

Now, I have always had a tendency to judge people by my first impression of their physical appearance. A reliance on externals that has let me down as often as not, but there it is. For me, a man's features, bearing and the degree of frankness or duplicity in the eyes were key signals. There was a lot to like in Weldon from all these angles: what I guessed to be military posture; a broad forehead, continually teased by a stray shock of straight brown hair; clear blue eyes that looked straight into yours; a straight, small nose – well, small by our standards – and teeth forever gripping a straight-stemmed pipe, sometimes smoking, often just chewing it.

On the morning of the second day after the evacuation, a sailor found me and said the captain would like to see me on the bridge. I was, of course, terribly excited, climbing the iron stairs two steps at a time. Weldon showed me the varnished wheel, the brass-mounted ship's compass in its own mahogany pillar and the logbook, which had a different name on it, written in some kind of antique-looking script.

'What kind of warship is this? It looks kind of, ah, unconventional,' I asked.

'Not a warship at all, Vartan, but a captured German cargo ship originally named *Aenne Rickmers*. She was converted to military use by the addition of light cannons fore and aft, but that's about all. With her two masts and single funnel, she still has the look of an old sailing ship. One of the most useful things about her is the flat area amidships where the cargo winches stow the seaplanes. There's one on deck now, a French one; take a close look later on, if you like.'

I had never seen an aeroplane close up and vowed to do just that.

Weldon went on. 'The ship is seaworthy but slow, which makes her vulnerable to torpedoes. She has already had one hole knocked in her by a German submarine off Smyrna. Fortunately, the naval base at Mudros was not far, and the hole was above the waterline once we jettisoned our water and cargo. Ah, am I speaking too fast? Can you follow me all right?'

'Yes sir, no problem, you speak very clearly.'

'Well, now you speak, if you will. Tell me more about Musa Dagh and these four thousand farmers who stood off the Ottoman Empire.'

'I was not there for the beginning, sir, only the last week or so.'

'So you're not from Musa Dagh, young man? How did you come to be there?' I began to explain, but when I said I was from Aleppo, Weldon interrupted: 'Aleppo, eh? So I presume you speak Arabic?'

'Of course, sir, that is what we speak at home. The Armenians from Cilicia and the east call us *arapahoz*, Arab-speakers. My family has been in Aleppo for generations; we are not even sure where they were before Aleppo. Maybe Constantinople, since Nakashian means "painter" or "artist" and the Anatolian villages where most of our people live – *lived* – had no need for such skills. Anyway, that was centuries ago, maybe.'

'And why in the world do you speak such good English?'

'Well, I spent five years in Jerusalem learning mostly English and classical Armenian. I worked a lot harder on English than Armenian, and still don't speak our language as fluently as the people from Musa Dagh. My mother spoke Armenian as a girl in Cilicia and I learned some from her, you know, mostly household words. Mainly we speak Arabic and Turkish.'

'Interesting,' said the captain, after reflecting a moment. 'Do you know what this old ship is doing out here, besides acting as a floating hotel for refugees?'

'No, sir.'

'Our job is to find out what is going on in the Turkish-occupied sectors of Syria and Palestine. We send seaplanes out to reconnoitre army positions and troop movements. We also land agents ashore, local people or people who can pass as local. We take them ashore, alone or in pairs, and pick them up at agreed places and times, usually at a spot where our boat can beach at night and get away without being noticed. The information we gather is very useful to the Allied war effort. Do you understand?'

'Yes, sir,' I answered, pushing my glasses up my nose.

'Do you know where this ship is taking you and your people?'

'Port Said in Egypt, sir, that's what my uncle who was part of the first delegation told us.'

'That's correct. To a holding camp. It should be safe and relatively comfortable. But what about you? It will be very difficult to get back home to Aleppo once you have disembarked at Port Said.' I had been thinking along those lines, wondering how I would even get a message to Mayrig from Egypt, which was cut off from Syria by the war zone at Suez and Turkish-occupied Palestine. Weldon chewed on his pipe for a minute or two. 'Let me think a little. I may have an idea for you,' he said, and opened the door to the stairs down to the main deck.

I went to see the seaplane, an amazing contraption of wires and canvas with two seats, one behind the other, perched on two cigar-shaped pontoons. The propeller was of beautiful varnished wood and the engine was incredibly complicated and ingenious. I then went to the bow, from where I could look out at the sea and feel the breeze and spray on my face, without the noise and smell of the engines. The land was clearly visible on the left, with a brown blotch I thought might be a town in Palestine, somewhere around Acre or Jaffa. Suddenly a sailor tapped me on the shoulder. 'The captain wants to see ya, young man.' I hurried up the steps to the bridge.

'You sent for me, sir?'

'Come with me, Vartan Nakashian. I want you to think about something.'

Weldon led me to his cabin, which was not at all what I expected. A largish room but with no luxury. In fact, he had had a plywood partition made to separate his living and sleeping areas, and on this he had pinned maps: Egypt, Gaza, north and south Palestine, Syria, Aegean Turkey. These were marked by numerous scribbles in pencil. 'Have a seat,' he said, and I sat on a bench under the porthole, while Weldon sat in the desk chair. He lit his pipe and offered me a cigarette from a packet on the table. I thought of accepting it but did not want to look foolish smoking my first one in front of the captain.

'Before being summoned by the *Jeanne d'Arc* to pick up refugees from your great adventure, we had spent the night off the coast of Syria, north of Tripoli. We had put an Arab ashore the week before with instructions to go to Aleppo and bring back a report from one of our agents there. He was supposed to meet our boat at the beach. We looked for his signal all night, but he failed to turn up. This is a dangerous business and the Turks are not such fools as you may think them. They have spies and double agents everywhere, and our people sometimes fall into a trap or betray themselves inadvertently. Or even turn out to have been double agents themselves. I don't think that was the case with the man we call Ibrahim, the one who didn't return. Now we'll probably never know. Part of the game.'

I adjusted my glasses and listened attentively. Clearly the arrival of the warships was neither a miracle nor the result of waving banners at the sea. Weldon went on: 'We need someone who can pass for a native in Syria, who can make his way from the drop-off point on the coast to Aleppo and return with a report from our man there. You are young for this sort of thing, but if you are willing to undertake such a mission, your age might even be an advantage – good cover. Highly dangerous work, need I say, and if you get in trouble, there is no way for us or anyone else to assist you. Whatever happened to Ibrahim might well happen to you. If so, you will probably be tortured to death, and if they find out who you are, your family will likely suffer as well. But if you succeed, it will help those of us who are fighting the Turks, for whom I don't imagine you have an undying affection. What do you say?'

I could feel the familiar flush creeping up my cheeks, and my heart was beating fast. 'I would give anything to be able to help. You can trust me to do my best, and not to say a word if captured. I may be young but I have already been involved in helping our people resist Turkish oppression. I smuggled bombs through the bazaar in

Aleppo, which unfortunately did not kill the Turkish governor they were meant for, and our friends were captured and hanged. So I am fully aware of what can happen if things go wrong. That's just one more reason to hate them, you are right about that. I killed several of their soldiers on the ramparts of Musa Dagh and took a bullet in my, ah, hip; you may have noticed that I still limp a little. Please do not hesitate because of my youth.'

'Well, you have a fair bit more under your belt than I did at your age, I'll say that. Here's the plan then: we'll disembark your people at Port Said, then sail north for a couple of reconnaissance missions, including dropping you on the beach. You will learn by heart a message for our principal agent in the city. If you want to see your family first, do, but don't breathe a word to anyone. Information can be a mortal danger to all concerned, as well as to our mission. Our chap will give you a report which you will bring back to the same beach where you were dropped. Don't bother reading it, it's in code. We have time to drill you on the signals and the other details you need to know about, generally get you ready. I would say we can be back up here, off the Syrian coast, that is, about four days from now.

'Do think about it, coldly, not emotionally. If you decide you would rather not get involved in something as risky as this, I will understand perfectly and think no worse of you. Intelligence work behind enemy lines is not for everybody, that's for sure. We will offload you at Port Said with the others, and no more said about it. But I need to know before we get there. If you decide not to do it, I will need to take another of our chaps. And don't think of breathing a word about this to anyone, not now and not ashore, whether you carry on with the assignment, or not. Understood?'

I looked at the captain, taking a moment to process what I had just heard. Then I said, in my most grown-up voice, 'You can count on me, sir!' Weldon smiled and held out his hand, which I shook firmly, looking him in the eyes, though mine were brimming with emotion.

I am afraid that I followed the captain around like his shadow from then on. The only awkward moment came when a delegation of male refugees came up from their steerage accommodation to complain about the food. When I translated their description of tinned rations as 'inedible', the captain laughed and said they were an ungrateful rabble, which I did not translate.

As soon as I had come down from that first momentous conversation, it hit me. What had I done? What about Shoushan? I felt sure the bond we had forged in a few short days was for life, something I would rather die than betray. And yet – I would have to lie to her. Worse, I would have to let her disembark while I sailed off again on the ship. Shoushan, my love, the one I had promised never to leave. 'Forever', I had said, and I meant it. God knows how I would ever find her again, where she and the others would go from Port Said, how I could travel around in a war zone looking for her. A war which nobody knew the end of, where it was open season on our people. Would she ever forgive such a betrayal?

I walked miserably around the deck, half hoping not to run into her until I had composed myself enough to know what to say.

I held off on sending another message for us to meet, though I knew she expected it. But she came up anyway, right on to the deck, and found me first. 'Vartan, where have you been? They said the captain sent for you?' I felt the blood run into my face and knew I must be blushing again. 'Some spy! Vartan the *mastool*, the idiot,' I thought. She was looking at me with a question in her big eyes, frowning. I did my best to avoid her gaze. 'Well?'

'Ah, yes. Oh, nothing, really, he just had some Arabic papers he wanted me to translate. It's marvellous up there, where they drive the ship. I wish you had been there to see it!'

I felt uneasy at the ease with which I had lied. Disgusted with myself. But what else could I do? I was trapped. She either believed me, or pretended to believe me. 'Oh, is that all? I thought it was something important. Well, I ought to get back to helping the ladies, today we're mending clothes.'

I spent the day and a half before arriving in Port Said trying to act normal. Shoushan continued to ignore the ban on women on deck, and the sailors did not interfere. I think my visits to the captain must have given me a sort of official status in their eyes, one I was not sure I wanted just then. Despite my inner turmoil, I thought I was behaving normally during our conversations as we paced the deck on calm days, or held to the railing when the sea was rough. During one such stroll, she stopped walking, turned to face me and asked, 'Vartan, are you all right? You seem distracted. Is this strange food disagreeing with you?'

'I'm fine, don't worry about me! I'm just anxious to get off this ship and see Egypt!' Again, a lie just came out. Digging myself in deeper. She gave me the same frown as when I told the first big lie, the one that led to the others. I felt like a fly snared in a spider web of deceit.

The disembarkation of the 'rabble' (I knew that's what they looked like to an English eye) went a lot more quickly than getting them on board the ships. The three French cruisers and the former German cargo hulk were all able to dock at the quays, sending their passengers ashore on gangways. I went down to the dock with Shoushan and together we went looking for the Bedrossians among the large group that was straggling down from the *Jeanne d'Arc*. We couldn't find them in the long triage queues.

As we threaded our way through the noisy, smelly crowd of tired and impatient refugees, I knew I had to tell Shoushan. Finally, after we had pushed and shoved and been shoved in return for a while, still without finding the Bedrossians, I stopped and took her by the arm, guiding her to a bench in the shade looking out at the great ships docked along the quay. Her bushy eyebrows pursed in a frown above her wide, questioning eyes.

'Shoushan, I have something to tell you. I am not staying here. I must leave again with the ship. Captain Weldon needs me for something important, something to help with the war against the Turks.' She was looking at me with such a look, sadness tinged with anger.

'So that's it! I knew something was afoot. Why in the world couldn't you have told me that before? Of course you have to help with the war if you have the opportunity. Lucky you to be able to do something! If you had just told me I would have said, "Godspeed, *janim*, only come back safely to me as soon as you can." And I still say that, but you have broken my heart with your ugly lie.' With that she got up and walked back towards the crowd of refugees and was soon lost to my sight as I sat paralysed on the bench.

'Damn!' I cursed myself. 'Just when I was going to explain. To ask forgiveness. To tell her I love her. Who knows when there will be another chance? Never, maybe. But I must at least say goodbye to Minas and his parents.' I jumped up and hurried after her, but before I could get very deep into the throng, I heard the whistle I had been warned to expect, meaning that *Anne* would be sailing in half an hour. I gave up and returned to the ship. In a way it was just as well, as I had no convincing explanation as to why I was going away. 'Better to vanish than to lie again,' I thought. 'Goodbye, Shoushan,' I whispered. My chest was tight and my eyes misted up as I climbed the gangway.

The sailor guarding the top end saluted me as I boarded, making me feel both embarrassed and proud. I hadn't yet done anything to deserve it, but I was going to be entrusted with a dangerous mission that would help the enemies of the Turks in their struggle to defeat the Empire. Such an opportunity for someone like me had to come at a cost. I felt a lot older than only a couple of weeks before.

I watched as the great hawsers were hoisted off the bollards and winched back on board. The ship's whistle sounded again and soon Port Said was receding astern, the colourful throng of refugees waiting to be processed still as large as ever. Besides my conflicted feelings about leaving Shoushan, I felt guilty about not saying goodbye to Minas. I could feel a strange air of disapproval whenever my cousin looked at me, especially when Shoushan and I were together. I swore to myself I would seek him out as soon as I could. As well as Shoushan of course. When that might be I could not guess. I went forward again to my favourite spot on the ship's bow. I was surprised to get a tap on the shoulder, a sailor sent to tell me that Captain Weldon would see me on the bridge.

'Well, Vartan, old chap, any second thoughts?'

'None at all, sir.'

'Then let's talk about what you are going to do.' Weldon spread a city map of Aleppo on the polished wooden navigation table and gestured for me to join him on the navigator's bench. I had never seen a map of my city before, in fact I had hardly looked at any maps at all.

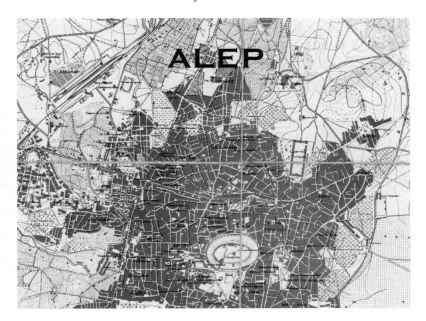

I soon got my bearings: the huge oval citadel in the middle, the souks to the north and west along with the Jewish quarter, Bahsita; Muslim quarters to the east and south; and Christian neighbourhoods north of the souks and Great Mosque, first Jdeide and then our own Atawi a bit further out. It was like being an eagle and flying back and forth over the city.

'Here is our man.' He pointed with a pencil at a spot in the middle of the bazaar. 'Irfan Hamadi, a rope seller. A Druze. Have you ever met a Druze before?'

'Yes, of course. There are not many who live in Aleppo, but they come to town selling horses or mules, which they are experts at rearing. They live down in the Hawran, the Jebel Druze, or across in Lebanon, in Wadi Taym and the Shouf. My father always said, "Trust a Jew before a Druze, a Druze before a Muslim, a Muslim before a Greek." He had a lot of prejudices but I think he must have had his reasons to feel the Druze were people you could rely on, relatively speaking.'

Weldon laughed his short, loud bark of a laugh. 'We feel about the same. Don't trust them all, and don't trust any of them completely. A good rule to navigate by. The Druze have been as helpful to us as anybody. Britain has taken their side over the past century or so, while the French stood with the Maronites and other Catholics, the Russians with the Orthodox and so on. We joined the game late and seem to have been left with the Protestants and the Druze. This Hamadi has proved himself more than once. But nothing is forever in the Levant, especially loyalty. So watch your back. Something certainly happened to Ibrahim, and he was supposed to meet up with Hamadi, just like you.

'Anyway, your task is to find his shop, in the central alley on the north side, just before the Great Mosque. *Souq al-hibal*, bag and rope sellers. Do you know it?'

'I know the souk like my hand, Captain.'

'Just ask for the shop of Abu Ghassan Hamadi. His son is called Ghassan, obviously, must be about ten by now. Always at his father's side. When you find it, and a fattish dark-skinned duffer with no beard but long moustaches, usually wearing a white kepi rather than a fez, squatting behind coils of ropes of all sizes and colours, you'll have found him. You are to ask him whether he has leather mule traces.

'He will answer that he doesn't, that he can have them sent from Damascus if you can wait a week but you will have to pay in advance. If he tells you that, then you are on, he has a report for us. You will hand him this purse.' At this, Weldon produced a leather change purse which made a pleasant tinkling sound when he shook it. 'Gold, old son, fifty fresh sovereigns with the image of our patron, good old George. Well, not *too* fresh: all used, and dated before 1914. We are always careful about that. Irfan could not safely spend them if they were dated after the war began, could he? Even as it is, if he's not discreet, people will see our hand in this. Anyway, that's a big purse to pay for a few mule traces, but nobody has to know how many sovereigns it holds. Irfan apparently has to pay dearly for some of the information he sends back to us, and he is definitely not in this for patriotism of any sort.

'He will say that he will write you out a receipt, which will be for a few *lira*, but on the back of the sheet of paper will be a message written in ink that cannot be seen until a certain chemical is applied to it. You won't have to worry about that, just fold it, thank him courteously and tell him you will return in a week for the harness. Does that sound clear enough, so far?'

'Yes, sir, I see no problem. Where will you leave me?'

'We will put you ashore at a beach about three days' walk from Aleppo. We usually drop our chaps at a place south of Iskenderun. Just north of Musa Dagh, in fact, a beach from where you can easily get to the Aleppo road, about two and a half days' walk if you go briskly. We'll give you a bag of oranges, you can pretend to be on your way to sell them, and eat some along the way, if you don't like our food any more than your ragged cousins did.'

I thought about this for a moment and looked at him, pushing my glasses up and clearing my throat. 'With respect, sir, that is Turkish territory. I can speak Turkish, but no one would ever take me for a Turk. If you leave me south of Musa Dagh, I will be able to pass for more or less what I am: an Arab, a Christian Arab from Aleppo. Not an Armenian, of course, I don't speak Arabic with an accent.'

'Hmm,' said the captain doubtfully. 'That makes sense, but the question is where? We need a beach we can find not just once, but again when we come to fetch you. In the dark of night. Let's look at the chart and see if there is such a place.'

I could tell Weldon loved maps. We hunched down together to look at the map of the Syrian coast. It even had al-Basit on it, the little harbour where we had found Uncle Sarkis's sailboat – hardly three weeks ago, but it felt like three years to me. I pointed to an indentation in the coast just north of there.

'Just north of al-Basit is a perfect little beach. I have recently walked from Aleppo to there, so finding my way will be easy. It's no further from Aleppo than Iskenderun. They grow oranges on the coast, so my story will make sense. What do you think?' The captain studied the chart and the numbers in the water off the beach.

'These are nautical soundings, my boy. Tell me how much water we'll have under our bottom. It looks like a good place to anchor while we send the boat to shore with you, though I would have preferred not to take *Anne* quite so close to the recent theatre of operations against the Turks. Hopefully we can get in and out under cover of darkness. All right. Here's the procedure: we will steam within a mile of the coast, in complete blackout conditions, drop anchor and send you ashore in a small boat, camouflaged for night operations. The old ship will be safely out to sea again, and you well inland, before dawn breaks. Understood?'

'Understood, sir.'

'So that's the plan. We will have to discuss your return. Do you think you can visit your family, carry out your instructions with Irfan Effendi, and make it back to the same beach near al-Basit two weeks to the day from now? We are to cruise up to Smyrna for the next ten days and will be back there at two o'clock in the morning of the night from Thursday to Friday, in two weeks' time exactly. Can you do that?'

'Yes, Captain, or die trying,' I said, and immediately felt I was being over-dramatic. The English have a way of talking about matters of life or death as though they were talking about a dog. I tried to look blasé. 'But how will you know I am there, to send the boat?'

'We will give you an electric hand torch.'

'A what?' My only experience of electricity had been the few public spaces in Aleppo, Damascus and Jerusalem, where electricity had been installed.

'A hand torch, a portable light that works with a battery, with an on–off switch. You will flash it three times quickly, then wait a minute before flashing again. We will not signal back, but will send the boat right away. Do you have a watch?'

'No, sir, but once in Aleppo I will take my father's pocket watch.'

'Take this one, just in case,' said Weldon, producing a battered silver repeater with a silver chain. I opened it and saw the hours were marked in Ottoman numerals, and the watch was a kind I had often seen, made in Constantinople. 'These *Ingleez* think of everything!' I thought.

The next day *Anne* steamed up the coast, past Gaza, Jaffa, Haifa, Acre, Tyre, Sidon, Beirut and Tripoli, then slowed down in order to pass Lattakieh around dinner time. The idea was to arrive off al-Basit by midnight, well after dark: the days were getting shorter now, and dusk would be around eight, dark by nine. I repeated all my instructions to myself and Weldon had me recite them once to him: the mock transaction with the Druze, the exact day and hour to be back on the beach, the operation of the hand torch, the need for complete discretion even with the family. I said goodbye to the captain and the few sailors I had got to know, as well as the Egyptian cook and the French pilots of one of the reconnaissance seaplanes.

The launch was swung outboard, dangling from its davits, and the crew began lowering it to the water. While I was watching this operation, Weldon came to find me and took me aside. 'Good luck to you, young Vartan. You will need some luck, we all do, but the best luck a man can have is native intelligence – brains – and I sense you're all right in that department. I shall look forward to seeing you again in a fortnight. We need that report, but we also need good men, and you will have a future working with us if you wish it. Now go, and Godspeed.' We shook hands and I saw a strange look on his face. I climbed down the rope ladder into the launch, excited by the thought of the coming adventure but mainly moved by the expression on Weldon's face. He was, of course, too English to say anything but I could tell he was concerned for me. I swore to myself that I would give satisfaction.

It was quiet at sea, the only sound being the dull splash as the oars, their blades wrapped in burlap sacking, dipped rhythmically in and out of the water. As usual, the sea breeze had died down after dark. The stars were almost as bright as they had been on the moonless night, not three weeks before, when Minas and I had sailed towards Musa Dagh. I was startled out of my thoughts by a loudly whispered 'Get ready!' and jolted as the boat ran up on to the beach and stopped. A sailor helped me, clutching my bag, and in a moment I was on the ground, dry except for my shoes. The sailor whispered 'Good luck!' and they were gone.

I suddenly felt very strange, standing alone on the dark beach, the only sound being the mindless lapping of the waves. 'What am I doing?' I thought. 'Did I ever intend to do something like this, or have events just carried me along with them?' I wrenched my thoughts back to the present. 'I had better get moving or I will botch this task, it's too late to go back now.' I felt a lump in my throat every time I thought of Mayrig, of having to lie to her, or at least tell her less than the whole truth. For her own good as well as that of my 'mission'. I shouldered my bag of oranges, carrying my knapsack filled with food, a canteen of water, the electric torch, some clean underwear and a thin bedroll, and started the trek to Aleppo, fifty miles to the east. I was just thinking how my bullet wound was healing well and hardly bothering me at all, when I swung my knapsack a little too far back and bumped it painfully.

Shoushan's face also drifted across my thoughts as I walked: I imagined her sad, and felt sad myself despite my exhilarating mission. I swore to myself, 'If I get out of this alive, I'll find her, somehow. Make it up to her, wash away my lie with truth and faithfulness.' I shook my head. 'Big words, and there is no way from here to "somehow". Just walk, keep your mind clear and concentrate on your task, so much more important than you, even than you and her. Everything else is a luxury that can wait, that *must* wait.'

The climb up from the beach was easy, but soon the terrain turned into scrub pine and oleanders with the odd canebrake, and it got hard to stay on the track in the dark. A good excuse to catch some sleep. I curled up on a bed of pine needles, my head on my knapsack. It felt as though I was just dropping off to sleep, when the first rays of the sun rising behind Kilich Dagh warmed my face. I awoke with a start, at first not sure where I was. I stood up stiff with cold, stretched, shouldered my bags and began the long hike home.

The road to Aleppo seemed longer than when Minas and I had walked it in the other direction. Of course, it was mostly downhill then. The trail led past a makeshift hunting cabin I thought must belong to the Turkmen mountaineers whose territory this was. At first hesitant to spend the night in a space where I would be cornered if anyone came along, I decided to take the risk, grateful for the shelter as the night was promising to be quite cold up there. In the morning, the path took me downhill past an Arab village called Bdama, then across the Orontes River on the bridge at Jisr ash-Shugur. Then a nice easy walk down to the plain, towards Idlib. I avoided going into that very Muslim town by skirting it to the south and at Ariha found the long, straight road to Aleppo, across a plain studded with thousands of graceful pistachio trees.

The railway tracks near the munitions depot were a welcome sight; after following them for a while, I turned into town, skirting the souk and heading up towards home. My long walk almost done, I could feel my pulse – and my pace – quickening as thoughts of home invaded my mind: Mayrig and my brothers and sister, a flash of worry about Anahit's cough, Halim's irresponsible behaviour, Mayrig's tendency to worry in silence.

Mayrig gasped on seeing me at the door and pulled me inside to a torrent of words, she who was usually so taciturn. 'You are so thin, my son! But look at you! You have grown up these three weeks. Come sit – no, go kiss your sister and brothers and tell us all. Is Minas all right? We heard about the evacuation on to French ships, just as the Turks were attacking. But why do you come home covered in dust, looking like a pedlar with that bag of oranges? Oh Varo, I have so many questions! While you are seeing the little ones – Halim is not here – I will put some kebab on the coals. Yes, kebab! We managed to get some good lamb from a neighbour who has a farm, old man Keshishian, remember? I'll cook it in pomegranate sauce, as you like it, and you will eat *kebbad*...' Bitter orange peel preserve, my favourite.

Mayrig had obviously been seriously worried about me, to gush like she did, so unlike her. I was now a secret agent, but under her roof I reverted to childhood habits. But now I had to stop her: 'Mayrig, I cannot stay now. I have an errand, that is why I am here. Give me a little cheese and bread and *ayran*, and I promise to come back later and eat all the kebab in the world. And *kebbad*. And your good *lavash* bread, if you have some.' She stopped in mid-flutter, starting a fire in the *mangal* and chopping meat and parsley and onions all at the same time.

'Cannot stay, Varo? How can that be? We've been so worried! Where must you go? You are not a *fidai*, are you, hiding bombs among those oranges? You should eat first, but if you just want cheese, here,' she said, fishing out some string cheese from the earthen pot where it was soaking in brine.

'Don't worry, Mayrig, I'll be back for supper,' I said, while gobbling a hunk of the slippery, salty white cheese, which I washed down with gulps of *ayran*. 'Goodbye for now, Mayrig.' I hugged her as a man hugs his mother, not like a child. As I closed the door I saw her standing alone in the middle of her kitchen, with a curved parsley-chopper in one hand and a stunned look on her face.

I made my way past the Forty Thieves and headed due south towards the souk. The vast bazaar was as busy as ever and should have felt utterly familiar to me, but something had changed in the past month and I was not sure if it was me or it. I threaded my way through the throng, passing the western entrance to the Great

Mosque and soon found myself in the rope souk. I had no trouble finding the Druze rope seller, sitting just as Weldon had described him, cross-legged on a *kilim*-covered bench in a sort of cave made of coils of rope of every possible material, thickness and colour. Whatever you needed to tie, bind, harness, restrain or connect. Suddenly, I realised I knew this place. Years ago, Father had sent me for twine or rope, I forgot what, but when I looked at the droop-moustachioed owner, I recognised him at once. 'If I know who he is,' I thought, 'he may know who I am, unless I have changed more than he has. If this mission goes wrong, I will be linked to my family, and who knows what might happen. Maybe I should forget this whole crazy idea about playing the spy for the *Ingleez*.'

I stopped to collect my thoughts before addressing the Druze, who I could tell was watching me out of the corner of his eye, while apparently busy splicing a rope, his fingers seeming to twirl the silvery fids. I tried to bolster my self-confidence: 'I am on an official mission on behalf of the British Empire,' I told myself. 'To this Druze rope seller I will look like Vartan Nakashian from Atawi Saghir, son of Hovsep the gunsmith, if he remembers me at all, otherwise I will look to him just like another teenage Christian *halabi*. Please God that he does not.' Then I realised I was not sure how to greet a Druze: with *salaam aleikum* as I would a Muslim? Or a generic greeting? I remembered my father saying they were part of the Islamic world, but were not accepted by most Muslims as belonging to the *Ummah*. That they had been persecuted for their beliefs. I decided to use the Muslim greeting, common in the souk, as anything else would sound as though I were condescending.

'*As-salaamu aleikum!*'

'*Wa aleikum as-salaam, ya hala*! I know this face, but the body is all grown up now. Are you not the son of Hovsep Nakashian, Allah have mercy on his soul?'

'Yes, *sidi*, it is I, Vartan, second son of *al-marhoum* Hovsep.' So much for that, I thought.

'How is your mother, Hajji Marie?' He called her that because she had made the pilgrimage to Jerusalem.

'Praise Allah, she is well, may He keep you well also, but it is not she who sends me to you today. I have come to buy leather mule traces. Do you have any of the first quality?'

On first hearing those words, Abu Ghassan looked as though he had seen a ghost, but quickly recovered, looking intently at me under his bushy eyebrows. 'Leather mule traces, did you say?'

'Just so,' I confirmed, looking him in the eye with all the mature assurance I could manage, resisting the impulse to adjust my glasses. 'Leather mule traces. I asked you, do you have any in stock?' The rope seller paused before replying, never taking his eyes from mine.

'Sadly no, *ya khawaja* Vartan. Not at this moment. However I can send to Damascus for any quantity you require. It will take about a week for my order to travel there and the merchandise to be delivered. The cost is three silver *ghurush* per *dra'* for the good quality traces, which is what I assume the son of Hovsep would require. Payment in advance. Are the terms satisfactory?'

'Entirely satisfactory, *ya* Abu Ghassan.' I pulled Weldon's purse from my pocket and showed it to the Druze, who nodded and spoke the words I was waiting for:

'Very good, we have agreement. I will write you out a receipt immediately. *Ya* Abu Ali, bring coffee for *khawaja* Nakashian and myself. How do you take it?'

'*Mazbout*, just sweet enough, thank you.' The *ferrash* scuttled off to bring the coffees. Abu Ghassan removed from a pile of papers and files a leather-bound ledger marked 'Receipts', opened it and carefully slid a loose sheet of paper from between two pages at the end of the copies of receipts. He took an old-fashioned quill, dipped it in ink and began to write.

I had a sudden flash of intuition. '*Ya* Abu Ghassan, please do not make it in my name. Just to the "bearer" will be sufficient.' The rope seller nodded, looking as though he expected the request, though the idea just struck me that instant. If I were to be caught, the receipt in my name would be a death sentence and would incriminate not only me but my family. I wondered whether I could keep the secret if they tortured me but put such thoughts out of my head. At least I would not know the content of the report.

The Druze watched as I carefully folded the receipt and put it deep in the inside pocket of my linen jacket. Just in time, I remembered Weldon's request that I see if I could find out anything about the fate of Ibrahim, my unfortunate predecessor. 'These are tumultuous times, *ya* Abu Ghassan,' I said, after taking my first sip from the small cup of strong Turkish coffee that Abu Ali had brought on a copper tray, along with a few dates and powdery *lokoum*. 'Our empire is defending itself heroically on several fronts. But life is uncertain in times of war. For instance, take a fellow I know, name of Ibrahim. He went for a walk, down to the seaside, and has not been heard of since. We think he may have been conscripted by the press gangs that roam the country, as they say. What do you think?'

The Druze sipped his own coffee and looked past me, rather than meeting my gaze. 'Everything is in the all-powerful hands of Allah. What you suggest is quite possible, since the law of universal conscription of last year. But I think he might just as easily have been the victim of an accident. The beach is a dangerous place, with all the storms that get up this time of year.'

'Ah, yes,' I said, closing the subject and the discussion. I had earned the right to go spend a few days with my family. There would be time to think about making my way back to the 'dangerous' beach. I blessed the intuition that had made me ask to change the landing-place. The unfortunate agent must have been spotted landing on the way in, or perhaps followed on the way back. Abu Ghassan did seem to be well informed, which meant that word of Ibrahim's 'accident' had filtered back to Aleppo. Assuming the Druze to be loyal. At least he did not know where I was expecting to be picked up and, unless I was followed, Ibrahim's fate would not necessarily be mine.

'*Daimi, ya* Abu Ghassan, may your house long endure. With permission, I shall take my leave now,' I said as I stood up. I handed the heavy purse to the Druze, almost as though the money were an afterthought. They're always pretending that in the souk, where everything is only ever about money, even the social niceties that surround it, like the taking of coffee and sweetmeats before consummating anything more significant than the purchase of a pound of bulgur. The rope seller took the purse without examining it and stowed it in his waistcoat pocket. 'Allah be with you, *ya khawaja* Vartan; my best regards to your good mother.' I took my leave and headed for Atawi; I knew myself to be an incurable optimist, but couldn't help feeling that I could trust the Druze, that if my mission were to fail, it would not be through treachery by the rope seller.

6

Beirut: December 1984

IRAN IN 1925 *was a new place for us. Swarthy men with tall astra-khan hats, all bearded, every one bristling with knives and guns, glowering at us foreigners, especially Christians who didn't speak Farsi. We had to learn it fast, and I had to make that Model T pay for itself. Until Bedros joined us, there was no way I could handle everything by myself. God, how the business grew! Within a year we had given up the*

Aleppo–Baghdad–Tehran route and started the first real trucking service in Iran. The petrol carriage for Anglo-Persian, over all those thousands of kilometres, just grew and grew until we had a hundred big White Motor Company trucks roaring this way and that. All those drivers and clerks to be hired: I learned how to weigh a man's worth just by looking at him, the way he stood, and, of course, the way he met my eyes, or didn't.

I was so busy. I settled her comfortably in the big house in the fashionable part of the city, with its splendid garden, but I did not have much time to spend with her, not quiet time anyway. There were always parties, dinners with other Syrian businessmen, Englishmen from Anglo-Persian or the embassy, visiting Americans from White Motor Company once I was given the agency. Occasional Iranians: Qavam-e-Sultaneh, other high government officials, each more corrupt and charming than the next. The rector of Tehran University, what was his name? So cultured, such a knowledge of Persian poetry, a real civilised man, were it not for the opium.

And of course Dashti: she thought him a bit rough, but he was genuine to the bone, such a rarity in the land of courtly hypocrisy. And such a mastery of their poetry. I learned fast, and not just the language. But Persia, Iran as it is now, was an enigma inside a conundrum, or whatever Churchill said about Russia.

Who could *understand Persia? Maybe* she *does. Let me take a look at her.* With a groan, he hoisted himself up from the armchair where he had been sitting for most of the day re-reading the *Masnavi*, Rumi's sprawling, almost epic saga drenched with mystic meaning.

Today he had started at the beginning, the sometimes salacious or funny anecdotes illustrating the carnal self, the urge to rise above the everyday. He slowly straightened up, got his stiff joints more or less operative and went into the library with its pile of books still lying where they fell. Above the fireplace was his favourite possession. A Qajar courtesan, painted on wood in the early days of the previous dynasty. *Those were real shahs! Not like the fake dynasty founded by the stable-boy usurper, nor his vain and indecisive son. Thank God she was* not destroyed in the bomb blast, just a few scratches of glass shards from the windows.

Vartan looked up at her, alone on a white wall. *There she sits, cross-legged: she's holding a glass half-full of a pinkish wine, such as Khayyam calls golgun, rose-coloured, the rosé from Sardasht I used to love. Look at her tartan pantaloons: the painter didn't make the slightest attempt to model the shape of her legs, it's as though the fabric has been glued flat on the board. Same with the floral Kashan carpet she sits on: it's perfectly depicted but also flat, with no perspective. The painter was not ignorant – he was daring.*

His eyes took in yet again the details he knew so well: her jacket of black-and-white striped brocade, with only a diaphanous under-garment, open to reveal her small, white, perfectly round breasts, their faint pink nipples. Beneath thick black eyebrows that meet in the middle, a pair of dreamy black eyes; a half-smile, not lascivious but serenely inviting. She's clearly a bit tipsy. She holds a pomegranate in one hand, a glass of wine in the other, held by the base as though offering it to the onlooker. Her dainty foot is turned sideways, so you can see it's stained with henna…

What sort of rooms did she grace for the century before I found her? Who has met that gaze before me? Who was this Mirza Baba who signed his name? He had seen other Qajar paintings in Tehran, but nothing this fine until Dashti asked him if he would be interested to see the home of one of his friends, a disgraced politician from an old noble family, a proud man who had just lost everything through a whim of Reza Shah's, before the bailiffs came. And there she was: *I must have her*, he had thought, and a few bribes later she had been wrapped in blankets and smuggled out.

Vartan groaned, that old hip pain lancing down his right leg, lately sharper and more persistent. He leaned against the mantel-piece, bending the leg at the knee until the pain subsided. *'Vilayet-e-faqih' indeed, the reign of the medieval clergy, of that rat-eyed fanatic the French cooped up in a suburb for a decade, then suddenly released just as his return could do the most possible damage. My poor Persia! What they did to Dashti...*

Vartan was lost in his digressive thoughts, staring into space, until he suddenly remembered the Qajar girl, and looked up at her once more. *You know better, don't you?*

Now, that painter is not dead. Nor is the girl, even if she was only a model. They are here, alive as long as I thrill to her gaze, to his skill. Is that why I took up painting? More my thing than writing poetry, that's for sure. The walls of this old barn are covered with them, my productions, and the attic is full; I wonder what will happen to all these worthless canvases after me. Good stretched canvas is not worthless, you can always paint over it. That would be good. But I suspect they will go by fire one way or the other; an incendiary shell like so many they fire down from the hills, or a bonfire just to get rid of them. But my God! I loved the hours, the thousands of hours I spent with my paints and canvases and easels, smoking pipe after pipe while I worked out compositions and colours. A few I am not ashamed of.

He went to the entrance hall where he had hung a half-dozen of his paintings, a hand on the cool marble of the hall table to steady himself. *Ah! The Mazandaran boats! Now that was a day for painting, on the bank of that great, lazy river. A spring day, not unlike this one, I believe, though I have not even looked outside. But then – the First Day of the World in that flat landscape of great rivers and infinite skies; like Khayyam:*

ruz-ist khosh u hava na garm ast

Neither too hot nor too cold, the day is fine;
A cloud sweeps the dust from the rose's cheek,
While the nightingale calls in mystic Pahlavi:
Always, at all times, you *must* drink wine!

I did just capture the immobility of the boats, tethered to the shore and half-sunk, not going anywhere soon, maybe ever; but their real purpose was to provide strong diagonals jutting out into the river as it cuts an arc through the land, with those strange thatched houses on the shore. They are not badly painted either. But where did I get the idea of the red colour, surely the tree was not red, but how strong it is, how fauve, *against the deep, almost Prussian blue of the sky. Today I would never have the courage to be so bold, to break the rules, if I were still painting. If my hand didn't shake like this. If I still had the* desire.

Everything I painted after leaving Persia was just a studio exercise, the artificiality of my carefully composed still lifes, all those models sitting stiff and bored. You can sense their boredom, I suppose that's an achievement of some kind. Damn hands! At least I can still smoke and pour a glass of whisky, when that goes it will be high time for me to go too. In fact it is time already. Anyway, I loved it, painting, but had more or less run out of things to try.

Towards the end I was more interested in the models than the painting, ha ha! Margaret especially, the little English one, was a sweet thing, a little thin but she held me tenderly, or rather put up with me holding her, just an embrace, chaste enough – more's the pity, but what can I do at this stage. But feeling that warm young body against mine, tender and willing, or at least passive, a long embrace, her breathing, her smell: soap and a pretty awful floral scent with a bit of body odour, clothes not washed often enough. She was like a rejuvenation tonic. No, not rejuvenation, that's the wrong word: not possible and, anyway, not really what I was after. Just the touch of youth, a reminder that it still exists, that I once knew it; to be close to a young woman after all these years.

My niece came in once. She must have thought, 'Dirty old man!' She will understand one day, I imagine, if she didn't then. How old would she be now? Forty? How I miss her, she is like the child we never had, she brought fresh air and sunlight into my life. All those hours in a stuffy sick-room shuttered against the light. I could not bear the thought of having another woman in my life – I never saw Maria again, not after the funeral anyway. But my niece brought a feminine presence; just that would have been enough. To my surprise she turned out to be naturally refined and receptive to everything I care about: art and poetry especially; even about food or books we agreed – that's why I called her 'Jouni', my soul. The only kindred soul in that morass of mediocre relatives. I wanted her to have the education I never had, pushed her to apply to Oxford, so can I complain that she married and stayed over there? Thank God, if there is one, that she did so, otherwise she and her family would be in the middle of this nightmare.

I suppose my whole life has been heading for this ending, alone and surrounded by madness, even if I am not quite mad, yet. I don't think I am. I have had my good moments, but there are stains nothing can erase. Like you, Hafez –

> I have drunk deep of whatever He poured into my cup;
> The wine of Paradise, or mere wine – I drank it up.

7

Aleppo: October 1915

A H, THE KEBAB with pomegranate sauce! I ate like an ogre, my hunger sharpened by the long walk in the fresh air and the horrid food on the ship. Mayrig stood watching me eat with an expression of satisfaction mingled with unease. Finally she spoke: 'Varo, now you must tell me where you have been. Why of all the refugees from Musa Dagh were you brought to Aleppo? What sort of errand is this, and for whom?' I pondered what to tell her while chewing on a large bite of succulent, gamy lamb.

'Well, I told them I was from Aleppo and asked if I could be dropped off closer to home, since Palestine is a war zone. They agreed there was no reason to leave me at Port Said, since I had a home to go to. The captain of the English ship was kind enough to oblige, since he was heading north anyway. My errand is simply that I was given a letter to deliver for that captain, as a return favour.' I found it very difficult to tell her that I would have to leave again in about ten days. There would be time for that.

I did tell the family – Mayrig, Halim and Anahit, Bedros and the elderly couple from the cellar, who spent much of the day upstairs with the family – the story of the siege and rescue on Musa Dagh. About Shoushan, not much other than that she was there with the Bedrossians. 'What about here, Mayrig? Are things no better? Are refugees still arriving?'

'Varo, you may not believe me, but things are much worse than they were three weeks ago. Every church and even the synagogues are overflowing, there are still thousands of people sleeping in the street. There is more and more cholera, some typhus. They send around donkey carts every morning to collect those poor souls who have died in the streets overnight. Now that you are here you can come with me as you used to, distributing what bread we can get. You will see for yourself. There are many, maybe hundreds, of people like us who want to help, but so many mouths to feed and so little money and food. At least with the cooler weather, one doctor told me, there will be less disease, but then winter will come and you know how cold it is in Aleppo in winter. I simply can't imagine how it will be for them.'

I went to sleep in my childhood bed. Just by being there, I felt a sense of security – but I knew it was false. My mother looked suddenly older. Not surprising, given all she had to bear. Halim the same selfish and unreliable character as always. Anahit still an angel of a girl, full of compassion for others, but still coughing and weak. My thoughts kept turning to Shoushan. 'Have I lost her? Can she ever forgive my lie? Will I ever be able to find her, or is her forgiveness or otherwise pointless, because we will never meet again? And my mission, my return to HMS *Anne*. Will I be able to carry it off and deliver the report safely to the captain? Or will my acceptance of a fool's errand on behalf of some foreigners lead to disaster for my family? How could I have given the *Ingleez* preference over Mayrig and Shoushan?' With all that buzzing in my head, I gradually sank into a fitful sleep.

Over a breakfast of cheese, olives and *lavash*, Mayrig told me about the Armenian school, which had been turned into an orphanage and refugee centre while continuing to provide what lessons were possible in the midst of such chaos. 'They need a teacher, Vartan. You could teach Armenian and English, well, English for sure.'

'Mayrig, I have to tell you something. I will have to leave again, in a week or so.'

'Leave?' She looked at me in disbelief, her chiselled face almost expressionless, except very tired. I tried to change the subject, and told her more about Shoushan. Mayrig remembered her from many years back, some wedding or funeral; a small girl, she said, 'shy but with a nice smile, dark eyes remarkable even for an Armenian.' She did not comment on my leaving, but her own dark eyes, framed by the lines of her forehead and the furrowed corners of her deep-set eye sockets, looked at me with a mixture of curiosity and weariness.

We spent the week doing what we could for the refugees, as we had before I left with Minas – a journey that seemed years ago, rather than a few weeks. At the school, we helped the nuns and the solitary priest who ran the orphanage. We bribed and wheedled the police on behalf of deportees needing permits to stay in Aleppo. We took bread, which Mayrig sent to be baked in much larger quantities than needed for the house, and distributed it to the homeless. If anything, the situation seemed to me to be getting more desperate than during the summer. The miserable survivors still straggling into the city were mostly at death's door. The interminable hot summer was finally, reluctantly giving way to slightly cooler weather, but the air was still heavy, the atmosphere oppressive. There was, at least, a decrease in the cases of typhus and cholera.

Just before the end of my time at home, I thought of Consul Jackson. 'Why have I been avoiding the idea of visiting him?' I thought. 'Because I know he will ask what I have been doing, what my plans are. And I don't want to lie to him. But I must find out whether it was he who managed to get a message to the warships. It could *not* have been a coincidence! It was so unlikely, after all those weeks on the mountain without seeing a ship. Or miraculous, if one could believe in such things.'

On my last day at home, I walked over to the consulate. Jackson received me immediately. He looked older and more tired, but with the familiar kindness in his plain Midwestern face. 'Well, Vartan, you've had some adventures, I believe. Sit down and tell me everything.' Which was just what I could not do. The consul joined me on the brown leather settee under the windows, with the early autumn sunshine filtering pleasantly through the gauze curtains. I described Minas's and my trip to Musa Dagh on foot and under sail; my wound, a 'scratch', I said; the heroism of the defenders, the ingenious organisation of the camp, the shrewd use of the pitiful supplies of ammunition, weapons and food. And the dramatic rescue, of course.

'We wondered whether you had managed to get word to the blockading fleet. It seemed so amazing, so miraculous that they appeared just when they did; now I think I have understood that it was no coincidence. Anyway, it is probable that in another few hours, we would have been overrun by the Turks. Even if we held out yet again, starvation was taking hold and people would have started dying within days.'

Jackson coughed. 'We sent discreet messages by, ah, every means we could think of, but never heard back, which is not surprising. So your guess is as good as mine. I would take credit for the brilliant outcome if I could! But now tell me how you came to be here, and what your plans are.'

I looked at the consul, then at the floor, wavering between replying with a lie, truth, half-truth or evasion. The story of my life these days. I pushed my glasses up to the bridge of my nose and looked him in the eye. 'I also wish I could honestly tell you everything, Mr Jackson. All I can say is that I have some business to do. Whether or not your intervention was decisive in saving all those lives on Musa Dagh, my friends and I will never forget that you tried your best, risking your neutral status here. If there is ever anything I can do for you, I'll gladly do it on behalf of my people.'

His slightly amused expression made me think he guessed more than I had intended to convey. We talked about the war, which America was still reluctant to enter. 'However,' he said, 'this is changing. First the *Lusitania* last May, lately the German atrocities in Belgium which have received a lot of publicity. The Ottomans are still associated in the public mind with "Abdul the Red", after the massacres of Christians in 1895 and '96. So there is no doubt about which side we are on. Our president, Wilson, is committed to neutrality; he would rather stay out, keep the economy on a peacetime basis, while appeasing public opinion and Congress by supporting Britain and France with copious loans. Money, weapons, but not bodies, so to speak.'

The mood at home was sombre during my last evening with the family. 'I will leave at dawn, Mayrig, no need to bother you or anyone else at that hour. Please don't get up.'

'Nonsense, Varo. Who will make your picnic?'

When I came downstairs, I found her already busy, having prepared my bedroll and packed food for the road: a slab of pungent *bastirma*, a hunk of braided white cheese, a loaf of *lavash*, black olives and a sticky folded sheet of *amardeen*, dried apricot paste.

I wound the captain's Ottoman watch, wrapped his electric torch in the bedroll and strapped Viper snugly in its place down in the small of my back. I took the receipt with the coded message given to me by the Druze a week ago, wrapped it in a piece of oilskin and sewed it as neatly as I could manage in my belt, just like the letter Minas had carried down from Musa Dagh one short month ago. Mayrig and I kissed silently, though I could tell she was saying the Saint Sarkis prayer to herself. Can't hurt, I thought. I set off through the dark streets of Atawi, retraced my steps back to the train tracks by the hippodrome and was soon walking briskly on the still-deserted road past Idlib to the coast.

Walking as fast as I could while the sun was up, I had to stop when the lengthening shadows turned into a darkness that obscured the roots and stones and other obstacles on the trail. After eating my picnic, I flattened myself a bed in a clump of oleander, like a dog. I found the road down to al-Basit before sundown on the third day, crouching on a knoll under some umbrella pines to wait for night. From there, I could make sure I was not being followed, with a clear view of the path on which I had come as well as the track down the coast from the north, at least until it was pitch-dark. It was October now, and the days were growing shorter and the nights cooler. I drew the bedroll around my knees as I leaned against a tree and dozed a little while waiting for two o'clock. I had decided to start signalling at half past one, just in case *Anne* was ready to send the launch early. Assuming the great ship with an English captain had not found something more important to do than keep a rendezvous with Vartan of Atawi Saghir, not yet eighteen years of age.

Weldon's watch chimed at one, and I started keeping a lookout for any sign of a ship. Surely there would be a glow from the funnel, or the gleam of a cigarette or porthole? I had seen nothing by the time it was nearly half past one. I put the torch in my pocket, rolled up my bedroll and walked as quietly as I could down to the beach, as near as I could manage to the spot where I had been left two weeks previously, though it had been dark then too. The moon was down. The surf was moderate, with tiny flashes of light every few seconds as the waves hissed on the small pebbles and coarse sand of the beach. Nothing that would hinder the launch from picking me up; if there had been serious surf, I could have swum out, but I did not want to contemplate that as I was afraid the seawater would make the report disintegrate or render its secret contents unreadable.

Three times I flashed and waited. Nothing. Half an hour later, at precisely two o'clock, I flashed again, pointing the torch as level as I could, and waited. I was beginning to think I would have to flash again, if indeed they were out where they should be, when I saw the ship's boat emerge from the darkness, the oars muffled as before, rowed by four sailors with a fifth at the tiller and a sixth at the bow with a rifle. The oars were shipped and the surf brought the boat right up on to the beach; all I had to do was throw my gear on board and climb over the gunwale, rolling clumsily into the boat. Once again, I didn't wet more than my shoes. The sailors nodded in silent greeting before pulling the boat back through the surf and rowing smartly against the freshening wind and waves back to the dark hulk of HMS *Anne*.

Captain Weldon was standing at the railing, silently, his wide forehead creased in a frown. Probably had to be roused from his bed for this. I ripped open the stitches on my belt, unwrapped the paper from its oilskin and handed it to the captain. 'All right, Vartan. Glad you made it safely back to us. But you made a mistake tonight. A nearly fatal one.' My heart sank. I looked at the captain, racking my brain for what my fault might be. 'When we say "signal at such-and-such an hour", we do not mean "signal half an hour early if you feel like it". If you had been an experienced agent I would have left at once, seeing your flashes at half past one. It might just as well have been a Turk who had cut your throat, found the torch and started flashing in the hope of attracting a landing. Now you know. Don't make such a mistake again.'

'No, sir,' I mumbled, my face flushing with shame and embarrassment. 'I am sorry, sir. Never again, sir.'

Weldon took the report to his cabin. I stood there aimlessly for a moment, my face burning, confused and bothered at having botched my first assignment and disappointed the captain. I went to my cabin, undressed and crawled into the bunk, thoroughly tired out by the long walk but unable at first to sleep. I kept revisiting that impulse to signal earlier than the appointed time, and had just about decided that I was, after all, a beginner and that no harm had been done, when the rhythmic motion of the ship and the constant vibration of the great engines all combined to draw me into a heavy sleep.

Next morning, I was in the officers' mess, devouring the Egyptian cook's impression of an English breakfast, when an orderly came to summon me to the bridge. I left my breakfast, having eaten most of the food but found, as always, the 'coffee' to be unworthy of the name, and hurried up two decks. 'Yes, Captain?'

'Sit yourself down, Vartan.' I sat on the bench, relieved at the friendly tone and at being called 'Vartan', instead of 'Young Vartan' or 'Nakashian'. 'Did you learn anything from our Druze about Ibrahim?'

'Nothing very clear,' I replied. 'I told Hamadi that a friend of mine by that name went down to the coast and disappeared, probably conscripted. The Druze said he likely had an accident: "The beach can be dangerous at this time of year." I took that to mean that he had been followed to his rendezvous on the beach, or intercepted and captured there.'

'Hmm. That fits with what our agent who wrote the report had to say. Makes me glad you had your ideas about which beach to land on. Better vary your route in future, all the same.' I wondered what the 'future' held as he had not said anything about what would come next for me.

'May I ask something, sir?'

'Of course, Vartan, but depending on the question, I might answer, or I might not,' he said, a slight smile crinkling the corners of his blue eyes.

'Will we be going to Port Said again?'

'Ah,' Weldon replied, 'that one I can answer. We shall. I have a Palestinian agent – a Jew – and his wife to pick up at Athlit. Interesting place, an old Crusader fort, I think the last one they abandoned when the Mamelukes finally chased out the last Knights Templar. Our man wants out, with his wife; seems he has been compromised somehow. It's the least we can do, and if they make it safely to Athlit, we'll drop them in Port Said before getting back to our coastal work. Why, my friend, do you have relatives there with the Musa Dagh crowd?'

I was afraid I was about to blush again; adjusting my glasses, I cursed that childish habit, and said, 'Well yes, in a way. My aunt and uncle are there, and I couldn't find them before we sailed a few weeks ago. I'd like to make sure they are all right, and to give them a little money if they're in need.'

'That should be altogether possible,' said Weldon, after sucking life back into his pipe. 'As for money, we need to settle up with you for work already done. And properly done, despite my grumbles last night. The report was very informative. But you know the drill. Not a word to anyone about our work on this ship, or what you did for us, or what you will do. Even to your aunt or uncle or whichever of your relatives it makes you blush to remember.'

'*Will* do, sir?' I asked, trying hard to ignore the jocular barb and without thinking how my question would sound. 'I don't know anything about that!' The captain chuckled.

'I suppose I ought to have cleared it with you. We have a new mission for you, away from your home territory, if you are game. If not, of course, you're free to say so, and we will either leave you in Port Said or drop you back on the beach near Aleppo. Sworn to keep the secret for all time, need I say.'

'I'm "game", as you say, sir. I only hope it is not hunting season.' The captain laughed his sudden, frank thunderclap of a laugh. 'Your English is damned good for someone who only spent five years in Jerusalem, as I think you said. You'll have a chance to use it in Palestine – in Jerusalem, in fact. Would you still know how to find your way around the Old City?'

The night was dark. I went up to the bridge to watch as we approached the coast. *Anne* moved slowly inshore, a sailor at the bow pitching a sounding line to test the depth forward as the old ship edged towards the beach. 'Eight fathoms, sir! Six fathoms, sir!' I could see the gleam of rocks on the shore, just appearing as a wan quarter-moon peeked out from behind the clouds. The launch was lowered. Its crew climbed quietly down and it dissolved in the darkness, the muffled oars making hardly a sound in the still night. The clouds drifted away from the quarter-moon, faintly lighting up the terrain and showing the silhouette of the ruined Crusader castle on a raised promontory to the north.

One could just make out two very faint sets of lights on the shore. 'Two villages, Vartan. One Arab, one Jewish; one called Atlit and one called Athlit by the people who live there. Insignificant, but one day there will be hell to pay after the big war is over and they can get back to their little ones. Two dogs, one bone; sooner or later, another war, I am afraid.' I found it hard to concentrate on 'after the war is over'. Just then I heard whispers and a dull thud, and went to the railing to watch the agent and his wife climb aboard. I glimpsed a man and woman carrying only two small bundles; Weldon sent their baggage below and escorted the couple to his cabin.

When I went to the mess for breakfast next morning, they were already there, poking at the food on the plate, carefully avoiding the rashers of bacon. I collected my plate and came up to their table, introducing myself in English and asking if I might sit with them. The man replied in a strange English that included a lot of words that sounded almost like English but were obviously something else. He was brown and wiry, with a bald head like a coconut shaved in the middle and fringed by stringy locks. A noble nose that could almost have been Armenian.

'Shimon Sorokin, this Esther, my wife. Good to meet with you, Vartan, you say?'

'Vartan Nakashian. An Armenian name, they are all rather difficult. From Aleppo.'

I looked at the woman, who had not spoken a word and looked extremely tired and sad. She had certainly been fair-skinned and probably quite beautiful before years of working the land had tanned her skin to a rich leathery tone and etched lines in her face. These made her less attractive but in no way ugly, merely old beyond her thirty-five or so years, as I guessed.

Shimon spoke: 'We originally from Bessarabia, you know where is?'

'No,' I answered, 'sounds strange, like "Arabia".' Shimon smiled.

'Sounds like, but is in south Russia. There was beeg pogrom in our town, Kishinev, I think you say Chisinau, in 1903. You know what is pogrom? So we decide to become Zionist and come here, journey take all our money. For ten years we been planting, growing oranges.' He paused, fumbled for a cigarette. 'Then six months gone we meet English agent. We help their people find way around, bring reports to Captain Veldon or agents he send to us. He tell us if we get trouble he take us away with him. We no believe, but see: he did it. He is real, ah, *mensch*, you know?'

'No,' I replied, 'I don't, but if it means what I think, you are right, he is a good man. A gentleman, they say in England.'

'Anyways,' Shimon continued, 'life here not easy, Turks very suspicion of us after war start. We enemy, Russian subjects. Not worth much in Russia: there, Orthodox don't like us; here, Turks. We think it good if England and France win war. England don't care, Jew, Christian or Mussulman, just keep quiet and pay tax, yes?'

'I can understand you,' I said. 'We also hope for English and French victory.' I thought to myself, 'If only there were a Palestine to which *my* people could emigrate in safety.' 'But why did you leave, it looks like permanently?'

'During past few weeks,' Shimon went on, 'we see young men in Arab village of Atlit watching me. When I take oranges to Jaffa, I usually meet English agent to take or give message. One Arab he follow me from far, I see him. Esther she used to work as, how you say, middle wife? In Kishinev. A few months ago, she help Arab woman with baby, very difficult. Turn out healthy boy. Woman risk life, tell Esther I suspected to spy for England, soon arrested.' He stubbed his cigarette out in the ashtray. 'We preparing to leave last night when we hear screaming and shotgun – *okh, neyn*, how you say? Gunshot, yes? From Atlit. We not know for sure but Esther think her friend found out. Pay big price.'

The couple were subdued, and so was I. We sat in silence for a while, deep in our thoughts. Over dinner at the captain's table, Weldon was anything but subdued, enjoying a glass of whisky. The Sorokins and I listened distractedly as he talked about the Ottomans' use of Islam to mobilise support for the war effort, trying to foment trouble among Muslims in British colonies, especially India. How the Germans were helping them, a tactic that would, he said, come back to haunt all of us one day. I felt like telling him that people like Shimon, Esther and me, we feel like pawns in someone else's game. Win some, lose some: 'part of the game'. He must have noticed that we were not sharing his jolly mood, not interested in the politics, and gradually he too fell silent and smoked his pipe, so that we all sat staring at our hands or into space, each in their own world, lulled to a torpor by the constant throbbing of the engines and the regular roll and pitch of the ship as it steamed through the dark.

Next morning, HMS *Anne* docked at Port Said. As the passengers waited for the gangway to be put in place, I went up to Shimon and Esther to say goodbye. I asked them what their plans were; they looked at each other. 'America,' Shimon answered, without enthusiasm. I could not tell whether he was pessimistic about the chances of making it there, or what life would be like there if they succeeded. 'We try to get visa for America. First, we go to main synagogue in Cairo. Most Jews in Egypt are Sephardim, but we sure they help us.'

I had promised the captain to be back on board within three hours, and hurried down the gangway and off towards the camp, unmistakable across the main road from the port. I felt elated, but my excitement was tinged with apprehension at the reception I would receive from Shoushan. Assuming, of course, that she was still in the refugee camp, though I could not imagine where else she might have gone. The camp looked like an improvisation: stone buildings in the middle, surrounded by a tent city. Sturdy English army tents arranged in neat lines. They were obviously inhabited by civilians, and not English ones: the washing flapping on the lines strung between the tents was a mixture of white interspersed with multi-coloured and flowery textiles, with a preponderance of pink. A touch of Cilicia in the Sinai desert.

A soldier stopped me at the gate, but let me through when I explained I was on furlough from HMS *Anne*. There were guards filtering visitors going in and controlling those leaving as well. Like a prison, I thought – this could not be what the defenders of Musa Dagh had in mind. But then I saw the children playing happily in their restricted but clean surroundings, the babble of people talking and shouting in Armenian, the men sitting, smoking and sorting out events over their coffee while the women did their washing and gossiped over the cooking pots. All that spoke more of routine and security than anxiety. 'A fence protects as well as confines,' I thought. I asked an old man sitting in the sun in front of a tent if he knew the Bedrossian family, and of course he did. He directed me to one of the stone buildings.

Inside, each former office was a dormitory, with rows of army cots, sheets or blankets hung here or there to offer a measure of privacy. Children ran around, their mothers and older siblings chatting while keeping an eye. There was a general smell of olive-oil soap and some spice, maybe cumin. I was looking around, taking all this in, when I was startled to hear my name bellowed: 'Varo!' Aunt Azniv stopped in her stride, with a basket of laundry on her ample hip. Her shout stopped the conversations around us for a moment and all faces turned towards me. I felt a blush coming on, but kissed my aunt.

'How are you? How is everyone?' I asked.

'We are all well, thanks to God, well enough for people in limbo. Your uncle and Shoushan are down there in our space, to the left of the first stairway.'

I hurried towards their 'space'. When she saw me her face lit up and I knew she did not, could not, hate me. I first hugged Uncle Artin, then Minas and finally turned to Shoushan. We stood looking at each other awkwardly, until Artin said, 'You young people run along and do your talking now, you will tell us old ones soon enough. Now go!' I gave Artin a grateful glance, took Shoushan by the arm and guided her towards the door of the building. Minas started to say something, then stopped himself and watched us go with a frown.

We stole glances at each other as we walked, on my part looking for signs of change after a few weeks' separation. I found her even more beautiful than when we parted: her cheeks fuller, the hunger circles under her eyes mostly erased. 'You've come back,' she said, 'but not to stay?'

'No, Shoushan, I must leave again in a few hours. But I had to see you. I was so confused the last time we parted. I still cannot tell you very much, but I really wanted you to understand…'

'I understand more than you think, Varo. You need to trust me: don't say more than you should, but don't lie to me, ever again.'

'*Never*. I swear. And some day this will be over: we will be together and there will be no more secrets between us. Can you forgive, can you live with that, and will you wait for me?'

She looked at me. The faint smile that usually lit up her dark eyes was not there. 'Vartan, why do you ask what I will do? Who knows what our future is? We're in the hands of the English now, I don't need to tell you that. I think their plan is that we return to our homes when the war is over, *if* they and the French win. But my home is not at Yoghun-Oluk. I still don't know for sure what happened to my family – whether I will have a home to go back to, whether I could do so if I wanted to. If I have to leave before you return, I'll make sure the people from the Armenian Red Cross, the Armenian people of Egypt who have been helping us so much, know where I have gone. That is about all I can promise now.'

We walked in silence for a while, around the camp perimeter, arm in arm. I stopped and turned to her: 'You are sensible, compared to me. I get so confused when I think about the future. Of course, you must look for your family, and as soon as I can, I'll come back to find you and we will look for them together. A few people from Killis made it to Aleppo and not all of them went on to Deir az-Zor. You mustn't give up hope. It's all we have now.'

'We don't really know what we have now, do we? You are off on an adventure, a useful one, I hope. Minas, for one, is seething – at his impotence, at your freedom. We are almost prisoners in this camp, living on the charity of the English. Swear you'll come back to me soon, Varo.'

I had no idea what to say to that. I looked down at the ground for a moment, then at her: 'Shoushan, I will try. I am no more master of my fate than you are. I will not promise something I am not sure is in my power. But I will try, *janim*.'

She held my arm more tightly and we walked around some more, mostly in silence. Impending separation, the fearful unknown, weighed heavily on us. After an hour or so, I said, 'Now I must go and talk to Artin and Azniv – and Minas. I don't quite know what to say, but I'll think of something. I hate to lie: my face looks like a tomato if I even think about telling a lie. As you know.'

My aunt and uncle quizzed me about where I had been and what I had done since leaving them. I took a deep breath and said, with a sideways look at Shoushan, that I was doing some translating 'and other things' for the English sea captain who had ferried Shoushan and me from Musa Dagh. Aunt Azniv, of course, insisted that I share their food, which was a treat after the *Anne*'s shipboard fare. She even had some rose jam, a fragrant Armenian concoction that took me straight back to Atawi and my youth. I didn't say so but Mayrig made the best *gülbesheker* in the world, according to a family recipe from Killis, and before that from the high Caucasus, so she always said. With the blood-red petals simmering for hours in the huge pot, the fragrance filled the house and spilled into the street – you could see passers-by stopping to sniff the air and look around. And now its cloying sweetness wafted me home, not just home but back to childhood. 'You like it, Varo?' asked Azniv. 'You *should*: Vartan means "rose",' she told me, the thousandth time I had been reminded of the embarrassing meaning of my name.

Minas sat silently as we ate and talked, not exactly surly but it was obvious that something had changed. I could tell he did not approve of the unofficial, but now public, bond between Shoushan and me. I wondered whether it was simple jealousy, in a society where first cousins often married. But I had never noticed that Minas had a penchant for her, only that he seemed to resent mine. Finally, after I had eaten to my satisfaction, and even Aunt Azniv's, and praised her *gülbesheker* to the skies, I asked Minas, 'You seem sad, or angry, Minas. What's wrong?'

'What's wrong? I want to fight but the *Ingleez* keep us locked up in this place. Even *you* get to help them with the war. I don't believe for a moment that you are just translating. We – I and the other young men here – would join any army that would have us, if we could fight the Turks, but none will, not so far at least. They even refuse to give us back the guns we brought from Musa Dagh – apparently they threw them in the sea. There is talk of organising an Armenian legion officered by the French to fight the Turks; I have put my name down. But there is no sign of it actually happening, or not yet. That is all, Vartan. You are lucky and I wish you well.'

I hugged each one in turn before leaving, and was relieved to feel a little of the old warmth between Minas and me. But there had been an edge, almost a tinge of anger to his words. I felt sure that Minas had secretly counted on marrying his prettiest cousin, as one did in 'Turkish' Armenia. He was a country boy, but not the sort of backward peasant who would seek to marry her against her will, and now there was the unspoken but obvious fact that Shoushan and I were in love. I had seen it in the faces of Artin and Azniv: they knew. In normal times I would have asked Artin to make it official. I looked at Shoushan one last time, and when I saw her eyes begin to glisten, I turned and left before making a fool of myself. 'Please God not to make these cursed times last so long that they become normal. There I go again. "Thank God", "please God", "if God wills". He is added to every sauce in these godforsaken countries of ours, even by people who don't believe he is really there. But who else?'

HMS *Anne* sailed at the appointed hour and soon I was at the broad stern railing, watching Port Said – and with it, the dusty brown expanse of Africa – fade away again into the afternoon haze over the Mediterranean. I was not surprised when an orderly came and summoned me to the bridge. The captain seemed in a jovial mood: 'Good visit, I hope?'

'Yes, sir,' I replied, 'everything in order.' I had a feeling that Weldon guessed more about me than I ever cared to disclose.

'Excellent,' he said, drawing on his pipe. 'Now to the future. Our first stop will be Athlit again, to drop off two agents who boarded while you were ashore. You must meet them, Sarah and Yussuf. The Zionist settlers are a rich source of information about Ottoman forces and troop movements, at great risk to their lives, and she is one of our most valuable agents. A different category from the Sorokins, if I may say so, but for each task there is a profile. To think the British authorities in Cairo didn't want to deal with them at first, just because they offered to help without asking anything in return! Old Clayton and Wingate are too experienced in the ways of the Levant to trust anybody who is not out for himself. And Sarah is… well, enough said, I think you will enjoy meeting her. After dinner, come to my cabin as we need to discuss your next mission, for which you said you were on board. Still "game"?'

'Of course. Jerusalem, I think you said?'

'Jerusalem. I will explain everything tonight.'

At mess time, I found the new pair of Jewish agents at table, obviously Yussuf and Sarah, and I immediately knew what Weldon had meant. The man was ordinary-looking, rather coarse, with unkempt reddish hair and small, almost mean eyes. I told myself not to judge too much by first impressions. But the woman… was nothing short of a revelation. Sarah was tall, blonde and blue-eyed, not like any Turkish, Arab, Armenian or Jewish woman I had ever seen. I had seen quite a few European women and thought she would stand out even among a crowd of those of her age, which I thought must have been in the mid-twenties. Beautiful she certainly was, but more than that: she had an unusual aura of freedom and openness about her that made her disturbing to look at. She wore her clothes, at this moment a cotton shift that seemed to hug the generous curves of her body, in an unabashedly *sexual* way – that's the only word I could think of. But not *vulgar*. Nothing to do with the lurid charms of the prostitutes I had seen (and nothing more) in the slums of Aleppo. I have rarely felt so intimidated and could already feel the warm flush of my usual change of colour creeping up from my collar.

'Um, may I join you? Captain Weldon suggested we, ah, get acquainted. I am Vartan Nakashian.' Yussuf frowned up at me, and looked as if he would answer but before he could do so, Sarah smiled at me and patted the bench next to her, saying in clear, almost unaccented English, 'Oh! So you're the young Armenian our captain seems to think so highly of! Now that we are colleagues, you must join us for some of the chef's interesting cuisine. And tell us about yourself – I hear you've had some adventures quite out of the ordinary for someone your age.'

I sat on the bench a little further away from her than the spot she had patted. I adjusted my glasses, looked at her and said, 'First tell me your names. I think the captain said Sarah and Yussuf? Is that an Arabic name?' The man laughed, a dry and controlled chuckle.

'He calls me "Yussuf" but my name is Josef, Josef Lishinsky. Almost pronounced the same. Immigrated to Palestine many years ago, from Poland, and work at the agricultural settlement at Athlit, Zichron Ya'akov we call it. This is Sarah Aaronsohn, sister of the renowned scientist and scholar Aaron Aaronsohn, maybe you heard of him?'

'Ah, no,' I said. 'But I have heard about the settlement. Apparently the Turks were very grateful for the useful work that was done during the locust plague a few months ago.'

'Grateful, maybe, but that hasn't made them like us or the whole idea of Jewish immigration. We have no illusions: they'll do to us what they are doing to the Armenians, as soon as they can get away with it. Sarah has seen for herself, haven't you, Sarah?'

She had not stopped looking at me, making me squirm and adjust my glasses. And blush even deeper, of course.

'I am afraid I have, during a trip to Constantinople last August. The devastation in the former Armenian villages and countryside is unbelievable. The worst things that we had heard are true. I won't repeat the details, but it is beyond imagination. I am sorry to tell you this, it must be very painful. You probably know all about it already, but unless you have seen it for yourself, you cannot *really* know.'

'I haven't seen all that with my own eyes, Miss, ah…'

'Just call me Sarah. Officially Mrs Chaim Abraham but my husband and I don't live together. Where were you during the massacres?' I thought Mr Abraham must be an idiot or unworthy.

'In Aleppo, Miss… Sarah, and what we saw of the deportees, the survivors, was bad enough. But there were no massacres in Aleppo and we resident Armenians were not deported or bothered unless we got caught helping the deportees.'

We sat and talked through dinner and what passed for coffee. I was intrigued by these people who had come from Europe to live in Palestine, struggling against huge odds. They were risking everything to make a new life for themselves. 'How many of our people,' I thought, 'would give anything to get themselves and their families *out* of this cursed part of the world. But this is where our ancestors lived and died, our bond is not found in some old book. And…' my thoughts wandered, 'what an admirable woman Sarah is! And *so* beautiful. I hope she is not involved with that ratty Josef, though he is nicer than he looks. Anyway, I must go...' I excused myself to report to the captain. I found him bent over a pile of maps and papers, apparently reports of troop concentrations and movements.

'Sit down, Vartan, and tell me how you found Sarah and Yussuf.'

'Well, Captain, if the Zionists have more like her, male or female, they will succeed.' Weldon pushed aside his papers and re-lit his pipe, savouring a cloud of pungent smoke. He looked at me:

'You are right there, she's a marvel. And quite a beauty, wouldn't you say? Makes me wish I was ten years younger. Though I doubt she'd be interested in an old lapsed Presbyterian even so.

'Now, more to the point, your next assignment: after dropping our friends at Athlit, we will drop you south of a miserable little Arab village called Isdud, which the Jews call Ashdod, though there aren't many Jews there. Yet another one of those tricky names, like the shibboleth in the Bible, you know? No? Never mind. You will just walk east, all paths from there lead to Jerusalem. About the same distance from the coast as Aleppo, I'm afraid. Once there you will go to the Old City. Enter by the Jaffa Gate and go through the Armenian Quarter, which, I imagine, you know well. From there go through into the Jewish Quarter and head for the Eliyahu Hanavi Synagogue.

'You will ask for the house of Eliezer Ben Negrila, near the Yeshiva where he teaches. He is an old Sephardi, whose ancestors were *wazirs,* ministers to the kings of Granada, and got kicked out of Spain with them in 1492, if memory serves. Damn Spaniards discovered America and exiled their best talent in the same year! He still speaks that funny Spanish at home, Ladino they call it. You will say you are visiting from Aleppo and have a message from a mutual friend, an old sea captain. Here, take this.' He removed a folded document from his drawer and handed it to me. 'A *laissez-passer*, in the name of a fictional Orthodox from Aleppo, Georges Habib, a couple of years older than you – you really don't look as young as you are. If the Jews ask whether you know any of their community in Aleppo, say you know the Dayans. No way for them to check up unless one of that powerful Jewish tribe happens to be visiting, which is not likely just now.' Weldon stopped talking to take the dottle out of his pipe and stuff it with a new wad of his tobacco mixture.

'And then, sir?' I asked at length, after Weldon had got his pipe burning and began filling the air with pungent smoke.

'And then… this, the usual thing.' He opened his desk drawer and removed a purse, shook it, the familiar tinkle of gold coins. It looked heavier than the one I had given to the Aleppo Druze, Hamadi. 'You will give this to Eliezer and tell him the following message. You will repeat this after me until you know it by heart. It's in Arabic, by the way.'

'But, do you know *Arabic*, sir?'

'Well, yes, it would take a bit of a thick skull to live in Cairo for fifteen years without learning the lingo. Though many of the Brits do just that, for their sins. Actually it's a bit of a hobby of mine, and a chum at al-Azhar taught me what he could of Classical Arabic. Their poetry, especially the older stuff, has some really smashing bits. And with people like Eliezer, who is a *real* scholar, in Arabic as well as Hebrew, I play around. I actually don't like for the Arabs, other than our chaps, to know I speak the language. Keeps them on their guard. Half of this intelligence business is giving the other side a sense of security. Of superiority, if you can. Knowing more than he does but making him think you know less and are generally stupider than he is. Using silence: making them feel they have to talk. And that's usually when people make mistakes.

'Anyway, what you have to tell Eliezer is dead simple. Listen carefully.' Weldon recited a line of Arabic poetry, well enunciated, perfectly understandable despite a slight English accent. I could hardly believe I was hearing this from the captain.

'That is strange Arabic, sir.'

'Yes, it is, for you and me, but not for Eliezer's forefathers. It's part of a poem written a thousand years ago in al-Andalus, as they called

Spain back then. Well, not the Jews, who called it Sfarad. They used to stick refrains from colloquial Arabic, or even medieval Spanish, on the end of poems in Arabic or Hebrew; shows you how close the two cultures were, back then. Three cultures, I guess I ought to say, though the Christians were country bumpkins by comparison to either of the others. Do you understand the refrain I just recited?'

'Yes, sir, the meaning is clear: "The gazelle ran through the fire, but the flames could not catch him."'

'Spot on. It's a code for Eliezer, and will set in motion a chain of events that will cause a few problems for the Turks in Palestine. Better you should not know in more detail.

'There is one question you can ask him for me, in private, of course. Last week we sent a seaplane to do a reccy – reconnaissance mission – over the Turkish camp at Beersheba. It must have gone down, because it never returned. French pilot and English observer on board. You might have met them? See if he has anything about them and their aircraft.

'Once you have done all that, he will give you another refrain for you to memorise and bring back to me. Not any longer than the one about the gazelle. It's a little game we play, the good rabbi and I, but it works, at least when the agent is literate. You will then return to the beach at Isdud, seven nights from tonight – that is the night of Tuesday, October 28th to Wednesday, October 29th, at midnight precisely. Three flashes from your torch, and at midnight, *not* half an hour earlier.' His right eyebrow arched in an attempt to look severe. I looked chastened but knew that my error the week before had been forgiven.

'Can you use a pistol?'

'Yes, sir, my late father was a gunsmith. I can shoot and even fix simple firearms, he taught me when I was a boy. But I would rather not carry a pistol. It would look odd on someone my age. I do carry a concealed knife, a dagger – actually I can use it better than many people can a pistol, especially at close quarters.'

'You surprise me, Vartan. No pistol then, just your *arme blanche*, a bag of money and a scrap of poetry. Do keep your wits about you: the Jerusalem road is known to be infested with robbers and there's no law enforcement to speak of. Get some victuals from the *usta*, our dear cook. Here's the purse and a little more local money for you to spend on necessities, or for opening doors of all kinds. While you are ashore we will move along the coast and deploy the new seaplane we picked up at Port Said. We need to find out whether Jemal Pasha, General Jemal as he is now, is getting ready for another go at crossing the canal. In a few weeks, you will go to Aleppo again, this time with a message in both directions. Is all that understood and acceptable? Any issues or questions?'

'Of course, sir, no questions. I will be happy to go to Aleppo as I will be able to check on my family.'

'Just so.'

I left the captain to return to his maps and went to bed early; the next night would be long and the sleeping rough. Sleep did not come easy, between imagining the unlikely mission to recite Arabic poetry to an old Jew in Jerusalem and thoughts of Sarah Aaronsohn. I fell asleep thinking of her and in my dreams found myself kissing her full lips, feeling her generous, yielding body under her cotton shift… I awoke with a start (and an erection) before things could go any further, feeling ridiculous and ashamed, unworthy of Shoushan. And secretly hoping that the same dream would return, and perhaps not end so abruptly.

The *Anne* steamed slowly offshore all day, so as to arrive at Athlit well after dark. The night was moonless and the sea quiet. I watched the loading of the tender that would take Sarah and Lishinsky ashore: the sailors lowered down a heavy bag, that I surmised must contain gold, and several lighter packages which the sailors handled warily, obviously explosives of some kind. As they rowed away, Sarah turned and waved at the ship, just before the darkness swallowed them. I imagined her wave was meant for me. 'Brave woman,' I thought.

'Brave people, heading off into the Ottoman Empire at war, bringing gold to pay spies and bombs to cause havoc, helped of course by the *Ingleez*. I wish our people had such support. Finally, it was only at Musa Dagh that there was any effective resistance, or any tangible outside assistance. And that was, as the captain would say, "a damned close-run thing".'

In less than an hour the tender was back and since the sea was calm, was towed behind the ship rather than hoisted on board, for my turn would come soon. The lights of the little town were clearly visible as we approached, with the ship in blackout conditions as usual when landing agents.

I spent the last few hours of the night huddled against the wall of a ruin. On this dark night I could not tell what it used to be, but I guessed it was an old *khan*, a caravanserai. My dreams were troubled, maybe by ghosts. I awoke with a start at first light, shook the night stiffness from my joints and started walking along a vague path leading inland from the sea. At first, I crossed a plain with intense agriculture on both sides, orange groves and wheat, it looked like. Then the landscape got more arid, prickly pears in bunches and scrub pine and cedar.

On the third morning, I was passing well-tended vineyards and a working windmill, with tanned people in casual European dress coming and going; there were women as well as men, some had blonde or reddish hair. I think it must have been one of the Jewish settlements. Suddenly it was there, the hill with its holy city in the distance, its ramparts seeming to float above the flanks of the hill with their rows of olive trees. How different the world, my world at least, looked since the last time I saw Jerusalem! It was just over a year since I had returned to Aleppo.

I passed the railway station, a pleasant square stone building from where I had heard there were occasional trains to Jaffa. Three hours to cover the same distance I had walked in two and a half days! I climbed up the hill towards Jaffa Gate, a square tower of huge sand-coloured stones. The Arabs call it Bab al-Khalil, Abraham's Gate. A Turkish soldier stepped out of a recess and stopped me with an unfriendly gesture. I produced Georges Habib's passport, which he looked at as though he was reading it carefully. There was a swirly illegible signature at the bottom, authenticated by an ornate Ottoman seal impressed in red wax, and this seemed to deflate his desire to make trouble for me. He handed it back and gestured for me to be gone.

I soon found myself in the Armenian Quarter, passing by the grey stone walls of the convent and school dedicated to Saint James. They seemed part of a distant past. I decided it would make sense to get rid of my bedroll and freshen up. I went into the convent and found the doorman, Brother Hagop, in his lodge. We embraced warmly and I was relieved that he didn't question me. I just said I was back for a brief family visit, which I think he knew was not true as I had no family there. He let me leave my things in his room. I washed my hands and face at the fountain in the courtyard; the cold water washed away the memories and thoughts that distracted me from my mission. I tidied up my clothes as best I could, then went out and across the invisible line into the Jewish Quarter, which I found dark, confined and unsanitary after the relatively airy streets of the Armenian neighbourhood.

In a few minutes, I was standing outside the synagogue of Eliyahu Hanavi. I admired the ornate doorway, nestled in a cul-de-sac. The door was locked, but just then a group of three religious students passed by, all dressed in black but without the long ringlets of the Ashkenazi. I stopped them and said in English, 'Good afternoon. Can you kindly direct me to the house of the scholar, Rabbi Eliezer Ben Negrila?'

The three bespectacled students looked at me suspiciously, at first. I suppose my youth, fluent English, maybe my spectacles even, made me look more like a student than a terrorist. They murmured something in a strange language, then one of them finally said, pointing to an alleyway going off at an angle near the synagogue, 'Down that street, third door on the left.' I thanked them, found the door and knocked with an ancient brass lion's-head knocker, its muzzle worn down to a kind of grin. The door opened and I was received by a barefoot young servant girl in a dark blue robe I think they call a caftan. Her uncovered dark hair hung down her back in a single thick plait. She looked at me pointedly, obviously surprised to find a young Christian at the door. I didn't know what language to speak, but finally asked for the scholar in Arabic.

'Wait here, if you please,' she replied in the same language, but her words and accent were strange. I watched her feet as she padded away on the marble floor with its black and white squares. When she returned, she led me through an interior courtyard, around a faintly gurgling marble fountain almost hidden behind a dense growth of green leaves and dangling tendrils. A few white gardenia flowers in pots perfumed the still air of the courtyard. I felt the stark contrast with the treeless city outside, on its stony hilltop, hemmed in by tombs. When the last trumpet sounds, there will be a stampede of skeletons of all three faiths, rising up and jostling with each other to be the first to enter Paradise.

I was struck by the quiet beauty of the house, its atmosphere so different from austere Aleppo houses or what little I had seen of other Jerusalem houses. Even the servant girl had a serene, alien brown-eyed beauty. Could this be a corner of Granada? I had no idea of Spain, new or old, but I imagined it something like this lush and fragrant courtyard. Then I saw him, an old man wearing a skull cap from which white hair fell in curls almost to his shoulders, like an icon of a patriarch. He was sitting at a desk in an alcove facing the courtyard, framed by two columns with capitals that did not match which I imagined had been recovered from the ruins of even older buildings. Surely not brought all the way from Spain!

The man was dressed in what looked to me like Arab robes but with an embroidered shawl over his shoulders. He was poring over a scroll I assumed to be the Talmud, the biblical commentary the Jews were endlessly commenting on, and commenting on comments on comments, and so on, and will be so doing until the end of time catches them unawares, according to the religion teacher at my old convent school. He was not especially fond of Jews but reserved his bitterest scorn for the Roman Catholics, Protestants and, especially, Greeks.

The scholar took off his glasses and looked up at me. 'What is your name and family, young Armenian, as I judge? And what brings you to call on this poor old Jew?' I suspected he knew exactly who had sent me. His gaze was penetrating in a way that was not unfriendly, but gave me the disquieting impression that he could read my innermost thoughts.

'Sir, I am not Armenian, I am Georges Habib, Orthodox from Aleppo. I have a message from a mutual friend, an old sea captain, who would like to share with you a favourite verse of Arabic poetry, of which he says you are a connoisseur: *Al-ghazal shaqq al-hariq…*' I recited. 'Do you know it?'

'Ah, yes,' replied the old man after a thoughtful pause. 'Ibn Baqi of Cordoba, a beautiful poem, a *muwashshaha*. Wonderful how the old poets knew how to spice up their compositions with popular song. To us nowadays it sounds like a breath of fresh air, a voice from the street – the street of a thousand years ago. But what is a thousand years to the mind of man? We have not changed, we merely forget. Do you know any others, *khawaja* Habib?'

'No, *ya ustadh*, not of that kind. In Aleppo, I learned some of the poetry of one of our city's most famous poets, a knight who fought the Christians, though his mother was a captive Byzantine princess.'

'Ah, the noble Abu Firas. And what do you know of him?' I tried to remember the verses Omar had taught me. He was intensely proud of his great ancestor (so he claimed).

'I think I can remember one verse, written when he himself was a captive: '*Aqulu wa qad nahat*... I love the way he describes the lonely turtle dove on his prison windowsill, beginning with the word *aqulu*, which sounds just like a dove cooing. But that's all I can remember of it.'

The old scholar finished the verse in perfect Arabic, with an accent I had never encountered before. I wondered if it was the way they spoke back when the Arabs were kings in Spain and the Ben Negrilas were their ministers. 'I will be pleased to hear a verse from you, if you have one you would like me to hear. But first, I have a question from our mutual friend. May I speak freely here?'

'You may, young "Orthodox". You may even tell me the truth about yourself.' I was embarrassed, not sure if I had offended the scholar with my clumsy attempt to hide my identity, but also unsure whether complete frankness was in order. Not for a spy, surely? I decided to give up the ridiculous pretence.

'I am indeed Armenian, and you will forgive me if I don't go around announcing it. These are terrible times for our people.' The old man nodded, half shutting his heavy-lidded eyes as though he understood only too well. 'Our friend would like to know if you have information about the crew of a small aeroplane that went missing last week while on a reconnaissance mission near Beersheba.'

'That I do, sadly. Their machine came down accidentally in the sands near a Turkish military camp, in the Sinai. One of the two, a Frenchman I believe, was knocked unconscious by the impact. That probably saved his life. The other, an Englishman, unwisely shot at the Turks who came to arrest them and was himself killed, but not before killing two of the enemy. The French officer, the pilot, I believe, whose name is something like "Say-zoo", was treated for his wounds, which are not serious, and interned in a prisoner-of-war camp near Beersheba.'

'You are exceptionally well informed, *ustadh*. I shall tell our friend, and I am sure that he will be grateful to you for putting an end to his uncertainty, even if the news is not good. Now perhaps you will share your verse with me.'

'Indeed.' With this the old man recited a line from a poem unknown to me, but which I understood perfectly: an exiled Moorish king pining about love, loss of a homeland and a throne, that of Seville. 'Can you repeat the poem for me?'

And so I practised the poem of an exile, in the house of an exile, and wondered if I myself was becoming an exile. A wanderer, that's for sure, as Shoushan would say. I'm not sure my father ever went further from Aleppo than Damascus; he certainly never visited me in Jerusalem. I repeated the poem three times and the old scholar nodded his approval. I pulled the heavy coin purse from my waist-band: 'And there is this; you will know from whom it comes and for what it is intended.' The old man took the purse and bowed his head slightly.

'You will take some refreshment with me before you leave, I hope? We could talk about poetry over a modest meal, which I believe will be ready in the kitchen. A dish of lamb cooked in an earthenware pot along with aubergine, seasoned with cumin, saffron, almonds and honey, a dish from our Spanish homeland.'

I was starving, but had put off thinking about my stomach until my mission was accomplished. Now that he reminded me of it,

I could smell the enticing perfume of the cooking, wafting in from the kitchen nearby. So different from what would be waiting for me back on shipboard! '*Ya ustadh*, that is most kind of you. I am afraid my contribution to a discussion of poetry must prove very inferior to the meal you propose.' Eliezer Ben Negrila laughed and said we would talk some but mainly eat, as I must have strength for the journey that still lay ahead.

The meal outdid even the promise of its perfume. We discussed many things: the likely outcome of the war, the fate of minorities if the Ottomans and Germans won, more poetry. I tried to eat slowly, but between my hunger and the succulent and fragrant lamb, I am afraid I must have looked quite uncouth, my mouth too busy to do much talking. Eliezer made it unnecessary, talking about al-Mu'tamid, the exiled poet-king of Seville.

'He lived during troubled times, and made a fatal mistake. The uncultured and fanatical Christians were pushing down from the north to threaten his kingdom along with the various other city-states, as al-Andalus had become since the fragmentation of the great Caliphate. Perhaps he had no choice, seen from where he stood. Anyway, he appealed for help to one of the Berber tribes from North Africa, Muslim fanatics who wore veils over their faces. And that's the *men* I am talking about. Despite the veils, they were warriors, not poets, and they won a famous battle against the Nazarethans, one which postponed the inevitable destruction of al-Andalus for a century or so. And then what happened? Of course, they took over al-Mu'tamid's palaces, his gardens and his *jariyas*, the slave girls who would sing poems to him against a background of water playing in the fountains, the song of nightingales in the orange trees with their fragrant blossoms adding yet another dimension to sensual perfection.

'It is a wonder they only exiled him, rather than apply the more expedient and permanent method of the sword. I suppose they wanted others to follow his example; and theirs, if their turn should come. Which it did, of course: seduced by the beauty of the place, the sweetness of life there, and yes, eventually by poetry, they grew soft. The Christians did not, and resumed their advance. So – perhaps you can guess? – the new masters of Seville asked for help from a still more warlike Berber tribe, the Almohads. And so the wheel turned yet again. The Arabs' great medieval historian, Ibn Khaldun, described it accurately, the relentless cycle of an empire won by the sword, of a civilisation rising, becoming refined and soft, only to be destroyed in turn by a new wave of hungry barbarians from the desert.

'We learn nothing from history, my young friend. Our temple was destroyed by the Romans, our people scattered. Some of us were fortunate enough to spend a few centuries in the gardens of Sfarad. I take some pride in remembering that, advised by clever Jewish *wazirs*, the Nasiri kings of Muslim Granada made themselves useful to the new Christian masters of the country. They held on to their jewelled existence for a few generations after Cordoba and Seville and all the rest had fallen; Ibn Zamrak was still writing poetry to be carved on the walls of the Alhambra two centuries after all the great libraries had been burned. I digress. But I think you understand me. Is the lamb to your taste? Might Rachel serve you another morsel?'

Once the pot of lamb was seriously diminished, I talked about my family, about my time in Jerusalem, and told the epic story of Musa Dagh. Finally, a little tipsy from the glass of strong, sweet wine, I rose to take my leave. The old man took my hand and held it in both of his. There was a long silence, but not uncomfortable. I felt a surprising sense of kinship with this elderly Jew. I felt he was trying to tell me something, but not with words. In a way I imagined was fatherly. Finally, he spoke. 'Now go safely. If you return to this city, I should be pleased to see you again, even if you have no message to give or receive – if we have not moved outside the walls by then, of course. If an old man may permit himself a word of advice, it would be to take time to reflect, avoiding impetuous actions, which your story and my instinct suggest you might be inclined to.'

I looked at his kindly face, wrinkled as crumpled parchment, and could not take offence. I thanked him 'for everything'. Having said goodbye to Eliezer, I poked my head into the kitchen to say goodbye to Rachel, and not only because of the best meal not cooked by Mayrig I had ever eaten. She smiled and lowered her eyes at the intrusion, which I thought she was glad of. My eyes travelled down to her small, shapely bare feet, and for an instant found myself imagining what the rest of her might look like. I shook off these distracting thoughts and set off on my journey back to the coast.

I first stopped by the convent to pick up my bedroll. Brother Hagop suggested I should go and say hello to the Superior, Brother Onnig. I did not want to have to lie or worry about what to say: I needed quiet time to think over all the strong impressions I had just received. Excusing myself, I hitched the bedroll over my shoulder, walked through the gate of the holy city, past the Turkish guard who merely scowled at me, and descended through olive groves past the windmill and the train station and down towards the sea. I thought about the city: ruins on every side, broken columns, toppled walls, stones standing mute, their messages rubbed off by the centuries. 'A city of fanatics, besotted with the past, with too many ruins and too little of everything else. At least they are not massacring each other for the moment.'

As I walked downhill, my thoughts kept returning to the words of the old rabbi. 'He makes complicated things understandable, if not simple. He lives the life of the mind: a life more real than that of all the soldiers and builders, merchants and gunsmiths, for that matter. And yet he is part of the struggle, part of Weldon's world. He has his Talmud, his poetry, the music of his own fountain, but is not blind to the real world outside. I wish I could follow him in the search for knowledge, for wisdom, not dead facts like I was taught at school, that waste of time. They hardly taught us any poetry! Perhaps after the war there will be time for study, or at least access to a library, if the new barbarians don't burn them all first. "After the war," he says. How sweet that sounds! Sweet but unreal. Now just walk, here you are dawdling along dreaming about poetry while the real world burns. Or lusting after half the women you meet, first Sarah and now Rachel. *Tfou*! What a despicable wretch.'

Back on board *Anne*, I recited my verse for Weldon, who seemed satisfied, even pleased, though as expected he refrained from sharing its coded meaning with me. Then I told him about the crew of the seaplane. Weldon banged his pipe on the table. 'Poor de Saizeu, a Turkish POW camp for the duration will not be pleasant, but at least he survived. But Ledger! The observer, if you don't know him. He was a good man. Just like him to take out a Turk at the cost of his own life. Damnation! We don't have many casualties in our operations. Except,' he added, 'for agents, of course. We have lost several of them. Occupational hazard, you might say.' This might have sounded callous, said in my presence, but I knew it was anything but. Weldon stopped talking and looked at me pointedly, as though inviting me to retire from the spy business while there was still time. I commented as neutrally as I could, 'Naturally.'

The captain puffed on his pipe for a moment, then changed the subject: 'I suspected the railway had reached Beersheba by now. With all the German help they are getting, it will eventually push right up to Suez if it's not stopped. I hope our chap Lawrence with his Arab irregulars can pull off a few more sabotage actions, bridges and the like. This damn war is not won by a long shot, not here in the East any more than in France.'

I had not met poor Sergeant Ledger, but I had the opportunity to get to know several of the English officers. My favourite was one of the younger officers, Harry Foster; shy and not much older than me. We had become acquainted when I saw him reading a book of

English poetry and asked if I could have a look. It was *The Oxford Book of English Verse,* most of which was difficult for me, having only read a few poems at school in Jerusalem – Victorian verse put on the syllabus but which I found long, complicated and boring. Foster walked me through several poems, starting with Donne's 'The Ecstasy', which amazed me by being so easy to read despite the date, and so daring in subject matter.

I realised I was beginning to like intelligence work. I liked playing a game where the other players were so much older and more experienced than I was. Like my furtive escapades with Omar in the dry bed of the Kweik, Aleppo's mostly dry riverbed: turning out the pockets of a murder victim for pathetic souvenirs, or wagering who would have the courage to steal figs from the garden of the head of the Musketeers, the *tfenkji agha*, an old janissary with a bloodthirsty reputation. Only now I was a player – a bit player with hardly a speaking role – on a stage where the actors were empires.

Such enthusiastic thoughts would inevitably give way to guilt, a feeling that my real duty, looking after my mother and siblings – my dying father's last command – was being neglected. I was not going to defeat the Turks or save Hayestan, but I could at least try to protect Mayrig and the children. And that could not be done while steaming up and down the Levantine coast on HMS *Anne*, or spending days walking to deliver messages I understood no more of than a carrier pigeon would.

Despite the captain's promise, the forthcoming assignment to Aleppo was delayed for reasons that were not shared with me. I knew better than to nudge: questions like when to drop an agent were strategic considerations to which only Weldon and his superiors were privy. I was invited to join the officers in their New Year's celebration, which seemed to me long and loud and full of forced jollity enhanced by alcohol. 'An interesting time for a German torpedo to whack us,' I thought. There was a German submarine on the prowl in the eastern Mediterranean, and several ships had been sunk or damaged. I remembered Weldon telling me that the *Anne* had been holed by a torpedo once.

I liked a glass or two of *arak* with my favourite kebabs in sour fruit, and enjoyed exactly one glass of red wine, if not too rough or sweet, but I had no taste for hard liquors such as whisky or gin and found the Greek brandy the sailors drank to be particularly horrible. So I was glad when the year 1916 had been duly inaugurated without out a torpedo attack, but went to bed feeling sick from the unholy mixture of drinks the English had insisted on sharing with me. The next morning I expected the officers to have a lie-in, but the mess was as full as usual. I was just finishing my greasy and unpalatable English breakfast when a sailor came to say the captain wished to see me on the bridge.

'Feeling all right, Vartan, or did we damage your brain cells last night with that awful Metaxa stuff?'

'I am fine, sir, but glad the year only changes every so often.'

Weldon chuckled, tamping his pipe and re-lighting it.

'I think the Orthodox Christmas is coming up in a few days, is it not? What we call Epiphany, on the sixth?'

'Why, yes, sir, it is, I had forgotten.'

'Well, perhaps this is a good time to send you home for a while, even though the mission I mentioned has been postponed for various reasons. Don't you think your mother would like to have you around on Christmas? We need to go to Mudros on naval business which is of no interest to you and that's not your turf. I suggest we drop you off wherever you like and come back to pick you up in three weeks or so. What do you say?'

'That would be wonderful, sir,' I replied. 'I would really like to check on things. And yes, my mother would be happy, I am sure.'

'I rather imagined you would feel like that. Do you still have the *teskere* in the name of good old Georges Habib?'

'Of course!'

'Good, keep it handy in case you get stopped by what passes for authority in that benighted country.'

Three days later, I was once again walking along the railway tracks towards the Christian Quarter, past the Italian consulate and the little house where Garabed Boyajian had disappeared from our lives on his way to Adana and death. I thought of the Armenian phrase, *esh nahadag*: 'donkey martyr'. 'Garo, poor fellow, was no donkey, but his death had not served any useful cause. But what was to be done? Work for the *Ingleez*, having a good old time among the 'chaps', but neglect the family? Find Shoushan and go far away, to America or Australia and build a new life, in a place where there are no deportations or tuberculosis? What then of Mayrig? What about our people? Who would we *be* in America?'

I cheered up as I turned the last corner into Atawi Saghir: the prospect of days with Mayrig and the children, even Christmas together, was enough to make me forget for a moment the desperate situation of our people. I loved this house, this secure hive where Mayrig was the solitary queen. 'There is nothing wrong in snatching a few moments of personal happiness, is there?' I asked myself. I climbed the stairs to the front door and knocked my special knock, which I knew Mayrig would recognise: TOCK tock tock tock. The door opened immediately and at once I knew something was not right. Mayrig literally pulled me inside and closed and bolted the door. Her chiselled face was grim. 'What's wrong, Mayrig?'

She held me by the shoulders and looked at me with what I felt was a new sadness in her eyes. 'They were here. The police, *chetes*, the lot. Looking for illegals, they said, but especially looking for you. And for what they could steal, of course. Then they took Halim away, conscripted him into the *taburlar*. I have been trying everything to find out where they took him, to try and buy his freedom. What have you been doing, Varo?'

I was about to say something, but was not yet sure what, when the unmistakable cries of a young baby came from the kitchen. 'Come down, Varo, I must attend to Garabed.' I followed, confused; that was the name of my little brother who died at birth many years ago, as well as Bedros's late brother. But it was definitely a live baby I saw in her arms, perhaps six or nine months old. I thought it looked like a small, wizened brown monkey, with a precocious shock of curly black hair.

'I was at the railway station a few weeks ago,' she began to explain, 'taking bread to the deportees packed into the wagons, the ones who had no money and were being sent on, towards the desert. The deportation trains have almost stopped now but when they do come through here, the people are more dead than alive. In fact, some of them *are* dead, but they don't allow them to remove the corpses until they get out of the city, into the desert. Suddenly this woman holds the baby out of the window and says to me, "Take him, *hanum*, take him and save him, please, for the love of God." She didn't know I was Armenian, even. I looked at her, then at him, and knew it had to be. I told her in Armenian that I would care for him as if he were mine, shouted my name and neighbourhood as the train began to move, just in case. And soon it was gone and I was standing there with this poor thing, just skin and bones. I'm sure his mother had no milk since she had no food either. At first I wasn't sure he would live, but as you can see he has put on weight. Garabed. What could I do?'

I looked down at the thin baby on my mother's knees – his eyes too big for his head, dark pools in an olive-skinned, elfin little face – and saw her face shining with a light I had not seen for years, as she smiled and cooed at her little foundling. 'Of course, you had to take him, Mayrig. He is lovely, my new little brother. *Mabrouki*, congratulations. But tell me, what makes you think they were looking especially for me?' She finished swaddling the baby, now wrapped up tight like a sausage, the Armenian way, and it stopped crying, looking up at us with its huge black eyes.

'I don't *think* it, Varo. They had an official paper with your name on it, a warrant or whatever. "Vartan Hovsep Nakashian of Atawi Saghir, Aleppo. Wanted for treason and other crimes against the State."' I was silent, conflicting thoughts and ideas racing in my mind. Mayrig looked at me and asked again, 'What *have* you been doing?'

I could not lie to her. 'I've been working with the *Ingleez,* Mayrig. Ever since the escape from Musa Dagh. I help them with information about the Turks, I take messages and bring reports from their spies in Aleppo and Jerusalem and other places in Palestine. I cannot imagine how they know about it, I've been so careful and the English would never betray me. Now you know, but you must never tell anyone, even though they apparently know something already. I am not doing this for the English, but for Hayestan and for all of us. For the future. But I am dreadfully sorry it has put you and the children in danger. What a *fool* I have been, to think they would never find out! I only wish there was something I could do now, for you. For poor Halim.'

I was fighting the tears that were trying to flood into my eyes. Her eyes glistened as well. Her voice was hoarse but firm: 'There is only one thing to do now, Varo. You must *go*. Can you get back to the *Ingleez*?' I smothered the tears, gathered my wits.

'No, not for almost three weeks.'

'Then you must go somewhere else, get out of Aleppo. You could hide here, God knows I would like that, but you would not be safe. They can come and search any time: they saw the secret room and realised that people had been staying there, though thank God there was no one just then.'

My mind began to clear. I had to decide what to do, *now.* There was no going back. *Anne*'s launch would not come to al-Basit for almost three weeks; there was nowhere in the city I could hide until then, no way to communicate with the ship. I was tempted to go to the orphanage, to ask if I could stay with them and help with their work, which seemed so important to me, more so in fact than landing and retrieving spies and reports. But my presence might put them in danger. If the Turks were looking for me, that might mean they know about the beach landings anyway, so I would just go from the pan to the fire. I would have to miss the rendezvous with the launch, disappoint Captain Weldon, who would think I had been captured, killed or – I thought with a shudder – turned traitor. I would have to go inland, not towards Cilicia of course, but towards the desert, along the railway tracks. I was not deported and even had a *teskere*, of sorts. How the wheel turns.

'I will leave town along the railway line, Mayrig, and try to get to Nisibin or wherever they are working on the Baghdad railway. I speak the languages they need, except German, but the *Alman* speak English, I think. I will pretend to be Orthodox, I have a *teskere*. Maybe once there I can find a Turk who will look for Halim on the *taburlar*, if he is still in the area. I know they use them on the railway. I will try my best, Mayrig, without endangering him or you any further.'

Mayrig silently began doing all she could – that is, to prepare a picnic for my journey. She put together a parcel of cheese, bread, olives and *bastirma*, the usual, but in larger quantities than for my two- or three-day walks to the coast. I went to my room and changed into fresh clothes, fixing Viper securely in its place, and took a further change of clothes, wrapping them in my bedroll. I changed my shoes for boots, sturdy ones that had been my father's. I looked around my room before leaving its familiar cocoon: when would I see it again? I went downstairs to find Krikor. He was trying to roll my old hoop in the courtyard but the confined space and uneven surface of river-smoothed stones defeated him. 'Help me, *khayyi*,' he pleaded.

'I can't little brother, I must go. The next time I come, I promise. Now come and kiss me.' His little arms squeezed my neck. A bleak childhood he was having; at that moment I would have given anything to have time to play with him, and to go looking for the other brother whose life I had endangered. I felt doubly guilty about Halim, knowing I didn't like him.

Last of all I kissed Anahit, who had watched all this with big eyes while lulling Garabed to sleep on her knees. I could hardly bear to meet her gaze. 'How are you, my dear one?' I asked her.

'I am well, *khayyi*, much better, hardly coughing at all, now.'

As I patted Garabed's little head, she had to fight back a spasm of coughing, but managed to quell it, or at least to postpone it. I put my hand on her forehead; it was cool. Our eyes met, joined in a wordless current of sadness, fear, hope and love. '*Allah yahmeeki*,' I said: 'May God protect you.' God again, but if not now, *when*?

'Here, Mayrig, these are my wages from the *Ingleez*,' I said, putting the coins in the pocket of her apron. 'Not everything – I'll keep some to get information about Halim, if I can. Now God protect you, and forgive me for causing you this distress.' She took both my hands in hers.

'Don't be foolish, Varo. You are fighting for us. God gave you the means to oppose the Turks in your way, as you did with our brothers on Musa Dagh. Now go with God, we will be all right here, and come back when this is all over. Go while there is still time.'

We embraced, she on her tiptoes so that she could rest her head, eyes closed, just for a moment on my breast. A wildly emotional gesture for Mayrig. My chest was in an iron clamp as I left.

8

Beirut: April 1985

*D*ASHTI WAS *in a foul mood that day. I was pretty gloomy too. I think somehow we could sense that we would not meet again. It was late summer or early autumn, about ten years ago, maybe 1974, just before the war started here. Five years before the Shah fell. Ali was in Beirut, no longer as ambassador; it was indeed to be his last visit here. We were up on the mountain. I remember having a smoke and talking about our usual things, Persian poetry and Middle Eastern politics. But he was not his usual jocular self. In the Senate a few weeks before, a senator had accused him of being in the pay of the British; another stood up and denounced him for atheism. His friends in the Parliament had only just avoided his being impeached for the mixed bag of corruption and heresy. He got angry just telling me about it. I tried to calm him down.*

'That Shirazi is a fool, and a notoriously corrupt one at that; all Tehran knows he is for sale to the highest bidder. No one will pay the slightest attention to his accusations; besides, they would secretly admire you for taking money off the *Ingleez*. But the charge of atheism is more dangerous. That book you just published is a bombshell: who ever heard of reducing the life of Muhammad, his twenty-three-year career, to what we know from historical sources, discounting his miracles and even looking for the origin of the ideas in the Quran?'

'I know,' Dashti said, running his fingers over his bald head, as if to tidy his long-lost hair. 'But someone had to tell them. Someone had to apply historical methodology to Islam, the way the Christians and Jews do to the history of their religions. Well, not all of them, not the American fundamentalists who think the world was created on a certain Thursday in a year when the pyramids were already ancient. Not the Orthodox Jews, who think the world begins and ends with the half-legendary wanderings of their tribe. But look at the corpus of work by reasonable scholars of both those religions; they might have burned people for translating the Bible in the sixteenth century, but they have moved on in the West. Why should we not do the same? Are we condemned to stay in the Middle Ages while the rest of the world advances? You sound almost defensive. But I know you have had your personal disappointments.'

'Ah, I have. You must be thinking of my childhood friend Omar. I know I have told you about that – probably many times. I will never really understand. I am not defending anybody, except maybe *you*. Ali, you studied Islamic theology in the holiest places of Shia Islam. You have sat at the feet of the most venerated imams and Mollahs. Surely Vartan Nakashian does not have to tell *you* that to question the revealed nature of the Quran is darkest heresy? To treat the Prophet Muhammad as an ordinary human being is worse than *kufr* – 'blasphemy' – it is a capital sin. People have been lynched in the bazaar for less – all it takes is for someone to shout *"kufr kard"* and the mob bays for blood, and no historical methodology will save the poor sod in question. Are you suicidal? What if the French let Khomeini return and the Mollahs raise the rabble to kick out this indecisive, sick Shah and take his place?'

'No, I suppose you are right, I have pushed the envelope a bit. But sometimes one just has to speak out against idiocy. So far all it has caused is a few pointed questions in the Parliament. Sometimes I wonder why I ever bothered sitting in that talking shop. The message is too important to bury: we must modernise, become more secular, or our countries will end up fossilised, antiquated relics for the worst dregs of society to exploit, or for foreigners to take over. Senseless violence destroying our precious cultural achievements, in either case. In a rational, modern society, what happened to the Armenians, or to your poor family, would be impossible.'

'What happened to my family had nothing to do with religion – not true Islam, for sure,' said Vartan. 'Those thugs were motivated by ancient hatreds, lust and sheer greed; in fact a lot of what is done in the name of Islam is cynical manipulation, poorly disguised greed and general bloodthirstiness, over which Islam has no monopoly, not now and not ever. But I'm talking about *you*: I wonder why you would waste your time trying to stir things up. Your books about Hafez, Saadi, and Khayyam are pearls. Not that you avoid controversy even there: you praise Khayyam for his irreligious verse, which most Iranians studiously ignore. Your people are such a cultured people, such a love for poetry! Surely that is more *your* world than trying to undermine their religion, a hopeless endeavour that will only land you in trouble!'

Dashti thought for a moment, then looked up. 'Cultured people, you say?' He walked to the balcony railing, looked pointedly at Vartan, put a finger alongside one nostril and blew his nose juicily. He then repeated the operation on the other nostril, wiping his fingers on his trousers. '*That's* how cultured we are!' Vartan decided to drop the subject, but was concerned for his friend. As the day waned, they sat in silence, Vartan smoking his pipe, Dashti his cigarettes, and watched the sun inching down beyond the darkening pine-covered hills punctuated with the occasional red-roofed village, dissolving into the bluish-pink haze of the distant Mediterranean.

The last evening before Dashti's return to Tehran, they sat again on the terrace watching the sun primping for its daily performance. Even the poetry they chose to recite, in the give and take form their sessions usually took, where the challenge was to find a stanza or quatrain that answered the previous one, was on a sombre note.

Vartan remembered starting with this:

Guyand behesht-e adni

They say that eternal Paradise is beautiful, with its Houris;
I say that the juice of the grape is more lovely still!
Take this ready cash, and leave the credit aside:
The drum-beat's sound is pleasant enough – from far away.

Dashti thought a mere second or two, and recited:

zan-e pish ke bar sarat

Don't wait for troubles to pile up on your head
Ask for a cup of rose-hued wine instead
Don't think you're gold, oh foolish man –
That once buried, they'll dig you up again!

'Notice,' Dashti said, 'how Khayyam takes apart the basic tenets of Islam, and of any of what they call the Great Monotheisms: Paradise in yours, Resurrection in mine. Not with arguments or facts, but with poetry. And generally, he got away with it. He was "Hakim", the "Doctor", respected for his genius as a mathematician and astronomer, so they could choose to ignore his poetry if they liked. Sometimes he goes further, though, like this quatrain which I am not sure you know – it has also been attributed to another poet, Attar, but no matter:

shakhsi didam

I met a man sitting on a patch of bare ground
Not a Muslim, nor a heathen; no mystic, with no creed;
No grace, no revelation, no canon and no call:
In this world or the next – who ever had that man's *guts*?

Vartan pondered the stanza for a moment. 'And after all your theology, on most of which you have turned your back, what are you left with? Do *you* have his guts? Are you comfortable with the void?'

'Certainly not "comfortable". I am tortured because I cannot be sure even of the void, nor what it's all about; as Khayyam says:

award ba-idtiraram

> I was dragged against my will into this world;
> Other than my own bewilderment, nothing have I understood.
> Now we're forced to depart, and still have no idea
> What the meaning of this coming, this staying, or this leaving
>   might be.

'Seeing the state the world is in, probably always *has* been in, I don't trust whoever created such a mess. He may have one of his practical jokes in store for either or both of us, or for the whole sorry human race, which he must be sorely tired of by now.' He threw away his cigarette half-smoked.

Vartan chewed on his pipe stem for a while, then recited a quatrain he knew Dashti loved as much as he did:

az ruy-e haqiqati

> Not mere metaphor, but literally true
> We are pawns, Destiny chess-master;
> We play a little game on the Being Board,
> Then he drops us in the Nothingness Box, one by one.

'Did you hear that drum-beat of doom: *yek yek BAZ*, "one by one"? Even I can see that it is so much more powerful in Farsi than in any other language I know. And the question "where do we go?"

is as unanswerable as "why are we here?" All we can do is pass the time, finding comfort where we can, beauty where it lies, even in the smallest things, and ask ourselves, or Him, or *someone* – for not finding answers is no reason not to ask.'

Dashti countered, as he so often did, with a quatrain: 'You taught me this one:

an qasre ki ba charkh

> That palace whose crumbling walls still stand high –
> The faces of kings once gazed out from its ramparts;
> But now a lone turtle dove is all that's left behind,
> Ceaselessly calling, '*ku, ku, ku, ku?*'

Dashti shook his head with a wry smile. 'You have to admire his virtuosity: not for complicated conceits and clever figures of speech, but for giving the stage to a humble dove, forever repeating, as they do: "Where, where, where – oh where?" "*Ku*" just *happening* to mean "where" in Farsi. Perhaps that is what makes a poem truly great: you read or hear it and think, "How simple! How obvious!" But just try to write something that says so much, so beautifully and with such economy!'

'I tried once or twice,' said Vartan. 'It came out a pastiche, doggerel. So I decided two things: I don't have whatever it takes to be a poet, but – thank God! – I can still recognise and enjoy a good poem.'

Dashti smiled, his mood clearly improved. 'You do, of course, know a good poem, but I sense you connect more with Khayyam than with the master of masters, Hafez, or the supreme mystical genius, Rumi. Our finest poetry is all about music, and Khayyam had something of a deaf ear to the higher forms of mystical poetry, where the music blends with the sound and meaning to make something truly sublime. Close your eyes and listen:

bar sar-e torb-e man

Bring a minstrel, bring some wine, sit down upon my grave
Enticed by your heady perfume, dancing! *I will rise*

Oh slender, lissom goddess, like a cypress standing there
Fill me, my soul, the world, with desire: clapping! *I will rise*

Yes, I'm old, but if you hold me close for just one night
In your embrace, I'll wake up: young again, *I'll rise*

The day I die, just visit me the space of one brief breath;
So that, like Hafez, from desire of soul and world – *I'll rise!'*

They sat in silence as the last colours faded in the west. The evening
star made its appearance, as bright and cheerful as if it had just
been made.

9

Near Aleppo: January 1916

T HE EARLY WINTER night began to fall as I passed through
the northern reaches of the last suburb, then headed out
of town. I walked quickly; soon the last signs of the city
had given way to the featureless gravel desert, the railway tracks
gleaming as they seemed to join before disappearing in the twilight.
Somewhere out there lay Nisibin, my destination. As it grew dark,
I left the level ground beside the tracks and started walking between
the rails. At first, I stumbled over the stones and wooden ties, but at
least they told me I was going in the right direction.

Through the night I walked, and worried, and tried to understand how this catastrophe had come about. And to come up with some coherent plan. 'Secret agent' indeed! I had put my mother in danger, probably sent my older brother to his death, neglected my sick sister and sweet little brother. The English will come for me and find no one. 'Pity,' the captain would say, 'part of the game.' I could not help wondering who tipped off the Turks: 'Could they have identified me as the young *halabi* who fought with the defenders of Musa Dagh and was evacuated with them? They are known to have informers everywhere. Or maybe they were tipped off by the rope seller. The Druze was ideally situated to do so, knowing exactly where I came from and who my family are. Perhaps someday I will know.'

The night was dark, the clouds hiding any sign of moon or stars. And long. Towards three o'clock, according to Weldon's watch, I started feeling really fatigued. I had walked most of the day and night, all the way from Jisr al-Shugur to Atawi and now God knows how far out of town. I started stumbling over every other railway tie and finally had to stop. I went down the short bank of the right-of-way, not daring to get too far away in the darkness; I shuddered at the thought of getting lost in that arid wilderness. There was not much vegetation close to the tracks but I finally found a wintry clump of stiff, flowerless broom. I curled up in its lee, with my bedroll spread over me like a blanket; that helped, but still the biting January cold of the plateau made me shiver, until at length exhaustion carried me away. I slept till dawn.

I awoke with a start, the morning sun on my face, but thoroughly stiff with cold. How could I have stayed so exposed in plain daylight? I got up and stretched, folded and shouldered my bedroll and started to walk again, my head still heavy with foreboding and remorse. I also thought of Weldon. So different from my father, the cold patriarch. Someone never seen to laugh, the stern, stingy, always-working Hovsep. And then I felt guilty for feeling like that about my own father, who must have loved us all in his way. I stopped about mid-morning, squatting by the tracks for a dry breakfast of bread and cheese, having left behind the gourd of water Mayrig had prepared for me and that even she forgot in the emotion of the moment. I ate mechanically and tried not to think.

Suddenly, a voice from nowhere made me jump, speaking in familiar Aleppo Arabic: '*Marhaba, sidi*, hello there, mister!' Walking the same way I had come there appeared a young man, maybe a year or two older than me. I froze and instinctively reached my right hand back towards Viper. 'May I join you?' said the new arrival. I saw he was dressed like an Aleppo Christian, in better clothes than mine.

'Of course,' I replied, standing up to shake his hand. 'Welcome!'

'Rafiq Sarraf, at your service. From Aleppo, on my way to look for work on the railway. I hear they need clerks at Nisibin, so that's where I am headed. There's nothing to do in Aleppo, with all the starving refugees and filthy *chetes* extorting money from everyone, and the conscription gangs seizing every able-bodied man or boy they can find.'

'Well, that's more or less my case as well.' I put out my hand: 'Georges Habib, also from Aleppo.'

And so now there were two of us walking along the tracks, both I think feeling more secure than when we were alone. We were very cagey about opening up too much at first. In the Levant, it was unusual, even suspicious, for two men to identify themselves only by first and last name. As we walked, we both gradually realised something was amiss, and we each came to the same silent conclusion. And realised the other had done the same. It was Rafiq who asked first.

'*Hay es*? Are you Armenian?' To which I blurted, 'Yes I am!' Soon we knew each other as Vartan Nakashian from Atawi Saghir and Rafi Sarrafian from Aziziyeh, neighbourhoods so close we could have met, and we probably had seen each other in church or elsewhere. We swore not to divulge our true identity to anyone, but to corroborate each other's story if needed. We went on speaking in Arabic.

Rafi told his story first. 'My mother is dead, poor thing. My father runs, or I should say ran, an ironmongery in the souk – everything from nails to nails, we used to chide him. He was caught harbouring illegals, refugees with no papers, and taken to prison. My brothers were arrested and taken off to the *taburlar*. I decided not to wait my turn. I have no *teskere* but my father had hidden a cache of money before they took him, and I brought that. I think that will be just as good as official identity papers, maybe better, if I am bothered by *zaptiehs*, *chetes* or other ruffians. I have a pistol under my jacket, along with the money, just in case. Now tell me about yourself!'

I told my story, omitting, of course, everything about the *Ingleez*, the *Anne* and all the rest. 'My short career in espionage will go to the grave with me,' I promised myself, 'and probably quite soon.' I was glad to have found a companion. Rafi's presence probably saved me from falling into depression during those first few days. Towards mid-afternoon, we heard the unmistakable huffing and rumble of a train coming towards us, heading west to Aleppo. We hid behind a tall growth of prickly pear, while the train clattered slowly past. The passenger cars seemed mostly empty, except for a few Turkish officers, some civilians in European dress and a group or two of railway workers.

There were boxcars with open doors; if we had been heading for Aleppo it would have been easy to hop on. If we could stand the smell. There was no doubt what the outbound cargo had been. It was not an animal stink, but a more unbearable odour, an odour of human sweat and waste and suffering, mixed with fear and death. 'If a train like that comes along in the other direction, let's try to ride it for part of the way, at least,' said Rafi. 'We can always hop off before it gets to a station. If they find us and insist on tickets, I am sure we can make an arrangement with them.'

'If one does come,' I cautioned, 'let's look first to see what kind of train it is, what kind of people are on it. You don't want to join a deportee train, do you, *Baron* Sarrafian?'

'Ah,' said Rafi, 'you have a point there. But if we see a passenger train with proper passengers, I am sure we can talk ourselves into a seat, paying whatever they ask. My feet are already tired!'

I looked at his scuffed city shoes, one of them already beginning to lose its sole at the front. 'You need better walking shoes, Rafi,' I said.

'Let's stop at the next shoemaker's stall and buy some!' he said, with a hearty snort of a laugh and I joined in. We chuckled at the thought as we trudged through a particularly desolate patch of arid, salty wasteland that looked like no one had ever lived there, nothing had ever grown there except the odd prickly pear or thorny desert acacia.

There was no sign of a train in either direction for the next three or four hours. Towards evening, we thought we heard something, and soon enough we knew for sure: there was an eastbound train coming up behind us. Soon the chugging and puffing sounds of the steam locomotive caught up with us. We hid as best we could, and once the massive locomotive had passed we watched several passenger cars go by carrying men in military uniforms and well-dressed civilians. Then a freight car rumbled by, its sliding doors open, and we stood up to assess our chances of making it; the train was going slowly enough that one could just about jump on, if one could only run alongside the train without falling. Suddenly, as we began to run, we could see to our utter surprise a man sitting cross-legged near the door. On spotting us, without hesitating he waved his arms and shouted, '*Yallah*, come on, lads!' Now he was kneeling, holding out one hand while holding on to the sliding door with the other. First Rafi, then I threw in our bundles, and then took his hand, letting him pull us in as we clambered up to the boxcar floor, sliding on our stomachs until our legs followed and we were safely on board.

'Thanks, brother!' I gasped, turning to look at our benefactor. I was still unsure how much I should relax or stay on my guard even with such a helpful stranger. We looked at each other as we got our breath back and the train continued its slow progress across the barren landscape. Rafi was the first to speak: 'Well, I think we're probably all going to Nisibin looking for work, aren't we? I am Rafiq, this is Georges, both from Aleppo. May we know the name of the kind person who invited us into his private rail car?'

Our host was a plump, well-dressed fellow of twenty or so, with curly black hair escaping from his fez, clean-shaven except for a neatly trimmed black moustache just covering the larger-than-usual space between his prominent nose and upper lip. He wore the trousers, pleated shirt and black jacket of a Christian townsman. Looking at each of us in turn, he smiled and began: 'I am Haig Chilinguirian, Armenian from Aleppo, just like you fine gentlemen, unless everything about you deceives me except those made-up names. On my way to take up a position in the materials department of the railway, promised me by an Italian acquaintance of my father, recently deceased of natural causes, God rest his soul. You might have known our business in the souk, Chilinguirian Brothers. Primus stoves and other useful implements, all imported. Ceased trading due to the blockade, hence my desire to find gainful employment.

'My brother is selling off the remains of our stock and, I trust, taking care of our mother and sisters with the proceeds. Nothing for me to do except sit around and eat – not my cup of tea. You may call me Haig in private, or the name I intend to use at Nisibin, Kamil; a Christian or Druze or just possibly Sunni name, sort of non-denominational, if such a thing could exist in this crazy world where a man's identity is determined by his name and whether his thing is circumcised. And now it's your turn. You may tell me your real names, or not, I don't mind. We are in the same boat, more or less, and I propose we stick together and help each other. Three is a better number than one, or even two, I think you will agree, if you have as much experience of the wider world as I have.'

Rafi and I looked at each other and burst out laughing. Each told his story and before long we were sharing the remains of Mayrig's picnic and drinking from Haig's water bottle. Haig, Kamil in future, had been to Nisibin before: 'We will have to get off the train at Ras al-Ain and walk the remaining ten miles or so, along the track which is still under construction. There is a horrible camp of starving refugees at Ras al-Ain, which we will do well to avoid completely. If we show any interest in the wretched people, we will probably be recognised for what we are and invited to join them.'

We jumped off before the train stopped and headed out into the plain before turning towards the direction of the unfinished right-of-way. Night caught us in the open, another cold night even in the semi-desert country we were crossing; a gusty north wind blowing down from the distant mountains sharpened the cold. 'There are no trees around here, and it's awfully cold, maybe we should carry on,' said Rafi, rubbing the sleeves of his light jacket as we walked.

'No, Rafi, think a little,' said Haig. 'If we show up at Nisibin in the middle of the night, what will they take us for? Marauders or spies, or desperate Armenians. Let's sleep here; Vartan has kindly brought a bedroll and I think we can all swallow our manly pride and huddle up together.' And so we did, arms around each other in a three-way embrace, with my bedroll on top. The wind blew it off us once or twice, but we made it through the night, shivering, dozing fitfully, occasionally talking in whispers.

We arrived at the construction base mid-morning on a brilliant winter day, cold but sunny. The north wind had dropped off a bit but still kept the sun from providing much warmth. Rafi, as always, was suffering more than Haig and me, in his town clothes and disintegrating shoes. I was glad of my boots and jacket but wished I had something to share with Rafi, cheerful as always despite his painful feet. We stopped to get an idea of the place from a safe distance before approaching the gate. The construction camp was a collection of mostly single-story frame buildings arranged around a large warehouse, with four long barracks and six smaller units which looked like officer or senior staff housing. Several military vehicles and flatbed trucks were parked in a fenced-off area behind the warehouse. There was a wire fence all around, topped with rolls of barbed wire, and a single entrance flanked by a small guardhouse on either side. A sleepy-looking Turkish soldier sat observing us, perched on a box in front of one of the guardhouses, his rifle leaning against the wall.

Haig assumed command of our trio and led us up to the gate; the soldier rose, took his rifle by the barrel and stood stiffly, legs apart, blocking the entrance, his face all surly authority. Haig addressed him in formal Turkish, sounding for all the world like an official *firman*: 'We are coming to take up positions in the materials department, invited by Ingegnere Signor Ortalli, head of materials and accounts in this establishment.' He flourished his letter which was, indeed, a promise of employment signed by Sig. Ortalli, but which of course only mentioned Haig, that is, his pseudonym Kamil Kharrat. I started pulling my *teskere* out of my pocket, but did not need to show it as the guard stood aside and waved us past. Haig led us briskly towards the warehouse. Another guard at the door informed us that the *ingegnere* was at headquarters and could be found in his office on the second floor.

We crossed the open space, which I thought was strangely clean and tidy, and headed towards the only two-storey building, obviously the headquarters. Turkish and German flags waved above the door. Officers and orderlies, mostly in uniform, scurried around with papers or satchels in their hands. Others, in civilian overalls, were busy loading equipment on to Italian flatbed trucks. We three impostors were soon seated in the waiting room outside the office marked 'Capo' and 'Bashmühendis': 'Chief Engineer.' After a few minutes, the door opened to produce a German holding some sort of polished black stick under his arm and wearing a tunic of brown corduroy with one row of buttons, black trousers with a beige seam, black jackboots and a black astrakhan calpac, which went splendidly with his turned-up moustache. Except that the effect was comic rather than imposing, I thought. The elegant officer looked at us three aspirants in our motley garb and travelling dust, slapped the stick against his leg and snorted before turning smartly and leaving the room.

Ortalli appeared in the door to his office, also inspecting us. He was a rumpled middle-aged man, with a paunch, a large bald spot extending up an already high forehead and a narrow nose pinched halfway along by half-round reading glasses. Straight brown hair streaked with grey decorated the sides of his long head. His eyes looked tired; crow's feet in their corners and creases around his mouth suggested an easy smile. He did smile, a little, as he looked over our three hopeful but anxious young faces, then said in heavily accented Arabic, 'You gentlemen wish to see me, I believe?' Haig answered, speaking slowly and enunciating clearly:

'Yes, Excellency, I am Kamil Kharrat, of Aleppo. I believe you knew a relative of mine, now deceased, and kindly wrote a letter offering me a position in the materials department. These are my friends and colleagues, Messrs Sarraf and Habib, who also would like to apply for employment in this august enterprise, putting their considerable talents and language skills at the service of the Empire and the furtherance of this great railway.' Ortalli could not repress another smile at this pompous speech and gestured to us to follow him: 'Come into my office, gentlemen, and we will discuss all this at leisure.'

The end result was that Haig was employed, as promised, in the materials department. As he had no demonstrable skills in the keeping of ledgers or accounts and no language he could admit to speaking other than Arabic and Turkish, that meant basically helping to carry things from the warehouses to the lorries and vice versa. With my knowledge of English and comparatively advanced education, I was put to work in the accounts department. Ortalli told me I would act as liaison between the Turkish commander of the camp and the Germans who were financing the work on the railway and who spoke English. In my spare time, I was to learn the rudiments of bookkeeping. Rafi had less immediate success, but was housed with us in the barracks pending the opening up of a vacancy for which his experience in ironmongery, especially nails, could be brought to bear. Before long, one did in fact turn up, the need for a literate stock person to keep a record of the arrivals and withdrawals of the all-important rails and the spikes used to hold them to the ties. And so, in a short period we were all three in official employment under the protection of the Empire, in the person of Capo Ortalli, which was much more important than the modest wages we received.

We had arrived at Nisibin on Orthodox Christmas, 1916. Thanks to Weldon's generous gesture, I ought to have been enjoying the holiday surrounded by my family. My heart sank when I thought about that, but fortunately I didn't have much time for brooding: it was my first day on the job and there was no festive atmosphere in the camp. Two weeks later, I had another realisation, that late that night, the launch from HMS *Anne* would be made ready to row to shore as soon as three flashes of light were spotted. At exactly the prescribed time. I felt heartsick to let Captain Weldon down. In a sense, I was working for the enemy, for the Turks and Germans rather than the British. Not a choice I had made, and I felt some comfort that at least the military usefulness of my services was close to zero.

I failed to notice when, a month after our arrival, my eighteenth birthday came and went; it only hit me several days later. One thing I did notice was my beard: previously a silky moss, it had started growing with a vengeance and becoming stiff and scratchy. Soon I had to shave every day or look like a vagrant. I had always been on the stocky side; some of the fights I used to get into at school were caused by the insult 'Fatty' in the mouth of some lout. I think I had a growth spurt and put on another inch or so in height so that I was no longer pudgy, much less fat, just squarely built and medium height for the Levant, rather than short.

Ortalli seemed glad to have someone he could talk to in the camp. I think he had been quite lonely before. His Turkish was only a little better than his Arabic, and he spoke no German, but his quaintly accented English was quite fluent. He was very well informed about the progress of the war. He never gave me any hint that he suspected my Armenian identity, or that of my friends, but in private conversation he expressed horror at the deportations. One day when I had brought in some papers to his office, he asked me to close the door and sit down.

'Georges, the thought of what is happening to all those innocent people is very troubling. And not very far away. At the camp – a prison, really – at Ras al-Ain just down the way, there is a Sergeant Nuri who is known to rape refugee children. He even boasted about it to one of our German engineers, Spieker, who reported that and worse horrors to our superiors and told me. Spieker and some of the German project directors tried to protect our Armenian engineers and skilled workers, who were vital to the construction and operation of the railway. This was refused; they were deported soon after, replaced by Arabs and Turks. The work suffered even more than the Germans had feared. And, on top of that, trains that could have carried construction supplies, and of course military ones like ordnance and even troops which were in such short supply on the Eastern Front, were clogged with deportees instead.'

There were long moments of inactivity as the war dragged on and work on the railway became more sporadic. I started smoking the cheap, pungent Turkish cigarettes stocked in the commissary, partly out of boredom: you could dream of anything while watching a puff of smoke rise, curl and dissipate. Soon, of course, out of need. Ortalli started teaching me the rudiments of Italian, which he said he spoke with a Tuscan accent. When he learned that I had a basic knowledge of French, Ortalli (who had studied engineering in Lyon) decided that we would speak that instead, which improved my ability to converse in the language my mother had tried to teach me. I welcomed the opportunity: I saw foreign languages, which I must admit I have a facility for, as a means of escape. Especially English and French, the languages of those noble pillars of civilisation. In return, I taught Ortalli Arabic grammar and in a few months he could manage respectably, his pronunciation sounding less Italian.

One baking summer afternoon, when a hot wind scoured the steppe, annoyingly blowing sand and grit at about eye level, I stayed in my office rather than crossing the courtyard for the siesta that was the privilege of the office workers and officers. On board HMS *Anne*, my friend Foster had taught me an English poem, Shelley's 'Ozymandias'. Taking inspiration from it, I had drawn a landscape with broken columns and a 'shattered visage' as I imagined it; the columns I had seen at the ancient ruins of Nisibin, which Ortalli told me used to be a town with an important Christian bishopric, as well as having older ruins he did not know the origins of. Suddenly, Ortalli opened the door, just as I was carefully writing the two lines I could remember from the poem underneath my pen-and-ink sketch. I was so surprised and embarrassed that my pen jerked, leaving a large blob of ink on the text.

'Please let me see what you are drawing,' said the Florentine. I fought a blush, which as usual made it worse, but pushed the ruined drawing across the table. 'Not bad, my boy. I had no idea you had such talents. Or appreciation of the words of that great poet, who came to Italy for inspiration and found only death by water. At least his poetry is still there to inspire us.' I began to mumble that I had finished my work for the day; Ortalli cut me off.

'Have you not understood? *This* is important too. If we live only by stock counting and ledgers we're already dead. Had you been born in Florence you might have had a very different life, if your untaught talent could have been nurtured to real ability, then who knows? It's nothing to be *ashamed* of, for God's sake. Please share your drawings with me in future.' With that, he left me very confused.

I looked down at the line I had been printing: 'Boundless and bare, the lone and level sands stretch far away.'

Months dragged by, the year turned, with me unable to confide my innermost thoughts and feelings to anyone. I was often prey to dark forebodings, to suspicions about even Captain Weldon: did he suspect the Druze rope seller was a double agent, that he was sending me into a trap, just to find out for sure, with the only risk being the life and family of a random young Armenian in whom their Empire had invested practically nothing? After a spell of such doubts, I would inevitably return to base, to a certainty that Weldon was on the side of the angels, and that he would not have sold his new recruit, not me, so cheaply.

I was also troubled by thoughts of Shoushan. Not an acute anxiety, as in the case of Mayrig, but a dull ache, a vague yearning which my body felt as partly, but not entirely, physical. I thought that at least she was safe, with her relatives in the English camp at Port Said. But our future together was about as uncertain as the outcome of the war, which was not looking good during my first six months in Nisibin.

March 1916 came and with it the first signs that the rude but short winter of the steppe was nearing an end. Then came catastrophe. In April, the Poona Division of the Indian Army under General Townshend were besieged at Kut al Amara in Iraq. The camp at Nisibin was in a flurry: a British victory would open the road to Baghdad, making the whole railway enterprise pointless. Our excitement did not last long. The British had to surrender after horrendous losses. Ortalli said this was a result of political interference from London and poor logistics on their part, more than brilliant soldiery on the part of the Ottomans. But the result was a terrible humiliation.

Those who made it as far as Nisibin were marched past the railway camp. We three Armenians stood at the fence and watched sadly as the wretched, starving English and Indian officers and soldiers staggered by, goaded to exhaustion by the most miserable class of Arab and Kurdish *zaptieh*. Such was the state of the great Empire that was going to defeat the Turks and save our people, whatever was left of it.

I had forgotten about another birthday. Nineteen – over a year of my life in this place! It was Ortalli who noticed it, from the employment register, and invited me to dine with him and the senior German officer in the camp, whose name was Schlugel. I think he was expecting me to be a rustic Arab or Turk; anyway, he smiled as though pleasantly surprised when I greeted him in English. He welcomed me in Arabic, the funny ancient Arabic of the Quran that foreigners seem to learn in their countries, pronounced in a very German accent. He cited the first verse of a famous poem to see if I could continue; I understood it all right, but did not know it. He tried again, and to my luck it was the well-known dove song by Abu Firas, Omar's supposed ancestor, which I had last recited to Eliezer deep in the Jewish Quarter of Jerusalem, what felt like decades ago.

After that very pleasant dinner, which I enjoyed despite drinking so much wine that I think I talked too much, I realised that it had not been just a birthday celebration. Ortalli needed Schlugel to meet me so that he could approve my promotion to chief bookkeeper, a total surprise to me. I was now by far the senior in position to my two friends but they did not seem to mind. I was invited to move from the barracks, where I shared a corner space with my comrades, to a bunk in a senior staff house but I refused.

Soon after the promotion, I went to see Ortalli: 'Capo, I have not taken a day off work since I came here over a year ago. I would very much like to visit my family in Aleppo: they do not even know I am here, and I have heard nothing of them. My brother Halim was conscripted to the *taburlar* and I must try to find him, at least to find out what happened to him. May I have a week or two off and a pass on the railway, to Aleppo and back?' Ortalli offered me a cigarette and lit one himself.

'Georges, normally I would be happy to grant your request, were it within my authority. However, it will be no secret to you that the war is not going well for "our" side. There have been huge numbers of desertions, especially by the Arab conscripts. We are under orders not to grant any leave and to keep a sharp eye on all Syrians and other Arabs in our employ. I could give you a pass but I am afraid it would not mean anything to the military police, and even less to the murderous irregulars. Jemal Pasha has hundreds of police combing the area for deserters and they are rewarded for the number they turn in. I fear you must wait a while yet.'

'I see. Do you think I could at least write to them?'

'Ah, George, think a little. To whom would you address such a letter? It would be seen by the postal workers and I am afraid might cause trouble both for you and for them.'

I pondered his words. 'He *knows*,' I thought. 'He knows and wants to protect me. But I must, somehow, tell them I am all right, where I am, and try to get their news. Try to find Halim. But how?'

I tried to keep as busy as I could. I spent long hours in discussions with Ortalli, about the war of course but also, thankfully, hundreds of other things. Like Renaissance painting for example, about which I knew nothing; but I was spellbound by the way he talked about it, by the treasures he described in his native Florence, which sounded like Paradise. I vowed to visit it one day, to discover it myself – but especially to share it with Shoushan.

I also made another friend. The head of accounts, my immediate superior after my promotion, was a Turk from Stamboul, as he called it. Vedat Bey Urul was his name, the descendant of an old and aristocratic Ottoman family. He never told me that: of course, it was Ortalli who said that the Urul family owned one of the sumptuous *yalis* on the Bosphorus, a magnificent wooden palace right on the water, with its own boathouse from which family members would be rowed to their destinations in the great city. Vedat's father was a *damad*, literally 'bridegroom', someone who had married the daughter of a sultan. The princess was not Vedat's mother but one of his other two wives.

'To marry a princess,' Ortalli said with a wink, 'is less impressive than it sounds. Between wives and concubines, a sultan could have literally scores of children of both sexes. There are always unmarried daughters to find suitable husbands for. Even Enver Pasha is a *damad*!' Vedat was past middle age; I thought he must be about fifty. We never talked directly about politics, but I got the impression that he detested the Young Turks. He said several times that he was ashamed that his nation should be responsible for the program of extermination inflicted on the Armenian subjects of the Empire.

My worries about my family nagged at me, intruding on every quiet moment. There was nothing I could do to help them. And I couldn't even send word, any more than I could to Shoushan. No question of making enquiries about someone taken to work on the dreadful *taburlar*. I felt so helpless, sitting out the war in this unreal place, this no-place. Over time, I had sort of given up and let myself become absorbed in the meaningless business of bookkeeping, writing or having others write tiny words and numbers on this or that side of a ledger, one that no one would probably ever look at; and so passed the weeks and months. From time to time, a cold shadow, like a cloud covering the sun, would pass over me. I would throw myself into my work, surprising everyone, from Ortalli and Vedat to Haig and Rafi.

The war was going better for the Entente side. There was a definite increase in testiness on the part of the German engineers and senior staff. I witnessed a couple of unpleasant confrontations between the Turkish officers and their German 'advisers'. We heard about terrible massacres among the concentration of refugees at Ras al-Ain and especially Deir az-Zor. These were said to be carried out by a collection of deserters from the army, *chetes* and the veterans of earlier massacres known as *hamidiyes*, joined by common brigands, including many Kurds. One particular group of marauders was known as the Khamseen ('fifty'); that being how many of them there were. That is also the name of a relentless, dirty wind from the desert. The Arab staff at the camp did not openly discuss the Fifty or their depredations. Most of the staff were Christians, and I suspect we were not the only secret Armenians.

12th February 1918. 'Twenty years old,' I thought. 'And what am I doing here – still here for God's sake?' I did notice that birthday, thinking of my dear ones, so far away. Well not so far, but a world away. My dreams often took the same form: I was bound or otherwise held down while Mayrig or the children or Shoushan, sometimes all of them at the same time, passed by on the other side of a wall through which I could see, but not hear or be heard. So they went their way, never noticing me or hearing my screams. As 1918 advanced, the war was going worse and worse for the Ottomans and, despite the lack of any real news, we three gleaned bits and pieces of information from new arrivals at the camp, or from clues inadvertently dropped by the Germans or Turkish officers, especially from the *capo*. The spring must have been a time of serious setbacks for the Central Powers and by the summer we knew the outcome of the war. We began dreaming of seizing the first opportunity to return to Aleppo.

Then an actual dream, one of Rafi's, almost got us into deadly trouble. The cubicle in the barracks where we had our cots was separated from the general sleeping area by a sheet on one side and a hanging blanket on the other. These hung from a rafter and provided a measure of privacy, not for the ear but at least the eye. In the middle of one warm night in August, Rafi must have had a nightmare, because he shouted out in Armenian, 'No, don't do it, please stop!' The sheet was roughly pulled aside by one of the Turkish other ranks who bunked nearby.

'*Siz Ermensiniz*! You are Armenian, I knew it! I will denounce you to the commandant! You will be shot as traitors!' By then half the barracks was awake.

Haig predictably had the most presence of mind, jumping out of bed and taking the enraged Turk by the arm. 'Now my good fellow,' he said in Turkish as flowery as he could muster, 'that was not *Armenian* for God's sake! What a joke!' He pointed at me (the soldier had no way of knowing who had shouted in his sleep): 'That was English; our friend Georges here is half *Ingleezi*, and even dreams in that language. You can ask Ortalli or Commander Schlugel; they will vouch for him. But I don't recommend it, he is a favourite of theirs and you will find yourself in hot water!'

The soldier was not convinced. 'Speak your *ferengi* for me then, and we'll see whether it's Armenian or not!' Fortunately, he seemed unable to imagine that one could speak more than one foreign language. I obliged with a stream of vocabulary I had learned on board the ship:

'You fucking arsehole, hoist your stinking idiot carcass out of my sight this instant!' The soldier stood and stared, his face an image of confusion, as though unsure whether what he had heard was English or Armenian, or Chinese for that matter. There was also the reference to Ortalli and the commander, the two senior foreign staff officers in the camp. He glared around at the unmilitary arrangement and general mess of our cubicle and backed out, pushing his way past the sheet and muttering to himself as he shuffled back to bed.

At the beginning of October, it became apparent that the war in the Middle East was over, or at least ending. We had observed large numbers of Turkish military, officers at first and then soldiers, walking past Nisibin towards the railhead at Ras al-Ain. Law and order were rumoured to be breaking down all over the country but life in the camp went on as before, except that no real work was being done. I decided to take the first opportunity to leave, and debated with myself as to whether I should tell Ortalli. Soon, however, I began to sense that he was also thinking of leaving. With work stopped on the railway, there was no point in keeping books. For the moment, the warehouse and access to the camp were guarded, so order was maintained, but I found the *capo* nervous, hesitant. He had removed the few personal possessions he kept in his office. I decided that I had to tell him, that I owed him that courtesy, and was sure he would not try to stop me this time. I would not tell him everything, only that I really wanted to get back to Aleppo and see about my family.

'So, Georges, we must part. I have enjoyed your company as much as that of anyone's out here, perhaps more than any. I will not be staying much longer, either, but must wait for an official order from Rome so that I can be paid my full wages for the – almost – four years in this godforsaken place. I will pay you yours, of course, and give you a letter of good conduct with an official seal which ought to serve as a *laissez-passer* back to the city. No official value, of course, but these cretins don't know the difference, believe me. You will have to tell me which name you want on it: Georges Habib, or your real, Armenian one.'

'So you knew all along?' I blurted.

'Of course I knew. First of all, look in the mirror; I have been in the Levant long enough. Then you were travelling with young Haig Chilinguirian, whose father I had done business with for years. Did you think I was stupid?'

'Certainly not, Capo. I suppose we were so anxious not to give ourselves away that we, well, gave ourselves away, at least to some-one who knew what to look for. Do you think the commandant knew as well?'

'What do you think? We were all lucky to have that good Bavarian rather than some doctrinaire Prussian.'

I looked at his tired face, his age showing more than it ever had. 'Well,' I said, 'I know I'm lucky to have met you, Capo. I would love to think we might meet again. Please address the letter to Georges Habib; when I get near home and can use my real name, I won't need such protection, or so I hope. Unless the Turks have long memories and are still in the persecuting mood. I will tell you my real name, in case you come to Aleppo. It is Vartan Hovsep Nakashian, of Atawi Saghir, son of the late gunsmith of some reputation in the city. I would be so happy to receive you in my home, and I expect we will be safe there now that the war is ending. Don't you think they will have more important concerns now that everything is falling apart for them and the Allies are, so they say, going to occupy Damascus and Constantinople?'

'I would hope so too, though they are a surly race and one thing they *can* do is hold a grudge. You should expect to find very little law and order in the city. Before, the refugees were not safe; now, I expect everyone will be at the mercy of the worst dregs of society. Humans like to take their frustrations out on the weak and defenceless, so if I were Armenian I would not relax too much just yet. Be careful!'

The next day, I said my goodbyes. I found Vedat sitting at his desk, looking sad but not busy packing like almost all the other senior staff. But not working either, just leaning on his elbows at an empty desk. 'What will you do, Vedat Bey?' I asked.

'A good question. My only son was killed at Gallipoli. My wife was driven nearly mad and our beautiful house is a place of tears and shadows and silence. I was content in this desert place, believe it or not. Now I must go back but, frankly, nothing means anything to me at this stage. Hopefully there will be a few quiet moments with any of my friends who are still around, and reading to myself the holy pages of our beautiful Quran. The monsters who drove our country to ruin violate it at every turn and I trust Allah will judge them as they deserve. May He watch over you, Georges, and keep you and those you love safe from harm.'

I embraced my friend and started to leave but at the door I turned back and said: 'Vedat Bey, I am not Georges, but Vartan, Armenian from Aleppo. I cannot leave you under a false impression. You will understand the reasons for the falsehood, and forgive me, I hope.'

'There is nothing to forgive, Vartan. It did not take me long to realise. A case of *force majeure* if ever there was one. Did you think so little of Vedat that you thought I would object, or like you less – or betray you?' I blushed, predictably.

'Of course not, Vedat Bey. I also should have known. But these times have taught us to stifle our trusting nature. May God, if he does anything at all, keep you safe as well. Thank you for your kindness and patience.'

Rafi and Haig said they would wait a little longer, save a little more money if the railway continued to honour its payroll, and follow me in a few weeks. We swore to meet at Mayrig's Atawi house. I went to the payroll office, collected my pay and my letter, left the camp through the now unguarded gate and started the long journey home, towards Ras al-Ain and Aleppo.

At Ras al-Ain, a train was about to leave, but it was packed full of officers and soldiers being demobilised and there was no room for me. I started walking towards Aleppo, hoping that another train would come along. Instead, a few miles further along, I came across the same train, stopped for some mechanical problem. Many of the soldiers were walking around, talking and smoking and waiting. The engineers shouted at each other and waved their arms, which I did not think likely to get the train moving anytime soon. No one stopped me from climbing aboard, and I soon found a place to squat on my bedroll, in a corner in front of the closed counter of the baggage car.

Finally, the engine began to hiss and clank again, and everyone re-embarked. No one paid me the slightest attention. The swaying and bumping of the train lulled me to sleep and after I don't know how many hours of fitful dozing, I awoke to find myself at the Sebil station. I was elated to be within a short walk of home, at last: *home*, Mayrig and Anahit and little Krikor. Time to take care of them, to do what I could to find Halim. I picked up my bundle, stretched, jumped off the train and hurried off.

Turning the corner into Atawi Saghir, I knew instantly, without question, that something was terribly wrong. The front door at the top of the outside stair was ajar, which it *never* was under the severe regime of Mayrig. I dropped my bundle and stood staring for a moment, uncomprehending, and just before I was about to run up the stairway was startled to hear a *'pssst'* from ground level across the narrow alley. I looked down and saw the face of Sitt Sarah, the strange old lady who lived across from us. She had always given me the creeps, with odd habits like nursing her many children, the last born when everyone thought she was too old, for five or six years. Mayrig always called her 'Miskini', poor soul, and went out of her way to be kind. Sarah had opened her cellar window a crack and looked terrified. She whispered, 'All gone! All dead! Poor Vartan!' I stared at her aghast, then crossed the alley and ran up the stairs, leaving my bundle where it fell. Pushing aside the battered door, I went into the house.

It was a wreck. It had obviously been ransacked by thieves looking for loot. The beds and settees were upside down, cushions and mattresses slit open and cotton stuffing strewn everywhere, like snow. There was no sign of life, other than the dreadful stains that could be nothing other than blood, reddish-brown on the kitchen and sitting room floors, still bright red on the white stuffing, a horrible patch on the white kitchen wall which ran down to a dried brown pool on the tiles. 'Could it be we were once so happy in this house? Could *this* be? What I am seeing? *What* has happened?'

I ran all the way upstairs to Anahit's room. It was in the same mess as all the others but without bloodstains. There was nothing stirring anywhere. Something gleamed at me from the pile of books and stuffing on the floor: Anahit's little gold cross, the Armenian cross she always wore on a chain around her slender neck. The chain was gone. I picked up the cross and put it in my pocket, unconsciously.

I ran all the way down to the cellar: Mayrig's precious domain had been devastated. A terrible disorder of broken jars and pantry doors wrenched open, the wardrobe shoved aside, its contents dumped on to the floor. The secret chamber door had been ripped off its hinges, its lock being too sturdy to break. 'All the keys were in her apron,' I said out loud, 'they could have asked. But I know what she would have told them.' No one, but no more blood down here either. It all happened upstairs. Whoever they were, they were looking for something specific, not just an ordinary robbery. In this modest house? Suddenly a smell jolted my senses: *gülbesheker*. A jar of fragrant rose-petal jam was smashed on the floor. I ran back upstairs.

The house was lifeless. The kitchen door was open; I went out into the courtyard to find a strange spectacle. Two trenches had been dug across the ground, unearthing the rounded river stones that had once paved it and were now piled up alongside the fissures. One of these trenches went clear across the courtyard, just passing by the well in the middle. The other started at a right angle to what must have been the first and then, about five feet along, it stopped, its furthest extent marked by a hole roughly two feet deep. At the bottom of the hole, I could see an elongated rectangular outline in the clayey soil.

My thoughts raced. Despite my confusion, I knew what must have happened: 'They came looking for Hovsep Nakashian's gold, following the rumour I had never believed. And they found it, buried right here, in the middle of the courtyard. He must have spent years secretly filling a *tanakeh* – an eighteen-litre petrol jerrican – with the savings of each year, dropping in there coin by coin the gold *lira* and perhaps sovereigns he was paid for his work. And when it was full, buried it in the courtyard in the dead of night. That shape in the hole is exactly that of a *tanakeh*.' I had felt that we were living very poorly compared to the high prices fetched by his handiwork: now I understood. He didn't expect to die so soon, perhaps ever, like many people, and took the secret to his grave. The rumour mill knew more than we did! I was sure that Mayrig herself had no idea about this; she might have jealously guarded her provisions, but if she had known about the existence of a fortune in gold, she would have spent it on helping the refugees.

I saw them all in my mind's eye: Mayrig, Krikor and Anahit. Little Garabed, the one who escaped, only to… then I remembered Sitt Sarah. I found her still at the cellar window and fell to my knees, my face inches from hers as I beseeched: 'Tell me, for the love of God, what has *happened*?'

'All gone! All dead! Poor Vartan! Poor Mayrig and Krikor, only Anahit, only Anahit!'

'Only Anahit *what*, Sarah? What happened to them? You must tell me. When did this happen? Who has done it? Where is Anahit?'

'The *chetes*! They came to look for Hovsep's gold, *Allah yarhumuh*. God rest them *all* now, they killed them with the long knives on the end of their rifles, dear Hajji Marie and sweet little Krikor. Thank God baby Garo was here, I had been nursing him.'

'When, Sarah?'

'When the pistachios were drying, Vartan, maybe three, four weeks ago.'

An overwhelming sense of unreality came over me. This simply could not *be*. 'Where are they now? What happened to Mayrig and Krikor? And for God's sake, what about Anahit?'

'In the Armenian cemetery, Vartan, the *Katholikos*, Sahag himself came to bury them. He cried, Vartan. And Anahit, they beat her, poor dear thing, then tied her hands behind her back and took her with them, pulling her with a rope like a donkey.'

'And where is Garo, then?'

'Sleeping, the little darling, in my house. He doesn't know a thing, bless him.'

I stood up, paralysed for a moment. Impossible to absorb such things. My mind raced in all directions: 'Three or four weeks ago! What was I doing? What was I thinking three or four weeks ago?

Why didn't I come sooner? On *time*, for God's sake?' Then I thought of the baby, Mayrig's little Garabed saved from the catastrophe, and now saved again. 'Sarah, let me see Garo,' I said. I had to see someone – one of ours – alive, to see for myself that someone had survived the massacre. She let me in and quickly bolted the door behind me, leading me to a cot in the corner of her bedroom. I leaned over and looked at the blissfully sleeping three-year-old, sucking his thumb as he dreamed. He was darker than anyone else in the family, with real Armenian features: already well-defined dark eyebrows, a tangle of curly black hair. He had filled out marvellously since I left for Nisibin. I felt my heart go out to him. Mayrig's mercy, the miraculous one. I bent down and kissed his forehead. 'Sleep, my little brother,' I whispered, my eyes brimming.

There was not much more to be learned from the dim-witted Sarah, and nothing to be gained by staying around in Atawi, in a desecrated house of death and horror. I looked at Sarah with my mouth open, unable to speak, and left. I ran to the Armenian church next to the cemetery, looking for a priest to ask where they were. Aleppo looked very strange to my eyes: dirty, strangely dilapidated and poor. The refugees seemed to have gone from the street, at least in this part of town, but it seemed that almost everyone else had as well and many shops were shuttered. The church was locked. I went down into the cemetery and immediately found the two fresh graves with wooden crosses and the names of my loved ones, my Mayrig, my impish little brother Krikor. But not, by some miracle, the little baby whose mother had made the final sacrifice so that he could live. Another Garabed, almost another martyr. I vowed to take care of him, when I could, once I had done what I was beginning to know I had to do.

I sat on the stony ground next to the mounds and put my face in my hands. My mind was tortured with visions and questions: had they bayoneted Mayrig in front of her little son, or had they killed Krikor while she looked on? Did they die quickly, at least? And my dear *Anahit*? I thought of the red stain on the wall. I could not cry tears for some reason but my body was convulsed with sobs. When they finally subsided, I got to my feet and walked unsteadily to the lime tree that shaded the cemetery, holding on to it as I vomited until the dry heaves had given up trying to empty me of everything I contained.

I left the cemetery and wandered through the streets, once my familiar surroundings, now foreign and hostile territory. I felt a horrible, crushing sense of guilt. It was taking time for me to realise that it was all true, but even before I actually knew it as knowledge, I felt an unbearable certainty that I was to blame. I suppose I had thought they were immune, that it could not happen to them. As though we were somehow exempt from the wholesale misery all around. 'How thoughtless, how selfish and blind I have been! Adding up numbers for the Turks, while they were...' But it had happened, and there was nothing I could do to change it. There was probably not much I could have done if I *had* been home, except offer myself and any money I had. At least I could have died fighting, died with my loved ones. But now... I had to find out who had done this. And what had happened to Anahit.

I was talking to myself like a madman. 'Who, in this infernal city, could tell me? Not poor simple Sarah. *Who* then? More likely a Muslim than a Christian.' I tried to collect my thoughts, and in the end resolved to go and see Omar. I walked south through Jdeide, then turned into the prosperous Muslim area where the great Jabri house stood on a small square named after their family. I knocked on the familiar door and the old manservant I had known for years opened and greeted me with the usual '*Marhaba ya khawaja Vartan*', but with a grim, funereal expression on his face, his head bowed. He knew, so Omar knew too. In an instant Omar was there, his arms around me. We both cried, and now my tears came in a flood. I couldn't believe I was weeping on my friend's shoulder, and he on mine, we who had tried to act like tough guys in our explorations of the city, to act like we thought men were supposed to. I knew Omar had a special fondness for my stony-faced mother, as well as for the little boy who always tried to tag along after us.

Finally, I pulled myself together enough to ask, 'Do you know anything about this?'

'A little,' said Omar, his arm still around my shoulder, as we both looked down at the floor. To look each other in the eye would be unbearable. 'I simply could not believe it when I heard. They say it was a band of *chetes*, a half-dozen of them, mostly Kurds. Not local thugs. Old *hamidiyes*, I heard – you know, veterans of the 1896 disturbances. They must have, somehow, heard the rumour about Hovsep Nakashian's gold. It had nothing to do with you, by the way, though we all wondered where in the world you had disappeared to, first on and off and then for the last few years. Apparently they found a whole *tanakeh* full of gold coins, bought themselves a truck, an Italian Tipo Due, and left town. That's all I know.'

I looked at my friend. 'I have to find them. They must have taken Anahit with them. She was not killed with... with the others. I *will* find her, and as for them... Will you help me? Maybe you could send some of your people to find out who exactly they are and where they went?' Omar looked down again.

'My heart is broken by what happened, *ya akhi*, my brother. I wish you only well. But I cannot do more than that.'

'You *can't*? Why not, Omar? What do you mean?'

'Don't you see? They are Muslims, Varo. You are not. It hurts me to have to tell you this, believe me. There is a bond between every Muslim, every believer in the true faith. I cannot help you take the lives of Muslims, and I can see that this is what you are set on.'

I interrupted: 'But friendship, Omar? That is nothing to you?'

'Of course it is important. I value your friendship and would do almost anything for you. But not help you to do deliberate harm to a Muslim, no matter what foul deeds he has done, and nothing could be more vile than this. Allah *will* punish them, of that I am sure. He is all-knowing, and He is just. If he were sentenced to die in an Islamic court, I would wield the sword myself. But I cannot help *you* to do it.'

I stared at my best friend. Already in a state of shocked numbness, I realised that, for me, at least, our long friendship was dead. It was like a second bereavement in one day. 'How is it I never realised that until today? I would have done anything for you: died, killed, whatever. But you… I understand. It is not the same for you. There is a gulf between us now that we are not children any more. But please, for the sake of our friendship that was, tell me everything you know. Don't *do* anything, just tell me what you can, and I will go and trouble you no more.'

Omar sat silently for a moment, a look of grim sadness on his face. Finally he spoke: 'Well, I only know a little more than I already told you. The band is led by a Kurd from the mountains around Van. He goes by the name of Karakurt – "Black Wolf". Apparently he and his gang of five or six left for "the city". About a week ago. That could be Istanbul or, more likely, Smyrna. They talked about how they were going to spend the fortune they had suddenly come into. Your fortune. That is all I know, all the help I can give you without going to extremes I am not willing to go to, as I said. But that does not mean I love you less as a friend.'

'Friend? Perhaps I will understand how you can mean that, one day. But that is secondary. What you tell me about this band is not much to go on, but I will find them. The gold means nothing to me but, just possibly, it might help me track them down.'

We parted in silence, sorrowing like two strangers who, having each taken the other for a friend, suddenly realised their mutual mistake. Strangers is, in a way, what we had just become. I left his house and wandered through the streets of the city I knew so well, feeling foreign and helpless, wounded and rejected. Orphaned. I could not bear to go back to Atawi. I felt exhausted and slightly dizzy, in no condition to go after the *chetes*. As I walked, my mind

filled with confused and painful thoughts of those I had lost, mingled with feelings of my own indelible guilt and a physical sensation
of something cold and sharp in my abdomen, a metallic taste in
my mouth. I somehow found myself in front of a third-class hotel
called the Frat (Euphrates). I looked dumbly at the sign, and realised
I must rest before whatever it was that lay ahead for me. The clerk
was an Armenian who recognised me and obviously knew what had
happened. '*Parev, Baron* Nakashian. Condolences.' The whole town
knew, while I was counting rails in Nisibin. I stared at him and took
the key without a word.

Inside the room I fell on the bed in my clothes. Suddenly the
sun was flooding in through the curtainless window, so I must have
slept at some point. The night had been a sort of delirium: images
of horror, pitiful screams and cries of voices dear to me echoed
through my mind, but I did not know if they were dreams or not.
I forced myself to rise, and saw in the mirror a haggard, unshaven
face that did not look in the least familiar to me. I splashed water
on it, tried to arrange my hair and clothes in some kind of order.
My movements were stiff, mechanical. Somewhere in my brain
was the knowledge, more like an instinct, that I needed strength
and resolve, and that somehow I would find my sister, my dear,
loving Anahit, who never harmed so much as a fly. I put a hand in
my pocket: her little cross was still there. Somehow I would make
those responsible pay for brutally ending the tight little world of
Atawi Saghir, the only world I had known as mine. Ours. The lives
of good Mayrig and her little ones.

I went to pay the bill, and realised I had quite a lot of money, my
back pay for over two years in Nisibin. My time there already seemed
ages ago: again I recoiled at the thought of my unconsciously placid
days in the camp, even the day when all this happened. Unbearable.
The money weighed heavily in my pocket, dirty, defiled. I realised
I would have to bury such thoughts for now, exclude everything that
would distract from my purpose or weaken my resolve. I stopped in

the souk to buy food and supplies for the road. Only once I was kitted out for a journey, bag of provisions and oddments over one shoulder, did I remember that I did not know where I was going or, even if I did know, how I was to get there. I sat on a stone wall alongside the esplanade in front of the Great Mosque. I struck a match on the stone and lit a cigarette, smoking mechanically, just to do something. I looked across at the great square building from the past. Somehow, since my encounter with Omar, everything about Islam had begun to seem threatening. Another subject for future reflection. Now I had to think clearly. I had to find a half-dozen *chetes* travelling towards Constantinople, or perhaps Smyrna, in a kind of truck I knew well from Nisibin. Somehow holding a young Christian girl against her will. With gold to spend and a head start of over a week.

I found it very difficult to concentrate. My brain was mired in a treacly fog of pain and grief and confusion. I tried to shake it off, to begin to come up with a plan. There was nothing I could accomplish by staying in Aleppo. Even my best friend would not help me. Especially him – my former best friend. If they left a week ago they must be far away by now, perhaps all the way to Smyrna or Constantinople.

Somehow I suspected Smyrna, rather than the sprawling capital. I had heard it was a place where all pleasures could be bought, where Ottoman law did not interfere with either Muslims or Christians enjoying the most extreme debauchery. Besides, I had heard rumours before leaving Nisibin that the English were planning to occupy Constantinople. I had to follow them quickly and, if they were not to be found in Smyrna, continue on to the capital city, where finding them would present a much more difficult task. The prospect of a challenge cleared my mind a little more. I had my letter from Ortalli and the old *teskere* from the captain, which I could try to use to talk my way into a *laissez-passer* to ride the railway.

But first there was little Garo. I had to provide for him, the miracle boy. And that meant going back to Atawi Saghir. Sitt Sarah was at her station, the cellar window. I took a handful of the money from my purse and handed it to her through the window. 'Take this and use it to take care of Garo. Please promise.'

'Of course, my son, I don't need money for that. Garo is my baby, my last, littlest baby, do not worry about him. You should go.'

'I am going, *ya sitti*. But there is more. Please listen carefully. You know my uncle, Sarkis Nakashian, the carpet merchant who lives in Ramadaniyye?'

'Of course, such a nice man.'

'For sure he already knows what happened. Send someone to tell him Garo is with you. Tell him I am all right and have gone after the murderers, looking for Anahit. If you need anything, I am sure he will help. Tell him I will be back one day. Do you understand?'

'Yes, *ya ibni*. I will do as you say. God protect you.'

I took a last look at the house. Every time I had come back to it, it was like coming back to childhood. Now it was deserted, desecrated, had lost its soul: Mayrig, and the little ones who gave it life. I got up and walked the twenty minutes to the Sebil. There was an atmosphere of chaos, with people in uniforms and civilian dress of all kinds arguing with each other in Turkish and Arabic in front of the ticket desk; much waving of arms, baggage piled helter-skelter in the waiting room and on the platforms. One of the soldiers was exclaiming that the *Ingleez* had taken Damascus; his companion shouting back at him that such a thing could not be. I pushed my way past them, waved my documents at the ticket clerk and said, 'I am a senior employee of this railway, just released from duty two days ago at Nisibin, as you can see from this certificate.' He looked up at me with a sarcastic smile and did not even glance at the papers. 'I am required urgently in Smyrna and must take the next train. Will you allow me to ride for free, as is my right, or must I pay for a ticket?'

He took the bait. '*Efendim*, if you do not already have a ticket issued by the railway, I cannot give you one for free. Perhaps you can claim reimbursement in due course, but you must pay.'

'That is most irregular but I really must be on that train, which appears to be about to depart.'

'There are only first-class seats left, *khawaja*. Two gold *lira,* ten *paras*, including first-class transit past the tunnels at Beilan and Bagche.'

I played my part, complaining that I would lodge a protest on arrival. He and I were accomplices. The Empire was disintegrating, the victors about to carve it up: who cared about a railway ticket? He probably suspected I was bluffing. He inspected the coins carefully and made a show of putting them in the cash drawer. I knew that as soon as I left, they would find their way into his pocket. I took the ticket with the seat reservation and went to look for my carriage. It took a huge effort to look normal, but I knew I had to, so I played the role of an officious clerk about to enjoy a ride in a first-class compartment and boarded the train that had 'Constantinople' written on the doors. I was not sure this would get me to Smyrna, or indeed where exactly Smyrna was in relation to the capital.

During the hour-long carriage ride past the unfinished tunnel through the mountains at Beilan, I found myself sitting next to an Ottoman Army officer, a captain. I offered him a Muslim greeting, in Turkish with a strong Arabic accent, and a cigarette. He said he was on his way home to Konya at last, praise be to Allah. As we lit up, he asked me where I was from. 'Aleppo, in the grocery trade, praise be to Allah. Travelling to Smyrna to buy figs and currants.' My neighbour smiled; solidarity of the *Umma*.

'This will be my first visit to that city. Do you know it?'

'I do indeed, but prefer my own city of Konya, a good Muslim town. Hardly any *giaours* left, since it was cleansed of Armenians. Smyrna is crawling with them: you are more likely to run into three Orthodox priests than one imam. The Turks and other Believers are mostly in the manual trades and blasphemously discriminated against.' He spat on the floor.

'Ah,' I replied. 'A place best avoided indeed. I will endeavour to make my stay there as short as possible. Does this train in fact go to that cursed place?'

'Not this one, *alhamdulillah*. At Afyon there is a branch that goes down there. I get off at Konya, as I said, but Afyon is the next stop so you cannot miss it.'

'Thank you, Captain Effendi, you have been most helpful.'

The train ride resumed for a spell, making a stop at Adana. The railway was interrupted again at the Taurus tunnel, again with continuation by carriage for those travelling in first class. Back on the train, after what seemed like an hour's delay, it finally began the long rail segment. At the tunnel's mouth, I could see that the blasting and digging operations had been abandoned, with equipment lying where it had been left. 'It serves them right,' I thought. 'They clogged up their trains with deportees who had done them no wrong, even engineers and employees. And lost the war – and maybe soon, their empire. Is it possible that the British are in Damascus? Would they carry on to Aleppo, then Cilicia and the mountains of Armenia? If so, what will that mean for those of our people who somehow survived? So many questions, so few answers.'

My thoughts turned black every time I had no specific occupation for them. I tried to concentrate on the landscape, quite spectacular as the train began the long descent, following the twisty bed of a river. I needed to start thinking what I would do if and when I made it to Smyrna. 'Has anyone seen a Tipo Due truck with six or seven *chetes*?' I would ask a passer-by, and probably end my days in the hands of the police.

Whenever I was not thinking, or trying to think, of anything else, Shoushan's face would appear. Not speaking: her face calm, a statue to Loving Patience. How I wished I could share my grief with her, bury my face in her shoulder and weep. Seek her forgiveness for what I had done to her – and for what I hoped I was about to do. I sometimes felt like a child, at others like a man. Just now

I did not feel like 'Vartan' any more, boy or man. I was Vengeance. Everything else about my life would have to wait.

The train chugged and hissed its way through a country of rolling hills, passing the city of Akshehir. I had what must have been a wonderful view of its lake on the right-hand side. In Aleppo we had seen hundreds of walking corpses from this town, survivors of some of the most barbaric massacres.

In the morning, the train stopped at Afyon, which they also call Karahisar ('Black Fort'). You could in fact see a sinister black fortress overlooking the town. I wondered what kind of town it was, with a name I thought meant 'opium'. I stood with my bundles on the platform, watching the other disembarking passengers arranging for transport, piling up baggage, greeting relatives and generally moving on, continuing their lives. I felt utterly alien, with no life of my own to continue, like a dead thing, an empty cicada shell from which the life had withdrawn. I went to the ticket office and was told there would be a train going all the way to Smyrna in the mid-afternoon. I showed my ticket, had it clipped and a seat reservation written on it. Now I was bound for Smyrna. It was 15 October 1918. An empire that had lasted for more than half a millennium was in its death throes. 'Perhaps there is a little justice, sometimes,' I thought, 'even if it comes too late.'

I waited on a bench on the platform at Afyon, drenched in golden mid-October sunlight, still quite warm at that time in the afternoon. Under other circumstances I would have been quite happy to play the lizard. Now my mind was in turmoil; I was nervous and anxious to be on my way. But unsure of what I would find, not to mention what I would do about it, what I could do. What I *ought* to do. I lit one cigarette after another, absent-mindedly throwing them away half-smoked, fidgeting and drumming my fingers on the wooden bench. The train did not appear to be coming. Would the train keep to any sort of timetable, at this time in history, with victory assured for the Entente, now including the Americans? Defeat was a certainty for the Turks, no thanks to me. A hollow victory, too late to save who knew how many innocent people, a whole way of life.

Finally, the train came puffing up from wherever it had been, then screeched to a halt with steam still billowing from the locomotive. I asked the platform attendant if he was sure it was bound for Smyrna, which he swore it was. There were only a few people waiting to board but the train arrived already over-full. Again, most of the passengers were men in various kinds of Turkish uniforms. They filled the carriage with my reserved seat and I was not about to wave my ticket at a Turk in uniform. I pushed my way through the crowded seating area of one carriage after another, until I saw a corner with a bit of empty space, behind the last benches of a second-class carriage. I ensconced myself there, leaning on my bedroll with the strap of my shoulder bag wrapped around my arm. Once the train lurched into motion, I spent the hours dozing fitfully, oppressed by horrible dreams; jostled awake by gloomy thoughts and memories and the numerous stops in the night of what was obviously a local train.

I was roused by the rising sun's rays streaming in through the dusty train windows. My mind was still clogged with disturbing visions from my dream, but these gradually dissipated. As my head cleared, I realised that I was feeling stronger than I had since discovering the horror only a few days before. Stronger physically, but as though anaesthetised. I had a vague feeling that my power of reasoning was gradually being restored. The train meandered along the edge of a plateau, then turned to descend through a landscape of hills and valleys, following the course of a river. By the middle of the day, the train was chugging its way through an area of rich farmland dominated by long rows of fig trees and well-tended vineyards, punctuated by poplars and sycamores with the first metre or two of their trunks painted white. I wondered, idly, why they do that. The poplars were already putting on their autumn colours of yellow and orange, while the vines were blood-red.

There were a few Turkish-looking villages, but as we approached the suburbs, I was struck by the European style of the houses, each enclosed within a walled garden of orchards and ornamental trees, guarded by iron gates, finer and richer than the houses of the wealthiest landowners in Killis. Mayrig's town. And now, all those houses, and their owners, and Mayrig... I focused on the landscape to avoid sinking back into the despair that had dogged me since Atawi.

As we crossed a hilly area of less opulent suburbs, I caught the occasional glimpse of the distant sea. Then the train pulled into the station and stopped. This was an elegant building with a sign saying 'Gare de Basma Khane', though why it was only labelled in French I couldn't say. It did seem to be the main station and, anyway, was the end of the line. I got off the train and looked around at the throng of people buying tickets, struggling with luggage and shoving their way along the platform, with porters wearing fezzes and neat uniforms carrying boxes or pulling handcarts, bearing steamer trunks decorated with labels like 'Cunard' and 'Shepheard's Hotel Cairo'. The people in European dress were in a state of excitement, the Turks sullen: what you might expect at the end of a bloody war, when you have victors and vanquished all mixed up together. From the esplanade in front of the station I could see, just down the hill, the twin bell towers of what looked to me like an Orthodox church, either Greek or Armenian, but grander than anything in Aleppo. A good place to start.

I shouldered my bag and walked down towards the church, and was surprised to see shop signs in Armenian as well as French. I asked in English a man in European dress coming out of one of those shops and he looked at me strangely and answered that this was Haynot, the Armenian Quarter. In some ways it reminded me of the Christian areas of Aleppo. People went about their business as though everything was normal, but I thought I could sense a tension in the air. Maybe I brought it with me, but people looked pensive, hurrying silently on their way, rather than lingering to chat or shop on such a fine October evening.

The church was even more imposing from close up: 'St Stepanos,' I read, 'Armenian Cathedral.' The door was open and I went in. Old ladies were sweeping and arranging flowers on the altar, as if for mass. I saw a young priest passing down the aisle, and addressed him in Armenian. The clergyman was a handsome fellow, perhaps eight or ten years older than me, in a black robe with a white collar, just like in Aleppo. He smiled as though my speech was amusing, which I suppose it was, a mixture of Jerusalem literary language and the colloquial dialect of faraway Cilicia. 'Where are you from, my friend?'

'From Aleppo, Vartan Hovsep Nakashian.'

'Abraham Khatchik Hartunian, honoured to meet you, *Baron* Nakashian. And what brings you to Smyrna at this momentous time in history?'

'Er, a family errand of sorts. But I have been travelling for a week and was out in the desert before that. Please tell me what is going on.'

'The war is over – I imagine you know that. Jerusalem, Damascus and Baghdad have all fallen to the English. The armistice is expected to be signed in a few days, on a British battleship, so they say. We expect Smyrna to be occupied by the Entente powers, like Constantinople, but no one knows when or by whom exactly. This city is mostly Greek; Greek-speaking Christians. Some of them are *reaya*, Turkish citizens, but they are all in a frenzy, hoping and expecting Smyrna and all of the Aegean, perhaps even the capital, to be occupied by Greece.'

My mind was not fully focused on what he was saying, but I made an effort to follow. 'Were there deportations of Armenians from here?' I asked.

'No,' said the priest, 'not generally. We have been lucky, so far, except that law and order has broken down and there are bands of thugs roving the countryside. They carried out a terrible massacre in a Greek town just up the coast. During the war, they did intern many nationals of enemy states, those who could not buy their exemption. A few thousand Greek *reaya* were moved further inland, the men taken off to the *taburlar*. You know about them, I suppose?'

'Yes, of course. My own brother was taken, from our home in Aleppo.'

'Your brother! I am sorry to hear that.'

'Father,' I said after a silence. 'I will tell you the reason I have come to Smyrna. There are also gangs of *chetes* and other brigands in our country.' I hesitated again before taking him into my confidence. 'A band of those rogues, led by someone they call Karakurt, attacked our house in Aleppo just a few weeks ago. They brutally murdered my widowed mother and young brother. They abducted my young sister, Anahit, and that is why I have come here. There is a rumour in Aleppo that they were coming to Smyrna, in a truck. They stole a large sum of money, my late father's savings. I must find them. I must, I *will* save my sister. The money is not important, except that they are probably spending it ostentatiously and that might help me find them.'

Abraham gripped my arm with his hand. 'How dreadful, brother. Will the trials afflicting our people never cease? You must come with me to my house. You will rest, we will have a meal and you will tell us your story, in private.' Whatever he was doing before he met me, he dropped it and led me to a modest house on a side street near the cathedral. I felt at home immediately: tables with embroidered linen *bashkir* textiles with their delicate geometrical patterns, the absolute cleanliness of the floors, the white walls bare of decoration except for an ornate cross on one, a lamp burning under an icon of a bearded saint in a carved corner niche. A carpet which I recognised from my uncle's shop: a 'dragon' design, old and very beautiful. An Armenian house, many hundreds, maybe a thousand, miles from any I had ever visited, but instantly recognisable, homely and welcoming. Abraham's wife came out directly; he introduced her as Araksi, the little boy sleeping in her arms as Calouste.

'Please forgive me, I was just putting him to bed. I will bring you coffee at once.'

'Araksi, I think our guest needs something more substantial. Give Calouste to me, I will hold him.' I thought of objecting but it would have been totally insincere since I was literally faint with hunger, having hardly eaten in three days.

Abraham listened to my story. 'Vartan, I will see what I can do. Our community includes some pretty rough individuals, nothing like a gang of *chetes*, of course, but the sort of toughs who can stand up to them when needed. People who work down in the port, mostly. I will send for one I know well and have him ask after your Karakurt and his fellow murderers, if he has not already run across them. If he cannot track them down, then I doubt very much they are in Smyrna. When you finish eating, I will send you to see the city with my deacon, a fellow about your age, from Chorum, in Angora Province. His family was deported while he was studying here and he has had no news of them. We fear the worst, of course, but I am sure it will do him good to talk to someone coming from Aleppo. Dear, would you mind?'

Araksi puttered about the kitchen for a minute, then returned and set a plate of steaming *harisa* lamb stew in front of me before going out to fetch the deacon. Another Armenian staple, a little different from Mayrig's… I banished sad thoughts and began devouring it, a taste of home and, mainly, food. A few minutes later she returned with a clean-shaven, thick-set young man with dark circles under heavy-lidded eyes, giving him a sleepy air. Abraham introduced us; his name was Vahram, and I could tell he had heard about me from Araksi. He sat patiently while I finished eating. As soon as I put down my spoon, he said, '*Baron* Nakashian, please come with me, we will walk around the city and talk, if you don't mind.' Abraham put his hand on my shoulder: 'That is a good idea, Vartan; get some fresh air and a first impression of our city; meanwhile I'll send for that, ah, gentleman from the port.'

I was in no mood for sightseeing but it was an amazing place. As soon as we went down the hill towards the port, the atmosphere became ostentatiously luxurious and pretentiously European – very different from Aleppo, where the few Frenchified streets and stores looked out of place and did not make more than a timid display of foreignness. Most of the people strolling on the seaside they call the Cordon were dressed and looked European; there was almost no one in the baggy trousers and turban of Turkish peasant dress. We sat in a cafe opposite the port and ordered coffee. Vahram asked me if I had heard anything about the deportees from Chorum.

'While I was still in Aleppo, I did meet an old couple from Chorum, but sadly cannot remember their names. They spent a few days at our home. Like many of those from the north, they had been deported by train rather than on foot, and some, like them, did manage to get off in Aleppo, the ones who had the means to bribe the guards. I know that's not much, I wish I had some real information for you.'

'Yes, it's frustrating to be so far away and to know nothing about what happened to them. I wish I could make myself believe that that old couple were my mother and father! Our family was relatively wealthy by Chorum standards, so perhaps they also managed to bribe their way to safety.'

I told my story. Vahram said he was sure that Father Abraham's contacts would help find the murderers, provided they were actually in the Smyrna area. I asked him what life was like in Smyrna during the war. 'This is not a city like any other. Its commerce is vital to the Empire, or was before the war – but the Turks hate it, "Infidel Smyrna". During the first year of the war, in May, the British navy bombarded the Turkish forts that dominate the city, one on a hill on each side of the bay. The Ottomans had just installed Austrian shore batteries, paid for by the Germans, of course. The *vali* of Smyrna,

Rahmi Bey, and all the rich foreigners, that is, the Smyrniotes of Greek, English, French, Italian or Jewish extraction, all the beau monde of Smyrna, they all sat drinking in Costi's cafe on the Cordon, just down the quay from here. Rahmi drinks as much as any of them, but holds his liquor better. There were cheers when a shell made a particularly good hit. On July the 14th this year, there were French tricolour flags everywhere, bands playing the "Marseillaise". Anthem of an enemy power. Strange place, don't you think?'

He went on to talk about a possible occupation by the Greeks, something that seemed to worry him a lot, a very complicated business involving the British and the Italians and the French. He must have noticed that my mind was not really focused on his story. 'I'm sorry, Vartan, I know you've been through hell and have a lot on your mind. Let's make our way back to Father Abraham's. He might have heard something by now. If not, tomorrow, I am sure.' We walked back up the hill, into the familiar-feeling Armenian Quarter, past the vast church with its ornate towers and knocked on the priest's door.

Abraham had news. 'I wish the news was better. There is indeed a gang of thugs from back east, led by a former *hamidiye* – you know, a cutthroat who took part in Abdul Hamid's massacres twenty years ago? Anyway, this one calls himself Karakurt, just like you said. He has four or five companions. One of the worst is an infamous brigand named Cherkess Ahmed, a Circassian, to judge by his name. They used to belong to a group of *chetes* called the Khamseen, who spent the whole time of the deportation plundering, raping and killing miserable refugees.'

'I know them all too well, Father. I did not know about Karakurt at that time, but the Khamseen were infamous. Do you know where they are, the Karakurt gang, I mean?'

'Yes. According to Hrant, my man among our Armenian *qaba-dais*, they have taken over the house of a Greek family who were deported inland, the father taken off to the *taburlar*. It is in a suburb on a hill called Tepecik, on the edge of the city, just beyond the Caravan Bridge and up past the Turkish cemetery. That bridge is a famous landmark, you might have heard of it. The ruffians spend their time drinking and whoring; apparently they have an endless supply of gold. But from what Hrant tells us, whores come and go, local Turks and Greeks, but there is no young Armenian girl with them, of that he is sure. I am sorry.'

It took me a moment to absorb the fact that they were here, nearby. But Anahit was not with them. *What* could have happened to her? I felt like I had been kicked in the stomach. I suppose I was stupid to have imagined I would find her safe and sound after weeks in the hands of such scum. 'Can someone show me this house?' I asked. Abraham and Vahram looked at each other.

'My brother Vartan, what would you do there?' asked Abraham. 'They are six at least, all bloodthirsty murderers. You are only one, and not even armed. Hrant swears there is no young girl in the house. You should not even think of approaching them, they would kill you just for pleasure. I don't want to say anything to hurt you more than you are already, but look at things clearly. They have killed your poor mother and little brother, that we know. Do you want to give them the satisfaction of doing likewise to you?'

'Father, I have no choice. I have come all this way. I have nothing to go back to and I cannot give up now. I will not take stupid risks, but I have at least to see for myself that my sister is not with them. If I can, to find out what happened to her. I don't need any help except for someone to show me the way and leave me there. Will you send someone with me to guide me? That's all I ask.'

Abraham was silent for a moment. 'It is not wise. But if you must, there is only one person: Hrant. He's a bit of a rogue himself, but he knows the way and can give you useful advice, I am sure, though I think even he will tell you not to try to contact them. Vahram, would you ask the verger to run up to the cafe where Hrant hangs out and bring him?'

Half an hour later, a man knocked on the door, one who actually did look very much like a bandit, or a retired boxer, with his cauliflower nose. 'Hrant der Simonian, at your service,' proffering a huge hand, calloused and tobacco-stained.

'Vartan Nakashian. Pleased to meet you, *Baron* der Simonian.' This formality was met with an alarming gap-toothed grin.

'Call me Hrant. Father Abraham says you want to see where the *chetes* from Van are staying?'

'I do. If you would be so kind as to show me the way, I'd be most obliged. Father, may I leave my baggage here until I return?'

'Vartan, of course you can. And you will sleep here. Are you sure you want to go up there today? It is late: soon it will be dark. Perhaps you could wait until tomorrow morning? Get a night's sleep and think about it, and if you must go, go in the morning.'

I stood up. 'Father Abraham, you are kindness itself. I will go now, if Hrant will show me the way. Thank you for the offer of hospitality: if I return before it is too late to disturb your household, I will knock.'

Hrant led me up towards the Tepecik hill. We walked up for a while and then down, crossing a river which Hrant said was called the Menes, then up another hill past a church and school, a large compound with a big blue-and-white flag flying from the flagpole in the courtyard. The houses around there all had a Greek feel about them, in fact some also had Greek flags in their windows. But as we climbed, the neighbourhood became a bit more mixed, some houses clearly Turkish; generally smaller, less tidy and closer together than the Greek ones. We passed the Ottoman cemetery on our right, a shady garden with small pointy stones, mostly without inscriptions, like poor Turkish graves in Aleppo. Hrant stopped and pointed out a large frame house, surrounded by a lush but untidy garden. 'That's the house where the fellow who calls himself Karakurt is staying with his henchmen. See all the lights: they are probably in the middle of one of their drunken debauches.'

I could in fact hear strains of plaintive rebetika music, bouzouki and flute accompanying a whining, repetitive vocal. There was a burst of garrulous laughter, with loud voices shouting from one of the upper storeys. Then the sound of breaking glass and more laughter. I turned to Hrant: 'Thank you, that is all I need, you have done what I asked. Please go back to town now, I will handle this on my own.'

'I don't want to leave you up here. Let me go and bring back some of my, ah, associates, with proper weapons. We'll make short work of those drunken murderers, but we need to be of equal number.'

'Thank you, Hrant. I appreciate the offer. But I don't need or want assistance. I hope to see you again, perhaps tomorrow. For now, thank you and goodbye.'

Hrant still hesitated. 'Father Abraham did not want me to leave you up here. But if you tell me to leave, I will leave. You remember the way back: downhill, cemetery on your left. Then across the bridge, follow the road around to the right; you will know you have reached the Armenian Quarter when you can see the cathedral towers. It will be dark soon, and the streets are not lit up here as they are in town. There will be a moon tonight, though. God be with you.' He shook my hand, frowning; then hesitated before turning and starting down the hill, leaving me alone. At first I felt utterly confused, a little dizzy and disoriented. Now that I knew the monsters were close, very close, I felt my emptiness being replaced by an overwhelming feeling of hate rising up like a deadly sap, cold oils coursing through my veins. My mind was in the grip of conflicting powers: the desire for revenge and aching love for those I had lost. A desire to know what happened to Anahit but a deadly fear of actually knowing.

I tried to shake off all such thoughts and turned to look up at the house. It was quite unlike the rather showy stone and stucco dwellings of the Europeans, but it was clearly not Turkish. It looked like what Hrant said it was, a house built long ago for a large but not wealthy Greek family, abandoned for at least a year. I walked past, studying the property carefully, without stopping to stare. It was open to the road in front, with no real garden, just a few odd bushes that must once have been ornamental. Everything had a neglected air about it, from the remnants of white paint flaking off the clapboards, to the untended vegetation. Only the tall cypress hedge that closed off the back yard of the house on three sides seemed to preserve an element of dignity.

There was a large open porch in front, a veranda with square pillars supporting the roof. A big old settee, its faded floral fabric in tatters with springs emerging from the seat, gave witness to times long past. I imagined a family gathered around, children playing in the garden, the father smoking contentedly on the settee. The ground floor was shuttered and dark, but the two upper storeys had their shutters wide open, some of which were hanging akimbo on a single hinge. I looked down the near side of the house towards the back. There, I could see abandoned rabbit hutches and chicken coops, their latticed doors ajar, along the cypress hedge. On the other side of the house, a driveway led back to where I could see, unmistakably, a Tipo Due truck, just like the ones I had watched loading and unloading at Nisibin. My pulse quickened: no doubt, these are the *ones*. I thought of Anahit. She must have ridden in that truck. But to where? Where could she be now? I repressed such thoughts and continued past the house, on up the hill where the last of the residential area gave way to umbrella pines with sheep or goat trails meandering among them, just visible in the failing light.

Then I came to a clearing with squared-off stones that looked like it had once been used as a picnic area. I sat on a stone and looked back down the hill, at the house and the cemetery beyond, the Greek school and the bridge. 'Caravan Bridge': I imagined camel-trains laden with figs ambling slowly down towards the port city. As the light faded completely, I could see very little of the house, except the brightly lit and unshuttered windows on the two upper storeys. I could just about make out the faint sound of music and voices from where I sat. I could discern the occasional dark shape crossing in front of a window, but could not see any detail at this distance.

I sat and thought, intensely, until it was very dark. What could I do against six armed cutthroats? A yellow half-moon began to rise slowly above the hills, off to the east. I could see the surface of the road gleaming faintly in the moonlight, and walked slowly and quietly back downhill to reconnoitre the house, staying in the shadows as much as possible. My right hand felt for Viper, snug in its sheath. I grasped it firmly and pulled it around to my side, easily and quickly accessible, ready. Unconsciously, I touched the pocket where I could feel Anahit's cross, with a fleeting thought of *'please'*, which was close to being a prayer, though I could not have said to whom or what. I was not yet sure what to do. I thought a closer look at the house might give me an idea. As quietly as I could, I followed the driveway towards the back. As I suspected, there was a back porch as well, much smaller than the one in front, its formerly screened outer door hanging precariously. An outside staircase had once led up to the first floor and a small balcony but the stairs had collapsed into a pile of rotten lumber and the balcony itself looked like it was about to follow.

I went across to get a closer look at the truck. On the flatbed behind the double cabin was strewn assorted rubbish, while against one side panel there were three *tanakehs*, eighteen-litre petrol cans secured by leather straps. I unsheathed Viper and cut one of the jerricans free from its strap: empty. The next one was full, or nearly, and so was the third one. I left them on the truck and circled the house, staying near the dark hedge, passing by the privy, a wooden hut from which there issued the unmistakable, unbearably cloying stench of years, or maybe generations, of accumulated human waste. I looked up at the house from the back: besides the front and back doors and the useless door to the balcony, there were basement windows on the two sides, low to the ground but too small for a man to squeeze through. With the upper storeys too high to jump from, the balcony staircase in ruins and the ground floor windows tightly shuttered, the two raised ground floor doors were the only possible points of entry or exit.

I decided not to rush into any action, mainly because I was not yet sure what I ought to do. For the moment, I had an idea or two, but nothing coherent. It was still early and the six were not going anywhere, to judge by the sounds of drunken merriment wafting down from the upper floor. I squatted against the hedge, with a clear view of the back door and an oblique one of the front veranda. I felt like smoking but repressed the idea. The music continued, with the occasional man's voice loudly shouting something in Turkish, then a woman's shrill laughter. A second woman squealed and there was the dull thud of something hitting the floor, probably a piece of heavy furniture knocked over, I thought. Suddenly there was the sound of footsteps, a man's boots clumping on the inside staircase, louder as he made his way erratically down. The back door was flung open with a bang and someone came out on to the porch. I could hear a man's voice shouting down the stairs after him in Turkish: 'Eh, Karakurt Bey, don't fall in the cesspool, drunk as you are! And if you do, don't come back inside! Ha! Ha!'

Raucous laughter lanced the night air. The man paused a moment on the porch, as though steadying himself or meditating a reply. I made myself as small and quiet as I could, hoping the shadows would make me invisible to someone coming out from the brightly lit interior. I could just make out his silhouette, a man of middle height, stocky, with black, baggy Turkish trousers and a headcloth half undone, now walking unsteadily towards the privy. *That. Is. Karakurt.* I knew what I had to do, without thinking about it, I just knew. I propelled myself to my feet, not even trying to be quiet, drawing Viper from its sheath as I ran forward to intercept him. He stopped on hearing the footsteps, but did not seem to fully take in the situation. In an instant, before he could react, I had tackled him and together we fell heavily to the ground, bound together by my arms.

He was strong and, despite his drunken state, was able to turn and wriggle free. He thrust his knee painfully up into my groin, then shoved me aside to extricate himself. During the instant it took me to recover, Karakurt, on all fours, seemed to be collecting his wits; he started to rise but before he got fully upright, I leaped on to his back. He collapsed heavily back down with me on top, pinning him to the ground. I brought Viper's sharp blade around and pressed it tight against his throat: 'Make a sound, dog, and I will slit your throat like a *Bayram* lamb!' To make sure he understood, I dragged the knife along his throat an inch or so, just below his Adam's apple, drawing blood and obviously causing pain. He started to shout a cry for help but I pulled the blade even tighter against his throat, cutting deeper into the soft flesh: 'So you think I am joking?'

The Kurd stopped resisting and entreated, 'All right, stop! For God's sake, *stop*! You're killing me! Who are you? What do you want? If you want money, I have plenty, look in my pocket, and there is more upstairs.'

'I am sure you have gold, the gold you stole from the Nakashian widow in Atawi Saghir, in Aleppo. But I don't want money. I want to know what you did with the girl you took away, after you killed the rest of the family. *Where is she?*'

Karakurt was still gasping from the struggle. He stopped resisting as though struggling to make sense of what he had just heard. I could smell on his breath a few inches from my face the sour stink of too much alcohol drunk over too much time, alcohol and cheap tobacco and garlic and his unwashed body in filthy clothes. 'The skinny little Armenian, you mean?'

'The same.' I resisted the urge to cut his throat to the bone, to feel his hot blood gush.

'She was sick, I saw her spit blood, I didn't want to catch the *sill*. We took her away with us, Ahmed wanted her, but I didn't touch her, I swear. What was she to you?'

'Everything, son of a pig. She was my sister, and the old woman was my mother. The little boy was my brother. *Now* do you understand? Did you ever have a mother or a sister?'

'I did not want to kill them, *khawaja*. I just wanted to find the gold. The others, Cherkess Ahmed and the others, they killed them while I was digging for the gold. I swear!'

'I don't care about that now. I just want to know what you did to my sister. If you can lead me to her, if she is alive, I will spare your life; if not, I will butcher you here and now, like the swine you are. Out with it!'

He made an effort to turn his head ever so slightly, so he could see my face. 'Easy on my throat, brother! You are cutting me! Stop it and I will tell you.' I eased the pressure of the blade against his bleeding fleshy throat but did not remove the knife.

'When I saw she was sick, I gave her to the others. They would… they used to take anything. And when they had finished with her, they… killed her. I tried to stop them, I swear I did, but they would not listen. She kept on crying, would not stop wailing and coughing, who would want to listen to that? Ahmed put her out of her misery, a bullet in the head.' I made a supreme effort to keep my mind focused, my thoughts together.

'And then, Karakurt? What did you do with her?'

'And then, well, what did you want them to do? They just left her in the ditch by the side of the road, and we drove on. Somewhere near Adana. That's all I can tell you, I swear, *vallahi billahi*.'

I closed my eyes tightly. I could not bear the thought of her horror at witnessing the massacre of her family, at the fright and degradation and pain of her last moments. Of her sweet, frail body thrown into a Turkish ditch and left for… I would *not* let myself think about Anahit now. A black rage came over me, a tidal wave of blind hate which overwhelmed every part of my body and mind. Without a word, still holding Viper tight against the man's throat, I reached my free hand under his belly and untied the rope which held his trousers up, yanking it free. 'Put your hands behind your back!' I growled, pressing Viper harder into the yielding flesh to ensure compliance. I tied his hands with a quick sailor's knot Uncle Sarkis had taught me, a secure knot you can tie with one hand. I unravelled his headcloth and, pulling back on his long, greasy ponytail until his mouth gaped wide, I stuffed a fist-sized wad of cloth into it, stifling a shout.

I was beyond any sort of conscious control. I sheathed the dagger, grabbed Karakurt by the ponytail with my left hand and the waistband of his trousers with the other, and dragged him forward through the low weeds that had taken the place of grass, as far as the door of the privy. Kicking the door open with my foot, I saw that the inside was an open cesspit, filled with mostly liquid sewage almost up to the two planks placed on either side for the sitter's feet. An overpoweringly putrid smell hung about the place; I quelled an urge to vomit. Kicking the planks aside, I called on all my strength to slide the bound but writhing Kurd up to the threshold. I went down on one knee, still gripping his ponytail, and looked him in the face. He went quiet; our eyes locked for an instant. His were wide with fear and entreaty. Mingled with all the other forms of stink in that place, was an acrid smell, I thought: the sour smell of mortal terror, of an animal's certain knowledge of its own death.

Karakurt's eyes opened even wider, as he began to comprehend what was in store for him. He grunted through the gag and struggled desperately against his bonds. With a final shove, I thrust him head first into the pit, well past his shoulders so that he could not lift his head above the surface, and knelt on his squirming legs. There was a ghastly noise of choking and gargling, a struggle that went on for about half a minute. All that thrashing and splashing roused even more stink, if that was possible. Gradually the noise ceased, the legs gave off kicking, the writhing stopped. I knew he was dead. On a last-minute impulse, I remembered what he had said about money in his pocket: I reached into his trouser-pocket and pulled out a bulging canvas purse, which I shoved into my own pocket. I had lost my glasses in the struggle and was relieved to find them intact near the spot where I had tackled him. My gorge rose and I leaned against the truck and vomited.

When my stomach stopped heaving, without stopping to reflect, I was lifting the two full jerricans off the bed of the Tipo Due. I put both on the ground, then carried one around to the front of the house, unscrewing the cap as I went. I poured about half the contents on to the doorstep and front porch, then ran with it around to the back, where I soaked the steps and lintel of the back door. Throwing the empty can aside, I ran back for the other full one, lugged it to the left side of the house and kicked in the cellar window. I dropped to all fours to look in and saw disorderly piles of what looked like corn cobs. The Greeks must have saved them for some reason, many years of them. Perfect! I poured about half the can's contents in that window, then carried it around to the other side and emptied it through the low window, which was already broken.

I pulled my box of matches from my pocket, went first to the front porch, struck a match and threw it in front of the door. The petrol ignited with a loud *whoosh*! sound and I had to jump back to keep from getting burned. I waited for a second to watch the flames lick and then begin to devour the old wooden door and the porch itself, all dry as tinder. I stopped on my way to the back of the house to throw another lighted match through the cellar window. I then set fire to the back porch. By the time I got to the cellar window on the other side of the house, the basement and its contents were already burning fiercely and did not need another match. Soon the fire had taken possession of the house inside and out, with the shouts of men and shrieks of women, the crash of toppled furniture and crazed footsteps as people ran around in a vain attempt to escape the smoke and flames. A sudden deafening volley of gunshots told me that the fire had reached the cartridge belt of one of the *chetes*.

I stood transfixed, watching and listening until at length the shouts and screams died out and finally ceased altogether. Now there was no noise except the roaring and crackling of the inferno, greedily consuming the old wooden house and all it contained, a monstrous pyre lighting up the night all around. My mind was not yet functioning normally, but something must have told me it was time to leave, for I found myself crossing the road and walking downhill towards the cemetery. I stopped in the shadows and turned back once more to watch the fire. Soon a small crowd had gathered in the street in front of the house. They all seemed to be shouting at once: fires are frequent among the wooden houses of Turkish towns, but this one was spectacular and there was noisy excitement among the onlookers.

I turned away again and began to make my way down the hill towards the town, without haste, with no particular thought in my mind, prey to a mental and physical numbness I had never experienced. Walking mechanically, like a sleepwalker. Then I thought of my father: 'Well, Hovsep Nakashian, you told me on your deathbed to take care of Mayrig and the children, and I failed you, I failed to protect them. But I did not fail to avenge them. With Viper, your last work.' Soon I had crossed the bridge, retracing my steps until I found myself in front of the cathedral. It had been no more than three hours since Hrant had left me opposite the house in Tepecik.

Captain Weldon's watch told me it was not yet ten o'clock, but I felt completely drained, I would sleep anywhere. The idea of a bed after the days and nights on the train was irresistible. I felt spent, as though a huge tension had been released from my body, like a long-compressed spring at last free to uncoil. Abraham opened cautiously, then recoiled physically from the sight and smell of me. I had not thought about that: some of the contents of both jerrican and cesspool must have splashed on my clothes. They were bloodstained, dirty and rank; I was totally dishevelled and the handle of my dagger protruded menacingly from my waistband. My cap was gone. 'My God, Vartan, what has happened to you? Are you all right? We were so worried about you!'

I suddenly realised how filthy I was. 'I am sorry, Father, I cannot enter your house in this condition. I will find somewhere else to sleep.' I turned to go but the priest took my arm gingerly and guided me into the house, closing and bolting the door behind us.

'Araksi, please get some water ready for Vartan to have a wash. I will bring you a change of clothes, we are about the same size. You will eat supper and tell us what happened.' As I sponged myself over the basin in their bathroom, I wondered what I ought to say. I decided I should tell them part of what I had done, but leave out the grisly parts, the Kurd's drowning in sewage and the fiery deaths of the women along with the other *chetes*.

When I emerged, bathed and dressed in Abraham's clean clothes, Hrant was there. The *qabadai* had heard about the fire and rushed up to see about it, and me: 'Just as I got there, there was this huge noise and the inside of the house collapsed. A few minutes later, the outside walls fell in, one by one. I never saw anything like it. Nothing was left but a huge bonfire of all the timber and contents, no sign of people. I asked someone what had happened, and they told me about the body found in the privy, hands tied behind his back. There were empty jerricans of petrol, no doubt it was arson. Everyone seems to think it was a band of Greek vigilantes, but nobody said they had seen any. The gendarmes didn't even bother coming.

'It was amazing how little was left of the house by the time I left. There was no sign of bodies except for one in the cesspool. I went around to see for myself, *tfou*! The neighbours said when the fire started, there'd been five or six men, plus two or three local whores, on the upper floor. Some of them said they would return in the morning, tomorrow morning, to search in the embers for the gold the thugs were known to have. For now, you can't get close – it's still very hot, some timbers are still burning. I've never seen such a sight. Those murderers got what they deserved, all right!'

I felt uncomfortable in the presence of Abraham and Araksi. The glee with which Hrant told his story did not help. Abraham sensed my unease and said, 'Vartan, I can tell you are troubled by these events, and rightly so. We can surmise what happened. Our Lord Jesus Christ said, "turn the other cheek", but what happened to you was not a slap on the cheek. You have avenged the brutal murder of your family. "Vengeance is mine, I will repay, saith the Lord", but sometimes He sets us trials which are beyond all human endurance. As you know, we are not like the Catholics, we do not practice individual confession and absolution of sins – there is a general absolution during mass. Perhaps you would come to mass tomorrow. I am sure the Lord will recognise your sincere contrition for what you have done; you will be forgiven, I know.'

I could not tell Abraham that I did not feel contrition, not towards his God anyway. And certainly not for the *chetes*. The priest's gesture was well meaning, I knew that. But I could not admit that what I had done was a sin. Even if it was, in the eyes of the Church, I was not going to feel any relief at having it forgiven by God or his surrogates. 'Let God explain his absence while innocents are being slaughtered,' I thought. I did feel remorse, but only for the women who had been caught up in the holocaust, probably poor girls just trying to earn a living, not guilty of the crimes of their customers. Maybe even Christians. Unavoidable, bad luck for them; I regretted that consequence of my act of revenge. However, I felt that – if there is such a thing as sin – the guilt belonged to Karakurt and his gang. They had endangered the lives of the unfortunate women by bringing them into a murderers' den. It was a miracle that I had managed to find out the unspeakable truth about Anahit, and to exact revenge on those responsible. That had been the goal of my journey, of my existence ever since the tragedy. But I could not tell Father Abraham any of that. I just said, 'Thank you, Father.'

I was so obviously exhausted that they led me to my bed without further talk or the supper Araksi proposed. I could hear Hrant and the Hartunians talking excitedly in the kitchen after I was in bed, but that did not stop me from falling into a deep, dreamless sleep. I woke with a start, not sure where I was, then sank again into sleep, but this time it was troubled by visions. More like a gallery of images than a dream: Mayrig, Krikor, Halim, baby Garo, Shoushan and, finally, Karakurt, each one appearing from the darkness and looking at me for a moment, then fading. None spoke except with their eyes. With Karakurt's grim face alone, there was a sound: the horrible, haunting sound of women shrieking. I woke again in a sweat, and when I had shaken off the visions, tried to conjure up Shoushan's face as I had last seen it. I felt again the same pain of separation I had felt on leaving her behind in Port Said. But not quite the same: her face had grown slightly out of focus during the almost three years we had been apart, the pain a little less sharp.

When I emerged from the bedroom, it was broad daylight, nearly ten o'clock according to my watch. Abraham had stayed home to see me. 'Vartan, you know that you can stay with us as long as you wish. I should tell you that Hrant came back a little while ago, to say that there was a rumour circulating of a solitary young Christian seen walking up and down past the *chetes'* house shortly before the fire. No one seemed to be actively searching, but news travels like the telegraph in Smyrna; as soon as one Greek or Turk, or Armenian for that matter, hears a rumour, all the others know it. I think you should avoid walking around alone. There will be crowds on the Cordon in the afternoon, the city is expecting the arrival of an Entente fleet, probably French and British and possibly Greek or even American warships. This would be the first such visit since the war began, and the Smyrniotes are in a state of excitement.'

I had an uneasy feeling, knowing that I might be identified as the solitary prowler. I felt no fear for myself: my mission was accomplished, and it would not make much difference to me or to anyone.

But I did not want to endanger my hosts. 'Abraham, thank you for the offer. However, I do not want to linger here. I'll try to make my way back to Aleppo, though I also ought to try and get to Port Said. Probably Aleppo makes more sense as it is on the railway. Yes, Aleppo first and, if at all possible, today.'

'If you do want to buy a train ticket,' Abraham said, 'I suggest you go to the agency down at the port, not the station, which is full of spies and informers. Vahram can take you into the city; two young men will not attract attention, especially as there will be lots of people around. You can leave your things here and pick them up on the way to the station, if you find a place on this afternoon's train. Or, better still, come a bit early and have something to eat and a rest before your journey.'

Araksi had put a plate of cheese, olives and bread out for me. I ate without appetite, to please her. When I finished, Vahram and I walked down the hill into town. He was talking but my mind was full of foreboding about the return journey on the train, questions about what I would find when I got to Aleppo. On the way out here I felt I was travelling through a landscape full of ghosts; now I was bringing my own with me. I was still vacillating about where I ought to go first. I had no idea how to get from here to Port Said. So I would start with Aleppo, if the trains were still running and if I could get myself a ticket without arousing suspicion.

We walked the length of Frank Street into the European residential quarter. Vahram sensed my grim frame of mind and tried to distract me with conversation. We passed ornate mansions, walking on clean pavements while expensive carriages and motorcars went by, horses' hooves and wheels clattering on the paving stones. After half an hour or so we found ourselves on the Point, the extremity of the city, which gave us a clear view of the port, the quays, and the segregated residential areas, each on its hill, more or less, according to Vahram. I could make out the towers of St Stepanos, the imposing hotels of the Cordon. Beyond all that, the more familiar-looking, lower houses of the Turks, spreading up the minaret-punctuated hill to the south. The Caravan Bridge and, as I imagined, the charred, maybe still smoking ruins of a house with a grisly secret, lay out of sight, somewhere on a hill across the river. I listened to Vahram absent-mindedly. Yesterday seemed far away; one phase of my life had closed. What lay ahead for me was a complete blank and I felt entirely indifferent to it.

Suddenly Vahram exclaimed, 'Look! Here they come! At least two, maybe three, big ships!' There indeed were the ships, three long grey shapes gradually emerging from the haze, heading into the Bay of Smyrna from the Aegean. I could not help but think of that day on Musa Dagh. We walked quickly back along the seafront into town, to find the Cordon packed with excited people from all of Smyrna's communities. There were fewer Turks than others, and those who were there clearly did not share in the general exhilaration. Fantastic rumours circulated among the excited crowd: the British will occupy the city. The Greeks will annex it. The Greeks and Italians will fight for it. The Russians have occupied Constantinople. The ships turned out to be two French and one British, come to show their flags, to reassure the local Europeans who were known to be worried about the future.

On approaching the roadstead, it was possible to see the names of the two French ships, their tricolour flags waving gently in the soft breeze. The British flag, which they call the Union Jack, was clearly visible on the other, much smaller ship, except that for some reason it had a blue background rather than the red one on HMS *Anne*. I could not make out its name. It was very different from HMS *Anne*, but neither was it a proper warship. I wondered if I could possibly talk my way on to it and out of Smyrna; I resolved to try and accost any British sailors who might come ashore.

The three ships dropped anchor in the bay, and soon were launching their boats, steam tenders chugging ashore with nattily uniformed officers and sailors from the French ships. The British one launched a rowing tender, much slower than the others but the uniforms were just as splendid. As they arrived, the crowd on the Cordon made a great fuss. The French consul greeted his country-men ceremoniously. Vahram pointed out the English consul: 'That's Charles Whittall, head of the English community, but born and bred in Smyrna.' I watched as a tall man dressed in some sort of formal European attire solemnly greeted the British crew and officers when they finally disembarked.

I pushed my way through the crowd to get a closer look and managed to get the attention of one of the sailors. 'What is that British ship and who commands her?' I asked in my crispest English. Before he could answer, one of the officers noticed me and waved me over.

'Well hello there, young Armenian! Isn't your name Varkan or something like that? Don't tell me you have forgotten old O'Neill, *Anne*'s bosun, now of course on *Managem* out there. Where have you been these three years or so? We thought you'd copped it back then! You'd better come with us: old Weldie will be chuffed as pie to see you again!'

'O'Neill! Of course I remember you – I'm just surprised to meet you here! It's Vartan, by the way. But did you say "Weldie"? You don't mean Captain Weldon?'

The burly bosun laughed: 'Vartan, of course! I do indeed, Weldon himself! He now commands Her Majesty's Yacht *Managem*, with Captain Smith at the helm. It's that small but elegant vessel you see in the bay, more seaworthy than HMS *Anne*. She's done mighty useful service during these last two years of the war. Will you come back aboard with us when we've finished our duties here? What are you up to in Smyrna, young man?'

'Ah,' I replied almost too quickly, 'that would be very kind of you. I accept with pleasure, and will be happy to see the captain again. However, I do have one bit of business to attend to, could I meet you back here at the quay in an hour from now?'

'That will do nicely, young Vartan – though actually you look a lot less young than you did the last time I saw you. Do be on time as we'll shove off in just over an hour.'

I hurried up the hill towards the Hartunians' house, making Vahram quite out of breath which I was glad of, as that way he could not ask me the questions I knew were on his mind about me and the English. Abraham and Araksi were surprised to see us back so soon, in such a rush. There was the problem of clothes. Araksi had washed mine and they were still drying in the sun outside the kitchen door, looking white and clean and innocent. Abraham said, 'Go, Vartan, you keep my clothes and I'll, ah, keep yours. God protect you and if you ever come back to Smyrna, our home is yours.'

Just before going out the door, I pulled the bag of coins from my pocket, the one I had taken off the just-dead Karakurt the night before. 'I don't know how much this is, Father, but please use it to help our people.' The priest's arm stayed by his side. 'It is my family's money, Father, stolen by those murderers. On my honour, it is not dirty.' Before Abraham could say anything, I had put the purse in his hand and started off towards the port. As I hurried down the hill, with the portly Vahram still puffing along behind, I remembered that I had never even looked in the bag, did not know what sort of coins or how many it contained. I assumed from the weight that it was gold, Hovsep's gold, at least I hoped it was and that I had salvaged a little bit of it for a worthy cause.

I said goodbye to the winded Vahram on the quay. 'Are you sure you'll be leaving with that ship? Why would they take you, Vartan?'

'I know them well, Vahram: it's the same captain and crew who saved some of us from Musa Dagh. Don't worry, if they don't take me I'll come back and buy a ticket for the first train to Aleppo; if it's tomorrow I'll spend the night in one of these hotels. Thank you, and please thank Abraham and Araksi for all they've done.'

After the brief trip out to the ship, I climbed the ladder up to the gunwale and stepped aboard. Weldon was on deck observing the boat's return and when he saw me, he barely saved his pipe from falling out of his mouth. 'Well, I'll be damned! He's not only alive, he's all grown up! Vartan, old chap, I couldn't be happier to see you! Let me debrief these fellows on their trip ashore. You can wait here or go down to the officers' mess; there are one or two others who will be as glad to see you as I am!'

I stayed on deck, watching the last motor launch making its way back to the French mother ship. The crowds were still thronging the Cordon, with British, French and Greek flags waving. 'But Smyrna is still an Ottoman town,' I mused. 'Surely this is a strange sight. I wonder if the Allies have any idea of the passions they are stirring up by their meddling?' Just then Weldon came looking for me and interrupted that train of thought. He led me straight to his cabin. Little had changed in almost three years; a different ship, this one he called a yacht, but with none of the visible luxuries I would have imagined. He had arranged his cabin just as it was on *Anne*: a plywood partition covered with maps, the maps decorated with scribbles.

I told him my story: the betrayal, Halim's arrest, the escape to Nisibin, the missed rendezvous and the more than two years in the desert. Ortalli, the return to Aleppo, the horrible discovery. The long train journey to Smyrna. I hesitated about telling him what I did to the *chetes*. 'I was lucky in a way, Captain. I found the wretches who destroyed my family and was fortunate, if you can call it that, in being able to exact revenge.' Weldon's right eyebrow arched, a tell-tale sign of interest that I had learned to read a long time ago.

'I suspect there is a good story there. Hopefully there'll be time. But dear God, what a tragedy you had to bear. I am terribly sorry, and afraid that your association with us may have been responsible. I suppose we'll never know. However, this is – or was – war, and life must go on. Will you sail with us?'

'Well, I must admit it would be, ah, somewhat convenient for me to be able to leave Smyrna without delay, or at least without going ashore again.' Weldon laughed his signature bark.

'Now I'm *sure* there's a story lurking. But I can wait, at least until tonight. This evening we sail for Beirut; you can come with us at least that far. The days when I could just cruise up and down, dropping and retrieving – or not – agents are behind us. Now it's peacetime, sort of, and I take orders. Mainly to show the flag here and there along with the Froggy ships, saves them having to spare a proper ship of the line. Would Beirut suit, or still too close for comfort?'

'No, Beirut would be perfect, Captain.' Weldon lit his pipe; I lit a cigarette.

'Ah, I see you've finally picked up this wretched habit. Anyway, now, Vartan, I'd like you to tell me more about what happened in late '15 or early '16, don't remember which, when you were supposed to return in three weeks, or was it two? Anyway, I think I can guess what happened; tell me what it looked like from your end, and I'll tell you what I know.' I told him the details: my uneventful walk from the coast, finding the police had raided the house, were looking for me.

'Beyond that, I don't know very much for sure. But the fact they had a warrant in my name made me suspect the Druze rope seller.'

Weldon puffed, then removed the pipe and said, 'You are not wrong in that. I regret terribly not having seen through him earlier. I ought to have suspected when that chap Ibrahim sank without trace, but I didn't want to believe that Hamadi was a traitor, at least not until you disappeared too. We sent him a test signal, which he promptly betrayed to the Turks. You will not find any Hamadi, father or son, selling rope in the souk, or anyplace else, I fear. But the harm is done, to you and your family and to Ibrahim before you, and to our intelligence operation. Not our finest hour, certainly not mine.'

I reflected on this for a moment, remembering how I had been inclined to trust the Druze, partly guided by my father's ideas about them. 'Hovsep was lucky, not to have seen what I saw. For that, however, I cannot blame the captain, nor the Druze, nor even the Turks. No one to blame but myself.'

Weldon smoked in silence for a while, his eyes straying towards me from time to time; I could tell he was thinking about me, perhaps wondering if he ought to say something. Then he said, 'Vartan, do you remember those two Jewish agents, Sarah and Yussuf, we dropped at Athlit while you were aboard?'

'Ah, yes, of course I do, I thought *she* was, er, remarkable.'

'I remember you did. And who wouldn't have? There was a lot to like, and there was more to Yussuf than met the eye. Bad news, I'm afraid. When the Turks realised the war was lost, they pulled out of coastal Palestine, a sort of scorched-earth tactic. They destroyed the agricultural research station that had been so useful during the locust plague. If you believe the gossip, they even ate the carrier pigeons and laboratory rabbits. Sarah's brother Aaron insisted on raising them for his research into the various endemic diseases of this area, against a lot of opposition from the chaps with curly sideburns. Not kosher, you see. Well, they allegedly ate the rabbits too, and I hope they acquired some rotten viruses. But the worst is poor Sarah. An informer told them she was our spy and they tortured her over several days. She never told them a thing, but did manage to grab a gun from a policeman and shoot herself.'

'Oh! Damn their eyes!' I said, stunned. 'But who could be surprised at anything they would do? And Yussuf?'

'After Sarah's death, he was hunted like a dog from village to village. Finally, they said they would kill all the Jews in one unless he gave himself up, which he did. They hanged him along with several others. Knowing the war was lost, they had nothing to gain except revenge.' That night I had dreams of beautiful blonde hair, of voluptuous lips and a generous body in a cotton shift, then woke up in a fretful sweat, horrified to be lusting after a dead woman.

For twenty-four hours, life on shipboard took on its familiar texture. I was made much of by the officers and sailors who had been on board three years ago, and by the Egyptian cook, who embraced me with sweaty affection. As the ship headed west towards

Beirut, I stood at my usual place on the bow, my face turned to the late October wind, offshore for once, dousing me with occasional dashes of salt spray. A sailor came to say the captain had invited me to the bridge.

Weldon wanted to know my plans. I looked at him blankly, unconsciously adjusting my glasses. 'Frankly, I have been so knocked about by events lately that I don't have any. I will need to get back to Aleppo at some point, to see about the young boy I told you about, Garabed. There's not much else for me there. I would dearly love to know what happened to the refugee family I went to see in Port Said, if you remember.'

'Vaguely,' said the captain. 'I'm afraid I can't take you to Port Said. After Beirut, we're being sent across to Athens. Apparently, the Allies are going to allow the Greek army to occupy Smyrna and its province and we are to ferry some of them. Not a very alluring prospect, I am afraid, and not very sound policy. If anything can get the Turks to come together and fight, it is the idea of a Greek army on Anatolian soil. However, orders are orders. As you may know, Beirut and the Lebanon, even Syria as far as the Euphrates, are to be occupied by the French. They have already set up a bureau in Beirut, which I think they hope to turn into a Governor General's setup. We also have a man there and, if you like, I could give you a letter of introduction to him. No more nocturnal assignations on remote beaches, more like an office job, clerk or translator or something. Of interest?'

'Of course!' I exclaimed – the first thought I had had about the future, my future, in a while. 'That would be really helpful. But does that mean that Aleppo will be under French control?'

'Yes, indeed, old chap. You have been out of touch with the news for a while, haven't you? If you ask me, a lot of things will change between drawing lines on a map and making the ambitions of empires and their petty officials chime with the lives and aspirations of people on the ground. I think some bullets still need to fly here and there, and Lord knows where or when people will be able to live in peace. The Ottoman state is collapsing, all right, but the Turks are still there. As you know all too well, the Levant is like a mosaic, with very little mortar holding the pieces in place.'

I sighed. 'It's true, whenever we have believed something good, or at least less bad, *might* be coming, events came along first and made fools of us. I am, or was, one of the worst for misplaced optimism. And far too trusting.'

A few hours later, as the sun set far away to the south-west, the *Managem* was anchored in St George Bay, off Beirut. A picturesque place, I thought, but so much smaller than I had imagined: not much more than an overgrown village, whitewashed houses with red stone roofs covering the hills rising up from the port. Beyond the town, the pine-covered mountains rose up majestically, the highest mountains I had seen, higher even than the Taurus chain I had crossed on the train. Church steeples here, minarets there, everything spoke of a mixed society, much more so than Aleppo. I recognised the clock tower of the Syrian Protestant College, the American missionary university on the seafront south of the city, which I had seen on postcards.

'What will *you* do, Captain?'

'Well, that's a good question. I've been in Egypt for fifteen years, and now almost four on these two old tubs. I have no desire to return to that cold and sodden island in the north. So, it's up to them. If they will keep me in Egypt, I'll happily go back to my job as Surveyor General. If I'm judged too long in the tooth, or if they need to find a job for a younger bloke, then who knows? Maybe I'll travel around a bit, see what some of these countries look like from the dry land, while there are still troops on the ground to keep the lid on things. A visit to Eliezer is always stimulating, and he's not getting any younger. Might come to see you in Beirut or Aleppo. Or wherever it is you end up!'

'That I cannot guess, either. But I would be more than happy to see you again, Captain. I wish you well and will never forget your kindness.'

'Hmm,' growled Weldon. 'Kindness that almost got you killed. But I wish you well, too, Vartan. You never told me exactly what you did to those heathens who murdered your family. Perhaps when it has receded in time a bit, you will feel more like talking, the next time we meet, as I hope we will. Meanwhile, Randall will take you ashore, and I'm sure my old friend Rawlinson will find something for you to do.'

The launch was lowered into the water. Weldon held my hand longer than just the standard English handshake. 'This is goodbye, for a bit at least. I've enjoyed knowing you, I must say. I do hope our paths will cross again. There's something about you I like. You take life as it comes, but put up a good fight when it does you a nasty turn. And no whining about it.' He paused a moment, as though deciding whether to continue. He cleared his throat. 'Thing is, you see, I don't have a son. Not much chance I'll have one at this stage. I don't mean to insult you – I know you're not a boy any more. But if I *did* have one, I wouldn't mind a bit if he turned out like you.'

I would never have dared express my feelings to the very English captain, even if I had succeeded in fully articulating them in my own mind. I felt that old sense of guilt towards the memory of my father. I was too moved to say anything, I just met his eye, with my own fighting to stay dry. And was glad when Randall said, 'Launch ready to board, sir!'

10

Beirut: May 1985

*A*MERICA! *What is it about America? So many of us have gone there. Bedros and Garabed and Minas have retired in Malibu, wherever that is, California I think, after spawning families. Minas apparently married an American and made a fortune selling sporting goods to those tanned half-naked blonde nitwits one sees on the television, unless that is Hawaii. They make a big deal over his lost leg and call him a 'war hero'. They all keep writing to say, 'Come, join us, with all our grandchildren you have more relatives out here than back in that godforsaken killing ground you insist on thinking of as "home". Can't you see there is no future there?'*

Well, today I might be forgiven for agreeing with them. The press is full of enthusiasm for some piece of paper the Americans and Israelis have made us, that is the Lebanese, sign. Empty words, as though there were any shortage of those around here. Now Israel will withdraw claiming 'mission accomplished', and things will go right back to where they were a year ago, only this time I think the 'Progressive' forces will go for the kill.

What is it about our countries? Maybe five hundred years of Ottoman rule have made us irretrievably, congenitally incapable of living sensibly. Maybe Dashti was right to try and wake them up. Anyway, it is not our century, that's for sure. There are Armenians who left Cilicia for Jerusalem in 1920 or 1922; then in 1967, they lost their homes again; and I know of a few of them who came here, thinking Beirut had so much to offer – what it offered was war and, for some, the road to yet another exile. But Lebanon was pleasant while it lasted. People of different religions living peaceably together, most

219

of the time; making money and enjoying life in this sunny Mediterranean tax haven. Now they are huddled in bomb shelters with their terrified grand-children, unless they have managed to get a visa to somewhere. I'm sure America would sound wonderful to them, but Mr Kissinger's sympathy does not extend to taking in the victims – the collateral damage – of his policies.

So there they are, and here I am. Every night it starts up again, the cannons ringing the city from the hills fire down on us like shooting fish in a barrel. Every morning it goes quiet again and, in this neighbourhood at least, there are people out there busily sweeping up broken glass, clear-ing up rubbish and burned cars, not to mention the odd corpse – a fighter dumped by the other side, or an unfortunate pedestrian who got in the way of a sniper's bullet or a piece of shrapnel. At midday the shops are full of people: at Dfouni's you can choose the year of your Dom Pérignon, but a kilo of tomatoes costs twenty times what it used to, before they ruined our currency. By sundown everybody is huddled again, watching the lying politicians or canned nonsense on television if there is electricity, trying to get the children to sleep before the cannons open up again. Some are making a fortune from all this, like their grandfathers did during the '14 –'18 war.

So this is where it led me, all those years, all that hullabaloo about making money, moving to Aleppo, then Tehran, London for a bit, Tehran again after the business went bust, making another fortune: taste of ashes, with her gone. Moving here thinking to come 'home', to 'our' part of the world, the familiar climate and food and mix of languages. Roots. And now all turned to dust.

    afsus ke bi gah

    Alas, time has passed and we are alone
    In a sea without a shore in sight
    The ship, the night, the chill and we sail
    In the sea of God, by God's wisdom and grace

How I wish Dashti were here! Poor Dashti. The only person in the world who would understand what Rumi meant by 'wisdom and grace'. Only he's gone over to the other side, through the veil at last: who or what did he find there? I am sure he would have got in touch if there was a way, ha! It was always hard to shut him up; and hopefully he is holding forth somewhere. In the company of Rumi and Hafez, if there is any justice.

How sharp the pain still is, Mayrig and Krikor and Halim. Anahit. Pain and guilt, guilt for not protecting them, guilt for the innocent blood I shed, which my poor dear ones would not have wanted. And her of course! How differently life turns out from what one imagines. We loved each other so much, each in our own way. And hurt each other. I blame myself mostly, so obsessed with the fight for money and success and status, and it was a fight, sometimes a war. I got used to winning all right, but what's left to show for it?

She must have been so lonely. That's when she got into her own brand of mysticism, Madame Blavatsky, Ouspensky's cosmic crap, finally the Rosicrucians. That was the last straw as far as I was concerned: just so much gloomy waffle. I told her too roughly, what need was there to hurt her? She was just looking for consolation. And then there was Maria, her head firmly on her creamy shoulders. I wish I could convince myself she did not know about Maria. She would not have understood that it was not about love, or sex – well, not entirely – but companionship, laughs, someone lively and funny to be with. And God knows Maria was that. But she was not the love of my life. Why do things have to be so complicated?

And then. Alone, a suffocating feeling of utter desolation, of a world bereft of life and love and youth and hope. That recurrent dream with me calling to her in a wilderness, a bitter wind carrying away my cries, menacing darkness all around. I tried to paint it, a desolate landscape I called 'No one There'. Nothing left but despair and regret, once the curtain has dropped.

az jumle-ye raftegan

Many have made their way along this long long road
Not a single one came back to tell us where it leads;
There's nothing here below save avarice and want,
So leave naught undone – once gone, you're gone.

11

Beirut: November 1918

I N THE PORT, I asked directions to the General Administration of
Occupied Enemy Territory, the address on my letter. Everyone
I asked looked absolutely blank. Finally, some sort of clerk
said, 'Ah! *Al-maktab al-askari al-ingleezi!*' And so off to the 'English
Military Office' I went, walking uphill through a pleasant Christian

neighbourhood of square houses with red roofs, shaded by cypresses and fruit trees in walled gardens, and further up through a more aristocratic-looking quarter, with pretentious palaces to rival those in Smyrna. Then I crossed a poor Muslim neighbourhood, which led to the central square called Burj, or 'tower', though I saw no tower. I was amazed at all the locals in European dress, even more so than in Smyrna. The Beirutis, Christian and Muslim, seemed to be trying to outdo one another in Westernisation. There were signs advertising nightclubs and hotels, with what I thought were daring posters of European-looking women. There were only a few people in Turkish or country dress, except a few Druze that I recognised by their baggy trousers and white kepis or turbans. I thought of Hamadi, but something told me he was a lot further away than just Beirut. Here, the average woman in the street was not veiled, with a few exceptions; in Aleppo, the opposite was true.

The English Military Office consisted of three or four rooms on an arcaded street further to the south, near the jewellers' souk. I asked for Major Rawlinson, and was told to wait. I showed the envelope I was carrying, its Royal Navy seal most likely helping to facilitate things; after half an hour, I was invited into an office with files and papers piled on the floor, obviously waiting for shelves or cabinets that had not yet arrived. The major was a tall, almost gaunt man, with thick glasses, busily sorting files and papers. 'An office soldier,' I thought, 'not a practical, active one, like Weldon.'

'My name is Vartan Nakashian, Major. I have worked for Captain Lawrence Weldon in the past, and he sends you this letter to recommend my services, should you have any need.'

Rawlinson stopped his shuffling of papers, looked at me, then down at the envelope, frowning as he opened it, and read the letter. He looked up with a smile. 'Well, young man, he recommends you very highly. Very highly indeed. What he may not realise, however, is that we are only here in a very temporary way. The Froggies will govern Lebanon, along with Syria, if they can. We have garrisons here and there, sort of where the boys were when the Turks gave up fighting. But this is to be French territory: any work with us would be short, to say the least. I'm not even sure if it is worth my while, getting the files sorted and all that. But one has to try and keep a semblance of order.

'I hate to give you the runaround, but really the best thing I can do for you is to send you with a recommendation to Colonel de la Villatte, Philippe is his name. A real soldier apparently, not a paper-pusher like me or like most of the French they are sending out here. A count of some kind, as the rumours have it. They seem to think this will be like administering Senegal; and as for us Brits, we can only think of saving money and demobbing our people as fast as we can.

'You probably haven't had time to notice the terrible state this country is in. We have promised to do what we can to help get things working again, but it is to be a French show, with us bowing out, stage left, as soon as we can decently do so. De la Villatte and his people have a huge amount of work on their hands, and little time: they have to win the hearts of the people away from this idea of one Arab kingdom including Syria, Iraq and Palestine. Colonel Lawrence has let them believe in it, for the purposes of the Arab Revolt, as it's called. Good tactics, bad long-term strategy. I assume you speak French?'

'Not that well. My English is much better, sir, but I get by.' Rawlinson wrote out a long note to the French colonel and handed it to me.

'I expect you will find many more interesting things to do over there. If not, come back to see me. Weldon says you performed some delicate missions for him, and some dangerous ones, where you acquitted yourself with credit. I regret not to have more going on at this time. Not sorry the war is over, of course, but... The French HQ is, naturally enough, in the old Turkish *vali*'s palace, now called the Petit Saray, not far from here: back to Burj and down the hill. Good luck, young Nakashian.'

I felt disheartened as I walked back across the centre of the city. I was not sure Weldon would have approved of my being shunted off on some Frenchman. The captain, I knew, had a lot of respect for French line officers and fighting men. I thought of de Saizeu and the other pilots of the reccy planes, who would always make a supreme effort to take off in their flimsy, under-powered seaplanes, even in bad weather. But he had little time for the political types. Then again, Rawlinson had said de la Villatte was a 'real soldier'.

The Frenchman was dressed in a uniform so impeccable that I wondered how much of a 'real soldier' he actually was, despite the rack of multi-coloured medals across his chest. He was a handsome, middle-aged man with the clipped moustache and proud bearing of what I imagined to be a French aristocrat, or perhaps someone posing as one. He received me cordially and asked me about my background, testing my French, which he must have found less than satisfactory. I had learned the rudiments at school in Aleppo and benefited a little from Mayrig's knowledge of the language and her fervent desire that I learn it; Ortalli had also tried his best, with modest success. The result was that I could understand most of what I heard, but spoke haltingly – with a thick English accent, oddly enough.

'We have a difficult task,' he began, 'establishing an administration in a country where our presence is ardently desired by part of the population, the Christians and especially the Maronites, and rejected by all but the elite of the Muslims. Despite your rustic French, I like the fact that you are not local. The Maronites may speak better French, or think they do, but they all seem to have an axe to grind, a cousin to employ. I will assign you to work as drago-man for me personally. Not being French, but a Syrian national, you will of course be paid a local salary. We have plenty of people who speak French and Arabic, of course, but you speak English as well and that should prove useful as we try to coordinate our activities with those of our departing British colleagues. Your Armenian and Turkish might serve as well, as I will explain.

'There are, as you can imagine, refugees from the deportations, and they include hundreds, even thousands, of orphans. The Turks tried to force the surviving children, the ones who did not get taken into Muslim families, into orphanages which they set up, where the children would be raised as Turkish-speaking Muslims. Over a thousand were brought here. They are being housed in two or three facilities, mostly at the former French college at Aintoura. This was set up by Jemal Pasha in person, as a centre for Turkifying and Islamising Armenian orphans.

'That is but one example of a priority matter. You will work for me personally when I require it, otherwise I will assign you to accompany my colleagues when they have sensitive missions that require your languages and, from what I read here, your tact and common sense. We have so much to do! The inhabitants, especially on the mountain, are hungry, with rampant diseases of all kinds. The banking system is broken. The roads are in a pitiful state. The political situation is in limbo while we try to agree with our British friends how to reconcile the aspirations of the Arabs with the region's need for stable government, which only a mandatory power like France – *only France,* in fact – is in a position to provide. Do you have any questions?'

'*Non, mon colonel,*' I answered, 'except that if I could have housing, as part of my employment, that would be very convenient. As you know I am not from Beirut and do not know anyone here.'

'That will not be a problem, provided you don't object to military accommodation. You can stay in the barracks here in the town centre, which is convenient as it is close to my office and, indeed, to my own quarters. And by the way, I would like you to give me and my family lessons in Arabic, if you would be so kind.' Without waiting to hear whether I would be so kind, or not, the colonel rang for an orderly and asked for me to be billeted in the Non-Commissioned

Officers' Barracks and my details recorded in the rolls of the Mission, as they referred to their organisation.

The colonel was right about there being a lot to do. It was like reinventing a government – in fact, a country. Five hundred years of Ottoman rule had melted away in the space of a few weeks, leaving deeply ingrained attitudes, habits and prejudices. Now General Gouraud was going to rule Lebanon and Syria, a majority Muslim region, and the general was known to be a devout, committed Christian without any experience of our region. I wondered how that was all going to work out.

There were several other Armenians working as clerks or drago-men for the nascent French administration, and from them I heard the news from Cilicia. Many of the surviving deportees had tried to go back to their villages, their farms and houses. They found them occupied. The French garrisons in the area could not – or would not – cope with the resulting unrest. According to one colleague who had been home to Aintab, the troops were badly supplied and badly commanded. They shared garrison duty with undisciplined Franco-Armenian troops who paraded in their French uniforms and insulted the Turks at every opportunity; I wondered whether Minas might have managed at last to join up. The region was a tinderbox; the end of the war had definitely not solved the 'Armenian problem'.

As soon as I was settled into the routine of my job, I began to worry about Garo, about whom I had had no news since the day I discovered the catastrophe. I asked if I could take a few days off and visit Aleppo; only after six months' service, I was told. The Postes Ottomanes had ceased operation, the new postal service of the French Mandate was not yet operational and I was therefore not able even to write. A colleague from Idlib was going on leave and I asked him to take some money to Sitt Sarah and to bring back news; the fellow returned with the money, apologising for not having found the house during the few hours he had in Aleppo. Intensely frustrated, I threw myself into my work.

I found myself one day accompanying financial experts who were trying to revive the banking system. The next day up on the mountain, that is Mount Lebanon, talking to silkworm growers, mulberry tree owners and weavers, as well as the owners of the silk factories they called *magnaneries*, all of whom needed to coordinate their activities in order to revive what had once been the principal economic activity of the Mountain. Then it was recruiting the labour needed to repair the roads and then to continue the Ottoman plan of road building, which had been abandoned with almost none of the roads completed to the extent that one could actually get anywhere.

And there was the orphanage at Aintoura. These visits were the hardest part for me, emotionally, but also the most rewarding. About seven hundred small children, between the ages of four and nine, all having lost their parents and siblings, their homes and native land. The Turks more or less abandoned the institution and children, once the outcome of the war began to be predictable. Now, with the return of Father Sarlout and other, mostly Armenian, teachers, their Armenian identities and names were steadily being restored.

Some of the volunteer teachers and nurses at the orphanage were from the local Armenian Red Cross Society. I asked one of the nurses whether they had any contacts with their sister organisation in Egypt, which she said they did. The next time I came to Aintoura, I brought a letter addressed to Shoushan at the Port Said Armenian Refugee Facility, care of Mr Artin Bedrossian. The nurse promised to send it with the next person from their group who visited Egypt, which she expected within the month. I felt strange writing to her after so long. I hesitated to tell her what had happened to Mayrig, Krikor and Anahit, and could not bring myself to put such news in a letter. I finally decided not to mention them rather than lie. So it was not much of a letter.

There was one part of my duties that really disturbed me at first:

the requirement that I teach Arabic to the colonel and his family. The colonel was too busy to attend more than the occasional lesson, which were held twice a week. His wife Denise was more interested, at first. She was an elegant Frenchwoman of about forty, a well-meaning soul who wanted to learn the language so that she could be of use to the women and children of the country. Of course, it turned out that most of her contacts with the local people were with the excessively Francophone elite, so she was not encouraged actually to do very much about that noble inclination. The Christian children did not need her well-meaning assistance; and the Muslims did not want it. But she persevered for a while.

My only prior experiences of teaching were my improvised effort with young Bedros, what seemed like ages ago, in another universe; and teaching Arabic grammar to Ortalli, which required little effort because of the quick mind and enthusiasm of the Florentine. At first I was quite daunted by the idea of teaching these French people. I soon realised that to succeed, I had to develop a method, and that method is just a matter of logic, of taking things in logical order: letters, then sounds, then words for the written language; basic phrases and idioms for the colloquial Levantine dialect, which is spoken in the kitchens, streets and souks. They did not need to parse the Quran.

My other pupil was their daughter Maude, about a year younger than me. And Maude is what continued to disturb me, even after I got the hang of teaching. She was like a miniature, fresher version of her mother: fine features, long, silky dark-blonde hair, blue-grey eyes setting off to perfection her creamy complexion. She had a coquettish temperament and no interest whatsoever in learning this odd language with the squiggles and pronunciation so harsh she said it made Spanish sound melodious. But she was drawn to one aspect of her Arabic lessons, and that was, I discovered to my discomfort, *me*. I could feel an animal attraction emanating from her. Every fibre of my own body reciprocated it. Not my mind, or my heart, particularly. But in her presence, as she did not take long to notice, *je perdais le nord*, I forgot which way was north as she said whenever I blushed or stammered. She made fun of my French, and she even made fun of my Arabic: 'How could anyone be expected to pronounce a sound like "ayn": *on dirait un cochon qui baille!* It sounds like a yawning pig!'

While I was busy translating for the French and working on my lesson plan for the family, the news from Cilicia went from bad to worse. Another colleague had tried to go home to Erzurum and was turned back at Harput, asked by the French for a military pass to enter the area. No one in Beirut had warned him he would need such a thing; maybe they did not even know. The elaborate administrative charts on the wall looked impressive, but often had little to do with the situation on the ground. He said there was growing unrest in Turkey proper and the French were anxious to withdraw their troops. If the Armenians were hated before for supposedly being disloyal to the Sultan, those still alive on Turkish soil were hated just as much. Now their crime was not being Turks – and having survived while the Empire perished.

I was concerned about the fate of those Armenians who had somehow managed to return to their homes, or were trying to, thinking that the French would protect them. No one could accuse me of not caring. But... more and more, my thoughts were drawn to the scented, dark-blonde tresses of the girl named Maude, especially when her father's business and her mother's increasingly intensive social life left us alone for the space of a lesson. We worked in the dining room of the Résidence des Pins, an elegant arcaded villa overlooking Beirut's ancient pine forest. I had never been in such a house before: the dining-room was panelled, with tall windows overlooking the forest and the sea beyond, precious carpets on the floor and a mahogany table polished like a mirror by the army of servants. A smell of furniture wax and lavender seemed to permeate everything.

But my attention was elsewhere: the girl with eyes the colour of mother of pearl, eyes which quickened my pulse and breathing when I was sitting across the table from her. Her effect on me was even more powerful when I came around the table to sit next to her, in order to show her how to form a certain combination of Arabic letters. Then her scent, her breath, sweet and warm as that of a kitten, the occasional – but, even *I* could tell, not accidental – brushing of her hand on mine or bumping of knees and her warm closeness all combined to fuddle my brain. Even if I had completely kept my wits about me, the boyish blushes I hoped I had left behind on reaching manhood made a spectacular return, providing the impish girl with another excuse to poke fun at me.

As the weeks went by, I found the lessons more and more of a trial, but one I looked forward to. I stammered when explaining simple concepts. The colonel and Madame hardly ever attended, as they became increasingly caught up in the social whirl of the capital of the French Mandate of Syria and Lebanon, as Beirut had become. When they did show up for class, they were hopelessly behind Maude, who was clever enough, and my improvised teaching method effective enough, to be actually making progress, almost involuntarily. The parents soon gave up altogether.

Then came a day in late spring, at the beginning of May. I arrived for the lesson at ten o'clock in the morning, with a sheaf of papers to translate under my arm, to find Maude dressed in tweed skirt and jacket for a country outing, looking her loveliest with the slightest blush (real or artificial, I did not know) setting off her hair and complexion to marvellous effect. '*Pas de classe aujourd'hui, mon cher*! We are going to the country! Boutros has had a picnic made and Selim will drive us in Papa's car to the Fleuve du Chien!'

'But,' I objected, 'I'm on duty today, I have these papers to translate, and after the class I'm to report to the finance office to assist with a bank inspection…'

'All cleared with the colonel, *cher professeur*. He thinks it is an excellent idea to go walking in nature on such a day and your services are not required other than to escort me on a picnic, if that is not too abhorrent a duty!'

We motored up the coastal road in the colonel's magnificent open Panhard staff car. When we crossed the bridge and stopped at a convenient place for climbing up the north bank of the river, Maude told me to wait a bit. She took Selim aside, put on her most charming face and told him something I couldn't hear. I could hear Selim's voice loud and clear, saying, 'That is impossible, Mademoiselle Maude, I have the colonel's clear and specific instructions not to leave you alone for a moment. He would never allow such a thing. I would lose my job if he found out!' She kept at him, and her determination, self-assurance and charm – together with some coins I saw her discreetly put in his palm – got the better of his scruples. The car pulled away and we were alone in the beautiful springtime of Mount Lebanon. I carried the picnic basket, Maude her bag and the rolled-up coverlet which was to serve as ground cover and tablecloth. She had brought her father's *Baedeker* for Syria (which included Lebanon) and Palestine. Once we got up on the hill looking across at the south bank of the river, we stopped and read about the numerous stelae we could see carved on the cliff face just opposite.

I had heard about the Dog River, and had resolved to walk up there one weekend, so the duty would not have been abhorrent, even if I had been less distracted by Maude's tresses. Having admired the inscriptions, we climbed up the hill until we had a panoramic view of the Mediterranean, with the Bay of Jounieh to the north and St George Bay further south. The roadstead was gleaming silver in the late morning sun, punctuated by ships swinging to anchor as they waited for a berth in the port.

Finally, after an hour or so, Maude said she was out of breath and thought we should find a place for a rest and lunch. A level space between two almond trees, where the wildflowers formed a frothy carpet about six inches deep. We still had a view down to the coast, but were shielded from the breeze (and importunate eyes) by an old stone wall just behind, one of those forgotten crumbling walls that decorate the mountain like tracery. Maude set about officiously arranging the tablecloth and picnic while I stood stupidly by, watching her fuss, fighting the beginnings of a blush. Her busy work finished, Maude took off her jacket and sat on the coverlet, straightened out her skirt and patted the space near her. 'Are you going to stand there all day?'

I gave up resisting and joined her as directed. We took off our shoes and socks and laughed as we wiggled their winter-confined toes in the spring sunshine. We looked past our outstretched feet at the panorama, bathed in the gentle sunshine of May on the Mediterranean. Then we looked at each other; she with lips slightly parted, grey-blue eyes looking at mine with tenderness and with a delicate but unmissable hint of invitation. She reached her hand to my face and slid my glasses off, putting them aside. Our first kiss, like my first kiss with Shoushan (I remembered for the briefest instant), was chaste; the second, less so; and soon our two bodies were entwined on the coverlet, our hands feverishly searching for, finding each other. I undid the buttons down the side of her skirt while she unbuttoned her blouse.

I had never known a woman's body before. Once I realised that I was about to do so, I worried for an instant that I wouldn't know what to do. She did guide me a little at first, but nature soon took over and my passion needed no assistance after the very beginning. The first time was a quick, violent clasping, leading quickly to a sweet and powerful physical surge such as I had never dreamed could be possible. The second time was slower, longer, more about us than just me, the end even more explosive. I had thought about this moment, of course, even obsessively at times, but it was more powerful, much more wonderful than my wildest imaginings. Afterwards we lay side by side, looking into each other's eyes, as though trying to pierce the mystery of being Other – and yet having suddenly, magically, briefly become One.

There was a long, sweet silence. Maude smoothed my hair, tenderly, her entrancing eyes drinking in my gaze. She said how beautiful my eyes were without the glasses. I basked in all these new sensations, enjoying the proximity of her body, her naked beauty that lay there, at my disposal. Her luminous, loving eyes fixed on me alone. Desire began to well up again. I was wondering whether she would be happy for me to initiate another round of that delirious dance, when she said quietly, *'Je t'aime, tu sais* – I love you, you know'. Gradually, I realised what she was saying and what was, or soon would be, required of me. Desire ebbed; the world seemed to turn gradually to stone. 'What's wrong, Vartan? Why do you look at me like that?' I was all confusion. I had taken advantage of her, as they say, and now all I had to do was say a few words. *The Words*. But I could not. I knew I would not be able to use the words that, deep inside somewhere, I had reserved for Shoushan. She looked at me, still tenderly but with a *pointe* of querulousness. *'Tu m'aimes aussi, n'est-ce pas?* – You do love me, too, don't you?' And now repeating, a touch stridently, *'N'est-ce pas?'*, as though it were unthinkable that I could not love her in return – that I would not even *say* I did.

I reached for my glasses and settled them on my nose. Espionage had taught me to lie, and I had become more adept at it since those first attempts, spoiled by my deep blushes and stammering. But it always disturbed me, and I felt the guilty weight of some of the lies I had told almost as much as the blood I had spilled. There could be no question of lying now. I felt too much tenderness for Maude, now tinged with pity at the thought that she had gone and fallen in love with me, or thought she had, or felt like she ought to *say* she had, which perhaps came to the same. But mainly, I could not do that to Shoushan, to her memory. It was my fault for forgetting myself, even if for the most irresistible reason in the world, the most intensely delicious instant of my life so far. But I was being true neither to myself, nor to Shoushan, nor to this girl who had given herself to me with abandon, as though it was a given that I deserved her affection now and would always continue to deserve it.

'What's wrong, Vartan?' She was alarmed, but still not believing. Gradually my awkward silence gave me away. 'There is someone else, isn't there? You were only playing with me? *Est-ce possible?*' We were sitting now. She started buttoning up her skirt, then sat looking at me with a piercing, accusing stare. I knew I had to speak, and it took more courage than my assault on Karakurt. '*Oui*, Maude. There is, or perhaps *was*, someone. Someone from a long time ago, someone I may never see again. I would never lie to you, Maude. I feel too much affection for you, affection and respect. I care for you. But so long as I do not know for sure that the other person is out of my life forever, I *cannot* say 'I love you'. You wouldn't want me to be dishonest with you, would you? That does not demean what just happened between...' She did not let me finish. She was on her feet. With sharp, angry gestures, she buttoned her skirt and blouse, pulled on her shoes and jacket, tidied her hair and brushed the flowers off her skirt. She pivoted brusquely to head downhill.

She suddenly turned back to me. 'I never want to see you again, Monsieur Nakashian! *Vous êtes ignoble! Je vous hais!*' Suddenly I was 'Monsieur', I was '*vous*' and she hated me. And she was gone. I stood stupidly for a moment, feeling dejected and clumsy, guilty of causing pain where I had least intended. An automatic gesture brought my hand to my nose and I smelled the new smell I had just discovered, the earthy, pungent smell of a woman's body. It came near to arousing me again, bringing back the thought and the sight of her, but I didn't allow my thoughts to wander further in that direction. I had to clear my mind – to act, somehow, I told myself as I got my own clothes in order. First, I had to see her safely back in the car; we would be much too early for the rendezvous with Selim. I put the uneaten picnic back in the basket, folded up the coverlet, which I noticed still had a large wet spot, and hurried down the path to the coast.

I found her sitting on a stone by the side of the road, her head on her arms, crying. I put the picnic things down and stood near her for a moment, knowing she sensed my presence and chose to pay no attention. 'Maude, listen. I understand how you feel. I am so, so sorry. You are so beautiful and kind, there is no man in the world who could resist you. I certainly could not, and if it were not for an old promise, made at a time of great stress, with death and bloodshed all around, I would have been entirely yours, body and soul. But I cannot be dishonest with you now. Can you ever forgive me? Can't you find it in your heart to forgive some-one who meant no harm, who had and still has only kind feelings towards you?'

She sat like a statue and sniffled from time to time. It seemed like an eternity before Selim returned, with both of us sitting silently on separate rocks and feeling separately miserable. When the car finally arrived, she opened the door and climbed into the back seat by herself, before the driver could get out to help her, slamming the door after her. I put the basket next to the astonished Selim. 'I will be making my own way back, Selim, God be with you.' I tried to catch Maude's attention before the great car pulled away, but she was staring resolutely ahead, her face a study in mortally offended womanhood, and then they were gone. I stood for a while, real-ised I was still stupidly holding the coverlet, and tried to get my thoughts straight before beginning the long walk towards Antelias, the largely Armenian suburb from where I knew I could get a ride back into town.

My thoughts were anything but straight. *Why couldn't you just say those words? Everyone says them.* I set off walking, following the road across the still new-looking stone bridge. As I reached the middle I hesitated, then threw the coverlet over the parapet down towards the fast-flowing river. I looked back once, and saw it spread out on the stream, bearing the last remains of our passion out to sea on the melted snows of Lebanon.

As I walked along the coastal road, I had a realisation: I was seriously hungry. I had a vision of a large bowl of *foul m'dammes*, fava beans stewed in garlic, lemon and olive oil, that I would order from a street vendor in Antelias. 'The day of the body,' I thought: 'first *that*, now the stomach. The world is going to hell, your family has been murdered, you have committed crimes they could justifiably hang you for and all you can even think about is your body. After hurting someone who did nothing to deserve it. Self-centred and stupid to boot, that's what you are. Where is all the wisdom you thought you acquired from Eliezer, where is the maturity you should have learned from working with people like Weldon and Ortalli? Or just from growing up. What is *wrong* with you?'

I trudged along, hardly noticing the traffic that went speeding past my elbow. Thoroughly depressed. Once at the busy crossroads of Antelias, a poor area which was being populated, and invigorated, by Armenian refugees from Anatolia, I did indeed indulge in a bowl of *foul*, and found it delicious and comforting, lifting my spirits even if it did not provide any answers to the questions and doubts that were nagging me. Life must go on. But how and where? Some things were about to change; I had no illusions about keeping my employment after the day's events. When I arrived at the barracks to collect my things, the French orderly said, 'Nakashian, you are to report to the colonel's office at once.' The sergeant looked inquisitively at me; I tried to look like a sphinx, and left without saying anything. At the office, I was shown in at once. The colonel drew himself up to his full height, about the same as mine, and glared at me. His face was brick-red. I thought he was about to burst with rage.

'So, Nakashian, this is how you repay my kindness? You have behaved most improperly towards my daughter, after scheming to be alone with her in a deserted place. Pathetic, ignoble behaviour, not even worthy of a boorish and servile race like the Armenians! What do you have to say for yourself?' I fought back a rush of anger at the slur against my people.

That actually cleared my mind a little. All I could think of to say, without further disloyalty to Maude, was, 'Sir, I understand your anger, and hers. I apologise for any offence or distress my actions have caused. I intended no disrespect to her or to you. She is, of course, entirely without blame.'

'Of course she is blameless, *espèce de canaille*! What else could she be, when you throw yourself on an unsuspecting, innocent, defenceless female who is under your protection?'

'Sir, I think we have said all there is to say about this unfortunate incident. I have removed my things from the barracks and have the honour to bid you goodbye.' The colonel took one step forward, as though he wanted to strike me. I stood my ground, arms to the side, looking him in the eye – not blinking once, impassive. He just stood where he was, with his fists clenched, his face if anything redder than before. I finally turned away and walked slowly to the door, which I opened, then closed firmly behind me. The secretaries and clerks in the outer office looked at me wide-eyed, with a mixture of hostility and curiosity. I tried to imagine the scene Maude must have made. I did not blame her, I could not even blame her father for his attitude. 'Which father,' I thought, 'French or anything else, would not believe his daughter's word about something like this? And who would not want to protect her, to crush anyone who tried to hurt her? Especially if the offending party is a wog, as my English friends would say. That's what we are to them, the great colonial powers. A "servile race" indeed! And we look up to them like supermen.'

Yesterday had been payday, so I had a little money and was spared having to go back to headquarters and ask for my wages. I had to smile: I had mortally offended one of the most powerful people in the city, who controlled the country's finances, police department, law courts, practically everything. I knew better than to go back and see Rawlinson. A decent man, but even with his personal feelings about the 'Froggies', he couldn't employ someone in such deep disgrace. And the *Ingleez* are leaving anyway, handing the Levant over to France after having won it from the Turks without any help from the French. Politics is a strange game.

Suddenly, I had one of those flashes of inspiration. I knew what I had to do. I went to Burj and took a *servis*-taxi towards Jounieh, back the way I had gone only a few hours before, with Maude. I got off at the junction with the road to Aintoura and walked up the hill to the orphanage. There I found Father Sarlout. We had met during one of the colonel's inspection tours, after the elderly Lazarist had returned from Turkish-imposed exile. To my surprise, he remembered me. 'Bonjour, Vartan Nakashian! What brings you up here, on foot and all on you own?'

'I am no longer working for the French, *mon père*. I left their service this morning. I would like to help you here, taking care of the orphans of the massacres. I have had a big disagreement with Colonel de la Villatte, and if that causes problems for you, I will go elsewhere and find another way to help.' The old priest tilted his grizzled head slightly as he looked at me.

'I can't imagine you getting afoul of our Gallic masters to that degree. But that is between you and them. There is much to be done here and you are welcome. We cannot pay, of course, but you can have room and board like the other volunteers.'

'Thank you, Father. Tell me about this place, about the children. We had such a brief visit last time, I think the colonel was late for lunch in Amchit.'

'It's a long and complicated story, Vartan. Let's have a cup of coffee.' Seated on chairs outside the back door of the school building, off the kitchen, enjoying the same May sunshine that had warmed our blood, Maude's and mine, that same morning, the priest began his story. 'This college has been here for a long time, since 1834 in fact. That was a great time of expansion for the French orders, the beginning of our *mission civilisatrice* in the Levant. The idea was not to convert the Muslims and Druze, but to ensure that the Christians, especially the Catholics among them, had good educational and medical facilities, everything they needed to remain the elite of the country. And to bind them to France, the protector they like to call *notre mère miséricordieuse*, "our merciful mother". A number of the good Muslim families, almost all of them Sunnis from Beirut and Tripoli, choose to send their children to our schools, where they are exempt from mass and the like. They generally love singing hymns, I must say!

'When the Young Turks decided to eliminate the Armenian "stain" from the Turkish motherland, there was a problem of what to do with the children who survived the deportations. I do not need to tell you anything about them, do I?'

'*Non, mon père.*'

'Well, it seems to be Jemal Pasha himself who had the idea of an orphanage for Armenian, and a few Kurdish, children, a sort of Turkification factory. The boys were all circumcised on arrival, yet another trauma for the poor lads. The punishment for speaking Armenian was known as *falaka*: beating on the soles of the feet, until they bleed. Little children! They were well fed in the beginning, when the head of the orphanage was none other than Halide Edib, the Turkish Jeanne d'Arc who is even now exciting crowds in Constantinople, or one should say Istanbul now, with her nationalist oratory. There are pictures of Jemal posing with her on the front steps. Talaat also visited. They were very proud of what they were doing. As the war went on, and things began to go badly for the Ottomans, she and the other celebrity sponsors of this enterprise lost interest. Funds began to dry up. The place was administered by corrupt and brutal men who just wanted to skim off the money intended for the children's well-being and put it in their pockets.

'In October of last year, the Turks left for good and we were allowed to return. To a heart-breaking scene. We found about four hundred children, all filthy and undernourished, many of them ill. Dozens died of the diseases they already had, weakened by neglect and starvation. Other orphans of the massacres were brought here, so there are over seven hundred now. After six months, they are much better than they were. They are learning to speak Armenian again, those who had forgotten. But they are all deeply scarred. By the time the Turks left they were totally confused about their identity. Their old Armenian names had been disfigured, preserving only the first letters: thus Hartun Najarian became Hamid Nazim, Boghos Merdanian became Bekim Mehmet, and so on.'

I felt an angry knot in the pit of my stomach. *Is there a* name *for trying to totally obliterate a people, an entire nation, to make the children of murdered parents forget their origins and disappear into the ranks of the murderers?*

'It will take a long time to reintegrate them into society. It is highly unlikely that more than a few will be adopted at this stage. I can see you as a teacher of Armenian, perhaps of English for the older ones. And a general mentor and big brother to the older boys. Have you taught before?' I managed a wry smile.

'Yes, Father, a little; I have taught Arabic to foreigners. My Armenian was learned at the Brothers' School, St Joseph's, in Jerusalem, and I think it will do. English is no problem. I'll do whatever you think useful.'

I did not make a conscious connection between what I was doing at the orphanage and what I had done in Smyrna. 'It couldn't be wrong to punish those who had committed such horrors,' I reasoned with myself. 'I could not have just left it to God, as Omar said one should. But I did without hesitation hurt innocent people, the poor girls I committed to a fiery death along with the murderers of my family. Surely I could have tricked them into coming out. Or something. But I was so drunk with the thought of revenge that I didn't stop to think, not for a second. And now they're dead; who knows whether they had parents, siblings or even children? An impetuous, thoughtless action, old Eliezer might say, if he knew. What right did I have? Did I think it would bring back my loved ones? It seems like the burden of what I have done is growing heavier with time, rather than lighter.'

My attention to the wounded souls of the orphans would not make them whole again, or make them forget the horrors they had seen. Some of the children were beyond reach, irretrievably isolated behind walls they had erected to keep out the monsters that still pursued them. All one could do for them was to make their daily life a bit easier. Others were more rewarding, in the sense that they responded to a drop of kindness with a flowering of personality. I could not help but have favourites, and two, a brother and sister named Vahe and Mariam, totally conquered me. They wanted to learn everything, so I ended up teaching them not only Armenian and English, but very basic French as well. I kicked footballs with Vahe and tasted Mariam's productions in kitchen science. I told them

stories, the Armenian legends I had learned from Mayrig. I felt her presence at those times.

The lessons for the older children were vocational: on 'graduation' they would need to earn their living. There had been a very small Armenian minority in Lebanon before the war; the refugees had swollen its numbers and taken over a whole dilapidated suburb, Burj Hammoud. As soon as they could, they moved to other, more elite, neighbourhoods, rather than staying in a ghetto. If things went on like this, I thought, soon there would be no more refugee camps in Lebanon. The need for the orphanage and similar ones continued, though, and I was settling quite happily into this new life.

I was so busy that I had little time to dwell on my yearning for Shoushan, though whenever she did appear in my dreams or imagination, my yearning was fierce. My experience with Maude had receded into a distant, dreamlike compartment in my mind, one I did not seek to revisit. I repressed, or rather refrained from dwelling on, my feelings of guilt for not having protected Mayrig and the children, and the bouts of remorse I felt for what I did in Smyrna. Sometimes I wondered whether I should – could – tell Shoushan about that. I did not want to, but I would have to, as though she could absolve me. An absolution which would mean infinitely more than anything proposed by the well-meaning priest in Smyrna. 'She will understand, if she really is my Shoushan,' I hoped.

Then there was Garo. I was still without news, and worried at having left him in the care of Sitt Sarah, who was kind enough but not by any standards normal. Finally, the new French Mandate for Syria and Lebanon managed to get the postal system working again. I wrote to Uncle Sarkis, to see how he and his family were faring and to ask whether he had heard anything with respect to Mayrig's foundling. A fortnight later, I had an answer: Sarkis and his wife and daughters were well and overjoyed to hear from me. They had given me up for dead in the wake of the silence that followed the deaths of Mayrig and the children, until they heard from Sitt Sarah. She had contacted Sarkis to let him know about Garo – and about me – and to ask for help. Sarkis and his wife had come over immediately, and fell in love with the miraculous little survivor. Sarah did not want to give him up but finally agreed that he would be better off with Sarkis and his wife. They started the procedure to adopt him (for once completely in agreement about something) and engaged Sitt Sarah to join their household and look after him. A son for Sarkis, at last!

I was relieved to know that Garo was safe and in good hands. I resolved to go see him as soon as I could. But my nights were troubled by dreams and half-waking visions of Mayrig and the children, of Shoushan, who always seemed to be on the other side of a fence from me, one with barbed wire and some sort of glass shield through which it was impossible to communicate. I fought with myself: 'How will she react when – if – I tell her what I have done? I've put myself beyond the pale, she could not bear to be with someone who has killed innocent people, I'm sure of that. If she hasn't answered my letter, it may be that she has given up on me, even without such knowledge. Perhaps it's better that way. Let her remember me as I was, as she thought I was.'

One Sunday, we had a visit from the Armenian Red Cross Society, a group that included the lady volunteer I had met months ago, the one who had promised to have a letter delivered to Shoushan at Port Said. She seemed pleasantly surprised to find me again. 'How amazing to find you here! I asked at the French headquarters and they said you had been dismissed. I thought that was strange, but no one seemed to know anything about your current whereabouts. And now I find you at Aintoura!' She fumbled in her bag and finally produced a rather shopworn-looking letter, the envelope addressed to me in English and Turkish. I thanked her and took the letter to the garden. I sat on a bench and slowly opened it, both fearful and hopeful of the news it might contain.

My Dear Varo,

I was overjoyed to read your letter and to hear that you are well and have not forgotten your Shoushan. I am still in Port Said with my uncle and aunt, both of whom send you their love. Minas has joined the Armenian Legion and fought the Turks in a great battle in Palestine under General Allenby. We are very proud of him. He wrote that he was wounded in a battle against the Turks, but that he is recovering and will come as soon as he can. The Legion has now been sent to Cilicia to help the French guard the people who return to what is left of their villages.

The past three years have been very difficult, living in the same barracks where we last saw each other, no change in any way, except that some people have left, moving out to join relatives in places like Damascus or Baghdad. The English have been very kind, as well as the Armenian Red Cross people, thank God for them. And bless the Armenian community in Egypt. When we told the English that we could not learn to enjoy the food they prepared in their kitchen for us, they let us take over the cooking, with them providing just the vegetables, flour, meat and fish. Now some of them come to eat in our refectory! Perhaps someday I will open an Armenian restaurant in London or America.

I have kept busy helping in the infirmary: with more than three thousand people still here, there are always some sick, but since the first few months there have been no more contagious diseases, like the typhus and cholera a few of us brought from Musa Dagh. How long ago that seems!

And how long ago it seems since we last saw each other. I have so often wondered what your life has been like. I know that you were helping the English in the war; I was and am very proud of that. You must be happy now that it is all over. I do hope your dear mother Mayrig, your brother Halim, Anahit and little Krikor are well? You didn't say in your letter. I would love to see them again one day.

However, I must tell you something. They will be closing this camp over the next few weeks. The Egyptian Red Cross have arranged for visas to America for those remaining refugees who are in good health and wish to go there. Many do, as there is nothing for us in our old homes, though there are some who insist on returning. I cannot understand those who want to go back to the scene of our catastrophe, after all those deaths and all that suffering, to live among the Turks. Uncle Artin has paid for passages for all of us: him, Azniv, Minas and me. We are expecting Minas back here any day.

We are booked to leave from Alexandria to Marseille on a boat called the Ismailia, *on the 2nd of July; then on a boat called the* Millinocket, *from Marseille to New York, about three weeks later. Uncle says that if you can get here and wish to come, he will get a visa and passage for you too. In fact, he has made a reservation, just in case; I said I would not agree to go unless it was possible for you to join us, if you want to. And if you find us in time.*

Of course, I do not know whether you still feel as you did for your Shoushan. I do not know whether you still keep our promise in your heart. I beg you, in any case, to send me a letter and this time tell me how you feel. Tell me whether you will join us in our journey to America. I have very little idea of what it is like there, but there are many Armenians already in a place called Los Angeles. Perhaps it will be possible to build a new life there. If you still love me as you did, as you said you did, then perhaps you will come. If not, if you have someone new in your life or have just grown away from me, then please be kind and tell me that, release me so that I can go off to the new world and hope, somehow, to find a new life there, far from the place of our pain and suffering.

Know that I remain, and whatever happens, will forever be,
Your

Shoushan

Port Said Armenian Refugee Camp, 28 April 1919

I sat on the bench in a stupor. *America*! Somehow it never occurred to me that she might actually slip away from me, for good. It had been almost convenient, I thought bitterly, to have her safely cooped up in a refugee camp while I was playing at espionage, scribbling in ledgers in Nisibin or tracking the murderers of my family. It was convenient, and it put off the day when I would have to tell her I had blood on my hands; not just the honest blood of a battle for survival but the blood of the innocent as well as the guilty. But to tell her, whatever the outcome, I had to see her! America! I could not go to America. But neither could I forsake her: 'She must *not* get on that ship!'

Shoushan in America, and me here! I looked again at the letter: they were to sail on the second day of July. That was in about two weeks. I had no identity papers, except for the old fake *teskere* in the name of Georges Habib, forged in the name of a now-defunct empire. I had to stop her, somehow. But how even to get to Egypt without papers? Her letter had taken six weeks to reach me. Writing to her was out of the question: there was no time and, anyway, what would I say?

I went to Father Sarlout and asked for a private conference. 'We will miss you, Vartan Nakashian. But I understand perfectly. Perhaps someday we will welcome you both here. *Que Dieu vous garde, mon fils.*' I left that afternoon for Beirut. The first thing I had to do was get some sort of travel papers. There was only one person I could go to: Rawlinson. On arrival at Burj, I went straight to the *maktab ingleezi*.

The major was busy with an endless telephone conversation but, finally, received me. 'Ah, Nakashian, I am glad to see you again. Your name came up just the other day. I understand you rather sullied your escutcheon with our Froggy friends!' At my blank look, he explained: 'Er, you seem to have left on bad terms. De la Villatte would not explain. But when I asked if it was some sort of corruption, or trafficking of political influence, or a crime of violence or theft, petty or otherwise, he assured me it was none of the above.

That only leaves one, or rather two things: his lovely wife, of about my years, and his beautiful daughter, of about yours. Which probably narrows it down to one of the two. I may be wrong, but you will admit there is a certain implacable logic in that reasoning.'

'Major, please let's not get into that. However, as you guessed, my offence was nothing despicable. Clumsy and insensitive, yes. But that is neither here nor there. Let me come to the point. For urgent family reasons, I need to be in Egypt within ten days from now. I have no identification papers, not genuine ones, anyway.' I showed him the *teskere* our mutual friend Weldon had produced, as well as the paper from Ortalli.

'Well, if these were issued by the current authorities, they might just get you from here to Egypt, assuming you could find transport. But what you have is no good, might fool a dimwit *zaptieh* but not an Anglo-Egyptian border policeman. You'll need an updated document issued by the proper authorities, preferably in your real name.'

'And where can I get one, in Beirut?' I asked.

'Only one place, at present. The French High Commission, as they're calling it. Born in Syria, you ought really to apply in Aleppo or Damascus. But it's the French who control what they call the État Civil now. Downstairs from Colonel de la Villatte's office and reporting to him, I regret to say.'

My heart sank. I did not see how I could ask the French. On the other hand, on what grounds could they refuse? I thanked the major and, with a heavy heart, walked to the French headquarters. I asked for the État Civil office, and was shown into the bastion of French colonial bureaucracy. I stated my purpose and was told to wait. After half an hour, a functionary (whose mother must have looked at him in the cradle and exclaimed: '*Mon fils*, you will be a *fonctionnaire!*') called me to the counter, and had me state it again, as well as my name, marital status, religion and place of birth. 'Aleppo? That is in Syria. You need to go to Syria.'

'But I have no travel document to enable me to cross the frontier.'

'You came here, didn't you?'

'I did, *Monsieur le Chef de Bureau*, but that was wartime. Now that the war is over and, thanks to France, conditions have normalised, I would not be allowed across the border. Surely it would be possible to give me a temporary identification paper?'

The *fonctionnaire* hesitated.

'Ah, yes, an *attestation provisoire*. But to obtain a temporary permit, you will need two persons of standing in the community to sign an affidavit swearing that they know you and are aware of your identity. I don't suppose you know such persons?'

I assured him that I did and gave all the information necessary so that the affidavit forms for Father Sarlout and Major Rawlinson could be prepared. I was told to return the next day. I stopped by the major's office and obtained his agreement. I then got a *servis*-taxi back out to Aintoura, where Father Sarlout also assented. Everything seemed to be falling into place.

I was back at the counter first thing in the morning and, to my surprise, the forms were ready – maybe I had misjudged the French. My first stop was Rawlinson's office. The major looked annoyed. 'Ah, Vartan, old chap. I am afraid I have some bad news. Your old friend de la Villatte was on the blower a little while ago to warn me about you and, in particular, that I should on no account attest to having known you. You really did, um, get up his nose, didn't you?'

I was crestfallen. 'Yes, sir, I suppose I did. But this is rather unfair, don't you think? I have the *right* to their damned *attestation*. But of course I cannot ask you to sign under these circumstances.'

'You may not ask, my boy, but if you give me the paper I'll sign it. Serves the bloody Froggy right. The cheek, giving me orders after we liberated the damned country and handed it over to them on a platter!' And with that, he took the form, signed it, blotted it, patted me on the back and sent me on my way without further discussion.

Back at the orphanage, I found Father Sarlout in a sombre a mood. 'Sit down, Vartan.'

'Ah, Father, you must have had a call from Colonel de la Villatte.'

'I have. And I will sign your form, as I promised. But first I must tell you about our conversation. The good colonel, in the most polite and elegant terms imaginable, told me that if I sign, the orphanage will see its subsidies from the French government drastically reduced. I cannot believe that he would do that, or that if he was base enough to attempt it, the higher authorities would agree to hurt these children, to hamper the good work we're doing, just to indulge a personal grudge. I will appeal and I believe I shall prevail: we have our own channels. But I thought you should know what you – what we – are up against. Where is the form?'

I was furious. What a reptile! And he dared call the *Armenians* 'servile'.

'Well, Father, there's no question of your signing this paper. The orphans and your work are much more important than my personal worries.' Seeing in his face that he was about to insist, I pulled the form from my pocket and tore it to shreds. 'I will find another way, Father.' I spent that night in the dormitory at Aintoura, tossing and turning. I toyed with the idea of trying my luck as 'Georges Habib'. Then I thought of just setting off walking, catching lifts when I could, and making my way to the Egyptian border. From there I could get word to Uncle Artin, who with his gregarious charm surely had enough contacts by now to talk the *Ingleez* into letting me across the border and into the camp. 'Am I not a refugee from Musa Dagh?' I reasoned with myself. 'Actually, my name must still be on the muster from three and a half years ago. If such a list still exists and if anyone cares who is on it any more. But how will I get to Egypt in the first place?'

In the morning, things were no clearer in my mind. I had no one to turn to, except Major Rawlinson, who I felt – despite his exceedingly helpful attitude (especially when it cocked a snoot at the 'Froggies') – must be getting tired of seeing me on his doorstep every other day. Back to the *maktab al-ingleezi* I went and, to my relief, he received me at once, with the usual laugh Englishmen use to disguise awkward situations. He scowled as I told my story.

'The absolute rotter!' exclaimed the major. 'Now that is low, even for a Froggy. We must see what we can do, mustn't we?'

'We must,' I thought to myself.

'Today I am submerged with preparations for a high-level Admiralty visit later this week. Come back tomorrow at this time, my boy, and I might just have an idea for you.' I was getting nowhere, and time was running out. But I was back outside Rawlinson's office at four o'clock the next afternoon.

'Ah, Vartan, sit down. Now, I cannot say anything about naval movements, can I? But there are, occasionally, boats going from here to Port Said. If I could find one, and get you on it, everything would be tickety-boo. Problem is, there isn't one, not exactly. What there *is*, is the HMS *Hannibal*, a battleship with all the top Navy brass on it, which will be calling here in a few days. Its exact movements have not been announced, an old wartime habit. But I know when it is due to call here, and I know that it has not yet been to Port Said; also, that it couldn't do a proper Mediterranean lark for the brass without stopping in Egypt. I believe I can talk your way on to it, as a translator, shall we say? That's all I can do, and there is a risk that they might decide to go to Athens or Mudros, Smyrna or Constantinople, for all I know. But I would bet that they will call at Port Said within the week. Nobody will question your travel documents if you disembark with a bunch of admirals. However, don't blame me if I'm wrong, and your deadline, whatever it is, comes and goes with you still on the high seas. What do you say?'

I was torn. My first instinct was to head off directly in the direction of Egypt, but that meant a long distance overland, several borders. Further discussions with the *fonctionnaire* would be fruitless given his superior's determination to thwart me.

'I will risk it, Major, if you really think you can get me on board. No hard feelings if it all goes, er, pear-shaped, as you say. Shall I return to Aintoura, or find a place to stay here in town?'

'We can billet you here, at our non-com quarters in the old Ottoman stables. Not as rank as it sounds, there haven't been horses in there for a century or two. Would send you to the officers' digs but they are full up. More of them around here than other ranks, not like when there was shooting going on, ha! ha! If you hang around here during the day, starting tomorrow, I will be able to introduce you to one of the brassy types and see if we can fix you up with a berth. Dixon!' An orderly appeared. 'See that Nakashian here gets a comfortable bunk in the non-coms' stable, if you please.'

It took three days for the *Hannibal* to begin her visit to Beirut, a visit which lasted two days. Rawlinson assigned me to interpret for the admirals and commodores during their tour of Beirut and the closer sites of Mount Lebanon. These included Deir al-Qamar and Beit ad-Din, up in the Shouf Mountains south of Beirut: two hilltop towns which had been the capital of Lebanon during different centuries, according to the guide I was translating for, a local teacher recruited for the purpose. I was surprised to learn from him that the rulers in those days had been Druze Emirs. The British were fascinated by the seaside ruins of Byblos, where a massive Crusader castle rubs elbows with a jumble of much more ancient ruins, Roman and Greek and God knows what. How it reminded me of Jerusalem! The pillars and temples of Baalbek amazed them; one of them said they were grander and better preserved than any Roman remains in Italy, which I could hardly believe. At another time, I would have been interested too. But not now.

They smiled at the stelae at the Dog River, while a couple of them tried to decipher the Greek and Latin inscriptions, I think to show off their learning. I was totally distracted during that visit. But the captains and admirals did not take to the food; they picked at their plates of meze, kebab and grilled chicken, sea bass on charcoal and baby lamb on a bed of fragrant rice with almonds and cumin, constantly worrying about hygiene. I thought with a smile about the Musa Dagh refugees and their issues with English food. Then I thought about Shoushan. Seven days remaining.

On the third day after their arrival in Beirut, having given satisfaction as an interpreter, I was duly conscripted for the remainder of the tour and took my place on HMS *Hannibal* in a midshipman's berth. The ship was much grander and bigger than anything I had experienced before, the berth much more comfortable than on *Anne* or *Managem*. But I was worried. We sailed at a leisurely eleven o'clock in the morning. I asked Lieutenant Pococke, my principal contact among the ship's crew, where we were headed. 'Smyrna, my boy! Do you know it?' My heart sank. The wrong direction, completely.

'Ah, why yes, I was there not long ago. And do we know how long we will stay there, and where we will go from there?'

'Oh, probably another two- or three-day stint. And then either Athens or down to Egypt – Alex or Port Said. They can't leave the region without seeing Egypt, can they!'

'No, I'm sure they can't.'

Four days left. We were swinging to anchor in the Bay of Smyrna, the vast ship glued to a mirror-calm sea. I cursed my decision to take my chances with the admirals when I could have at least retained control of my situation, even if the odds were against me. 'Why must you always count on others?' I reproached myself. And now

I was like a hostage, with no way of taking control of the situation. I felt very strange, touring the sights of the city with the British naval delegation, walking along the Cordon, wondering what Vahram, Abraham and Hrant would think if they saw me in such company. As far as I knew, they did not, and apparently no one recognised the solitary walker who had been spotted prowling around the *chetes'* house on Tepecik hill.

Finally, the great warship hoisted its two enormous anchors and got underway, its four huge funnels belching black smoke. HMS *Hannibal* at last began to steam south. I was anxious, but there was nothing I could do. Apparently, the commander-in-chief had not yet decided, or if he had decided, he had not told Lieutenant Pococke whether it was to be Port Said or Alexandria. So I took up my preferred station on the bow, smoking as I watched the Levantine coast slide by, its contours masked in midsummer heat haze. Somewhere out there was Athlit, from where Shimon and Esther had escaped in the nick of time. I wondered what had become of them. America, probably. The place to go nowadays. Poor Sarah and Josef; for an instant, her face glided across my mind. Further south, we steamed past Isdud, or Ashdod, names Weldon had called a shibboleth, past the beach where I was put ashore on the mission to Jerusalem and Eliezer Ben Negrila. 'Was that really *me*?' I wondered. 'And only three years ago?

'But not for me, America. My people are here, in this land, which holds the bones of those who died, and of my own loved ones. Of those who survived, some are in exile and all bear the wounds of these terrible years. But my people are not in Los Angeles. Those who go to live at the far edge of the world, to grow old where the languages, cultures and landscapes of the Armenians mean nothing, they are choosing a premature death. The death of Hayestan. Better to live near the Turks, with all the baggage that implies. Why should we leave our homes, this earth where our ancestors are buried, now sodden with our blood, just leave all that for the murderers to enjoy?' All kinds of bizarre and morbid thoughts crossed my mind. I was beginning to be sure that I would get to Alexandria just as the steamer pulled away from the dock, watching my love, my hope for the future, the possibility of building some sort of new life out of the ruins of the old, disappear into the distance.

One day left. The first day of July, 1919. I stood at the bow, trying to wish away the remaining sea miles. Directly, I could make out a distant camel-coloured blot along the horizon: Egypt. Suddenly Pococke was there. 'You wanted to know where we're headed, old chap? Well, it's Port Said! Be there before sunset.' My heart sank: 'She must already be in Alexandria,' I thought. 'At least she told me the name of the ship, the *Ismailia.* If ever we get in before it's too late, I'll have to make my way to Alexandria. How far could it be?' I reached into my pocket, mechanically feeling for my packet of cigarettes. I looked at the half-empty packet of Kensitas Lieutenant Scott had given me and I suddenly had no desire to smoke. 'A dirty habit. Waste of time and money and probably not healthy. No place for you in my new life!' With that thought I threw the packet out to sea, watching it arc and spin as the wind caught it, then dive and disappear into the blue-black waves of the Mediterranean. I touched my watch pocket, feeling as I often did for Anahit's little cross, my amulet, my constant reminder.

We got in to Port Said around teatime, which meant that having moored alongside the quay, the massive hawsers holding the huge warship tight against the fenders, there was a pause before the gangways were put in place. I was all ready with my few belongings, standing at the gunwale, waiting. I had said my goodbyes to Pococke and the sailors, who had been very civil to me, one of the ratings having served on the HMS *Anne.* It seemed like an eternity, and the sun was low in the western sky before I managed to run down the gangway. I had no idea how one gets from Port Said to Alexandria, nor how long it would take. All I had was Turkish money, still legal tender in Syria and Lebanon but I feared probably not in Egypt, where the English had been in charge for many years.

I ran up to a military policeman: 'How can I get to Alexandria tonight?'

'Tonoit?' said the Englishman. 'I wouldn't try to go there tonoit, oi wouldn't. It'd tike you at least six hours and cost you a bleedin' fortune. Wait for the trine in the mornin', that's what.'

'I don't care, I have to *be* there tomorrow morning. I have a ship to catch, the *Ismailia*, bound for Marseille.'

'Well, said the policeman, I knows a cabbie who'd get you there all roit, but 'e'll charge you bags of *floos* for it, 'e will. If you're gime we'll go see 'im.'

The policeman presented me to the driver of a battered car from before the war, a four-seater with a Wolseley badge on the radiator, and then went back to his post. The English driver, who looked like a demobbed soldier who had stayed in Egypt after the war, said he could have me there before midnight, but asked to be paid in advance. He smiled and shook his head at my Ottoman coins. 'Well, there is one other taxi, of sorts, still around. No fancy motorcar, neither. In fact, I'm not sure the old gippy would take his banger as far as Alex. If I introduce you he might not ask to be paid until you get there, assuming you do get that far. Do you want me to ask him?'

'Yes, please,' I begged, 'right away, if you please.'

We found the driver, an Egyptian in a blue *gellabia*, seated in a cafe facing the port, drinking coffee, playing philosophically with his toes and obviously enjoying the idea that his work day was over. Parked a few yards along was his vehicle, an antique two-seater phaeton with 'Austin 10' on it. It had obviously been in one or more serious accidents and showed signs of having been repaired using whatever materials could be scrounged in wartime Egypt – from baling wire holding the dented bonnet in place, to a metal plate with 'Tetley' upside down that served as a passenger door after its first career on a tea crate. My heart sank, but after some discussion, the driver grinned at me and carefully opened the door.

A few minutes later, just shy of six in the afternoon, we were on our way to Alexandria. I sat next to the driver as the old car chugged slowly along, the still-hot July wind in our faces. The cab driver was a simple man, an Egyptian with country speech but used to English ways. The English driver had introduced me as 'one of our lads', his English translated approximately by a familiar clap on my shoulder. The Egyptian did not think of demanding to see the colour of my cash, trusting the word of a sort-of *Ingleezi*. He looked a little askance on hearing me speak Levantine Arabic. For a moment, I was afraid he would get suspicious and ask to see my money.

We motored along, and I was comforted to think that at least I was heading in the right direction. Next stop Alexandria. I had often heard 'Alex' mentioned by the *Ingleez* on board HMS *Anne* as a desirable port of call. And now the most Europeanised city in the Levant, after Smyrna. Shoushan's face came to my mind, in sharp focus now. 'If only we can get there in time. A horse would go just as fast as this wreck!' With these thoughts in my head, I dozed in the heat, leaning on the makeshift door of the car. The driver shook me awake: '*Shway shway*, go easy; the door is not as sturdy as it once was!' I sat upright and soon dozed off again, this time slumping forward, my arms crossed on the dusty dashboard.

Sometime after midnight, the driver pulled the cab to a stop. 'I need some tea, *ya Basha*.' I had never heard myself addressed as 'Pasha', a thought that would have amused me at any other time. The teahouse was a tiny palm-frond hut, illuminated by a single lantern, along the road somewhere after Damietta. I had seen that name signposted in English and Arabic a little while ago. The proprietor made tea, squatting next to a Primus stove. It was obvious that I was expected to pay. I fished out a few Turkish *paras* and offered them to the *qahwagi*. '*Dhi eh, ya Basha*,' said the driver, 'here we use Egyptian money. I hope you have some to pay for the ride!'

'Of course,' I lied, trying to sound like a proper pasha, 'but no small change. I am sure our friend here can find someone to change these *paras*. *Tfaddal*, take another *para* to make it worthwhile.'

Soon we were rattling along again. I fell asleep for a while, this time with my head leaning on the driver's bony shoulder. When I awoke with a start, I saw that we were following a road right along the sea. There were breakers on the beach or rocks to our right, there was the sound of the surf and the smell of salt air, warm and rich with seaweed. There was a nearly-full moon high in the sky; Captain Weldon's watch said it was three o'clock. 'How much longer, oh Sir Driver?' I asked, beginning to get the hang of Egyptian polite discourse.

'As long as it takes!'

'Yes, but *how* long? How many hours?'

'God the Merciful alone knows the secrets of time and fate,' was the reply. I gave up, leaned back and tried to relax.

When I awoke again, we were passing Rashid, again marked by a signpost. The eastern horizon was imperceptibly lighter, the first sign of impending dawn. 'How far now, oh Sir Driver?'

'Less than four hours, *ya Basha! Inshallah!*'

'Four hours,' I thought. '*If* God wills it. It will be mid-morning before we arrive. All this, for nothing.' Suddenly the car's engine began to cough and the driver brought it to a halt. 'The car is too hot, oh Pasha, it must rest and cool down.' There was little I could say to that. The driver wrapped his hand in a cloth and loosened the radiator cap, producing a cloud of steam. I cursed myself for not finding some way of hiring a better automobile.

'Oh Sir Driver,' I said, as authoritatively as I could. 'Do you know the port of Alexandria?'

'Does a snail know its shell, oh Pasha?' A good image for this cab and its driver.

'Then do you know the *Ismailia*, the steamer that leaves for Marseille in the morning?'

'How could I not know the *Ismailia*, Oh *Pasha*? It is the cream of the Khedivial Mail line. Well, the slightly old cream. It goes around the Mediterranean, from Alexandria to Marseille, Genoa, Athens, Constantinople, Smyrna, Beirut, and then back to Alexandria to start all over again. The day of Allah is long, oh Pasha, and the business of merchants never ceases!'

'In that case, oh Sir Driver, if you get me to Alexandria before the *Ismailia* sails, in time to find someone who intends to sail aboard her, I will give you a tip such as a pharaoh would give, let alone a pasha!'

'*Inshallah, Oh Basha, inshallah!*'

I sighed: '"If God wills" again. If we are depending on him we are truly lost.' We resumed our journey after half an hour's rest and, once it had cooled down, a litre or two of water added to the radiator from the jerrican in the baggage platform behind the seats. I noticed a slight quickening of the pace, accompanied by the occasional cough and shudder from the engine. 'Just don't let the wretched thing give out on us before we get there,' I thought. The sun was just clear of the horizon when suddenly the cab left the coast and headed inland.

'What is this, oh Sir Driver? Is Alexandria not on the sea?'

'Indeed it is, oh Pasha, but the port is on the far side of the city. We will save an hour by going around, by the lake called Mareotis.'

By the time the tall cargo winches of the port and the masts and funnels of the ships moored along the quay or anchored in the bay rose into sight, the sun was well up – nine o'clock according to Weldon's watch. I found myself mouthing a prayer, though I would have been hard-pressed to say to whom it was addressed. 'Could it be that the *Ismailia* has not already sailed, oh Sir Driver?' The old car pulled out on the shadeless quay, the engine stopping with a grunt and a wheeze. The driver pointed up at a steamship, of about the earliest vintage still operating in the Mediterranean, clearly in the final stages of preparation for sailing. The davits were back in their sailing position, cargo stowed and only one gangway remaining in place, with sailors carrying a few last-minute messages and parcels up to and down from the old ship. I handed the driver a fistful of Ottoman gold *lira*, most of the remains of my pay from Nisibin. He started to protest, then realised that the gold in his hand, be it Turkish or Frankish or Chinese, was worth as much as his ancient cab. He grinned and pocketed it, lit a cigarette and sat watching his pasha trying to talk his way on to the gangway.

I tried to bluff my way aboard in English. The Egyptian policeman guarding the dockside end of the *passerelle* was not impressed: 'No ticket, no board.' I racked my brain for an argument.

'But you must let me find the Bedrossian family! Their grand-mother in Aleppo has died and they have inherited half of Syria! It would be a crime to let them sail for Marseille and America without telling them! I am sure they will reward you handsomely. And be assured, I do not wish to travel, in fact I want to take one of the family back with me, to begin the formalities!'

The argument, plausible or not, and in particular the mention of a handsome reward, seemed to give him some pause. *'Wallah, ya Bey?'* ('Now I'm a *bey*,' I thought. 'Is that more or less than a pasha?')

'Yes, I swear by God!' I was able to exploit his momentary hesitation and run up the gangway and, when I was almost to the top, I saw Shoushan among the throng of passengers at the rail-ing, holding her hands over her mouth. 'Shoushan!' I shouted as I ran, 'Shoushan! Come down, come with me!' I saw her standing immobile, frozen with her hands still over her mouth. Then Uncle Artin and Aunt Azniv were with her; Minas followed, leaning on a crutch. Soon I had shoved past an amazed steward and was among them, embracing each in turn. The ship's great horn began to sound, and the stevedores were preparing to loose the hawsers from the massive bollards on the quay. Holding Shoushan's hand, I addressed them:

'My dears, there is no time to explain. I must stay here. Mayrig, Krikor and probably Halim are dead, but many more are still alive. I understand your decision to seek a new life in America, but I cannot. Everything binds me here, to my people, to the work that must be done for them. I want Shoushan to stay with me, if she wishes. Together we will work for the future of Hayestan. I love her and will do everything in my power to make her happy. Please let her stay with me, if she wishes it as I do. I will get the *Ingleez* to marry us as soon as possible, I swear. But Shoushan, if your heart is set on America, if you do not need me as I need you, if your new life is in a new place, not the old ones, not with me, then you have my blessing. Go, go and be free from any promises we made to each other, go and be happy.'

I had never made such a speech before. All those words just poured out of me, as I stood at the top of the gangway. I know I must have looked and sounded to my relatives very different from the Vartan they had last seen three years ago. Shoushan still had not moved her eyes from me. There was a long silence. She looked at her aunt and uncle, who were standing with open mouths, like statues to astonishment. Shoushan burst into tears. I thought I had surely failed. Then, still sobbing, she threw her arms around her Aunt Azniv, then Uncle Artin, kissing them with her face still wet with tears. Finally she hugged Minas, who stood stiffly, looking dazed and sorrowful. I thought for a moment he was going to object, but he just looked down at the deck. Clutching her bag, she turned and looked me in the eyes. 'Do you mean everything you said, Vartan Nakashian?'

'I swear I do, Shoushan.' She looked back at the others, and said, 'It will be all right, this is what must be, this miracle. I will write to you, I have the address of the Armenian Benevolent Union in New York. Only, make sure they know where you have gone. I love you all and will never forget your kindness.' I embraced them in turn. Artin was about to say something when the sailors started removing the gangway, so I grabbed Shoushan's bag and her arm and pulled her away, passing through the gap in the railing without a second to spare. Together we walked down on to the quay as the ship's horn sounded three mournful blasts. We stood in the withering July sun of Egypt as the gangway was hoisted away and the hawsers winched up, waving up at those about to depart until the tugboat finished towing the hulking old liner out into the shimmering bay.

12

Beirut: June 1985

A BOVE VARTAN'S chair, the dust motes carried on their endless Brownian dance in the sunbeams. There were more of the latter since an artillery shell had landed in the garden of the other old Bustros house next door overnight, bringing down several of the surviving shutter slats on his house but, mercifully, sparing the glass this time. His mood was heavy with memories: his unintended callousness towards Shoushan, leaving her alone for so many days and nights in Tehran, never imagining what would happen. *I brought her there to die.* And the Greek girls in Smyrna all those years ago, their laughter and song turned to screams of terror and pain as the fire devoured the old house, the terrible sounds that had haunted his dreams for over sixty years. His failure towards Mayrig and his brothers, towards poor Anahit, never completely absent from his thoughts on such a dark day, but so painful that he tried his best to keep it from his consciousness.

More recently, his inaction when Dashti was arrested in Tehran. Surely there was something that could have been done for him, but what? The Mollah-led mob had taken over the country, and his books *were* provocative, from their point of view. And now Lebanon was in the throes of its own frenzy – it was all he could do to survive from day to day. Then the horrible news of his friend's arrest and torture: who could do anything for someone the guards were holding in Evin Prison? At least he was released, broken, to die at home.

And I, at least, am being left alone. The odd artillery shell or rocket, but not directed at me personally. Cold comfort. What fools men are! Khayyam says it best –

Gavi-st der asiman

There's a cow named Parveen, holding up the sky
Another cow below, holding up the Earth;
Open your eyes, man, and use your mind to see
Between those two cows – such a herd of *donkeys*!

Vartan Nakashian smiled again at the verses he had just recited for perhaps the thousandth time, and just as he looked up at the golden sunbeams, it hit him. A sudden feeling like a kick in the head, a searing pain like none other he had ever felt. He stiffened in his chair, gripping its arms for dear life, literally, as the pain spread, shooting down his right arm and right leg at the same time. *Could this be what it feels like to have a stroke?* Time ceased to have any substance; he sat for seconds, or minutes, or hours, he had no way of telling and it was irrelevant. Finally, the pain subsided, leaving him drained, exhausted by what felt less like a struggle than a beating in which he had been the passive victim. He tried to move his limbs: left side, no problem; right arm and leg, difficult. The right side of his face felt very strange, numb. He wondered whether he should call Maqsud. *What do I expect him to do about it? Is this the end? Oh, let it* be *the end, not paralysis, not half a brain and a body that does not work.* But it was not the end. As some unit of time passed without further crisis, his mind gradually began to clear. He felt returned to himself, though his right-sided members were still very recalcitrant. But they were not completely inert, he noticed gratefully. He wiggled the fingers of his right hand, though he could not raise the arm off the chair. His right foot moved back and forth on command, but he doubted it would support him if he tried to walk.

The afternoon was advancing, the familiar invasion of sunbeams nearly horizontal. A powerful feeling that he was at a crossroads descended on him. A need to choose, to act. But what were the choices, what in the world could he *do*? Gradually one thing, one big thing, became clearer and clearer: he had, at last, reached a definitive moment of some kind. The beginning of the end, perhaps, or perhaps not, but things would never again be what they were just a short time ago.

He had been aware, as his eighty-seventh year came and went, that it was *time*. Almost everyone he had ever cared anything for was on the far side of the veil. It was the exact timing and the manner of his departure that had been withheld, until now, and he accepted what seemed to him like a verdict – and a sentence – almost gratefully. Not a fulfilment; but somehow, perhaps, atonement.

He felt an overwhelming desire to go in a manner at least partly of his choosing while he still had the strength. Or at least to make best efforts. To go trying, fighting – not meekly. Musa Dagh spirit, if there's any left. He used his left arm to push himself forward and up, while willing his left leg and whatever control he had over the right one to extract him from the chair. This succeeded, but the wobbly right leg collapsed, leaving him on all fours, except that his right arm provided very little support. He dragged himself like a two-and-a-half-legged dog across the marble floor towards the door, where the ornate brass umbrella stand held a bouquet of umbrellas and walking sticks. Not being able to draw himself upright to remove a stick from the stand, he nudged it with his left shoulder until it fell over with a crash, a clang of metal on marble. Retrieving a sturdy cane from the pile, he gripped its head, an ebony *tête de nègre*, in his left hand and with an effort drew himself off the ground, achieving a hunched-over but basically standing position. Erect but comically wobbly.

Where he would go from there and what he intended to do were still taking shape in his mind, and coalescing into a sort of plan. *The sea. I must see the sea again. On the seashore I will know what to do.* He felt his hip pocket and made sure his wallet was there. He leaned against the left-hand panel of the wrought-iron front doors of the old house and with his left hand pulled the latch and awkwardly tugged the other side inwards. It seemed weeks since he had been outside. The ceaseless traffic on the street just outside the gate, with its hooting and revving noises, the shouts and the screech of brakes seemed unbearably loud and ugly. Somehow, holding the railing and leaning heavily on the cane, he managed to descend the steps to street level, hobble to the gate, dragging his right foot, unlatch it and pull it open. He could not signal a taxi to stop with his right arm hanging limp and his left gripping the cane, but the look on his face must have been eloquent enough, for directly a taxi came to a stop. 'Where to, Grandfather?'

'I am not your grandfather thank God, but I want to go to Byblos. Will you take me there?'

'*Byblos*! That's an hour away! The road is open but there are
many roadblocks. That will cost you twenty dollars, Grandfather!'

'Make it forty. But help me.'

The driver came around, opened the back door to help Vartan
take his seat, which he did basically by collapsing backwards into the
battered Mercedes. The driver said, 'Are you all right, Grandfather?
Shouldn't we go to the hospital?' Vartan struggled to right himself,
then pulled the door shut with his good hand.

'If I said Byblos I meant *Byblos*, now *yallah*, let's get moving!' The
old car threaded its way past the Power and Light Company, down
the hill to the port and turned northwards on the coastal road, past
the old Armenian slum of Burj Hammoud. Vartan had not been out
of Ashrafiyeh for over three years, never ventured north for twice
that long. He had not seen the former refugee camp called Karantina,
the old Ottoman quarantine station, since it had been destroyed
following a bloody siege. There was nothing recognisable left of
the shanty town that had been home to thousands of Palestinians:
now a no man's land, a rubble field with weeds sprouting, the occasional incongruous spring flower. He shuddered as he thought that
the exulting victors would not have bothered removing the bodies
before sending in the bulldozers.

It was a warm June afternoon, promising a hot summer; a drive
along the coast would have been pleasant under other circumstances.
The current unpleasant ones – other than his own bodily ailments –
were all too evident in the succession of roadblocks they had to
stop at: a Kataeb (Phalangist) one near the port, a Lebanese Army
one at Burj Hammoud and an unidentified one near the shuttered
former den of vice on the hill, the Casino du Liban. Vartan's obvious
age and the garrulous taxi driver got them through without Vartan
having to do more than flash his *hawiyye*, the national identity card
which sets forth for all to see the religious sect of the bearer. Like
the 'shibboleth' which he had finally understood the meaning of.
Here they used the cards to separate the sheep from the goats and

on a bad day this was as far as the goats would make it alive, unless it was the sheep's turn. Armenians were apparently OK today.

They passed the turnoff to the road up to Aintoura, the orphanage and school where he had taken refuge after his scandalous episode with Maude, sixty-something years ago, for God's sake. *Father Sarlout must have gone to his reward many years ago; and so must Colonel de la Villatte, damn him; but Maude?* For an instant, the colour of her dark-blonde hair, the faintest memory of her troubling scent, wafted across his consciousness, across the better part of a century. *If she's alive she's over eighty, like me, all wrinkled up like a toad. She's either ancient, or dead. Why are things getting all mixed up in my mind?* After the tunnel he looked up the Dog River ravine, a brief glimpse of the lowest stelae, two that were not even there during his fateful picnic with Maude – he had heard about them, carved by Allenby and Gouraud, the competing boasts of the British and French for having 'liberated' Lebanon. *One game that was definitely not worth the candle, if the current chaos is where it had to lead. But was it? Is there really a predetermination – was it written from the beginning, as the Arabs say – or could one, could they or we have changed the course of history through different actions?*

The taxi driver had given up trying to engage Vartan in conversation. His thoughts were too confused, too far away from the everyday chatter of the driver, an Orthodox from Marj Ayoun, a town in the southern highlands that had practically ceased to exist in the ebb and flow of armed conflict in and around it for the past twelve years. He wanted to sound Vartan out about where he thought things were heading, things that might affect his ability to return home one day, 'when all this madness is over'. Vartan heard him talking but was wrapped up in his own thoughts, immersed in the company of people long dead and events that meant nothing to anyone else alive. Suddenly the car stopped and the driver turned back towards his passenger and said, '*Khawaja*, we are in Byblos. This is the path to the ruins, since that is where you asked to be left. Can you walk or do you want me to help you?'

'Please give me a hand, *ya ibni*. I am not so steady on my feet these days.' That being an understatement, the young driver had to put his arm around Vartan and half-support him as he hobbled along, leaning on his cane but relying on his helper to keep from falling.

They found the ticket collector at the Gothic archway leading into the Crusader castle, its tower now acting as a sort of gateway to the archaeological site, with its jumbled palimpsest of stone walls and ruined buildings. 'We are closing, uncle, it is nearly sundown.' Vartan pulled himself as erect as he could.

'Here, my friend, is a small compensation for allowing an old man to watch the sunset from the ruins. I will not stay more than an hour, and God will grant you bounty for your kindness.' Saying that, Vartan extracted several twenty-dollar bills from his wallet and proffered them to the astonished guard, who pocketed them with a profusion of thanks and blessings. 'Will you help me down to the sea, son?' he asked the driver.

They picked their way along the stony and overgrown path, down the hill towards the sea. Vartan thought he could remember the way to the small Greek theatre, rebuilt – his archaeologist niece had explained many years ago – by the Romans, then left to decay until it was restored by a French mission. A gem of a ruin, with the marble bleachers weathered but still mostly intact, a semicircle facing a small rectangular stage with delicate engaged columns decorating its front, the sea gently lapping the pebbles further down. When they reached the theatre, Vartan asked to be left where he could sit on one of the surviving seats in the front row. The driver helped him get settled, but was obviously uneasy. 'Shall I stay with you, Grandfather, and take you home? I'm not busy and it is nice to be out here, away from the city for a while.'

'No, God reward you, I will be all right. I want to be alone for a while. Here is your fare, thank you.' With that he handed him several twenty-dollar bills, which the driver noticed were the last remaining in his wallet. But Vartan was oblivious.

'How will you get home, Grandfather? I will wait for you outside the gate, just call me when you are ready. As though you were my own grandfather, *wallah*.'

The young man withdrew, pausing several times to look back down the path. Vartan looked out at the sun preparing for its daily funeral, the usual, spectacular Mediterranean panoply of red and orange and violet clouds getting ready to shroud the sun as it buried itself in the horizon. *A theatre. What an appropriate setting.* As he watched, he was conscious of a renewal of the pain in his head, of a new tingle down his right side and members. *I think Act Three is about to end. Curtains, as they say. The veil, the other side, at last.*

With an effort of concentration and all his remaining strength, he pulled himself to his feet and, leaning heavily on his cane, lurched across as far as the stage; holding on to it with his good hand, he made his way laboriously along, a new flare of pain stabbing down his right leg as he dragged it behind him. He looked at the distance to the water's edge and knew he would never cross it erect. He threw aside his cane, which fell with a clatter among the old stones. Holding on to the marble edge of the stage, he lowered himself to all fours again. He used his good arm and leg to drag the rest of his body across the stony ground. Suddenly he stopped and laughed out loud. *Isn't that the Riddle of the Sphinx: 'What animal goes on four legs in the morning, two at noon and three in the evening?' I've been all three in one day, but backwards, ha ha!* A renewal of pain on one side of his head made him concentrate on making progress. He crawled past a marble pedestal of some kind. *These are not just any stones, old Vartan. What did Khayyam say?*

An qasre ke Bahram

That palace where Bahram used to lift his glass
Is now a place where lions rest, foxes have their cubs;
Bahram who so loved to hunt the wild ass –
Now just think! The tomb has caught Bahram!

Dashti loved that verse, gur *meaning both 'ass' and 'tomb'. Will* he *be there?* Vartan finally reached the water's edge, still on hands and knees and close to exhaustion. The nearly tideless Mediterranean caressed the pebbly shore, and the first touch of the water was cool but not cold to his hands. He paused a moment to savour the contact with the sea, but soon began to sense a return of the pain in his head. *I must make it now or it will be too late. Now!* He made a supreme effort and dragged himself another few feet along the gently sloping beach of small smooth pebbles and coarse sand. Gradually it fell off until he was just touching the bottom, his torso in the sea. He felt relief as the burdensome weight of his body was increasingly supported by the water. Another instant and he was floating, clear of the stony bottom. He was free, relieved at last from the discomfort of his heavy, painful, malfunctioning body.

The first gulp of salty water was a shock. He swallowed more water. He gasped as it entered his lungs, then relaxed. *Oh Mother, I am coming to you. I'm coming home. Shoushan, here I am, I am coming back. Please forgive me.* The waves at first hesitated, then bore him gently away from the beach towards the darkening copper of the sunset. He never heard the shouts of the young driver on the shore, for he was enveloped in a dazzling whiteness, a light so bright that it excluded any other sensation. All was silence, he no longer felt anything physical. No coherent thoughts restrained his mind. The last thing he was conscious of was an inchoate but overwhelmingly intense *yearning*, a tidal wave of yearning that rose up through the stars and broke to fill the universe.

Glossary of Arabic, Armenian and Turkish Words

Abu: vaulted ground-floor storeroom under a house
Alhamdulillah: 'praise be to God'
Allah yarhumuh: 'may God rest his soul'
Alman: Germans
Amo: uncle
As-salaamu aleikum: 'peace be upon you' (greeting)
Ayran: diluted yogurt with mint and a touch of garlic
Barghout: literally 'flea', the smallest-denomination Ottoman coin
Baron: 'mister' (Armenian)
Bashkatib: senior secretary or scribe
Bayram: Turkish for one of several Muslim Feasts
Belediye: town hall
Chete, Zaptieh, Bashibouzouk: irregular soldiers or policemen
Dra': a cubit, measure of length (arm's length)
Fatteh: Syrian delicacy with layers of chickpeas, toasted bread, pine nuts, garlic, *tahini*, lemon and yoghurt (on its own or with chicken or lamb kebab)
Ferengi: foreign
Ferrash: household servant (menial)
Floos: money
Giaour: infidel (non-Muslim)
Gülbesheker: rose petal jam
Halabi: inhabitant of Aleppo

Hamidiye: an irregular soldier who took part in the massacres of Armenians carried out at the behest of 'Abdul the Red', Sultan Abdul Hamid, in 1894-96.

Hanum: respectful form of address for a married or mature woman (Turkish)

Hayestan: Armenia

Ingleezi: English (plural *Ingleez*)

Janim: 'my soul', term of endearment (Turkish)

Kardeshim: 'my younger brother' in Turkish, term of endearment

Kebbad: bitter orange peel preserve

Keefik, mniha?: 'How are you, well?' (colloquial, to a woman)

Khawaja: a form of address used mostly in addressing Christians (*'khawaga'* in Egyptian Arabic)

Khayyi: 'my brother'

Lavash: flat, sometimes unleavened, Armenian bread

Lira: Ottoman pound

Mabrouki: congratulations

Marhoum: late, departed (dead)

Mütesarrif: Ottoman provincial official

Muwashshaha: a strophic form of Arabic poetry invented in Muslim Spain, also used by poets writing in Hebrew

Para: Ottoman coin (1/4000th of a gold *lira*)

Qabadai: tough, thug

Qahwagi: person who makes or sells coffee

Reaya: literally 'flocks', non-Muslim minority citizens of the Ottoman empire

Sidi: sir, mister

Sill: tuberculosis

Sitt: respectful form of address for a married or mature woman (Arabic)

Tabur, plural *taburlar*: short for *inshaat taburlari*, forced labour 'construction squads'

Tamam mı?: 'all right?' (Turkish)

Tamriya: or *tamriyeh*, dessert made with date syrup

Teskere: permit, especially residence permit

Tfaddal: 'please', 'help yourself', 'after you', 'be my guest', etc.

Tfenkji agha: 'head musketeer', head of the municipal militia in Aleppo

Umma or **Ummah**: the community of believers in Islam

Usta: cook

Ustadh: teacher, respectful form of address

Vali: Ottoman governor

Wa-aleykum as-salam: 'and peace be upon you' (greeting in response to '*As-salaamu aleykum*')

Wallah (also wallahi, vallahi billahi etc): '(I swear) by God'

Wazir: minister

Ya: 'oh' (invocation)

Ya haram: 'for shame!'

Yallah: 'come on!', 'hurry up!'

Ya salam: expression of surprise

Zaptieh: see *Chete*, above

Acknowledgements

Thanks to Stephanie Murphy, Maya Slater, Rone Tempest, Jim Muir, Nicholas Vester and Andrée for slogging patiently through various permutations of this story and providing infinitely helpful comments; and to Peter Jacobs, my editor at Quartet. All the warts and errors in this final product are purely my responsibility.

I am very grateful to Iraj Anvar and Anne Twitty for permission to publish their translation of the Rumi poem on page 220. It appears on page 108 of their marvellous translation of selected poems of the master: *Rumi, Say Nothing; poems of Jalal al-Din Rumi in Persian and English* (Sandpoint, Idaho: Morning Light Press, 2008). All other translations are mine.

The photographs are either mine, from my collection, or out of copyright to the best of my knowledge.